Red Path

Path Series

by:

Neri Lopez

Red Path

The Path Series: Book 1

Neri Lopez

Siren Book & Craft LLC

Reader Discretion

This work includes themes of sexual assault and rape that some readers may find disturbing or triggering. We advise reader discretion.

If you or someone you know has been sexually assaulted, please know that you are not alone and that there are resources that can help you through this difficult time. If you are or have been a victim of sexual assault, you can contact your local police department and call the number below.

National Sexual Assault Hotline:
800-656-4673
Or chat online at: http://www.rainn.org

RAINN (Rape, Abuse & Incest National Network) is the nation's largest anti-sexual violence organization. RAINN created and operated the National Sexual Assault Hotline in partnership with over 1,000 sexual assault service providers across the country.

For victims of a roofie assault, please contact: 844-960-2939
http://www.theedgetreatment.com

Also, help is available 24/7 on the Suicide and Crisis Lifeline.
You can call or text in English or Spanish.
The number is: **988**
http://988lifeline.org

American Indian Cultural Center

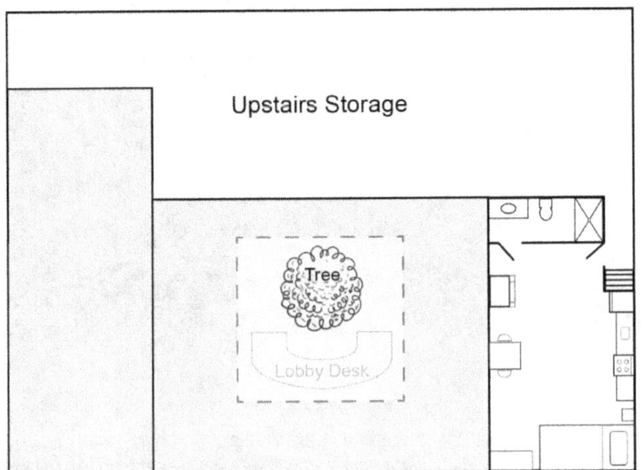

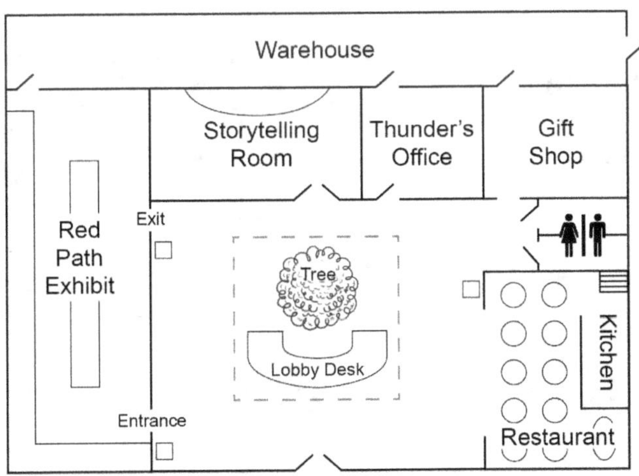

Path Series Family Trees

d.-deceased ❧ shaded box is a spouse

Thunderbird

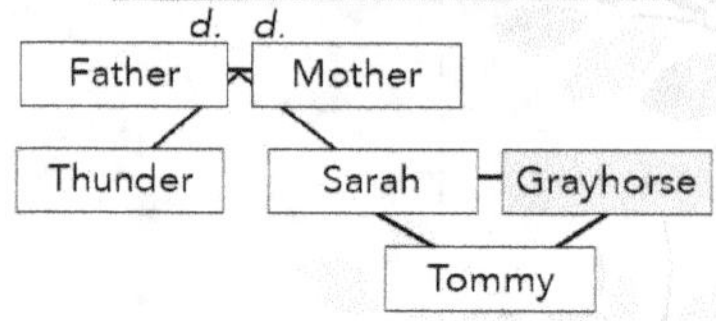

Shelter Boys

George (21-original)

Tim (17)

Luke (15)

Kenny (14)

Jimmy (13)

Bryce (6)

Gonzalez

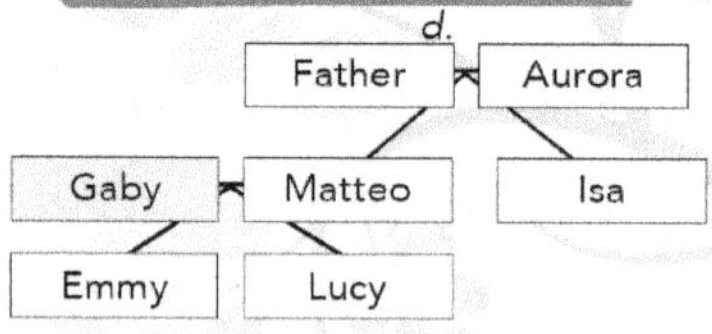

Spirit of the Eagle

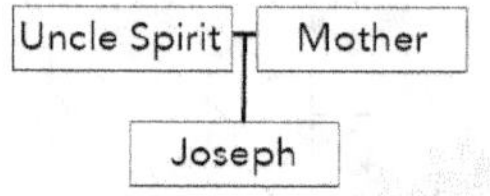

Doe Eyes

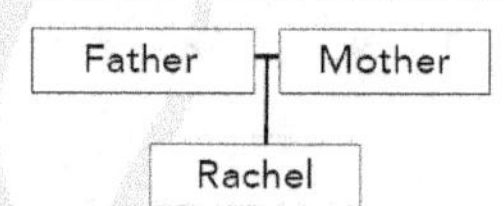

Holmes

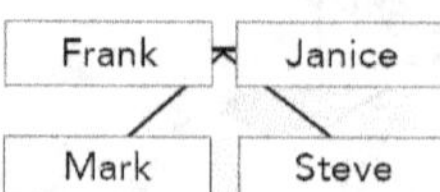

Walker

Ramon — Caridad
Maggie

Lakota

aké waŋcíŋyaŋkiŋ ktélo – goodbye, I'll see you soon
até – father
ciŋkší - son
cuŋkší - daughter (his)
cuŋwítku - daugher (her)
haŋ – yes
haŋ ciŋkší – yes son
hau – hello, you're welcome, or good morning
hecitu yelo, tuŋšká – that is true, nephew (it is okay)
higná – husband
híŋhaŋni wašté tibló – fine morning big brother
hiyá – no
hiyú wo – come on
hokahey - let's do it or let's roll
iná – mother
inala - aunt
kiktáyo – wake up
Kóla – friend
lekší – uncle
Mató Háŋska - Tall Bear
mitákola – my friend
mitáwicu – wife
mitáwicu thečhíhila – I love you, my wife
mitáwicu caŋté thečhíhila – I love you, my wife, my heart
Paha Sapa – The Black Hills
pilámaya – thank you
Súŋkawakháŋhota - Grayhorse
súŋkawakháŋhota cíkala – little grayhorse
taŋkši – sister
taŋyáŋ yahípi – you're welcome
tibló – brother
Tingleska Ista – Doe Eyes
tojáŋ - niece
tóhaŋ niš hwo – when did you arrive/come.
ťuŋšká – nephew
šičé - brother-in-law
suŋkáku – younger brother
úwo – come
Wakaŋ Táŋka - Great Spirit
Wakíyaŋ Hotóŋpi - Thunder
Waŋblí Kiŋ Wanági Uŋ - Spirit of the Eagle
wašícuŋ – white man
wašícuŋ wíŋyaŋ – white woman
wašté hwo, ťuŋšká – are you okay, nephew
wówaštelaka mitáwa – my love
wíŋyaŋ mitáwa – my woman
Zintkála Wakíyaŋ Hotóŋpi - Thunderbird

Spanish

abuela – grandmother
adiós – goodbye
ay – ow
¡Ay! ¡Dios mío! - Oh my God
bien – fine, well, or good
cómo está Isa – how is Isa
cómo estás – how are you
Fricase de Pollo y Arroz Blanco – Chicken Fricase and White Rice
gracias – thank you
hija – daughter
hola – hello
ingenioso – clever but not honest
mami – mommy
mija – Cuban slang for "my daughter"
mira – look
niña – girl
por nada, mi niño - your welcome, my boy
que – what
qué guapos – how handsome
qué lindo – how lovely
qué pasa – what's going on
qué pasó – what happened
si – yes
te quiero – I love you or I want you
tía – aunt
y tú – and you

Contents

Prologue   1

1. Pine Ridge Indian Reservation, South Dakota   3

2. Put Your Degree to Work   6

3. American Indian Cultural Center, Florida   9

4. Thunder's Office before Meeting   13

5. Lobby @ Teramar Studios   15

6. The Encounter @ Teramar Studios   18

7. The Meeting @ Teramar Studios   21

8. Let the Games Begin   27

9. Runaway Art Director   28

10. The Flyers are Coming, The Flyers are Coming   30

11. Tuesday...Still no Isa   35

12. Wednesday...The Night before Opening   37

13. Thursday...Red Path Exhibit Opening Day   41

14. Thursday...Red Path Exhibit Opening Night   45

15. This Exhibit was Awesome!   50

16. I am a Klutz   63

17. Yes...No...Maybe...Definitely Not Tonight   67

18. The Grayhorse's Drive Home   76

19. Rachel's Adventure in the AICC Kitchen   79

20. Friday...Day After the Opening   84

21. Joseph's Thoughts   89

22. Friday @ Teramar Studios   91

23.	Got My Wallet and License and Apparently a Date	95
24.	Friday @ AICC	99
25.	Friday Double Date...NOT	104
26.	Important Artifact...Missing	105
27.	Saturday in the Park	108
28.	A Pleasant Surprise	112
29.	Saturday Night Fiasco	118
30.	Sunday...Babysitting	126
31.	Sunday...Family Lunch and Fun in the Sun Day	130
32.	Monday Mixup	137
33.	Monday Night Misunderstanding	146
34.	Tuesday...The Morning After	156
35.	Tuesday...Prepping for School Field Trip	162
36.	Tuesday...School Field Trip	164
37.	Date Night at Thunder's	173
38.	Dinner @ Giovanni's, The Right Date This Time	179
39.	Time to Think about the Knife Later	186
40.	Save a Horse, Ride a Cowboy...Well, Ride a Horse Anyway	190
41.	Horseback Riding Lesson	194
42.	After Dinner Coffee	200
43.	Isa Formally Meets Her Future in Laws	203
44.	Police Scrutiny	209
45.	So Many Viewpoints as the Plot Thickens	212
46.	Play-by-Play Terror	221
47.	Joseph's Demented Games	226
48.	A Score to Settle	232
49.	Afternoon After the Shit Storm	238
50.	Epilogue - Happily Ever After	240
Special Thanks		244
About the Author		245

Prologue

THUNDER

Thunder's heart was racing as he listened to the fear in Sarah's voice. He spoke soothingly to her while booking a flight home on his computer. Two days after the head-on collision that took the lives of Carolyn and Tom Thunderbird, they scheduled the funeral. Many people attended the service. Carolyn and Tom had been very involved on the reservation with their people. Their father was a medicine man and their mother was a teacher.

Thunder considered dropping out of college. He still had one more year left in his five-year bachelor of Architecture Degree program. The night after the funeral, Thunder and Sarah stayed up late talking about their options. He could get a job on or near the reservation so he could take care of her. They also talked about moving her to his college town. But it was her senior year, and she really wanted to graduate with her friends. Not to mention where would they live? Thunder had a scholarship, so he lived in a dorm. It was hard to beat free room and board. He didn't have enough money saved up from tutoring to get them an apartment. Most of his money went to pay for his classes, art supplies, meal plan, and books. He would have to get a full-time job and take one class at a time, extending his graduation date. His degree was not conducive to night classes and he would still uproot Sarah. Even doing that, they still didn't know if they could afford an apartment there with one entry level salary.

Sarah didn't want Thunder to quit college. He was so close to finishing. His dream was to become an architect and help design homes and buildings for his people on the reservation. In high school, he tutored and helped their youth at the community center for free. He was so good with kids, she always thought he would be a teacher like their mom. But he loved designing buildings. By the end of the night, they talked to Uncle Spirit for some of his wisdom and guidance. They both went to bed, thinking about their options. Sarah didn't tell Thunder, but she was going to ask Uncle Spirit if she could stay at the house alone and he could check on her. He didn't live far, and she could take care of herself.

The next morning after the funeral, Thunder and Sarah went to talk to Uncle Spirit. She shared her plan of living alone - they were both against it. Neither one wanted to leave a single seventeen-year-old girl in a house all by herself. Spirit-of-the-Eagle had been a childhood friend of their fathers. He had always treated them like a part of his family. To them, he was an uncle, and his son was their cousin. Uncle Spirit informed them that his wife Morning Sunshine and their son Joseph would welcome Sarah into their home until

Thunder graduated from college. Thunder looked torn about the decision, but Uncle Spirit convinced him that his parent's dream was for him to go to college, get a degree, and continue to help their people. The entire family was proud of Thunder because not a lot of their people got to attend college on a scholarship. It would be a great experience to get off the reservation and learn about the white man's world. After graduation, Thunder would be back and he could help motivate others.

A year passed quickly. Thunder graduated, came home, and they moved back into their parent's house. Thunder and Sarah weren't as close as they used to be because Thunder was never home. He was having a hard time finding people who wanted a new house. Frustration led to his sour mood until he got a job as a cowboy at a ranch on the rez that worked with horses. Before long, he learned how to train horses.

One day, Uncle Spirit asked Thunder to come in once a day for an hour and teach elementary students about their culture. None of these jobs had anything to do with his architecture degree, but he loved talking about Native American History.

This really angered Joseph. He couldn't believe his father had not given him the opportunity to teach kids. Joseph had been taking college courses at the neighboring town's community college, but Uncle Spirit knew he was not attending regularly. Uncle Spirit was afraid if he didn't take school seriously, how could he run a business daily? But Joseph was angry and felt that Thunder was the chosen one and it wasn't fair. Sarah tried to talk to him to explain all sides, but after a while he just got angrier and meaner toward her. She hated Joseph had become so nasty and ignored him. She never told Thunder because she was afraid of what Thunder would do.

Thunder took the teaching job and realized he loved it. Soon it seemed Thunder was teaching all the time during the day to all the different grades. At night he was going out with so many unwed mothers or older sisters of his students that Sarah hardly ever saw him. Thunder was over six feet, well built, and handsome with his long straight black hair. Women flocked to him like bees to honey. Women were always after him, young and old.

Chapter 1

Pine Ridge Indian Reservation, South Dakota

THUNDER

"Mr. Thunderbird, can I see you in my office after class?" Principal White Feather said as he stepped into Thunder's classroom and interrupted the end of his lesson. "Oh, and I need you to attend the Council Meeting at the community center right after school."

Thunder found himself puzzled by this interruption and responded, "Yes, sir, I will finish up and be right there."

Principal White Feather nodded and closed the door. Some students started joking and saying "oooo, Mr. Thunderbird's in trouble".

"Mr. Thunderbird, are you in trouble?" Kenny asked.

"Alright, settle down, class. No, Kenny. I'm sure it's something about our next scheduled field trip. Nothing for you to worry about." Thunder smiled at Kenny.

Thunder gave his students their homework assignments and released them when the bell rang. Thunder taught Native American Art and Culture at Pine Ridge High School on the Pine Ridge Indian Reservation. He'd been teaching there for four years. His first-year teaching, he taught art at the elementary school. However, when they needed a teacher for the high school, he volunteered. He loved teaching children of all ages, but was truly enjoying his interaction and engagement with the older ones. Thunder's class was an elective and many of his students took his class from their freshman to senior year. He loved having returning students. Thunder taught his students about the Art in American Indian culture, as well as art around the world.

"Bye Mr. Thunderbird, see ya' on Monday," Kenny said as he walked out the door.

"Bye Kenny, have a great weekend," Thunder answered.

He didn't know what was going on. He didn't think he had done anything wrong. After packing up his backpack, he headed toward the principal's office, wondering if a parent had gotten upset with him. But would a parent go to the council members? Thunder was surprised to learn there was a meeting today. Meetings were usually once a month and, on a Tuesday—today was Friday. Thunder didn't attend every meeting because of his teaching schedule. He focused more on his students and their lessons than on council meetings.

Waŋblí Kiŋ Wanági Uŋ, Spirit of the Eagle, a Lakota holy man and tribal council member, grew up with his father on the reservation. Uncle Spirit was his father's closest friend. They were more like brothers than friends. When

Thunder's father died five years ago, Uncle Spirit took Thunder and his sister under his wing and became their closest friend and mentor. They had mutual respect. They're family now.

Maybe Uncle Spirit would know what was going on. This was the first time Principal White Feather had interrupted his class and asked him to go to a council meeting. Thunder called Uncle Spirit while walking to ask about this mysterious new meeting.

"*Hau*, you have reached the voice mail of *Waŋblí Kiŋ Wanági Uŋ*, Spirit of the Eagle. I am in a meeting, in the sweat lodge, or having a smoke. Leave a message at the tone and I'll get back to you."

"Hey Uncle Spirit. White Feather came into my classroom and requested my presence not only in his office, but at a council meeting today. I was just calling to see if you knew what this was about. I'll talk to you later," Thunder sighed and knocked on the Principal's secretary's door.

"Come in."

"Hi Janice. Is Principal White Feather in his office? He asked me to come see him."

"Hey Thunder, he sure is. He said you would come by to talk to him. He's waiting for you."

"Great, thank you."

Thunder walked back and knocked on the open door. "Sir, you wanted to see me?"

"Yes, I have something very important to discuss with you. We will do it at a special council meeting that is about to start in a few minutes." Principal White Feather looked at his watch and stood up from behind his desk. "Walk with me to the Community Center."

"Of course, sir, is everything okay? Is a parent angry with me and requesting a meeting?"

"No, but let's talk about this when we get to the meeting. Step outside for just a minute. I need to speak to Janice about another issue that came up today."

"Absolutely. I'll wait for you outside."

Now Thunder was concerned and worried about what this was all about. He'd had parent-teacher conferences but never with the council members.

"Ok, that's all squared away," Principal White Feather walked into the hallway. "Let's go."

"Sir, did I do something wrong?" Thunder asked as they walked down the hallway and out of the school, heading towards the Pine Ridge Community Center. The PRCC was only two blocks away, and it was a beautiful day for a walk. Many adults and children went to the PRCC because they had after-school programs, two basketball courts, a gaming room, a small cafe, a small library, and conference rooms. The tribal council always met in one of the conference rooms.

"No, you did nothing wrong." Principal White Feather clapped him on the back. "We just want to discuss something with you." When they entered the PRCC, Thunder saw several of his students playing basketball. He waved back to them as they called out his name. When they reached the conference room, Principal White Feather gestured for him to sit on the bench in the hallway.

"Have a seat here Thunder," Principal White Feather opened the door and turned before stepping through. "Someone will come and get you when we are ready for you."

"Yes, sir." Thunder took a seat. Principal White Feather proceeded into the conference room.

This meeting seemed very secretive, and Thunder couldn't wait to find out what was going on. As he sat on the bench outside the door, he leaned his head back against the wall and closed his eyes. He thought about his lesson plans for the next week. Being a Native American Art and Culture teacher, he needed to teach his students about Native American Artists in all tribes and their cultural differences. Next week, they would learn about Wendy Red Star. She grew up on the Crow Reservation in Montana. She had a painting that helped him teach his students about their warrior's clothing and weaponry. As he was sitting there, two teenage boys walked toward him down the hall and he could easily hear their conversation.

"Why do we need to learn all this history about the Little Big Horn? My parents say I should learn all this stuff, but I really don't care. It all seems boring to me. Besides, like reliving the past will get us off this reservation," one teen grumbled to his friend.

"Yeah, I know what you mean. I prefer to hang out in the city rather than being cooped up in a classroom. And who cares about Custer? We won and all those people are dead now, anyway."

As they walked by and continued their conversation, Thunder gritted his teeth in frustration and cracked his eyes open to see if he recognized them. They were not his students, but he recognized them as Mike Long Feather and Alex Red Fox. How could anyone say that the Little Big Horn was boring and not important? It was anything but boring. And to not want to learn about Crazy Horse, Sitting Bull, Red Cloud or any other great American Indian leaders and chiefs was ludicrous.

Thunder strongly felt everyone needed to learn about the past, so they didn't repeat those mistakes. He worked very hard to teach not only about the artists and culture, but some history in his class. Many teens were tired of their parents talking about how it used to be. There were a lot of traditionalists on the reservation who refused to change or accept modern ideas and not move toward the future. But there were others that wanted to learn and not repeat those mistakes. Some even left the rez for a different way of life. Most had a choice to make. As long as people had a choice, then others should respect them. As for the teens, how could they so adamantly want to live in the future if they didn't know who they were? Where their ancestors came from? Their hardships or what they strove to become?

Thunder hoped to educate the youth of his people and perhaps someday educate everyone else. He wished all people could come to an understanding about their religion and culture so they could all live in harmony, kindness, and understanding.

Thunder was going to follow the boys to talk to them, but as he stood up, the door opened and Uncle Spirit came out. He looked at Thunder with a smirk on his face and waved him in.

Chapter 2

Put Your Degree to Work

THUNDER

"*Hau*, why didn't you answer your phone?" Thunder mumbled as he walked past him.

"*Hau mitákcola*, I was already in council when you called and it was on silent, sorry," he mumbled back.

"*Hau*," Thunder gazed around the room to acknowledge all the elders. They were sitting in a circle and there was an empty chair for Thunder. He walked into the room and took a seat.

"*Hau, Zintkála Wakíyaŋ Hotóŋpi*," the room full of elders responded.

"*Zintkála Wakíyaŋ Hotóŋpi*," *Mató Háŋska* spoke. "We called you here today because we want to discuss where our children's future is heading." Tall Bear had been the leader of the tribal council for the past four years. "We have an idea which we want to share with you. We know how dedicated you have been to our children in the past, and we want to ask you to take on this new endeavor."

Thunder sat up straight and proud with a smile on his face. It was nice to be appreciated. His heart was racing as he listened carefully, as Tall Bear explained what they wanted him to do.

"We want you to set up cultural centers in several parts of the country to educate the *wasicun* about American Indians. The first one that we want to set up is going to be in Sunrise, Florida. We got a good price on property there and our Seminole Tribe friends, who own the guitar-shaped casino, assured us of excellent tourism exposure since it will be near a huge mall. That area is growing, and I think the casino will pique interest in Native American Tribes in the United State. Swift Antelope and I went there last month to see the building. It will take some work to turn it into a Cultural Center, but the Seminole Tribe nearby is also willing to help." Tall Bear said.

"I am honored, *Mató Háŋska*." Thunder was stunned.

"Does this mean you accept, *Zintkála Wakíyaŋ Hotóŋpi*?" asked Tall Bear.

"Yes, I accept." Thunder smiled at Tall Bear. This was the opportunity of a lifetime. Thunder couldn't wait to get started. With his knowledge, he could teach so many people about their culture, art, and lifestyle. He would miss his family, especially his sister and her husband, but what a great opportunity—they would understand. Maybe he could ask to bring them with him.

"When do I leave?" Thunder asked the council. "And if it's before school is out for the summer, who will replace me? I would like to prepare my students as soon as possible."

"You will leave in two weeks. We will set up a replacement for you to finish out this school year. It is our desire for you to open before the next school year begins. Although we have purchased the building, it will be your responsibility to design the space in order to bring our culture to life. We want to call it The American Indian Cultural Center. We want to showcase all Native American tribes. This AICC will also have a restaurant which will feature authentic American Indian foods. We are sending George Grayfeather and his wife, Mary. You can hire anyone else you need. Since this is our first attempt at this type of endeavor, we will have mostly Lakota and Seminole foods and exhibits. If this works out, we will speak to the other tribal councils and elders about exhibiting and teaching their culture and heritage as well."

Thunder's heart pumped with excitement, his chest puffing up with pride. He felt surprised to learn that they were considering opening a cultural center, especially in a state so far from home. Their trust humbled him. He would do everything in his power to make sure this cultural center was a successful venture.

"Thank you for trusting me with this opportunity. I will not let you down and I will keep you posted as I progress with the center." Thunder told them.

Tall Bear continued, "We will also send *Tingleska Ista*, Rachel Doe Eyes, with you as an assistant. She has shown the women's council that she will be an excellent teacher to the *wasicun winyan*. We will work on this project for two years and see if we are successful. Assuming we are, the decision is yours to either stay there, return to your people, or open the next one. If you decide to leave, we will replace you with another warrior. If you choose to stay, you can train the next warrior and we will send them out to the next location. We can also move your sister Sarah and her husband, *Sunkawakhanhota*, Grayhorse, so that you are not alone. Does this sound fair, *Zintkála Wakíyaŋ Hotóŋpi*?"

"*Han, Mató Háŋska*, again I am honored to be chosen as the leader in such an important matter and very grateful that I can bring my sister and brother-in-law with me."

"Then it is settled." Tall Bear smiled at me and stood up. "The council will meet here again in two days to plan your trip to South Florida."

All the council members went to Thunder and slapped him on the back. They all complimented Thunder for his bravery and courage, as they wished him good luck. It would only be Rachel Doe Eyes, George & Mary Grayfeather, his sister Sarah & Grayhorse (if he could convince them to come) and him. They had their work cut out for them, but Thunder wanted more than anything to prove to his people that he could do this. Teaching others about his culture could bring everyone together and make it a better place for future generations. He noticed Uncle Spirit walking towards him.

"I recommended you, *Wakíyaŋ Hotóŋpi*, Thunder. We have been talking about this for the past few years and I knew you would be the best warrior for the job." he smiled at Thunder.

"Uncle Spirit, I am humbled and honored that you suggested me to the council. I will do my very best to not let you down." Thunder hugged him.

Uncle Spirit grabbed his shoulders after their hug, looked him in the eyes, and said, "You have never let me down. Your inner strength, kindness, bravery, and courage are powerful medicines. Your father would be very proud to see his son now."

Thunder embraced Uncle Spirit again and held back his tears.

"I must be on my way so I can tell Sarah and Grayhorse. Tommy is only three and I don't know if they want to move, but I hope they come with me. Otherwise, I guess I will visit often because I will miss them so much. I must go, but I will see you in two days."

"*Aké waŋcíŋyaŋkiŋ ktélo Wakíyaŋ Hotóŋpi*, may *Wakan Tanka*, Great Spirit, always be with you in your new future." Uncle Spirit said.

"*Pilámaya, Waŋblí Kiŋ Wanági Uŋ*," Thunder replied as he headed out of the Community Center. On his way out, he glanced toward the basketball court to see if he could see Mike Long Feather or Alex Red Fox, but they must have left for home. He would inquire about their schedule during the school day and see if he could talk to them before he left.

Thunder couldn't stop smiling as he walked back to school and got his truck before heading out to tell Sarah, Grayhorse, and Tommy the good news.

Walking into the house, he heard them all in the kitchen laughing.

"Hey guys, what's so funny?" Thunder asked.

"Watching Tommy try artichokes," Grayhorse glanced over his shoulder at me.

"*Lekší!*" Tommy hollered, jumped out of his chair and ran to him. Ever since Tommy could walk, he would run to his uncle and either jump on his lap if he was sitting or into his arms if he was standing. Tommy knew his uncle would always catch him.

"*Tʳuŋšká*," Thunder caught him, "How was that artichoke?"

"Yuck," Tommy stuck his tongue out, still trying to spit it out.

"You had a spring in your step when you came in *tibló*. What's made you so happy?" Sarah inquired.

"Great news," Thunder put Tommy back in his chair, "The tribal council asked me to head up a new cultural center in South Florida and I can bring you all with me."

"Woo-hoo!" Tommy was jumping in his seat.

"Wait, a minute. Tommy, can you go to your room and give us a minute?" Sarah asked, helping him out of his chair.

"Ok, *Iná*." Tommy exhaled his breath.

Sarah waited until Tommy walked out.

"Now, what is this about?"

Thunder explained everything that had happened at the meeting. After many questions, Sarah and Grayhorse decided not to uproot Tommy until Thunder decided if he was staying in Florida or moving on to open another center in another state. They all agreed one move was enough for Tommy. Thunder promised to come home as often as he could - he would miss them.

Chapter 3

American Indian Cultural Center, Florida

Four Years Later… Thunder

Thunder rubbed the back of his neck with his hand as he reviewed the next day's schedule. He'd already closed the cultural center for the day and was totally exhausted. Things were going on schedule for the new exhibit. This time, along with the Lakota artifacts, they were also showing paintings, pottery, and jewelry from the Kiowa, Navajo, Hopi, and Seminole tribes. As he looked back on the previous four years, he wondered where all the time had gone.

When he came to South Florida, it was just hopes and dreams. Now it was a thriving business that was always busy. After working at the AICC for two years, he stayed because he loved his job and the location. Sarah, Grayhorse, and Tommy held to their agreement and moved down. Once they bought a house and Tommy started school, they didn't want to leave. They loved it there.

It was quitting time, and Thunder was more than ready to go home and relax. He stood up and left his office. His office was at the back of the cultural center, between the storytelling room and the gift shop. His side windows into those rooms had a reflective window film on the glass so he could see into those rooms from his office, but not be a distraction from anyone in those rooms. He didn't put the reflective window film on the glass front of his office, though. There he installed blinds he could close if he needed privacy. Most days, his blinds were open in case someone was looking to speak to him and so he could monitor the center.

Mark, his front desk employee, was sitting behind the welcome counter in the lobby talking to Rachel Doe Eyes. Their cultural center was open Tuesday through Saturday from 9 a.m. to 5 p.m., unless they had an opening night. George and Mary Grayfeather enjoyed the Florida weather and were still working for Thunder. They opened the restaurant from 11 a.m. to 2 p.m. Whenever they wanted a vacation, Thunder hired a temporary traveling chef from another tribe. Since the food, gift shop, and exhibits changed often, they had a lot of repeat customers and quite a following on social media.

"Bye, Mark, Rachel. See you tomorrow," Thunder said.

"Bye, Boss," they responded.

Thunder walked out the front door and got into his truck to drive home. He'd bought a house within walking distance of the beach. His white Spanish-style home with a clay tile roof was a two-story home with four bedrooms and three and a half bathrooms. It was on the Fort Lauderdale Intracoastal Waterway. A highly sought area because of its proximity to the beach, private boat docks, and walking access to several restaurants. It was a thirty to forty-five minute commute to work, depending on traffic and the time of day, but once he was home, he loved being able to run on the beach to relax. The waves at the beach always seemed to help him think and de-stress.

As soon as he got home, he parked his car and walked to the beach. He found a spot near the sidewalk and sat down on the sand. He lifted both knees and propped his elbows on his knees as his hands dangled between his legs. *How did I get so lucky to be chosen to open and run this center?* He thought as he watched the people sunbathing on the sand or swimming in the water. Thunder was proud of the path his life had taken. Staying in South Florida with Sarah, Grayhorse, and Tommy had been an excellent decision. Sarah was always complaining that he worked too hard, but he was used to putting in long hours. He'd had to work hard getting the center up and running in the early years. Then two years ago, the tribal council opened a new cultural center in New York. He'd commuted between both centers. Not caring for the hustle and bustle of New York City, he stayed in Florida. *Not to mention, you can't beat this weather,* Thunder thought, taking a deep breath of the salty ocean breeze.

The cultural centers were his pride and joy, but they weren't without sacrifice. Setting them up took all his time and energy and left little time for anything else, like a love life.

Thunder watched a beautifully fit woman jogging along the shoreline. There was a time when he would have jogged after her so he could get her number. But he was older now and was looking to meet someone special that he could get serious with and commit to. The female jogger had her blonde hair in a ponytail like Jennifer. Jennifer was his first love. He had fallen hard for her. But Jennifer had dumped him when she found out he lived on a reservation. Thunder grabbed a fistful of sand and threw it towards the beach. She'd thought once they graduated, he would move to the big city and become a world-famous architect or maybe have his own Architecture Firm and she would never have to work. He couldn't blame her for that assumption. He had graduated college with a major in architecture and a minor in business. Once Jennifer realized he would go home to his people, she stopped answering his phone calls and texts. After Jennifer dumped him, he was very bitter, to say the least. Thunder wasn't about to chase after her and not go back to the rez. So, from that point on, if she ignored him on campus, he ignored her.

Then his parents died in a car accident, and he had to focus on his finishing his degree and returning to the rez to take care of his sister. He sighed, remembering how lost he'd been back then.

During that last year in college after being dumped and his parent's death, he sowed his wild oats a lot. Especially knowing he would never see those girls again once he left. He swore he would never get serious over a female again.

Although he studied architecture, he never got licensed. When he went back to the rez, they needed an art teacher, not an architect, and the tribal council stepped in and asked him to become an art and culture teacher. He could never say no to the tribal council. They had helped him emotionally and financially after his parents died. Grabbing another fist full of sand, he looked down and watched it slide down between his fingers like the sands of time. So, designing became a hobby he only shared with certain people. Uncle Spirit knew this, which was probably why he'd recommended Thunder for this cultural center. Uncle Spirit knew he could fix any building design issues and then run it and teach people about our culture.

Watching the sunset, he noticed several girls walk by and smile. He smiled back but didn't engage in conversation. He wondered when it had all changed. When one-night stands stopped becoming appealing because now all he wanted was to have what his parents had. What he saw in his sister's relationship with Grayhorse.

He'd dated Rachel when they first moved to South Florida for almost two years. During that time, he realized Rachel was not the one. At first, she was very clingy. Then he could never find her after work. Several of his friends would say they saw her at local bars drinking with other men. Thunder couldn't prove she went home with those men, but he was pretty sure she had. She was horny when she drank, and she hadn't called him. They'd just drifted apart. He loved her as a friend, but their friends with benefits thing had run its course. He was not in love with her.

Rachel was flirting with Mark when Thunder left. Thunder wondered if they were together now. He couldn't imagine being with someone sexually anymore unless he felt something - a genuine connection. *Maybe I'm growing a conscience or just growing up*, Thunder thought as he watched another beautiful woman jog by. Sarah wouldn't believe he spent most of his nights alone these days. As a business owner in this area, he was part of the chamber of commerce and other business organizations and was constantly promoting his cultural center. Thunder met a lot of women, but he didn't sleep with all of them. Well, at least not anymore.

As the sun set over the ocean, his phone rang in his pocket.

"Speak of the devil," Thunder muttered to himself.

"Hey Rachel, what's up?"

"I totally forgot to tell you about the meeting you have tomorrow morning at 10 a.m. with Teramar Studios," she said.

"Is this the new company we are using for marketing since the last one messed it all up?" Thunder watched as the ocean swallowed the sun, making the water glow with red and orange hues.

"Yes, I will email you all the information they sent me with prices and the address," she answered. "You're meeting with John Cummings."

"Ok, thanks for letting me know. Can you please open the center since I can't be there until after the meeting?"

"Of course."

"Great. I'll see you tomorrow."

"Ok, good luck," Rachel said. "I can't wait to hear all about it when you get here."

"Thanks." Thunder hung up the phone. *Well, I guess I should walk back home and read all the documents to prepare for my meeting tomorrow.*

Thunder rubbed his hands to remove the sand. Then he stood up, swiped the sand off his pants, and walked home. They still wanted to do four openings a year, representing the four seasons. Even though in South Florida it felt like it was only one season—summer. Their next exhibit was in three weeks, and some of the tribal council members were coming in to help.

Because of the problems with their last ad agency, they swore to never use them again. Teramar Studios was recommended to him by some of the local businesses in town. So now he was at home looking over all the pricing and contact information Rachel sent him so he could be ready for his meeting tomorrow morning.

As he looked over the emails, he could see that it would cost him more, but if they did a good job, then it would all be worth it. This exhibit was very important to everyone involved. Especially the tribal council because it was the first exhibit since the center opened that would include more Native American Cultures, not just the Lakota and Seminole. The tribal council wanted to ensure equal and effective representation for everyone. It needed to go off without a hitch. This next month before the opening was going to be very busy. He needed a dependable agency so he could focus on other things.

Chapter 4

Thunder's Office before Meeting

THUNDER

After showering, Thunder wore a suit for the meeting. Teramar Studios was a prestigious ad agency based on the photos he saw on their website. He dressed in his black suit, white shirt, black tie with a subtle American Indian pattern, and black wing-tip shoes. Today, he needed to look the part of a successful business owner, so he opted to wear a suit instead of his usual jeans and cowboy boots at the cultural center. His goal during that meeting was to be taken seriously. He quickly checked himself out in the bathroom mirror, looking all professional except for his hair.

Lakota Warriors grew their hair long as a symbol of their life force and a spiritual source of identity and tradition. Their long hair equated to power, virility, and physical strength. Thunder's tribe wore their straight black hair long and loose. They'd sometimes add a braid on each side. Women usually loved his long hair loose, he recalled with a rakish grin at his reflection. But for this professional meeting, he'd pull it back into a low ponytail, definitely not a man bun. He grimaced into the mirror at the thought of a man bun. Brushing his hair out, he found his simple black hair tie and finished his ponytail. He added a splash of cologne and left his house.

After getting in his car, he looked at his watch and realized it was too early to go to Teramar, so he went to the office and got some work done before the meeting. Pulling into the cultural center, he noticed he was the only car in the parking lot. He remembered asking Rachel to come in early. He'd assumed she would be there by now, considering they opened in thirty minutes.

The front door was locked, but Rachel could still be there. Rachel sometimes walked to work because she didn't live far and she enjoyed the warm weather. They always locked the front door until they were ready to open because they couldn't see who was coming in. Rachel wasn't at the front desk when Thunder walked in, so he headed to his office and called out her name.

"Rachel, are you here?" He called out.

"In your office," she yelled, "I'm filing."

So, she came in early. When he got to his office, he saw her filing paperwork.

"Rachel, I'm going to work for about an hour and then go to Teramar Studios. Is there anything you left out from the emails that I should know about? Once I leave, I don't know how long I will be, but I am planning on coming back. I can't imagine a first meeting with them will take all day." Thunder walked to his desk, sat down, and booted up his computer. He wanted to print out all the emails she sent him yesterday so he could have them on paper for the meeting. He'd also written his questions on a notepad to take with him.

"Oh, Thunder," she cooed, "you look really handsome and smell divine." She winked at him. "I don't think I have ever seen you in that suit. I love the tie."

Her comments made him feel a little uncomfortable because he wasn't sure if she was just being her flirty self or if she actually wanted back into his bed. Lately, she had been a lot more touchy-feely with him. Sometimes touching his arm or running her hands down his back. He would have to talk to her about that. He was not interested in starting up a relationship with her again.

"Uh...Thanks," he tried not to make eye contact with her and continued to look at his computer. He didn't want to lead her on, especially since he saw her eyes roaming over him from head to toe before he sat down. Thunder went to the gym, ran, and stayed in shape. After all, he lived on the beach in Florida with a lot of hard bodies. His abs had to keep up.

Thunder placed his phone on the desk, tapping it to check the time.

"*Pilámaya*, Rachel. As for the clothes, you know I don't wear them often, but today I want the agency to take me seriously. It is important for our new exhibit. I don't want the fiasco we had with the last agency." As soon as the emails finished printing, he grabbed them from the printer and put them in his briefcase. Clicking it shut, he decided he would rather get to the agency early than continue the conversation with Rachel. He wasn't sure where she was going with it, but he knew he didn't want to go there.

"Well, this is all I need." He stood and checked his pockets to make sure he had everything. His phone was not in his pocket, so he opened his desk drawer. "Rachel, have you seen my cell phone? I could've sworn I put it on my desk."

"It's right here," she grabbed it from the coffee table, "you must have set it down here instead of on your desk."

"Huh, I don't remember doing that," he said to her as she handed it to him. He tried to make sure he didn't touch her hand, just his phone.

"What would you do without me, Thunder?" She said as she held onto it a little too long for his liking.

Okay, abort, leave, exit the building quick. This was getting strange. In the last two years since they broke up, she had done nothing like that.

"Uh, yeah, well I have to go or else I'll be late. See you later." He snatched his phone from her hand and dropped it into his pocket. Turning around, he left his office quickly. Rachel was acting strange. He really had to talk to her, but now wasn't the right time.

Chapter 5

Lobby @ Teramar Studios

THUNDER

The drive to Teramar was about fifteen minutes, but it could take longer with city road traffic. It was good that he'd left when he did—better to be early than late. His mom used to say, "If you are fifteen minutes early, then you are on time. If you show up on the dot, then you are late."

He was relieved to see the ad agency had their own parking with lots of spaces. Parking his truck, Thunder took a deep breath before he got out of his truck. Squaring his shoulders, Thunder walked into their lobby. When he walked up to the receptionist's desk, an attractive receptionist who was checking him out like he was a delicious snack greeted him.

"Good morning, my name is Johnny Thunderbird. I have a 10 o'clock appointment with John Cummings," he shot her his signature smile, that had served him well in the past. She was all smiles—her eyes continuing to devour him.

"Good morning, Mr. Thunderbird. I'm Maggie. It's nice to meet you," Maggie replied. "Please have a seat and I will tell Mr. Cummings you are here."

"Thank you, Maggie." He went to the couch, unbuttoned his suit jacket, and sat down. He set his briefcase on the floor and looked around the posh lobby. This place was classy, with expensive art on the walls. He wondered if they would ever let him place a painting or two in there. The floors were a light marble, which contrasted nicely with the circular black marble receptionist's desk. There were awards on the wall, along with the paintings. The awards were for their graphic designs and their exceptional ad campaigns. He cringed inside and wondered if the prices Rachel had sent him were correct or if he was in over his head. Well, he was already there, so he would have to ask a lot of questions and verify pricing.

"Mr. Thunderbird, Mr. Cummings will be with you momentarily. Would you like some coffee?" asked Maggie.

"Yes, thank you. I never got my morning cup, so that would be wonderful." Thunder stood and buttoned his suit jacket.

"Normally I would get a cup for you, but I'm waiting for another customer. I can tell you where it is if you don't mind making your own coffee?" Maggie winced.

"Not a problem. I don't expect you to leave your desk just to get me coffee. Just point me in the right direction and I'll get it." Thunder smiled.

"Great." Maggie stood and pointed down the main hallway. "Go down this hallway, pass the elevators and make a right. Please help yourself to coffee and any food you see."

"Thank you, Maggie. I'll come back after I get my coffee." Thunder passed her desk and followed her directions. He found a small kitchen with a lounge. He walked to the coffeepot, grabbed a mug, and poured himself a cup of coffee. Next to the coffee pot were lots of creamers, sugar, and sugar substitutes. Wow, what a setup. Hopefully, this coffee would settle his nerves for the meeting. This prestigious agency was an improvement from the previous one he used. He understood the significance of a first impression and wanted it to work out with this ad agency.

*** Isa ***

Isabel was working on an ad campaign for dog food when she heard her office phone ring. She glanced at the screen to see who was calling. She had been working on this campaign for over a month and the client continued to change his mind with the direction of his ad. He wanted the ad to match the commercial. However, in order to create his entire campaign, they had to get the importance of what he wanted to say about his product. Every time they came up with an idea, he loved it. They proceeded to storyboards, and then he would change his mind and ask for a different direction. The client wasn't sure if he wanted to focus on talking animals in the commercial, the ingredients in the food, or the dog's mental health. Isa was tired of spinning her wheels. She hoped this last idea, which focused on the nutritional value of the food extending the quality of life for the dog, would appeal to her client. These storyboards were due tomorrow, and she hoped that wasn't her client calling with changes. All they had left to do was to mount the boards and prepare the presentation.

If she didn't answer her phone, her secretary answered and took a message. She saw it was Maggie, the company receptionist, and her best friend. Before she could say hello, she heard Maggie's voice whispering.

"Isa, Isa, are you in there?" Maggie's tone was urgent and barely contained her excitement.

"Hey Mags, yeah, I'm here. Why are you whispering? What's up?"

"You have got to see the hunk that just stepped into our office and is going to be meeting with John this morning," Maggie whispered.

"You mean Johnny Thunderbird?" Isa replied. Isa was the Art Director at Teramar Studios. She knew who the sales reps were meeting with daily. She had to be prepared in case they asked her to come and sit in on their meeting for conceptual ideas.

"Yeah, that's the guy. He is soooooooo hot! I hope he asks me out before he leaves. Or maybe I'll ask him out. You have got to see him. He's getting a cup of coffee in the kitchen as we speak. That's why I'm whispering. Oops, gotta go, I think he is heading back to the lobby," Maggie cleared her throat, evidently seeing Thunder enter the lobby again.

"Yes, Mrs. Davis, I will have Jim call you back as soon as possible. Have a nice day." Isa knew Maggie could hear her laughing as she hung up the phone.

Isa loved Maggie. This job would not be as much fun without her. Isa and Maggie became friends on Isa's first day of work. They'd hit it off immediately. Since they were both single, they tried to get together once a week to go to clubs to dance, catch a movie, get dinner, or rent a chick flick. Sometimes they'd have a sleepover weekend.

Maggie was determined to either get a date for herself or set Isa up. Mr. Thunderbird must be really attractive if Maggie wanted him for herself. She rarely passed those up to Isa, which was fine. Isa didn't really have time to go check out a potentially hot client, anyway. She had too much work to do.

Chapter 6

The Encounter @ Teramar Studios

THUNDER

"Mr. Thunderbird, hello I'm John Cummings. It is a pleasure to meet you," John extended his hand out to Thunder.

"Mr. Cummings, it is a pleasure to meet you as well. Please call me Thunder." Thunder stood and shook his hand.

"Very well, Thunder, you can call me John. Let's go upstairs and talk in my office." John turned to Maggie. "Maggie, will you please hold all my calls?"

"Sure will," she smiled brightly at Thunder.

"I see you got some coffee. Do you need a refill before we head up?" John asked before he pushed the elevator up button.

"Sure, that would be great. I'm not one to turn down more coffee," Thunder answered and walked with John into the kitchen. John filled up his mug, and they headed back toward the elevators.

Thunder wondered why they didn't take the stairs since they only went one floor up. Then again, Mr. Cummings didn't look like the exercise type and this was a business meeting. Under the circumstances, the elevator was more professional.

As they exited the elevator, John said to Thunder, "Right this way. My office is the third one on the right. I just need to tell Bob something. Go on ahead, I'll only be a minute."

John popped his head into the first office on the right. Thunder walked toward John's office. As he passed an open doorway, a brunette burst out of the office. She was looking down, checking something on her phone, and ran right into him. He quickly dropped his briefcase and grabbed her with his left hand to steady her. Unfortunately, his right hand had been holding the coffee that she was now wearing.

"Ooof! Ow, holy sugar, that's hot!" she screamed, staring down at her shirt and pulling it away from her skin. She looked up at him and brushed a few strands of hair back from her face, her eyes filling with tears.

"Miss, I'm so sorry. Are you alright?" Thunder's eyes widened as he looked from her shirt to her face.

"Isa, are you ok?" John asked rushing over to check on her.

Thunder stared at the pretty, petite woman he nearly ran over. She was wearing a navy skirt and an off-white blouse that was now covered in coffee stains. He also got a pretty good look at her breasts inside her lacy bra when she pulled her blouse away from her body. *Dude, don't focus on that, he told himself. Remember to be professional. Having a tent in your pants is not professional behavior.*

"I'm so sorry. I didn't see you coming out of that office. I'd be more than happy to pay for your dry cleaning or buy you a new blouse," he offered. He didn't think running into her had been his fault, but he had spilled his hot coffee on her.

"That's alright. It was my fault. I should have looked before I ran out into the hallway," Isa sighed. "I'm Isabel Gonzalez, the art director at Teramar Studios."

"Isa, this is Mr. Johnny Thunderbird. He's here to discuss some advertising for his future exhibits at the American Indian Cultural Center."

"I'm pleased to meet you, Mr. Thunderbird." Isa pulled herself together and put her hand out to Thunder.

"Please call me Thunder."

Since Thunder's briefcase was on the floor, he switched his coffee from his right hand to his left so he could shake her hand. The minute their hands shook, he felt a burst of electricity run up his arm, leaving him speechless for a moment as he gazed into her eyes. The feel of her smaller hand enveloped in his made him feel very protective of her—she was the one, his future. Her smile caused his eyes to be drawn to her lips. He smiled back and wanted to taste her plump, luscious, red lips. However, they were in an office building conducting business. So Thunder resolved to conduct himself like a professional and not an oversexed idiot. Realizing he was still holding her hand, he released his grip, allowing her hand to slide out.

"I'm sorry for our crazy introduction. It is a pleasure to meet you as well. I look forward to seeing what your agency offers for our cultural center." He was quite proud of himself for that speech.

"Well, Thunder, I need to clean myself up. However, John will go over your project with you. If you have questions about the design aspect of your job, contact me directly. John can give you all my information. Gentlemen, have a good meeting."

*** Isa ***

Isa tried to keep her cool and took the stairs to the lobby. She headed toward the kitchen and grabbed a couple of napkins. That man was too good looking for his own good. Just knowing he was in the building was making her wet. Maybe she should go home and change her blouse and panties. Ugh, he was so hot.

Isa walked to Maggie's desk.

"Mags, you were so right," she whispered. "He is drop dead gorgeous."

"He is dreamy with those chocolate brown eyes that are so mesmerizing, tall, well built, so alpha male, confident walk, good manners, and smelled so good. I bet he's fantastic in bed." Maggie rested her head on her hand, adopting a faraway look on her face. Then she blinked and looked at Isa. "Wait, what happened to your blouse?" Maggie asked with a confused look on her face.

"I ran smack dab into a gorgeous brick wall that was carrying a full cup of hot coffee and I chose that moment to wear it. Ugh, just call me a klutz," Isa told Maggie. "I had to pull it away from my body quickly, but I think he still got a good look at my boobs in my lacy bra. Then I tried to dry it with napkins, but now it's worse. I don't have time to go home and come back, so I guess I'll sneak back upstairs and put my blazer on. Maybe I can leave early today. Anyway, gotta go. Come to my office for lunch."

Maggie just smiled and laughed at Isa during her whole embarrassing story. "Ok, see ya' at lunch," she told Isa before she picked up the next incoming call.

Chapter 7

The Meeting @ Teramar Studios

THUNDER

John and Thunder walked into John's office, and John closed the door.

"I'm sorry about your coffee," John lamented. "Can I get you another cup?"

"No," Thunder smiled, "it's alright. I'm just sorry I spilled it on her. I can always get another cup when I get to work."

"So Thunder, what are you looking for from our company? You said you had issues with the last ad agency and I want to make sure we help you the best way we can."

"Thank you. I appreciate you taking the time to meet with me."

"Of course, we pride ourselves on our customer service and creating the best campaign for our clients."

"We do several exhibits during the year. Our previous exhibit was called 'The Life and Times of American Indian Cultures'. The previous agency made a terrible mistake with the name of the exhibit and called it 'The Life and Fines of American Indian Cultures'. No one at the agency caught the typo, and they hadn't given me the proof until after the printer started printing the flyers. By the time I called to talk to them, they had already printed 2,000 brochures. At first, they wanted me to pay for it, which I refused, since they started printing before I signed off on the proof. Then they apologized and agreed to fix them and reprint my order. However, that show started two days after that conversation. The agency had the information for almost a month before they gave me a proof, and they didn't print them in time to distribute to local hotels, motels, shops, and schools in the area. Our opening night was a total disaster with utter confusion. We didn't have brochures with a price list, so all my staff and volunteers were constantly asking me about the price and descriptions of every item."

"Wow," John interrupted, "that sounds crazy."

"It was. We ran ourselves ragged and sold little. After that night, I created a simple brochure which was not great since I'm not a Graphic Designer. But I had no choice until we received their corrected brochures. By the time they delivered the corrected brochures and flyers, we had already been a month into the show. Because of the error, we didn't have as many visitors as we would have liked. I swore to never use them again."

"I assure you, we will work on your campaign efficiently. Let's talk about what this next exhibit is about and when it is opening." John took out a pad and began taking notes.

"Our exhibit was called 'Red Path' and it would contain original paintings, sculptures and clothing by American Indian artists from over 50 tribes. This is going to be our biggest exhibit to date. Because of the importance of this exhibit, we would like your ad agency to create a marketing flyer, brochure, and social media campaign."

"We can certainly do that. What is the date on your Opening Night?"

It was nearly two hours later when Thunder came out of John's office. The meeting went well. Thunder left John with a flash drive containing images of the displays, food, and items for sale during the exhibit. John told him they would be in contact with him within the next two days with a first draft for Thunder to approve and make any necessary changes. Once Thunder approved their ad campaign, they would print the brochures and flyers, and Teramar would publish everything on Thunder's social media platforms. John told Thunder he could expect to have the flyers at least a week before opening night, if not sooner.

That was music to Thunder's ears. He left that meeting a very happy camper. Even happier when he saw Isa in the lobby on his way out. She had great legs that would look even better wrapped around him in bed. He noticed she wore her blazer, trying to cover up her blouse. That gave him a great idea.

"Hello again, ladies. Ms. Gonzalez, may I have a word with you in the kitchen please?" he asked.

Isa looked at Maggie, then back at him. "Um, sure. Do you have some questions about your flyers? We can go to my office."

She started walking toward him. As she got closer, he noticed there was a bathroom next to the kitchen. He nudged her into the bathroom. Thank goodness it was a single stall.

"What are you doing?" Isa asked, her face riddled with confusion. "This is not the kitchen." She tried to get out, but he had already closed the door and locked it.

"Ms. Gonzalez, I will not hurt you. I just started thinking I can give you my shirt and you can give me yours," he told her calmly. He watched her panicked expression as she looked between him and the door.

"Are you crazy? Why would I do that? My shirt wouldn't even fit you?" She tilted her head quizzically.

"I will not wear your shirt. I'll get it dry cleaned for you. It is my fault that I spilled my coffee on you, and it's not even noon. You can't go to lunch and finish out your day with that shirt," he told her as he pointed to the stain that was clearly visible even with her blazer on.

"Well, what about you?" She asked.

"Ms. Gonzalez, I'm going straight to work after this. I keep several clean shirts at work because sometimes I work late and sleep on the couch in my office," he shrugged.

"Ok," she sighed, "I have several meetings today. How do we do this? And please call me Isa. The last thing I want to think about is my mom as I'm stripping in a bathroom with a man I barely know."

She placed her hands on her hips, waiting for Thunder's instructions.

"I'll take my shirt off and then turn around while you take yours off. Then I'll hand you mine. I know it will be a little big, but we can make it work in the back," he suggested.

"Okay, if you think it will work. I can't go home early, and I can't stay like this. Not only can the clients see my stains even with my blazer on, but I smell like coffee." She scrunched her nose.

As soon as she said okay, Thunder started taking off his tie.

"Can you hold my tie and jacket for me, please? I don't want to put them on the floor," he asked as he took them off.

She graciously held out her hand and took his tie and suit jacket. When he undid his shirt buttons, he noticed she was staring at his chest and abs. He was grateful for his workout regimen. She kept licking her lips, and it was driving him crazy. He wanted to be the one licking and tasting those lips. He pulled off his shirt and stood naked from the waist up. She was still staring at his abs.

"See something you like?" He grinned at her.

"Oh, sorry. You have nice abs—sorry shirt, a nice shirt, so white," she stumbled over her words, her face blushed a nice shade of reddish-pink.

"Okay, thank you, I think?" Thunder tilted his head, puzzled by her words, but loving her blush. "Hand me that other stuff." Thunder pointed to his jacket and tie in her arms. "I'll turn around. Let me know when you're done and we'll switch shirts."

Thunder grabbed his suit jacket and tie and turned around. Covertly, he watched her from the corner of the mirror as she unbuttoned her blouse. Since she was looking down, Thunder knew she hadn't realized he had a front-row seat to the show. And what a great show it was. She had perfect breasts and a body that could stop a truck.

"Ok, here's my shirt," Isa draped it over his shoulder, "hand me yours."

And then... the show was over. She was buttoning his shirt before his fantasies could get the better of him. There was something strangely erotic in seeing her in his shirt and knowing she'd be wearing it all day. Maybe she'd even go to bed in it.

"Thunder, you can turn around now," she said as she buttoned up the last button.

Even though his shirt was tailored to fit his slim waist, it still appeared enormous on her. He was well over six feet, and she was almost a foot smaller than him.

"We can fix it. Turn around," he told her. He unbuttoned and unzipped her skirt. She immediately held the front of her skirt so it wouldn't drop to the floor. Then he pulled the back center of the shirt away from her body and folded it lengthwise toward her. With one hand, he held the shirt against her butt while he tucked the rest of the shirt into her skirt. Then he zipped and buttoned her skirt, quickly lifting it to fix the shirt underneath. He got to see and feel her thong and nice ass.

"Are you trying to cop a feel?" She turned her head, staring at him, stunned and angry, as she slapped his hands away. Not only did he "accidentally" cop a feel of her nice ass and soaked pussy, he realized she felt the same sexual tension he felt and hardened even more.

"Uh, I'm sorry." Thunder lifted his hands and pointed to the back of her skirt and said, "I was trying to tuck in the shirt so it wouldn't look so bulky under your skirt." He looked innocently at her while lying through his teeth. He didn't want to scare her off and tell her, yes, he was trying to cop a feel.

"Well, I can tuck it in myself," she squinted at him.

"Absolutely. I was just trying to help." He raised his hands up and took a step back.

"Fine," she sighed as she stared at his chest in the mirror.

Thunder noticed she was panting and her eyes dilated. He wished he had more time, and they were in a different place. He counted to ten and got his big guy to calm down. This was their first meeting, and he had to be professional. He was just helping her out, and he still needed to walk out of the building with some dignity.

"Ugh, Thunder, I am never pulling this off. You are huge compared to me." She sighed, placing her hands on her hips, staring at herself in the mirror. He smiled at her because he knew he was huge everywhere, but she didn't know that yet.

"You can fix it a little more if you need to," he told her. He knew he had to stop touching her or he would fuck her on the bathroom counter.

"Maybe put your blazer on? That will help, I think."

"Ok," she put on her blazer and closed it. "I think this will work. Thank you, Thunder, I really appreciate it," she spontaneously hugged him. He hugged her back, of course.

"You are very welcome. I will get your shirt cleaned and we can exchange shirts later. How does that sound?" He kept his hands on her hips and quirked an eyebrow.

"That sounds great," she smiled.

He hadn't let go of her, and she wasn't pulling away. For a second, they just stared at each other, almost like they were playing a game of chicken and were trying to see who would break first. Thunder was never one to back down from a challenge.

Holding her gaze, he leaned in for a quick peck on the lips. But as soon as their lips met, he knew he wouldn't be stopping at a simple peck. She seemed to agree wholeheartedly with his decision.

Grabbing him by the back of his head, Isa opened her mouth, silently asking for more. She was much shorter than him, so he did them both a favor and lifted her up to his level. After a few minutes of losing himself in her, he pulled away and looked into her eyes as he slowly let her slide down his body.

"I'm not sorry about kissing you. Been wanting to do that since you slammed into me. But I am sorry our first kiss was in a bathroom at your place of employment," he whispered, gazing into her eyes. "I gotta go. Can I call you so we can see each other again?"

"Okay," she answered breathlessly.

He nodded his head toward her, brushing his lips against hers one last time, then turned around to grab his jacket and tie along with her shirt that were now on the floor...oops. He unlocked and open the door, like nothing unusual or inappropriate had happened in the bathroom. Thank goodness nobody had needed the restroom.

"Bye Maggie, thank you for your help today," he called out to Maggie on his way out.

"Bye Mr. Thunderbird, see you later," Maggie replied.

When he got in his car, he realized two things. One, he never put on his suit jacket. Two, he walked through the lobby shirtless in his dress pants. Well...so much for professionalism and dignity.

*** *Isa* ***

Isa waited a couple of minutes after Thunder left before she walked out of the bathroom and straight to Maggie's desk.

"Now there went a real hunk. I wonder if he noticed he wasn't wearing his shirt?" Maggie giggled. Then Maggie turned her head and looked at Isa, her eyes widening. "Is that Thunder's shirt you're wearing?"

"Yes," Isa blushed, "he let me borrow it so he could get mine dry cleaned. It was very sweet and crazy. Please tell me no one was in the waiting room when he left shirtless?"

"No one but me and I got an eyeful. That man is so hot. I think you should ask him out. Did you guys change in the kitchen, you crazy kids?" Maggie asked her.

"No, in the bathroom, and before you ask, we closed the door and locked it."

"Oooohhhh, did anything else happen? Do tell!" Maggie wiggled her eyebrows.

"Other than the kiss, no," Isa slipped up when she answered her. Oh no, now the questions wouldn't stop. What had she done? She didn't have time for this. She had fifteen minutes to eat lunch before her next client meeting.

Before Maggie could ask more questions, she held up her pointer finger and said, "Stop, I don't have time for details. Let's eat a quick lunch in my office and I'll give you a summary of my bathroom antics. But we've got to hurry because I have a meeting with Mr. Coleman at one, so grab your lunch and let's go."

"I'm on it girlie." Maggie grabbed her lunchbox and followed Isa to her office.

Once they got there, Isa closed the door. She didn't want their conversation to be overheard. Isa told her exactly what happened in the bathroom, the conversation, the changing of clothes, and the kiss quickly between bites. Maggie listened as she ate her lunch.

"You know, Isa, it's the twenty-first century. It's okay to ask him out. You need to get out. You haven't been with anyone since Keith, and that was almost two years ago." Maggie humphed.

"That's not true. I've gone on dates. Just not very often and they have all turned out bad."

"Name one, Isa," Maggie said between bites.

"Tom, the car salesman that came into the office. Remember, he wanted us to do his new commercial."

"Oh sorry, yeah, what a loser. But you went on a business lunch with him, NOT a date." Maggie responded. "You told me you mostly talked about work."

"Well, yes, we talked about work, but it was off the premises, and we ate lunch together. Doesn't that count as a date?"

"That's not a date Isa, but if you want to call it that to make yourself feel better, okay?"

"Ugh. Okay, he mostly told me I should buy a car from him and then asked me out on a date. Which I turned down because I don't need a car. Plus, after that lunch, I didn't want a date with him. Thank you very much." Isa told Maggie.

"If you had taken him up on his offer for a date, that would have been a date." Maggie held up her hand and stopped Isa's next comment. "Still, that's one in two years. You've got to go out more often. You're too young and pretty to stay home all the time. Besides, you must be growing cobwebs down there. Unless you've been using B.O.B." Maggie wiggled her eyebrows. Isa had named it B.O.B. which stood for 'battery operated boyfriend'.

Maggie had given Isa a vibrator last year for her birthday. It was rechargeable, looked like a man's penis with balls and came with a remote control. It was Maggie's not-so-subtle nudge to get back in the saddle.

"Thanks, I think. Anyway, 'true feel' has been getting a lot of action lately and I'm happy with that for now," Isa looked at her watch. This conversation needed to end now. "Wow, would you look at the time? Lunch is over. I guess Maggie's advice therapy is over for now."

"Okay, okay, I can take a hint. But keep me posted if or when he calls. I want all the details," Maggie said as she packed up her lunchbox and left Isa's office.

Chapter 8

Let the Games Begin

THUNDER

Thunder called Isa the day after their bathroom adventure and left her a message on her voicemail. Unfortunately, he only had the ad agency's phone number. He should've gotten her cellphone number when they were in the bathroom. He couldn't stop thinking about her.

Luckily, a couple of days later, Isa called the cultural center and set up an appointment with him through Rachel to see the sample brochure and flyer. He wasn't sure why she didn't call him directly. John had his office number, cellphone, and the cultural center's main number.

On the day of the meeting, Isa came into the room and sat in on the presentation. Thunder was so happy to see her. He wanted to talk to her as soon as the presentation was over. However, halfway through the meeting, she was called out. When the meeting ended, he thanked everyone. They presented him with two different ad campaigns. He chose the one he felt represented his exhibit the best. He told them he was so happy with their work, he would use them exclusively. An enormous weight lifted off his shoulder and he wanted to celebrate.

He didn't know which office was Isa's because the day he bumped into her, he never asked if that was her office she was coming out of. So, he went to see Maggie in the lobby.

"Hi Maggie."

"Mr. Thunderbird, how are you?" Maggie smiled.

"You can call me Thunder. I'm doing great. Can you please call Isa's office and ask her if she can meet with me?"

"Sure Thunder." Thunder waited at Maggie's desk while she dialed a number and spoke to someone on the other end.

"Hi Melanie, Is Isa in her office?"

"Ok, I'll let Mr. Thunderbird know she is gone for the day. Can you please leave her a message? He wants to speak to her."

"Thanks Melanie. Talk to you later."

"Thunder, I'm sorry she has left for the day, but Melanie will leave a message for you."

"Great," Thunder sighed, "Thank you Maggie."

Thunder left and went back to work. He had a lot to do in the next three weeks.

Chapter 9

Runaway Art Director

THUNDER

A week later, Thunder tried to see Isa when he met with John at Teramar and gave him approval to print the flyers and brochures. This time he walked to the office she came out of during the coffee spill and knocked on the door. The lights were off, and blinds were closed, and no one answered. On his way out, he walked to Maggie's desk and asked her to call Isa. Maggie called her office, but no one answered. Thunder left Isa another message and headed to work.

When he arrived, Rachel had already packed several of the artifacts from the previous exhibit that had to be shipped out to make room for the new exhibit. Some Lakota items from their reservation always remained spread out on display during exhibits.

Thunder walked into the warehouse and took an inventory of all the new artifacts that were coming in for the Red Path Exhibit.

"Thunder," Rachel walked into the warehouse, "Do you need help?"

"No, Rachel. I'm good. If you can continue to pack up, that would be great. As soon as I'm done with this inventory, I'll start laying it out in the display cases and you can make the labels."

"Okay, do you want to get some dinner tonight?"

"Uh, no thank you. I'm going over to Sarah's for dinner." Thunder moved to the next box.

"Oh, Okay. Maybe tomorrow night?"

"I have so much to do, I can't even think about tomorrow," Thunder sighed. He didn't want to go out to dinner with her. He didn't understand why she was doing this now. She never asked him to go out to dinner. "Is something wrong Rachel?" Thunder asked.

"No, why?"

"Um, because you've been acting strange lately. I'm your friend and I'm concerned about you." Thunder looked up from his clipboard. He called her a friend to define their relationship.

"No, I'm good. Just wanted to know if you wanted to have dinner, since I didn't have any plans."

"Okay, well, that's good." Thunder went back to his clipboard.

*** *Rachel* ***

Men were so dense, Rachel thought. Of course, she had been trying to go out with him. They had broken up a long time ago, but she still had not found someone as good as Thunder in or out of the bedroom. Despite her persistent attempts to make him see her romantically once more, he still regarded her as just a friend. You would think he had needs. Needs that she would gladly fulfill. It's not like he was seeing anyone. If she could get him in bed, he would remember how good they were. Damn, she hadn't gotten laid in months, hoping he'd take notice.

Rachel knew they could have a beautiful life together at this cultural center if he just gave it a shot and stopped putting her in the friend zone. Maybe she would have to become close to his sister. Sarah didn't like Rachel after the last time she dated Thunder. Sarah had even asked Rachel point-blank if she had cheated on her brother. Thinking that Sarah was just guessing and pulling at straws, Rachel denied it vehemently. Rachel hoped Joseph hadn't told Sarah anything, or she would be in big trouble.

Well, time to make nice with Sarah and persuade her to help get Thunder back. Thunder loved his sister and would do anything for her. Sarah was her ace in the hole.

Chapter 10

The Flyers are Coming, The Flyers are Coming

THUNDER

T hunder sat at his desk, staring at his phone. He had called Isa yet again, and she was busy with a client. Maggie said she left a message, and she would call him back. He wanted to tell Maggie—yeah, right? But he kept the call professional, thanked her, and hung up. He couldn't stop thinking about Isa, even though she was ghosting him.

"Thunder," Rachel called out from the lobby, "The flyers are here."

Thunder hurried out of his office, hoping Isa had delivered them. When he reached the lobby desk, he looked around and only saw the delivery driver.

"Thank you," Rachel signed for them and smiled at the driver.

"No Problem. Have a great day."

"You too," Rachel and Thunder both answered.

"Do you want to put them up today?" Rachel asked.

"Yes, let me call Sarah and Grayhorse and see if they can come over and help before they have to pick up Tommy from school."

"What about me, boss?" Mark asked.

"Can you stay here while we put them up? I really don't want to close the center."

"Sure, no problem. I have the easy gig." Mark leaned back in his chair and placed his hands behind his head.

Thunder laughed and walked to his office to make some calls. Rachel followed him.

"Why don't I go with Sarah, and you can go with Grayhorse?" Rachel volunteered.

"Let me talk to Sarah first and see if they are available. Can you please close the door on your way out?" Thunder called Sarah's cell right after Rachel closed the door. He wanted privacy, since Sarah didn't like Rachel.

"Hello?" Sarah answered.

"*Hau, taŋkši.* How is my favorite sister?"

"I'm your only sister. I obviously should be your favorite. What are you doing and what do you want?"

"Ouch, that hurts," Thunder dramatically sighs. "What makes you think I want something?"

"Uh, let's see. You are calling me during the day, you called me your favorite sister, you now sound dramatically offended, and I know you have an opening in a little over a week."

"Okay," Thunder laughed, "You got me. I got the flyers for the Red Path Exhibit featuring the Opening Night date and I need your help to distribute them." Thunder winced.

"Is that a question or a statement?"

"A question. Can you please help me distribute them?" Thunder asked nicely.

"Well," Sarah laughed, "Of course I will. Do you want me to get Grayhorse to help?"

"That would be great."

"I'll come by with Grayhorse in about thirty minutes and get them. We can deliver several before Tommy gets out of school."

"Uh, Rachel suggested that maybe you guys could do it together."

"Thunder," Sarah sighed.

"I know you don't like her. But something is going on with her and maybe you can get her to tell you."

"Fine, but I would rather do this with my sexy husband."

Thunder could hear Grayhorse in the background.

"You'd better want to do everything with your sexy husband and not someone else."

Sarah laughed and then starting moaning.

"Hey you two. TMI, I don't need to hear that. I'll see you in thirty." Thunder hung up the phone before he heard anymore moaning and groaning. Those were not the sounds he wanted to hear coming out of his sister's mouth. Stepping out of the office, he went in search of Rachel.

"Rachel, Sarah said she would go with you, and I'll go with Grayhorse."

"That's great," she beamed.

"Let's walk to our closest neighbors and put these up before they get here. Mark, we'll be back in a few."

"Sure boss, no problem."

Thunder and Rachel grabbed a handful and walked up and down the block, delivering the flyers. All their neighboring businesses would take them and replace them with the previous flyer. They all helped each other out.

*** *Sarah* ***

"So, what did you want to do with your sexy husband?" Grayhorse whispered into his wife's neck from behind.

"Thunder wants us to deliver some flyers for the new exhibit and he wants me to go with Rachel."

"What?" Grayhorse stopped and turned her around to look at her. "Since when? He knows you don't like Rachel. That's not like him to do that to you."

"I know," Sarah answered wryly, "But Rachel suggested it and he thinks she is up to something."

"Why doesn't he just talk to her?"

"I don't know," Sarah whined, "but I want to help him out. He's my brother and I love him. He is always doing stuff for us."

"Ok, do you want me to go with her? I can stare her down and interrogate her." Grayhorse crossed his arms and gave her his intimidating look.

"No," Sarah laughed and slapped his arm, "I'll do it. How bad can it be?"

"Famous last words." Grayhorse raised his eyebrow at her. "Alright, let's see how many flyers we can put up before we pick up Tommy."

"Lead the way, my sexy husband."

Grayhorse turned around and carried Sarah firefighter style to the car.

"Grayhorse, no. Stop, the blood is rushing to my head!" she screamed.

Grayhorse dropped her into the passenger seat, kissed her, and got into the driver's seat. Sarah was grateful to God every day for Thunder bringing Grayhorse home that one day so long ago. They laughed and joked all the way to the center. Walking in, they saw Mark behind the desk.

"Hey Mark, Where's Thunder? We are reporting for duty." Sarah saluted Mark, who chuckled at her antics.

"He went to distribute some flyers to the businesses on the block. He'll be back soon." Before Mark could finish answering her, Thunder walked through the door with Rachel.

"Hey," Thunder hugged Sarah and Grayhorse. "Are you guys ready?"

"Yup," Grayhorse answered.

"Ok, let's grab some flyers. Sarah, you and Rachel can go to the food stores and the local schools. Grayhorse and I will go to the gas stations, hotels, and nearby malls. Keep some to take home so we can spread them out around the city."

"Sounds good," Grayhorse said to Sarah, "*wíŋyaŋ mitáwa,* I will meet you here at 3:30. I don't want to be too late in picking up Tommy."

"Okay," Sarah kissed Grayhorse, "Rachel I'll drive, Grayhorse can go with Thunder."

"Okay." Rachel followed Sarah out to her car.

"So, let's go to the grocery store that's right by our closest elementary school. Then we can go to that elementary school and any other schools nearby. We'll visit as many as we can in the next couple of hours."

"That sounds like a smart plan, Sarah."

"So," Sarah said as she pulled out of the parking lot, "How have you been?"

"I'm good. Trying to stay busy with work."

"Dating anyone?" Sarah dove right in with her question.

"No, not right now. I've been single for a few months. I'm tired of one-night stands and losers."

"Well," Sarah nodded, "I can understand that." Sarah hoped Rachel would expand on her answer. If Rachel was seeing someone, then she would leave Thunder alone.

"How are you guys doing?" Rachel turned to face her.

"We are phenomenal!" Sarah exclaimed. "Tommy is loving school, Grayhorse is busy with the ranch, and I'm enjoying volunteering at the school. Oh, here's our first stop." Sarah parked at the grocery store. "Do you want to do the honors, or do you want me to give it to them?" This was one of their usual stores that always displayed their events.

"I'll go, so you can leave the car running. I'll only be a few minutes." Rachel got out and headed towards the grocery store.

Sarah waited in the car. Rachel didn't take long at all.

"They said thank you and they couldn't wait to see it. They would put the flyer up today." Rachel beamed.

"Woo-hoo, one down and several more to go," Sarah pulled out and headed toward the closest elementary school. Afterward, they went to one more elementary school, two middle schools, and one high school. Sarah felt completely exhausted trying to come up with small talk between deliveries. She couldn't wait to get back to the center.

"So," Rachel looked out the window, "Is Thunder seeing anyone? He seems on edge and keeps calling someone named Ms. Gonzalez?"

Boom, there it is! Isa knew it was just a matter of time. She was shocked it took Rachel all this time to get the courage to ask her about Thunder.

"I don't really know. He has said nothing to me about anyone."

"Oh, maybe he's just calling her about business. Do you know if he is dating anyone?" she looked innocently at her.

"Not that I'm aware of, but I haven't asked him. Have you seen him with someone?"

"No, I was just curious."

"Rachel, you know he thinks of you as family." Sarah rattled on. "You are a good friend to him, but he is not romantically interested in you. I would hate for you to get hurt."

"Oh, of course," Rachel looked angry at first, but then smiled as if nothing was wrong. "I was just asking because he seemed off and as his friend, I just wanted to help him if he needed a shoulder to lean on."

"That's nice of you, Rachel. Well, here we are. Thank you for going with me. It was nice to have girl talk." Sarah was grateful the conversation about Thunder started near the end of their trip and not the beginning.

"Yes, it was. Thank you for driving."

Sarah and Rachel walked into the center. Sarah went straight to Grayhorse for a kiss.

"How did it go?" Thunder asked.

"It was great." Rachel leaned on the lobby desk. "We delivered a lot of flyers."

"Excellent. Grab some more flyers and share them wherever you go. Thank you all for helping me out. You know it takes a village."

"We are a small village, but a village non the less," Grayhorse said as he escorted Sarah to the door, "See you all later, we gotta go."

"I'll walk you to the car," Thunder said as he walked behind Sarah and Grayhorse.

"Bye," Rachel and Mark said.

"So," Thunder looked at Sarah, "What is going on with Rachel?"

"She said nothing, but I think she wants you back."

"What!" Thunder shouted, his eyes bugging out, "Why? It's not like I've been acting like more than a friend."

"She didn't specifically say she wanted you back, but she definitely implied it. I told her she was family and a friend to you. I think she got a little angry, but then played it off. You need to be careful. Do not flirt with her."

"Me," Thunder pointed to himself, offended, "I'm not interested in her. Hell, I'm too busy fantasizing about a woman that won't even answer my calls."

"And who is this woman?" Grayhorse smirked.

"Isabel Gonzalez. She's the art director at the new ad agency that we're using. She keeps avoiding me and sending me to voicemail. Then she'll call me back and leave messages with Rachel."

"So, why are you still after her?" Grayhorse asked. "I've never known you to have to chase a woman for a date."

"Ugh, it's a long story, but I felt like we belonged together when I bumped into her with my coffee, and we exchanged shirts."

"Uh, I think you need to tell us the entire story *tibló*," Sarah stared at Thunder.

"Not now, he doesn't," Grayhorse spoke up. "We need to go. He can call you tonight and give you all the gory details."

"Fine, call me tonight." Sarah yelled before Grayhorse closed her truck door and headed to the driver's side. Sarah opened her window and heard their comments.

"I owe you one," Thunder mumbled.

"Not really, you only have a few hours to get your story straight," Grayhorse laughed and pulled out of the parking lot.

Sarah would call him tonight and find out who this woman was that was twisting up her brother. They always chased him, not the other way around. Thunder needed a challenge, and this woman might just be the one to give him a run for his money.

Chapter 11

Tuesday...Still no Isa

THUNDER

Two days away from the opening, Thunder still hadn't talked to Isa. It was now going on almost a month since he had seen her. Mark, Rachel, Sarah, Grayhorse, Tommy, and Thunder drove all over, posting the rest of the flyers at more hotels, motels, restaurants, schools, and malls. Teramar took care of all the information on their social media accounts. This time, the brochures had the descriptions and prices for all the items on sale.

Thunder put the final touches on the exhibit. He had to pick up the tribal council members from the airport tonight at eight. They were staying at the guitar hotel with their Seminole friends. He would bring them to the exhibit tomorrow so they could see it before it opened to the public. That would give him a day and a half just in case he needed to change anything. He truly valued their opinion and advice.

For tonight, he would take them to dinner before dropping them off at the hotel. He wanted them to rest after their long flight from South Dakota.

Everything was coming together like the pieces of a puzzle. Thunder knew Isa was aware of his opening day, but he wanted to send her a personal invitation. A quick email would suffice. He knew she read her emails every day because she always responded to him at different times throughout the workday. An email invitation seemed more professional. He wanted to be careful how he phrased it because he didn't want to come off angry or demanding. He still had her shirt and was tired of her ghosting him, plus he really wanted to see her.

Ms. Gonzalez,
I know you are very busy, but I would love it if you would come to the opening of "Red Path" at the cultural center on Thursday. The exhibit opens at 6:00pm. It would be my honor to give you a personal tour and introduce you to the elders in our tribal council.
I hope to see you here.
Thunder

If she didn't come to the opening, he was going to find her come hell or high water. For now, it was time to go to the airport.

Chapter 12

Wednesday...The Night before Opening

Isa

Isa was busy working long hours for the past three weeks. She felt bad about avoiding Thunder and playing phone tag. He never answered the phone at the cultural center, so she would leave a message with Mark or Rachel. If they transferred her call because he was in his office, she would hang up. If he didn't answer, she would leave a message. Despite knowing it was childish behavior, she felt embarrassed after the hallway and bathroom incident. She didn't know what to say. She knew eventually she had to either get her shirt or forget about it.

For now, Isa specifically told Maggie not to bother her in her office if Thunder was looking for her. When Thunder was in the building for a meeting, Isa either shut her blinds and locked her door or met with clients at their office. She tried to avoid bumping into him.

She knew she wasn't being fair to Thunder, but she was embarrassed and scared. He did not know that she really liked him and thought he was sexy. She was afraid of rejection after her last relationship. Her ex-boyfriend, Keith, cheated on her and left her feeling insecure and unattractive. He was the art director at a prestigious ad agency, and she worked for him as one of his graphic designers. Even though Keith was her boss, they dated for three years, and she really loved him. Unfortunately, Keith loved a lot of other girls during those three years. She was so oblivious. She gave him her virginity at twenty and said yes when he proposed to her. How wrong she was.

When they started planning the wedding, she should've known he was dragging his feet on all the decisions. While she believed he was busy with work, she also had a lot on her plate. She still vividly remembered the night she wanted to talk about the venue with him. They had not spent a lot of time together lately because of their work deadlines and she wanted to surprise him at his office after work with dinner and a tight dress with no panties.

"Honey, I'm home," Isa opened Keith's office door and stared at one of the other designers naked and laying over his desk as he fucked her from behind.

"What the fuck is wrong with you?" Isa screamed at Keith. When neither one realized they were being watched. Not really wanting an answer to the question, she quickly threw the bag of food at his back, turned around, and ran out of the room. Holy Shit and to think she was going to marry that cheating bastard.

"Isa, wait," he screamed as he chased her down the hallway, "stop, it's not what you think! I love you!"

Isa was waiting for the elevator, wondering why it was taking so long.

"Isa," Keith was panting as he zipped up his pants, "it's not what you think. I still want to marry you. We can work this out."

Isa turned to look at him. Unbelievable. He was fucking another woman, and he wanted to work it out.

"Are you fucking crazy?" Isa was shaking as she yelled at him, "I never want to see you again, you asshole! I was loyal to you. I never cheated!"

"I know and I'm sorry you had to see that. Once we are married, I will only be with you."

"Are you serious? You were supposed to be with only me while we were dating and when we got engaged." Isa was fuming as she took off the engagement ring and threw it at him.

When the ring hit Keith in the face, he realized Isa was not forgiving him and he got ugly.

"Fuck, you frigid bitch. You know what? I don't want to marry you. Fucking you is like fucking a dead fish. All you do is lay there and I have to think of other women to have an orgasm. You were just a convenient hole!"

"You asshole!" Isa yelled as she got in the elevator.

"I'm better off without you," Keith screamed one last insult before the doors closed, "quit since I don't want you working for me, you cold bitch!"

Isa remembered feeling heart broken, ugly, and worthless after that brief encounter. She had driven home and cried herself to sleep.

Fortunately, she hadn't put money down on anything. Her spidey senses had been tingling subconsciously because she hadn't booked the venue, church, flowers, DJ, or Videographer yet. Goodbye Asshole Keith and good riddance.

Unfortunately, she had lost three years of her life with the asshole. Well, really five years since she was still trying to get her life and self-esteem back. Since the breakup, she'd been trying to empower herself. There were good days when she felt her confidence returning, but then she would see him in or out of the office with a beautiful woman on his arm and her insecurities would resurface.

It became unbearable to work in the same company as Asshole Keith. He was the one who cheated on her, but since he was the man, she was the pitiful little woman who couldn't keep her mouth shut. Her cheeks burned as every time she met the accusatory glares of the other men in their agency. Not being able to take it any longer, she quit her job and looked for another one. Her self-esteem was at an all-time low, and it took her a few months to find a job. Luckily, when she interviewed with Teramar Studios, they loved her portfolio and immediately hired her as their new Art Director. That helped her work with self-esteem, but not her personal self-esteem. She didn't think she was pretty enough or good enough in bed to keep any man happy.

Focusing all her attention on her work, she convinced herself she didn't need a man to validate her. She convinced herself that dating was overrated. Besides, she had B.O.B, who didn't come with any baggage and wasn't a cheater. She put all her time and energy into her job and reaped the rewards. There were days she felt lonely—although she wouldn't admit that to anyone, not even Maggie.

Maggie, of course, didn't agree with her. She kept pestering her to go see Thunder and see if their chemistry was still strong. Then again, Maggie was a hopeless romantic. She wanted everyone to live in a fairytale with their Prince Charming, castle, kids, and live happily ever after. Isa had been a hopeless romantic once until Keith broke her down with his cheating and mental abuse. She would get better, but it would take time.

Isa went through her emails and saw one from Thunder. He emailed her an invitation to the Red Path Exhibit on opening night. That was so cool that his tribe elders were coming to see the exhibit. She knew they would be very proud of him and love what they saw.

Usually, one of her designers worked on a project and she oversaw it from beginning to end. However, when she saw all the images for the exhibit, she became so excited her creativity took over. She developed her own design. When Thunder came the day of his presentation, she asked her designer to present both designs. She didn't want Thunder to know she had worked on his project. She didn't want him to make a biased decision.

He ended up picking her design and Teramar became his exclusive ad agency for the future. Strange how she could have feelings for this man but kept pushing him away. She felt so messed up and confused.

Maybe she should go to the opening. She knew she would love it and Thunder would be so busy he wouldn't have time to focus all his time on her. Stupid thought—who wouldn't want a sexy man's attention? Wouldn't she want him to focus on her? *Ugh Isa, get out of your head and give this man a chance. Not everyone is Keith.*

She'd call Maggie later and see if she wanted to go with her. Thunder was super attractive, and he likely has good-looking friends. Besides, it was always better to go with Maggie to an opening. They'd discuss all the items they saw. It would be a fun night.

Now, back to work. Today was proving to be a very long and busy day, filled with client meetings and concept brainstorming sessions, which would probably go into the night. They needed to come up with a fresh new angle for an anti-smoking and anti-vaping ad campaign. That was a challenging venture, as we had already covered every angle with anti-smoking. Oh well, that's why she had brainstorming sessions with her design team. Eventually, someone would hit the bullseye and the sketching would begin. Isa called the local deli and put in a sandwich order to be delivered at 7 p.m. to keep the juices flowing. It was going to be a long night.

*** *Thunder* ***

After dinner, Thunder dropped off the tribal council at their hotel. He went back to the cultural center to double check everything one more time. By midnight, he had everything in order. They had placed all the exhibits either on the walls or in enclosed glass cases. They placed the sculptures on the columns scattered around the room. The caterers delivered all the food, and it was ready to be prepared, including hot and cold hors d'oeuvres. George and Mary Grayfeather cooked all their meals, but for an opening, Thunder hired caterers to help them out. The caterers made everything except the fry bread. George Grayfeather was adamant he would cook this traditional food.

His nephew Tommy asked if he could help serve the guests. He was reluctant at first, but ultimately, he gave in. Tommy could handle the situation, but he would make sure Tommy only carried the food trays, not the drink trays. There were three food trays, the Bacon wrapped Buffalo Meat Bites, freshly made Beef Jerky Sampler, and the Indian Fry Bread. Thinking about Tommy, he smiled to himself. He was a smart, kind, and responsible seven-year-old boy who was growing up way too fast.

Rachel and Sarah would serve the drink trays and Mark would help Tommy with the food trays. Grayhorse would greet and welcome the customers at the door in his full Lakota Warrior Regalia, sans face paint, and hand out their brochure about the exhibit. No face paint because they didn't want to frighten or intimidate any guests or children who didn't understand their culture. They wanted to educate, bring awareness, and spread peace, not scare people. Once everything was in place for tomorrow, Thunder drove home to relax. Tomorrow would be there soon enough.

Chapter 13

Thursday...Red Path Exhibit Opening Day

THUNDER

T hunder woke up at 7:00 a.m. and went for his daily run on the beach. He ran three miles and stopped near the palm trees on the beach to say his morning prayer. His father taught him how to pray to *Wakan Tanka*, the Great Spirit, in the mornings since he was a young boy. He learned to thank *Wakan Tanka* for all the good things he would receive that day. Even when he was in college, he always ran to a park or wooded area where he could be alone with his thoughts to pray. He knelt, closed his eyes, then raised his hands and head toward the sky.

"*Pilámaya, Wakan Tanka*, for being blessed with the beautiful sunrise before my eyes. May Father Sun continue to shine with his brightness on this beautiful day. May Sister Moon grant me the peace of an excellent opening tonight for me and our people. I pray all guests will enter with an open mind and heart. But most of all, I pray for them to listen and learn without judgment," he sang his morning song. When he finished, he hung his head down for a moment of silence.

*** Isa ***

Isa had driven to the beach before the sun rose to clear her head. She still didn't know if she should attend the opening that night. As she walked along the shoreline and watched the sun rise, she shivered as a weird feeling overcame her. She looked around to make sure no one was following her. As she looked toward the palm trees, she saw Thunder with his hands up. It looked like he was praying. His eyes were closed, so she walked closer to him and hid behind another palm tree. His prayer moved her. She didn't realize how important this night was to him. When she saw him stand, she stayed hidden. It worked. He didn't see her. After he left, Isa walked back to her car and drove to work.

*** Thunder ***

Thunder stood up and contemplated an average jog or a full run home. Energized after praying, he started jogging, but soon his arms were pumping faster, and he was running at full speed. During his run, he continued to reflect on the people who were coming to bless his exhibit. He realized he still had some last-minute preparations to do before tonight. By the time he entered his house, sweat drenched his body. He went upstairs to take a shower, get dressed, and head to the cultural center.

Thunder expected the tribal council to arrive at ten this morning. They usually ran a few minutes late, but he wanted to make sure he was there when they arrived. He dressed casually for the day, but took his Lakota Warrior Regalia for the evening. When he'd built the cultural center, he had them build a small apartment above the center so he could spend late nights there. It was a one bedroom/one bathroom loft apartment with a kitchenette. He installed a stackable washer and dryer in the apartment for quick washing of items from downstairs.

While he drove, he realized he needed to go over the schedule with the tribal council. He always wanted one or two council members in the exhibit room to answer questions. Placing the rest of the council members in the Storytelling Room to regale their guests with stories of their heritage.

He arrived at the cultural center at 9:45 a.m. and unlocked the door. No one was here yet. They kept the center closed until the opening at 6:00 p.m. This gave them time to make sure everything was ready. He saw some boxes on the front desk. Opening them, he realized it was the Navajo Jewelry they were expecting from Phoenix, Arizona. With great excitement, he discovered it had arrived in time for the opening. Carrying the boxes to the gift shop, he unpacked them and put the items in the jewelry case by the checkout counter. He noticed that the packing slip had a letter with the prices. He needed to print out the price tags and attach them to the jewelry.

*** Isa ***

That morning, Isa tackled her mail before she got started with her day. Melanie dropped off her mail daily and placed in on the corner of her desk. She usually kept up with her snail mail, but she had been so busy lately that it continued to pile up. She was much quicker reading and answering emails than checking snail mail.

Most of the mail would end up in the trash can by her desk, but every once in a while, there was an important letter. As she continued opening the envelopes and going through the letters inside, she saw the AICC brochure sticking out. She pulled out the brochure and remembered "The Red Path" Exhibit was tonight. She wanted to go but was nervous about seeing Thunder again. Between their phone tag and her ghosting him, she wasn't sure if going was such a good idea. Eventually, she would have to see him if she wanted her shirt back. Tonight was not the night. The opening was more important than her missing shirt. Ghosting him was going to make this evening uncomfortable if she ran into him. She needed to stop second guessing herself. He sent her an email invite so he must want to see her.

It would be great to see the exhibit since she'd designed all his advertising and displays. She knew the center had a museum for the artifacts and exhibits, a story telling room, a gift shop, and a restaurant. Not only were they listed in the brochure, but the local paper had written an article about the cultural center when it first opened. The article also mentioned that the storytelling room served as a playroom for the neighborhood children. She'd wanted to go since she read the article, but never found the time. American Indian culture fascinated her, but she'd been too embarrassed to go there alone. She thought she would make a fool of herself by asking too many questions about the exhibits and culture.

As she was thinking about this, John Cummings stopped by her office. "Isa, are you going to the opening tonight?"

"I was thinking about it. Are you?"

"I am. I'm leaving now so I can run home and pick up Jane and the kids. They are excited about seeing all the artifacts and hearing the stories. We wanted to get there early because we can't stay late since it's a school night," John said. Since he met with Thunder more than she did, he was aware of more details about the exhibit. He'd also stopped by a few days ago to see how it was going. He knew it was her design, and she was handling all the design stuff.

"How do you know there will be storytelling?"

"Uhhh...Isa didn't you read the flyer you designed about the opening? The schedule of events was on there."

"Yeah, I read it when I did it, but I guess I forgot everything I read." Isa scrunched up her nose and rubbed her forehead.

"Well, we have been pretty busy around here," John laughed. "Okay, I gotta go. I want to leave before the rush hour traffic gets terrible. I'll see you there."

John had been married for about ten years to his lovely wife, Jane. They had an eight-year-old boy named James, and a six-year-old girl named Juliet. His kids were the perfect age for storytelling, and she was sure they would have a great time.

Maybe she would be stealthy, and he wouldn't see her. After all, he hadn't seen her at the beach this morning while she watched him and the cultural center was pretty big, with several rooms. Tonight was her chance because she had a valid reason to be there. The place would be crowded, and she would try to blend in with the other guests. Thunder would probably be so busy, he wouldn't see her, anyway. She never responded to his email. If she ran into him, she would apologize for not replying. She would sound professional and congratulate him. Okay, now that she had a game plan, she was feeling better about going. She'd thought about asking Maggie to go with her and then forgot. With Mags, she wouldn't feel so self-conscience.

"Teramar Studios, Can I help you?" Maggie answered professionally.

"Mags, the opening at the American Indian Cultural Center is tonight. Do you want to go?"

"I can't tonight. Ryan finally asked me out, and I already said yes. But you should go. It's about time you got your butt over there and talked to Thunder. I still don't understand why you are avoiding him. He is such a nice guy and so hot. Besides, I'm running out of excuses to cover for you every time he calls. Just think about all he can teach you about all the stuff you always read about in your old west romance novels. Even if you don't want to talk to him, there will still be other people there to ask questions and learn from. Isn't his tribal council coming?"

"Yeah, Mags, they're coming," she sighed. "I was just hoping to have you there for moral support," Isa chuckled.

"Isa, you don't need me. He would love to see you and talk to you. Besides, you need to stop worrying about going alone. You're an attractive single female, and you certainly don't need a man by your side to have a good time. Just take a deep breath, stand tall, hold your head up high and mingle. If he doesn't talk to you, then you can talk to someone else. Ooohhh, you could meet a guy there tonight to date. You really do need to date. It's been too long and all work and no play makes Isa...boring!"

"Thanks a lot Mags. I know I need to go. I got this. Opening night will be packed, but I'll be good. But I still wish you were coming with me. Tell Ryan I said hello and he should have picked another night," she smirked.

Ryan had been working in accounting for over a year now. He was handsome, responsible, and very smart. Maggie usually picked losers, like Isa. Ryan was not a loser. He was nice and had manners—not usually Maggie's type. Isa really hoped they would work out. Maggie had been flirting with him for the past two months. It's about time he got the hint and finally asked her out.

"Ha, I will. Don't think I won't tell him what you said. I'm sorry, I don't want to cancel, since it took him forever to ask me out. I thought he didn't like me, but maybe he's just shy and oblivious."

"Well, he would have to be. Other than you just grabbing him and kissing him, you were obvious."

"I thought so too. Maybe someone from his department finally clued him in. It was getting hard to come up with excuses for me to be at his desk on the third floor. Especially since I could've stayed at my desk and called him with my questions." Maggie chuckled.

"Could be. It's a relief he finally asked. Have a great night! I want to hear all about it tomorrow."

"Oh girl, I will give you all the details. As for you, you'll be fine without me. Go enjoy yourself. You've been working too hard lately and you need to go do something fun."

"Okay mom." Isa rolled her eyes.

"Uh-oh, I gotta go. I've got a call coming in and I'm leaving after I answer it. See ya' tomorrow."

Isa hung up, sat back in her chair, and looked at her desk. By deciding to go to the opening, she would leave her computer at work and not bring work home. She looked down and realized she was wearing a nice cream colored linen dress. *No need to go home and change!* She still had an hour to go before she could leave, but her head was hurting from having her hair up in a bun all day. Opening her desk drawer, she got some ibuprofen and drank it with the bottle of water on her desk. Ibuprofen always helped get rid of her headache. Needing to relieve the pressure on her head, she walked to the restroom to let her hair down. Putting her head down, she fluffed out her hair. Then flipped her hair back. She looked in the mirror to see the effect and smiled. Much better. She went back to her desk to finish up a flyer she had been working on.

Chapter 14

Thursday...Red Path Exhibit Opening Night

THUNDER

By 5:30 p.m., Thunder had everything under control. He wore his tan and turquoise beaded buckskin shirt, pants, and loincloth that his sister made for him a couple of years ago. He'd asked everyone to come dressed in their best American Indian clothing. Since Mark did not own American Indian clothing, Thunder lent him his other buckskin shirt. Mark wore it with jeans because neither Grayhorse nor Thunder's pants would fit him. They were much taller than Mark. Thunder glanced over to the entrance of the restaurant and saw Sarah, Grayhorse, and Tommy had also dressed up. They were showing Tommy which trays he could carry. In the lobby, he could see Rachel placing the last of the artist cards on the sculptures, and Mark was behind the front desk. Everyone looked great.

The only thing Thunder questioned for the evening was whether to have alcohol at the opening. In the old days, the white man's firewater, as they called it back then, played a huge role in his people's downfall. Once forced onto reservations, warriors could no longer continue their old way of life and resorted to alcohol to escape. Some of them lost their pride and became stagnant lost souls. Granted, the white man did not force them to drink the firewater, but they made it accessible by destroying all that they could about their culture, heritage, religion, and way of life. Nowadays, the firewater still caused problems with the warriors, just like it did to everyone else.

This was one reason the tribal council didn't want him to serve alcohol during the exhibit. They were trying to teach everyone about their old ways. However, he noticed from visiting openings in other museums that they always served wine or champagne with hors d'oeuvres. They'd have a lot of non-native guests coming tonight, and he wanted to be accommodating. In the end, he'd had white and red wine along with soda and water. It was a last-minute decision. He hoped the tribal council wouldn't be too angry with him. He wouldn't serve any other alcohol, just wine.

He walked into every room with a checklist on his clipboard to make sure everything was in place. They all knew not to talk to him as he made his quick run through. He didn't want to get distracted. They would just nod to let him know they were ready.

To Do List

Lobby: Sculptures with artist information tags. Grayhorse was ready to open the doors and greet our guests. American Indian Flute music playing from the speakers... Check

1st Room – Museum – Red Path Exhibit: Paintings hung on two sides of the room with artist information tags. Display cases with clothing and larger artifacts set against the other two sides of the room—glass cleaned, no fingerprints. The center of the room displayed several hunting weapons and pottery items in cases with their descriptions. American Indian drum music with prayers and chants playing from the speakers... Check

2nd Room - Storytelling Room: Set up for storytelling with a small stage and pillows surrounding it. In the bookshelves surrounding the room, kids and adults could read some American Indian Culture children's books to their kids. Lots of dream catchers hanging from the ceiling. Train table was set up for small kids along the back wall and the doll changing station was next to it in the corner. In the doll changing station, they had several baby dolls of diverse ethnicities and their American Indian outfits from several tribes. The outfits were in bins in the cubbies, appropriately labeled based on the tribe. On the wall above the changing station, they had brief descriptions of the tribes, where they had been located before the reservation, and where they were now. American Indian's current fun, upbeat music was playing from the speakers... Check

3rd Room - Gift Shop: All the jewelry displayed with prices. An American Indian made everything they sold from several tribes. They also sold American Indian books, blankets, clothing, moccasins, dream catchers, and toys. Oh shit. He didn't have anyone running the register. Ok, change of plans. Mark could run the register. He would either ask one of the tribal council members if they could walk around with a tray of food or he would do it. They also played American Indian Flute music there since they propped the door open into the lobby... Check

Restaurant: All the tables were set up. The wine glasses were ready to be poured. Sarah, Tommy, Rachel, and Mark were ready to serve. George and Mary Grayfeather were in the kitchen prepping the Indian Fry Bread and organizing the caterers. American Indian Flute music was playing there as well since it opened into the lobby... Check

Grayhorse was waiting for him in the lobby, ready to open the doors and greet their guests... Check

Checking off each room as he went through everything on his list. He walked up to Mark when he finished.

"Mark, could you please run the register tonight? You are familiar with the items that are for sale and the ones that are for display only."

"Of course."

"Thank you, I really appreciate it."

Thunder took a deep breath and knew they were ready. Mark nodded his head toward the front door. Thunder turned around and saw Rachel open the door and let in the tribal council. He headed over to greet them.

"*Hau*," Thunder smiling while he hugged them, "What do you think? *Wakan Tanka* has blessed us today."

"*Hau*, he certainly has. Everything looks wonderful. You have done a great job *Wakíyaŋ Hotóŋpi*."

Immediate warmth and confidence spread through Thunder's body. They were all smiling and looking around, even though they had seen most of it yesterday.

"Where do you want us?" Uncle Spirit asked him.

"Can everyone come over here for a moment?" Thunder spoke loudly so everyone could hear, "Sarah, can you please get George and Mary?"

Sarah nodded and got them. They all gathered around Thunder.

"I want to go over tonight's schedule. Please let me know if you have questions." Thunder nodded to everyone.

"Mark will run the register in the Gift Shop all night. I'll need one of you to help with the food trays. Sarah or Rachel can explain what to do. One of you in the 'Red Path Exhibit' room to answer questions. Two in the Storytelling room, stories will be told at seven and eight. Tell the same story or change it up. Everyone else can mingle throughout," he told them. "Oh and switch the jobs around throughout the night if you want to move around."

"Sounds good." Uncle Spirit nodded and pointed toward the storytelling room. "Let's all go into the Storytelling room now and do a quick blessing for this night."

They all walked in and sat cross-legged while Spirit of the Eagle the evening. A sense of calmness settled over Thunder as he closed his eyes and slowed his breathing. They'd all put their blood, sweat, and tears into this exhibit and couldn't wait to experience it with their guests.

At 6:30 p.m., they opened the doors. They were ready.

*** *Isa* ***

Isa was so focused on finishing the flyer she was working on that she lost track of time. Oh no, it was already seven. Based on the address, it would only take her fifteen minutes to get there. However, since she had never been there, she didn't know if they had parking. She'd assumed so since it was near the casino and the big mall.

She saved her work but didn't turn off her computer. Teramar did computer backups every night. After grabbing her purse in the bottom left drawer of her desk, Isa sped out of her office, backpedaling a bit to turn off the light before slamming the door shut behind her. Most everyone had gone home by then and many offices were empty.

Maggie had already left for her date with Ryan. If Maggie was not at the front desk, employees were required to lock up when they left. Isa locked the front door on her way out. Heading to her car, her cell phone was ringing. She scrambled into her purse to get it out.

"Hello?" Isa sounded out of breath.

"Hi," Maggie said in a very loud and happy voice, "Why are you out of breath? Do you see him? Is he there?"

Isa could hear loud music and noises in the background.

"Hey, Mags. No, I'm not there yet. I'm just now leaving the office. What's up?" Isa smiled and realized Maggie must have had several drinks to be so cheerful.

"What?" Maggie screamed into the phone.

Isa heard Maggie say she was going to step out so she could hear her.

"Okay, can you hear me now?" Maggie giggled.

"Yes, I could always hear you. It's you that couldn't hear me. Anyway, why are you calling me on your date?" Isa asked her.

"Duh, because I wanted to make sure you went."

"I'm leaving work now." Isa reiterated.

"Aren't you already supposed to be at the opening?" Maggie asked.

"Yes, but I lost track of time." Isa got in her car, pulled out of the parking lot, and entered the traffic.

"Of course you did, you coward. You really are heading over there now, right? You're not just saying that to appease me?"

"No, I'm not just saying that and yes, I'm going. I promise. I will not chicken out." Isa adamantly stated.

"You'll be fine. Have a drink when you get there to help yourself relax and have a good time."

"Thanks, Mags. I still wish you were with me, but I hope you have a great rest of your date."

"Oh, I will," Maggie said before hanging up.

She arrived fifteen minutes later than she thought because of traffic. Grateful the parking lot was clearly marked, she found a parking spot near the end of the lot. After turning off her car, she put down her visor and touched up her lipstick.

Being in advertising, she always ran into someone she knew at museum openings around town. She had to look professional and well put together. There could be a potential client, peer, or another ad agency at this opening. First impressions were always key. She always said, "You never get a second chance to make a good first impression and the first thirty seconds are crucial."

Isa rarely attended a lot of openings because she didn't want to attend alone. She usually sent one of her designers. However, as Art Director, she knew she should be the one attending such events. The first one she attended after Asshole Keith had been very awkward, to say the least. Everyone in their art community knew they had dated for three years and did not expect to see her walk in alone. Rumors started circulating about what he did to her. She'd told no one, so she wasn't sure how they all knew. Office gossip always spreads like wildfire, especially when it had to do with sex with the boss. Most of the night, she wished the earth would open and swallow her whole. Everyone kept asking about Keith or saying how sorry they were. She'd left early that night and vowed to not attend another opening by herself again. Yet, here she was.

Asshole Keith's cheating had done a number on her, and Maggie was right. She had dated no one for the past two years. Isa crossed her fingers and hoped she didn't run into the asshole tonight. But if she did, she needed to show him she was doing great and was strong enough to be at an opening alone. *I am woman, hear me roar*, she thought. She'd be cordial and professional. She didn't need to air any dirty laundry tonight, especially not here.

Time for a pep talk.

"Ok Isa, you can do this. Just get out of the car and stop being a coward. Keith was an asshole and not worth it. There is nothing wrong with attending an opening alone. You do NOT need a man by your side to give you courage. You are beautiful, smart, kind and an all-around great person. If you see Thunder, be professional with him too. This is his big night. You've got this!" With that said, she took a deep breath, got out of the car, and walked toward the entrance.

Chapter 15

This Exhibit was Awesome!

Isa

The cultural center had a beautiful glass front facade which enabled anyone to see inside. Isa noticed it was very crowded. Wow, Thunder had done a good job of marketing this exhibit. As Isa went to open the door, an attractive male Indian dressed in his regalia smiled and opened it for her.

"*Hau*, welcome, come in and join us in our celebration."

"Hi, thank you," Isa said as she smiled at him.

"My name is Grayhorse. Let me give you a brief description of what we have tonight. To my left is the entrance to the museum room which has the exhibit 'Red Path'. In the back is the storytelling room, which will begin their next stories at 8:00. You still have a few minutes to grab a seat if you wish to hear our stories. Next to that is the Gift Shop. You may purchase any paintings, sculptures, jewelry and/or pottery that have a price tag. Most of which are in the gift shop. Items without price tags are not for sale. The artifacts enclosed in the glass cases in the museum are holy and are not for sale. Between the gift shop and the restaurant are our restrooms."

She smiled at him and nodded her head. "Okay."

He handed her a brochure—he obviously didn't know she was the brochure designer—and continued, "If you are hungry and want more than finger goods," he pointed behind her to the restaurant, "Our restaurant is open tonight and is serving a variety of delicious American Indian Foods including Indian Fry Bread. If you need any help, please ask someone dressed like me," he smiled as he pointed to himself. "We are in our traditional clothing and ready to help you. Again, welcome and have a pleasant evening," Grayhorse smiled as he finished his spiel.

"Thank you so much," she said to him and hurried to the storytelling room. She was excited to hear a story and wanted to experience everything the museum offered. On her way there, she ran into a beautiful Indian woman dressed in a very ornate dress that jingled as she walked. She was holding a tray of glasses filled with white and red wine. She stopped in front of her.

"*Hau*, would you like a glass of wine?" she greeted Isa.

"Hi, yes please, I would love a glass of white wine," Isa answered. "I love your dress. It is absolutely beautiful."

"*Pilámaya*, it is called a Jingle Dress. We wear it for one of our famous dances at our powwows."

"Well, it is stunning. Where did you buy it?" Isa was getting side-tracked from going into the storytelling room. But who could blame her? The dress had blingy bells all over it.

"I didn't buy it," she chuckled. "I made it myself."

"Now I'm even more impressed. Wow, great job."

"Were you headed toward our Storytelling Room?" she asked kindly. "Spirit of the Eagle is about to start."

"Oh, my goodness, yes, thank you." Isa checked her watch.

"You're welcome. Enjoy your evening," the woman said.

"I will, thank you." Isa pivoted and strode toward the Storytelling room.

The room was behind a glass door. As she went to grab the door handle, another handsome American Indian male dressed in his regalia pushed it open for her from inside. He must have seen her coming.

"*Hau*," he whispered, "Welcome."

"Hi," she whispered and smiled. Isa looked around and saw adults and children cross-legged on the ground, completely captivated by the older man's storytelling, the hush of the crowd broken only by his voice.

The Storyteller, Spirit of the Eagle, looked up as she came in, nodded, then continued with his story.

"... Father Sun burned his bright circle in the sky during the day and Sister Moon at night. Brother Hawk and Sister Meadowlark sang their sky song. And Brother Buffalo grazed upon the earth in great numbers, giving their lives so that his people could find nourishment and make shelter."

"My tribe was called the Hunkpapa. We were one of seven Lakota Tribes, and we have many famous ancestors like Sitting Bull, A Lakota Chief and Holy Man, who lived from 1831 to December 15th, 1890. We believe that there is a living spirit in all creatures and things. We call our sacred spirit Wakan Tanka, and we pray to him like you all pray to your God."

"This new world has changed many of our lives, but we strive to teach our culture and live in a world of kindness and peace. My name is *Waŋblí Kiŋ Wanági Uŋ*. In your language, it means Spirit of the Eagle. I am a Medicine Man for my people. That means I am a healer and have knowledge of magical and chemical potencies of various medicines and I'm skilled at administering these medicines during our rituals. I am so grateful to all of you for coming to see us today. I will be here all night if you have questions for me. I will now turn it over to our Pine Ridge Reservation Tribal Council President, Tall Bear, who will tell you a famous Lakota story told to all our children."

Spirit of the Eagle switched places with Tall Bear. Isa had been so engrossed in Spirit of the Eagle's story, she hadn't seen the older man sitting on a bench behind him.

"*Hau*, I am Mató Háŋska, Tall Bear, and here is my story for you tonight."

"Iktomi is a figure from the mythology and folklore of the Lakota people, a Native American tribe who lived in the Great Plains region of what is now the

United States. In their stories, the Lakota people depict Iktomi as a trickster
figure who exhibits cunning and a mischievous nature.

Iktomi is often depicted as a spider, and many of the stories about
him involve him using his web-spinning abilities to trick or deceive other
characters. In one well-known story, Iktomi uses his web to trap a group of
ducks, but ultimately fails when a wise old coyote outwits him and frees the
ducks. Despite his mischievous ways, Iktomi is also seen as a knowledgeable
figure in Lakota folklore. He is often called upon by other characters to offer
advice or guidance, and his stories often contain lessons about the importance
of wisdom and caution.

The character of Iktomi has become an important part of Lakota culture,
and people still pass down his stories from generation to generation. In modern
times, he has also become a popular figure in literature and media, appearing
in books, films, and other works that draw on Lakota folklore.

Overall, Iktomi is a complex and fascinating figure who continues to play an
important role in the mythology and culture of the Lakota people.

This is the Story of Iktomi and the Ducks:

*Once upon a time, in the vast grasslands of the Great Plains, there lived a clever spider
named Iktomi. Iktomi was known throughout the land for his cunning and mischievous ways,
and he spent his days spinning webs and playing tricks on anyone who crossed his path.*

*One day, Iktomi came across a group of ducks who were swimming in a nearby pond.
Seeing an opportunity for mischief, Iktomi quickly spun a web across the pond and trapped
the ducks in it.*

*The ducks struggled to free themselves, but Iktomi's web was too strong. They quacked
and flapped their wings in frustration, but they could not break free.*

*Just as Iktomi was about to claim his prize, a wise old coyote named Makatanka appeared
on the scene. Makatanka had been watching Iktomi's antics from a distance, and he knew
the spider was up to no good.*

*Makatanka approached Iktomi and asked him what he was doing. Iktomi tried to play it
cool, but Makatanka could see through his lies. He demanded that Iktomi release the ducks
at once.*

*Iktomi was no match for the cunning coyote, and he reluctantly agreed to let the ducks
go. As the ducks flew away, Iktomi scurried off into the grass, embarrassed and defeated.*

*From that day on, Iktomi learned to be more careful with his tricks, and he started to use
his cunning for good instead of mischief. He became a wise and respected figure among the
animals of the Great Plains, and his stories were passed down for generations to come.*

These stories enthralled Isa, and she eagerly desired to hear another one,
but she also had a powerful urge to see the exhibit. Spending a lot of time
in museums was her thing, being one of those nerdy people who read every
description plaque. She quietly stood up and headed out of the room, noticing
the handsome American Indian staring at her and smiling. He gently and quietly
opened the glass door for her.

"Thank you," she whispered.

"*Hau*," he responded.

When she was fully out of the room, she looked around the lobby, which was
decorated so beautifully that she didn't know where to look. Straight ahead, in

the center of the lobby, was a beautiful statuesque tree with an overabundance of vivid green leaves. She was curious if they built the cultural center around the tree or planted it afterwards. The gigantic tree was real and growing out of the ground, surrounded by a patch of grass. As her gaze followed the height of the tree, she noticed the skylight directly above it. It made sense to give the tree light during the day. They painted the rest of the ceiling to resemble the sky outside. How had she missed the tree when she walked to the Storytelling Room? The wine and beautiful Jingle dress had thoroughly distracted her. After all, wine and bling were two of her favorite things.

She looked around the lobby and noticed the decor, which included walls painted antique white and a border at the top that ran the length of the room. The border was a traditional Lakota pattern of brown diagonal lines in the shapes of triangles. In between the triangles, there were different animal hieroglyphics in a salmon color representing bears, wolves, bison, eagles, and horses. Hanging on the walls were several paintings by local American Indian artists depicting their lifestyle and culture. She saw two beautiful sculptures sitting on two, three-foot column stands. One at the entrance to the exhibit and one at the exit. Also, noticing an object on another three-foot column near the entrance to the restaurant. The interior designers made sure that the lobby had a peaceful and serene atmosphere.

Isa looked at her wineglass and noticed it was empty. Well, another glass couldn't hurt, right?

She walked toward another beautiful woman with a tray of wineglasses and took another one, placing her empty one on the tray. She thanked the woman and headed toward the Red Path Exhibit. On her way, a little boy came toward her with a tray of Indian Fry Bread. She'd read all about this in her novels, but she had never seen or tasted it in person.

"*Hau*, would you like some Indian Fry Bread to go with your wine?"

"Hi, thank you. I would love some," Isa said as her stomach growled, reminding her she had not eaten dinner.

"You're welcome. My name is Tommy. I'm not allowed to carry the wine because of my age, but if you want more bread, just look for me." His face beaming with joy.

"Hi Tommy," Isa took a bite and rolled her eyes. "Thanks. This is delicious. I will most definitely look for you. My name is Isa. It's nice to meet you." Isa held out her hand for a handshake.

"I'd shake your hand, Isa, but if I drop the tray, my mom will kill me," he said as he widened his eyes dramatically.

"I totally understand. It was crazy for me to do that. See you later."

"Bye Isa, see you later."

The Museum had display cases along the first two walls and paintings on the other two. The room resembled a stretched-out rectangle. In a circle, she walked the room from left to right, saving the items in the center rectangular glass display case for last. She didn't want to miss anything. Her first stop was the display cases on the left. These cases had different traditional buckskin clothing from the men, women, and children. They ranged from everyday wear to ceremonial outfits.

The next display case ran along the back wall. This display case contained buffalo hides which belonged to some survivors of the Indian Wars. Next to the hides were two life size mannequins of an Indian man and woman in authentic 1800s clothing. The mannequins wore traditional buckskin garments, resembling the clothing of the Lakota plains Indians. The man had on a long sleeve buckskin shirt, loincloth down to his knees with leggings, and ornate moccasins. She realized, looking at the male mannequin, that the Indians did not cover up their male anatomy as much as the white man. She kind of knew that from reading her romance novels, but it was different seeing it right in front of you. A rush of heat flooded her cheeks. He had a bow over one shoulder and arrows in the tall buckskin pouch over the other shoulder. In the waistband, he carried a knife sheathed in a beautifully decorated buckskin pouch. His hair was waist length and free flowing, and he wore a small medicine bag around his neck like a necklace.

The female mannequin had on a long sleeve buckskin dress that went down to just below her knees. She had on a pair of knee-high moccasins that looked like buckskin boots. She was carrying a buffalo robe in her hands and a baby in a cradleboard on her back. The cradleboard was gorgeous, made of soft rabbit fur and decorated with silver and turquoise beads. Only the baby's head was visible. There were explanations and information about every garment that was being displayed.

She stared at the mannequins for a long time, wondering what life must have been like for the people who lived like that. As she walked towards the end of the back display case, she saw all the larger weapons. There was a large assortment of lances, bows, arrows, larger tomahawks, and rifles from different tribes. She could picture warriors on their horses, with their long hair blowing in the wind and their faces painted, riding out in an open field ready for war. The tribes used these weapons for hunting, defending their loved ones from any enemy, stealing horses, or counting coup. She was awestruck by these magnificent yet dangerous weapons.

She didn't see price tags on anything being displayed in the cases, so all those items must be holy and treasured. She could easily imagine why it was a great way to teach others about their heritage for generations to come.

As she made her way to the right side of the exhibit, she saw paintings created by Native American Artists from all over the United States. All the paintings were beautiful and most of them were for sale. Some already had the "Sold" sticker on the price tag. She didn't exit out the door, but made her way to the next long wall to finish looking at more paintings. After seeing all of them, she moved to the center of the room where there were display cases with artifacts dating back to the 1800s. This was during the time of Sitting Bull and Red Cloud. There were knives, tomahawks, arrows, moccasins, dishes, cooking utensils, and sacred pipes. She also saw a letter from the "White Father", our president, addressed to the Lakota Indians about signing the treaty of 1868. Next to that letter was a copy of the actual treaty.

She'd read about that treaty. It was the one the whites ignored to take the land away along the Paha Sapa, the Black Hills. The whites had found gold in the Black Hills, and they wanted the land so they could dig it up and become rich. That forced the American Indians onto reservations.

As she worked her way back toward the exit, her wineglass was empty again and her stomach was grumbling. Tonight, the cultural center would close at 10:00 p.m. due to it being the opening. Glancing at her watch, she realized it was already 9:30. She had spent a long time looking and reading about all the items in the museum. Leaving the museum room, she headed across the lobby behind the tree toward the restaurant. As she made her way there, she realized the object she saw earlier was a lance. The column couldn't hold it because of its length, so they clamped it in front because it was tall.

The lance had a sharp, elongated arrowhead tip. A red material covered it, holding the feathers to the bottom. The description read: Feathered Lance, Lakota (Sioux), Northern Plains, ca. 1840.

Surely that belonged to a brave warrior. She stretched out her hand and gently ran her fingers over the feathers.

*** *Sarah* ***

Sarah was so proud of Thunder, everything was running smoothly. Thunder stood at the front door with Grayhorse until several guests wanted to meet him and get private tours. Sarah took it upon herself to check on Uncle Spirit and the Grayfeathers, since she was walking around the lobby with a serving tray.

"Hey sexy husband, how's it going?"

"Hi *mitáwicu*, better now that you're here." Grayhorse gave her a quick kiss.

"How's it going?" Thunder approached them. They both turned and smiled at him.

"Few are coming through the door, so I'm helping Sarah with the wine trays. Good idea, by the way. Everyone loves having the wine. Even if you got a lot of grief from the council." Grayhorse smirked.

"Yeah, I'm kinda surprised they let me move forward with it."

"Well," Sarah piped up, "you didn't give them much choice. When you were working on your checklist and they were in the museum, the caterers poured the red wine into the glasses on the table, per your instructions," she chuckled.

"True, but I'm sure I'll hear about it tomorrow."

"*Hau, lekší*," Tommy came over with his tray. "I have dropped nothing. Aren't you proud of me?" he boasted.

"*Hau*, Tommy, I'm always proud of my favorite nephew."

"*Lekší*, I'm your only nephew," he sighed.

"True, but you are my favorite." Thunder squeezed his shoulder and smiled at him. "And yes, you are doing a great job and I'm very proud of you."

"Oooooh," Tommy said suddenly, "I gotta go. Mary is waving me over to fill up my tray. Everyone is loving the Indian Fry Bread!" He shouted as he ran over to Mary.

Thunder chuckled at Tommy's antics, "You have a great kid. Now hurry and have another one so I can be an uncle again."

"Ha, ha," Grayhorse put his hand around his wife's back, "hilarious. You know you can meet someone, get married, and make one of your own. It would not be unheard of."

Sarah laughed and looked toward the restaurant. Mary was putting more fry bread on Tommy's tray, while he focused on not dropping it. While watching, she saw the same woman who had complimented her dress walk up to Tommy. The woman took a piece of fry bread and smiled at him. Tommy smiled back and said something to her before he walked off with his tray. She was now standing in front of Thunder's lance, reaching out to touch it. Sarah turned to Thunder and noticed him watching the woman.

"I think you are right *higná*. Serving wine was a good idea. *Wakíyaŋ Hotóŋpi*, I know it is not usually our way, but no one seems to take advantage of it." Sarah spoke, trying to engage Thunder in their conversation. But he seemed to be oblivious to her comment and focused on the woman across the lobby.

"The night is still young, *mitáwicu*," Grayhorse stated sarcastically.

"Well, that it is. However, I do not think we will have any trouble. I wish we would have done this for the previous openings. So far, we have sold more paintings early in the evening than before," Sarah mentioned, with a twinkle in her eye.

"And you think the wine has something to do with this?" Grayhorse raised his eyebrow to question her.

"Well, it just helps to loosen people up a little. They seem a little more social and happier. Do not make me sound like an idiot. You know what I mean," she slapped Grayhorse on his arm. "And besides, I take credit for this, because the wine was my suggestion," she beamed at Grayhorse and Thunder.

"Ah, so now we reach the significance of this conversation. You want some praise and attention, *mitáwicu*. As if you don't get enough of that at home." Grayhorse placed his hand dramatically over his heart. "Do you want me to tell the tribal council it was your idea so they can praise you?"

"Nope, they don't need to know. Thunder can take all the credit from the council. I just want you to reward me," she said in a sultry way to Grayhorse.

"I will always reward you *mitáwicu*, any way you want." He gave her a kiss on her cheek and whispered, "later," in her ear. He looked to Thunder, who hadn't been paying attention, and said, "So you see Thunder, your sister has excellent ideas and is always right."

Sarah nodded and looked at her brother. Thunder continued to stare at the woman, who remained very focused on his lance. The woman gently reached out to touch the feathers. Wow, no woman had ever captured her brother's attention like that. Sarah was pretty sure Thunder hadn't heard Grayhorse say she was always right. Thunder would not have agreed. But the look on his face was troubling Sarah. It was the look of a panther out on the prowl seeking his latest victim. He looked hungry. His eyes were full of desire. A look she had not seen him wear in a very long time. He was licking his chops and ready to go in for the kill. Not to hurt the poor woman, but to devour her. Interesting. She wondered if he would be mad that the woman was touching his lance or forgive her and want her to touch another type of lance. As Sarah was getting ready to question Thunder, he looked at Grayhorse and smiled.

"Well, I could've told you that," Thunder said wryly.

"Wow, you heard Grayhorse say I'm always right, huh?" Sarah's mouth dropped at her brother's comment.

"Yep, I heard. Now, if you will excuse me, there is someone I need to talk to." Thunder turned around and headed toward the unsuspecting woman.

"I can't believe he agreed with you. I wonder if he knows her?" Sarah stared at the woman.

"You know that we men will agree to you women being right if it ends an argument, right? Plus, he has something or someone else on his mind that has nothing to do with egging you on."

"Huh, well. We will discuss this later. I gotta make my rounds. Bye, *higná*," she saucily walked away, glancing over her shoulder, watching Grayhorse staring at her ass sway while he licked his lips.

"Later, *mitáwicu*, wait until later."

*** *Thunder* ***

Thunder got closer to the woman to see if it was Isa. He'd only seen Isa with her hair in a tight bun at work. The woman looked like her from behind. She was petite, with perfect womanly proportions and beautiful curly hair that looked soft and erotic. He could picture her hair draped over him while she rode him into the night. Save a horse, ride a cowboy or Indian in his case. Strange, he'd had many women, but none had ever affected him so quickly or driven him as crazy as Isa did. He felt this overpowering urge to protect and claim her as his woman. His cock hardened as he watched her run her hands delicately over the feathers.

In his mind, he pictured her hands doing that to his body. Those long delicate fingers running down his body until they reached his throbbing cock. When he walked up behind her, he could smell the aroma of fresh daisies in her hair. He reached out and touched the horsehair on the lance, stroking her hand.

"Hi, Isa," he whispered near her ear.

"Oh, you startled me," Isa jumped and turned around. "Mr. Thunderbird, I didn't see you come up behind me," she placed her hand over her heart.

"I'm sorry. I didn't mean to startle you. Are you enjoying the evening?" Thunder watched as her eyes dilated and she licked her lips, devouring him from head to toe. He'd worn his hair loose with two thin braids down each side tied with a piece of rawhide and dressed in his Indian Powwow Regalia. The way she kept staring at him was intriguing him. She usually wasn't so bold.

Thunder stood rooted to the spot as he watched Isa's obvious approval of his body. He didn't want to move or breathe, so she wouldn't stop her gaze from gliding across his body. Especially since she kept licking her lips. He could tell she liked what she saw. It felt like he was going to be her next meal. Which would be fucking fantastic. She could lick him all over any time. He was losing his battle over his self-control, and his cock was rising to attention. Counting to 100 was a good way to regain his control before he pushed her up against the wall and fucked her right here in public. Fuck the opening.

*** *Isa* ***

"I'm sorry. What did you say?" she asked breathlessly. Finally, listening to Thunder tell her about the lance. He said it was given to him by Spirit of the Eagle when he was a child.

"Several tribal councils of other tribes provided the other weapons you saw in the museum. We usually keep them in museums or community centers on our various reservations. Some date back to the late 1800s during the Indian Wars. Native tribes used others for buffalo hunts. The hunts provided my people with food, shelter, clothing, and cooking utensils, among other necessities. Are you familiar with Lakota culture or war weapons?"

Isa was not saying anything. She just stared at his mouth and his low husky voice asked her again.

"Do you know about these weapons? Are you familiar with Lakota or any other American Indian Culture?"

She finally looked up into his eyes. "Well, I'm interested in Indian culture and have read several books on the topic. That's how I could design a brochure and work on your advertising campaign." She didn't want to tell him that some of those books were romance novels. Most people don't think you could learn anything from them except smut.

"American Indians," he grinned at her.

"What?" she asked, confused.

"We prefer to be called American Indians or Native Americans, not Indians. And you can let go of the lance, Isa. I will not hurt you, even though you have ignored my calls." He smiled at her.

Isa realized she was gripping the lance and quickly released it. He must think she was an idiot. Obviously, she knew he wouldn't attack her. She got nervous because first she'd played phone tag and ignored him, then she'd ghosted him, and now she was holding his prized possession while she insulted him by calling him an Indian. This was not going well at all for her. Either the wine made her act like a slutty airhead or him standing so close to her had done the trick. He looked so hot. Isa looked down and closed her eyes in embarrassment and felt a rush of heat in her cheeks. "I'm so sorry. I didn't mean to be insulting, Mr. Thunderbird."

He reached under her chin with his finger and lifted her face up so she would look at him. "Ah, so you recognize and remember me. I was thinking you were a figment of my imagination. No reason to be sorry. I wasn't insulted. Frustrated and maybe a little hurt, but not insulted."

Isa was stunned by his smile. It lit up his eyes and showed his beautiful, perfect white teeth. She couldn't help but smile back at him.

Thunder held out his hand to shake hers. "Shall we start over, since our first meeting ended with you wearing my coffee and then my shirt? My name is Johnny Thunderbird, but my friends call me Thunder. And you are?" He raised a devilish-looking eyebrow at her.

"My name is Isabel Emelina Gonzalez." Isa was not sure why she gave him her full name except she was unnaturally nervous standing so close to him and it automatically came out. If he ever interrogated her, she would surely buckle and tell him everything while she stared into his dark, mesmerizing eyes. She swore he could see down to her soul and couldn't seem to look away. "My friends call me Isa. I'm pleased to meet you, Thunder."

"Likewise, Isa," Thunder lifted her hand to his lips. "So, we are friends now, Isa? No more phone tag or ghosting?" He winked at her and watched her blush again.

"No more phone tag or ghosting, I promise, Mr. Thun... Sorry, Thunder," she cringed at her mistake, peering up at him cautiously.

"No worries. You can call me Johnny, Thunder or Thunderbird, whatever works for you. I answer to all of them. However, most of my friends call me Thunder. Did John come with you tonight?"

Isa thought the name Thunder certainly fit him, especially since his presence was causing her body to tremble in certain areas.

Isa lowered her gaze to his wide shoulders and narrow waist. Silver and turquoise beads and tassels decorated his buckskin shirt and pants, resembling the mannequins in the museum. As her gaze continued to travel down his body, she noticed his thighs seemed to strain against his pants along with another part of his body which had tented his loincloth. Various silver and turquoise beads sewn in a bird pattern decorated his moccasins, hence his last name. Isa suddenly realized she had been staring at him again from head to toe like a juicy piece of meat. *Oh my god*, she thought, *I haven't heard a word he said and I'm acting like a hussy, eyeing him up and down like that.* Damn wine. She really needed to eat something. How could she be so bold? Her eyes widened, and she spun around and headed into the restaurant. Hurrying to a table, she sat down.

"Would you like something to drink?" An elderly woman asked her.

"Yes, some water would be great. Thank you," Isa watched Thunder sit at her table.

"Thunder, something to drink?"

"Yes, Mary. I'll have water as well. Thanks," he answered Mary, looked at Isa and asked, "So, I don't think you heard me earlier. Did John come with you?"

She was not making eye contact with him and kept staring at the menu.

"I...I...I'm sorry. Did you ask me something?"

"Yes, I asked if John came with you. You didn't answer me. But that's okay, I rather enjoyed watching your eyes light up and you lick your lips as you gazed over my body," he smirked at her.

"I really need to go now," Isa said in a rather raspy voice. She jumped up and turned around abruptly to walk away. She felt Thunder's hand brush by her forearm as he tried to reach for her.

"Isa, wait," Thunder called out.

She never saw Tommy coming from the lobby with a tray of food until she ran into him. The food on the tray spilled all over Isa and they both collapsed onto the floor from the impact. Unfortunately, Tommy had a small container of honey dipping sauce on his tray. Isa looked down at the honey she was now wearing. Why was she always messing up her clothes around Thunder?

"I'm so sorry, Isa, I should've seen where I was going," Tommy frantically apologized and glanced up at Thunder. "I should've been more careful since I was carrying a dipping sauce. Miss Mary trusted me and I ruined everything! I'm so sorry." Tommy whimpered.

Oh, could this night get any more embarrassing? Isa thought. "Tommy, it wasn't your fault. I wasn't being careful, and I didn't see you. I'm so sorry," Isa said. She looked down at her new off-white dress with splashes of honey. Isa took responsibility for the accident, acknowledging that she had run into the little boy and ruined her new off-white dress with splashes of honey. If she hadn't been so nervous and embarrassed by what Thunder had said, she would have stayed in her seat, ordered a meal, and flirted right back. Tommy was so upset, he kept apologizing to Thunder. A man and woman ran into the restaurant. They must have heard the crashing of the tray.

"*Iná, até*, I'm so sorry," Tommy was crying as the two people she assumed were his parents helped him clean up the mess.

"It's okay *ciŋkší*, accidents happen," the woman bent down and hugged Tommy, "your dad and I will help you clean it up."

"I'm so sorry. It wasn't his fault. It was mine." Isa released her dress and cleaned up the mess on the floor. "I should have seen where I was going. I'm the one who should be sorry and have to clean up this mess. Are you okay?" She glanced at Tommy.

"I'm okay Isa," he mumbled.

Thunder held his hand out to Tommy to help him up while his parents and Isa were cleaning up

"*Wašté hwo, tʿuŋšká?* We will speak of this later and you will tell me why you disobeyed me." Isa heard Thunder whisper to Tommy.

"*Han lekší*, I am so sorry."

"Please don't be mad at him. It was my fault. I should have been paying attention." Isa pleaded with Thunder. Tommy's lower lip was quivering and tears were rolling down his face.

"It's not like Tommy to not listen to my rules," Thunder seemed baffled. "Isa, we need to see if we can clean up your dress."

"My dress will be fine. He's just a little boy, and he was doing a great job until I ran into him. You were doing great Tommy." Isa complimented Tommy. She couldn't stand to see the boy crying.

"Thank you, Isa," he whispered.

Thunder sighed and looked at Tommy. "*Hecitu yelo, tuŋšká*, it was an accident. After we clean this up, you can stop serving. Most of the guests will leave within the next twenty minutes. Thank you for your help tonight. You really did a great job. I couldn't have done it without you."

"Thank you *lekší*," Tommy smiled crookedly.

Isa was trying to pick up a piece of fry bread that went under the table.

"Ma'am, you do not need to clean this up. We will take care of it. You are a guest," Grayhorse said as he smiled at her. He and Sarah were finishing up.

"A clumsy guest, it seems," Isa mumbled.

"Isa, are you okay?" Thunder asked her as he held her elbow to help her up.

Isa looked him in the eyes and said, "Yes, I'm fine. I think it's time for me to go. I've done enough damage."

"Isa, come with me. They will finish up and you need to clean that dress before it stains."

She looked down and saw the splashes of honey seeping into her dress. She grabbed a napkin off the table and tried to wipe it, but that was just making it worse. It kept sticking to the napkin and smearing.

Isa wanted to get to her car so she could have a good cry and wallow in her misery. She had humiliated herself tonight. Thunder was guiding her toward the kitchen in the restaurant.

"Where are we going?" Isa asked, panicking.

"I have an apartment upstairs. You can take off the dress and I can try to clean it for you. I have a washer and dryer."

"Wait, I'm not going upstairs with you, I don't really even know you." Isa stopped walking and pulled her arm away from Thunder. He seemed nice, but he was a stranger with a lot of weapons in the museum. What if he had weapons upstairs? A torture chamber? She was hyperventilating. If she didn't calm down, she would pass out.

Thunder stopped in front of the stairs and turned around, facing her. Holding her shoulders, he leaned down and looked into her eyes.

"I will not hurt you if that is what you're worried about. I only want to help you remove the stain from your dress before it becomes permanent. It seems every time we meet, I'm responsible for ruining another piece of your wardrobe." Thunder muttered. She could tell he was trying to set her mind at ease with a joke.

Thunder began pulling her up the stairs slowly. *Well, at least they weren't going to a scary basement*, she thought.

"Really, Thunder, it's okay, I should get home anyway," she stumbled and tried to pull away from him. He released her so she could hold the rail and not fall.

"I give you my word that I will be on my best behavior. Come with me please, we will leave the door open. My apartment is above this kitchen. We can leave that door open as well. You can change into my shirt while I wash the stain out of your dress. If it dries up, it will ruin the dress, and it is a beautiful dress."

Isa stared into Thunder's eyes as he talked to her soothingly. She didn't realize he'd continued walking backwards up the stairs while he held her hand. True to his word, Thunder left the door open downstairs. His hand was so warm and comforting, but because of his size, she knew he could overpower her in a minute. Opening another door at the top of the stairs, Thunder stepped aside and waited for her to walk through it. Isa walked into a small loft apartment. On her right was a bathroom, and on her left was a kitchenette. Beside the kitchenette, she could see his bed underneath a window. Just the necessities. It surprised her he lived in such a small apartment above the cultural center. Across from the kitchenette there were paintings hanging on the wall, a table for two and a stackable washer and dryer unit.

"Isa," she looked at him, "the bathroom is on your right. You can take off your dress in there. The door has a lock. Just toss the dress out when you're ready. I will hand you my shirt."

"Ok, thank you," Isa walked into the bathroom and quickly closed the door.

"Ugh," Isa mumbled to herself, "could this night get any worse?" Maybe she should not have said that because she just jinxed herself. She stared at her ruined dress in the mirror. "What have I done and how will I get out of this one?" she asked herself.

Thunder knocked on the door, startling her.

"Isa, are you okay? Did you say something?" he asked.

"No, I'm fine. I'll toss my dress out in a minute." Isa undressed and stared at the stain. Not knowing how he was going to clean it up. It probably just needed to go in the trash. Gathering the dress up in one hand, she stood behind the door, unlocking and opening it just enough to hold her hand out.

"Thunder, can I have the shirt?" she asked with her hand sticking out of the bathroom door. "Here's my dress."

"Here, use this one," he said. Thunder pulled his shirt off, and they switched clothing.

"Thanks," Isa replied as she slammed the door and locked it again.

Chapter 16

I am a Klutz

I sa looked at the shirt Thunder handed her. It looked just like the one he'd had on. *Wait a minute*, she thought. *If this was his shirt, then what was he wearing now? Was he out there shirtless?* She stared at herself in the mirror and took deep breaths while she fanned herself. He was so tall she'd hoped the shirt would fit her like a dress, down to her knees. She fumbled with the shirt, finally putting it over her head and arms. It was really soft, big, and dropped to her thighs.

"Thunder, do you have any sweatpants?" Isa screamed through the door.

"My sweatpants will be too big for you, Isa. They will probably fall off your body considering how small you are. Isn't the shirt long enough?" she heard him ask.

She closed her eyes and took a deep breath. Her heart was pounding a mile a minute. How was she going to be in the same room with this hunky guy and be half naked? When she thought back to all his interactions with her, she realized he was a nice guy. She was more afraid of sleeping with him than of him killing her. Plus, she loved the softness of his shirt.

"Isa, are you okay? Did you hear me?"

"Yes, I'm fine. I'll be out in a minute." Isa closed her eyes and took another deep breath. After counting to ten, she opened her eyes and looked in the mirror for her next pep talk of the night, "Ok Isa, it's now or never. You can't stay in the man's bathroom forever. Eventually, come out or he has to come in. Just walk out there and put your big girl panties on and face the music. You got this." she opened the door and stepped out. Thunder was at his sink, lightly scrubbing the stain on her dress. When he heard the door, he looked over his shoulder.

"I think I got most of the stain out, but I want to soak it for a few minutes. Would you like something to drink while we wait? I have soda, coffee, or tea?" Thunder turned around and leaned against the counter, his hands braced on either side.

"Tea would be fine, thank you." Isa was looking down while she walked toward Thunder, tugging his shirt down. She hoped by pulling on the material, it would miraculously stretch down to her knees.

"Don't you have to get back downstairs?" She finally looked up and realized she was wearing the shirt off his back. Wowza, can you say abs? He must work out all the time because his body was a work of art. She had an urgent need to touch and explore him with her hands and tongue.

"That shirt looks much better on you than me," he grinned as he stared at her legs before his gaze travelled up her body to her face. "My assistant, Rachel, will hold down the fort until I return," Thunder turned toward the sink and filled up the teakettle.

"Thunder, what kind of tea do you have?" Isa walked up behind him, leaning against his back as she attempted to look over his shoulder. She heard Thunder groan.

"How about you have a seat at the table, and I will bring it all to you?"

"How long do you think my dress will need to soak?" Isa stepped around him to see her dress soaking in the sink. She swished it around with her finger, looking for the stain.

"Only a little while. I got most of it out. In a few minutes, I will put it in the dryer on a gentle cycle and see if the stain came out. But if you want, I can get it dry cleaned for you? Every time I see you, your clothes seem to mysteriously end up in my possession, like a strange magnetic attraction." He turned and smiled at her. "It's a good thing I have a walk-in closet at home."

"You don't live here?"

"No, I own a house by the beach. I only have this apartment for when I work late and don't want to drive home. After I picked up your shirt from the dry cleaners, I took it to my house, so it's not here."

Isa was having a hard time breathing, with them standing so close to each other. He stretched his hand out to touch her hair just as the tea kettle went off. He closed his hand into a fist and dropped it by his side. Turning toward the stove, Thunder grabbed the teakettle and poured the hot water into their mugs.

"Have a seat," Thunder nodded to the table and placed her mug down. "I'll bring you a selection of teas so you can pick your favorite. Do you want some honey for your tea?" he chuckled.

"Ha, ha. Very funny," she grumbled. "Ugh, yes. I really do put honey in my tea."

"I'll bring it all to the table. Just relax."

"Okay, thanks," Isa sat and found the tea she liked. While dunking her tea bag, she looked around the apartment. On the table was a beautifully hand crafted American Indian designed pottery vase. Above the table on the wall was a painting on real cow hide. It depicted warriors on their horses running towards a herd of buffalo. In the room's corner, at the foot of the bed, was a shelving unit containing small drawings in frames and more sculptures.

Isa was looking around the apartment and noticed he had kept a lot of paintings and artifacts up here.

"I guess you can see the museum doesn't end downstairs." He set down the honey and walked back to the sink to let the water drain. "I like to be surrounded by my culture, especially since I am far away from home. I also keep a lot of artifacts at my house." He said while squeezing the dress gently in the sink so it wouldn't be sopping wet when he placed it in the dryer. Then he walked over to the dryer and set it on a low, gentle cycle before he sat down with her at the table.

"How is your tea?"

"It's good. You had my favorite, Black Tea."

"I'm glad. It's one of my favorites as well." Thunder dropped his tea bag into his tea.

"Are you Lakota?"

"*Han*, I am Oglala Lakota," he stated proudly. "Where are you from?"

"I'm American, but I'm of Cuban descent. My mom came to the United States on a freedom flight when she was two years old. She only remembers the stories about Cuba and what her parents told her while she was growing up."

He noticed a sadness in her eyes.

"So, you must have talented storytellers in your family also," he noted, trying to take away the sadness in her eyes. He loved to see her smile. She had a beautiful smile that lit up her face.

"Yes, I do," she smiled at him. "Someday I hope to go back and see where I was born and meet the rest of my family that is still living there. I would love to see the places that my parents have told me about."

"What did you mean by a freedom flight?" Thunder looked confused.

"After Castro came into power, he treated the country like his personal property. He suppressed religion and confiscated private property. He was ruling the country as a Communist and some people disagreed with his beliefs. After the Bay of Pigs, the U.S. watched what was happening in Cuba and created the Cuban Adjustment Act which assigned Cuban immigrants the status of 'parolee' because everyone assumed we would return to Cuba shortly. To make a long story short, in the late sixties and early seventies, Castro offered 'Freedom Flights'. A family had to file papers asking to leave the country, and if the government approved, they would receive an assigned flight to the U.S. My mom's family received approval, except for my grandfather, who couldn't leave with them because of emigration restrictions. Meaning he had to go work in the agricultural fields cutting sugar cane for six months and live like a prisoner. He ended up losing forty pounds, and when my mom finally saw him, she didn't even recognize him and freaked out.

"I did not know." Thunder watched her intently.

"Yeah, it was horrible from the stories that I've heard." Isa sighed.

"Would you have gone back?"

"I think we would have, but they would not go back to a Communistic Country."

"So, how does a woman of Cuban descent become so interested in the Lakota?" He asked her as he sipped his tea, watching her reaction over the rim of his mug.

"I have read a lot of history books, different cultures and religions fascinate me. I don't want to be like other people, that don't want to learn everything about the history of the United States. In order to avoid repeating the bad, I desire to be aware of both the good and bad that occurred. Maybe also because I feel like some Ind...sorry, American Indians do too. They took away my homeland, and now I can't live there anymore unless I want to live in communism. Granted, it wasn't the U.S. that took it away, but they didn't help us either. The Bay of Pigs is not a happy memory for me or my family. I'm sorry, I'm rambling. You don't really want to hear this." She looked nervously toward the dryer. "Do you think it's done drying? I should go, and they probably need you downstairs." She looked at him.

"Sure, let me check. You stay seated and finish your tea." he stood and pushed a button on the dryer. His stackable washer/dryer was right by the table, so they could keep talking.

"It's still a little damp and the stains are not totally out," he said as he looked at the stains. "I would like to keep it and take it to the dry cleaners. They might get it out and press it for you." He said before he placed it back in the dryer.

"Your story is very interesting to me, but I must be the one to apologize to you. I know little about the plight of the Cuban people or their culture and traditions. Teach me and maybe at the same time I will teach you about my people." He sat back down at the table, crossed his arms over his chest, and stretched out his legs.

Isa jolted a little when Thunder's leg rubbed up against hers under the table while he was getting comfortable. He looked so huge and out-of-place sitting at the tiny table, but the other option was to sit on his bed. Thunder noticed her discomfort and sat up. He placed his elbows on the table while he drank his tea and looked at her.

"Would you like some more tea?" He reached for her mug.

"No, I'm good," she said and reached for her mug at the same time. Their hands brushed and Isa experienced a spark of energy run up her arm. Thunder reached out with his left hand to touch Isa's curls.

Chapter 17

Yes...No...Maybe...Definitely Not Tonight

Isa

"Your hair is so beautifully soft, with curls so full of life. Why do you wear it in a bun at work?" He asked, gazing into her green eyes.

His provocative gleam mesmerized Isa. "Thunder, I, uh," she bit her bottom lip and watched his eyes widen as he licked his lips. He slowly put his hand behind her head and gently pulled her toward him.

He looked into her eyes and asked breathlessly, "May I?"

"Yes," she whispered. He kissed her lips tenderly.

Thunder ran his tongue along her bottom lip, prompting her to open her mouth for him. Isa closed her eyes and opened her mouth on a moan. Thunder tilted his head to the side and possessively slipped his tongue into her mouth. His mouth tasted sweet from the honey in his tea. Isa sensed a feeling of dizziness sweep over her. He was dominating their kiss and Isa loved it.

He stood up from his chair, never breaking their kiss, as he held her and moved backward to close and lock the apartment door. Then he walked her backward toward the bed. Moving his left hand to the back of her neck under her hair, he held her head at the right angle to devour her mouth, using his right hand to pull her into a firm embrace. The kiss was long, sensual, and getting very demanding. No one with this much passion had ever kissed her. Isa ran her hands through his hair, pulling the strands toward her.

Thunder broke the kiss, panting as he gazed at Isa's half-lidded eyes. Trying to catch her breath, Isa ran her hand slowly over his face and he closed his eyes briefly. Isa traced his eyes, then his nose, and finally his mouth. As she ran her fingers over his lips, he captured one gently and pulled it into his mouth, sucking on it as she imagined he would her breasts. She moaned as he slipped his right hand under her shirt.

Gliding his hand over her flat stomach on his way to her breasts, he unclasped her bra and brushed his hand over her nipple as he slid the material away from her breast. He captured her nipple and tweaked it with his thumb and forefinger until it became a hard nub, standing erect and ready for his attention.

Isa took her finger out of his mouth and ran her hand down his chest, panting because of the sensitivity of her breasts. She wanted to feel her naked breasts against his chest. Thunder grabbed the hem of his shirt and stared into her eyes as if asking for permission. Isa nodded, and he pulled the shirt over her head along with her bra, tossing them to the floor. Isa stood before him in only her barely there thong.

"You are so beautiful, Isa."

"So are you. Beautiful, that is."

Thunder chuckled as they both stared at each other's bodies with appreciation and anticipation of what was yet to come.

Thunder started kissing Isa's neck, and she moaned louder when he'd found her hyper sensitive spot. He turned them around and sat on the bed, pulling her onto his lap, so she straddled him. As she tightened her thighs around his body and got comfortable, she felt completely aroused.

"Isa, I can't wait to touch and taste you everywhere." Thunder looked into her eyes as he reached down to cup her ass. Pulling her toward him with his right hand so he could suck on her breasts, he played with her nipple on her right breast with his left and sucked on her left breast.

Isa threw her head back and moaned while she ground onto his cock. Wanting to give equal attention to her other breast, he switched sides. After both breasts were wet with satisfaction, he reached around with his right hand to her thong. She became drenched and ready for him to lick her dry.

"Are you sure about this, Isa? You are so wet for me. Do you want me to touch and taste you? Do you want to touch and taste me?" he murmured softly between kisses to her breasts.

Isa stiffened in his arms. Thunder's words registered in her mind, wiping away the last lingering effects of the wine and her sexual euphoria. She had only had sex with Keith and he wasn't a talker in the bedroom. Having Thunder explain his wants and needs so openly embarrassed her. *Oh no*, she thought, *maybe she'd gone too far.* It was her fault that she was sitting on his lap, half naked. He'd asked and she never stopped him. She started questioning herself. *What am I doing? Why have I let this happen? I barely know him. Is this really what I want? Am I ready to sleep with someone again? I haven't done it in so long, maybe I'm not good at it. After all, I was cheated on. It must have been my fault. Keith said I was a cold fish. I need to stop this before Thunder finds out I'm horrible in bed.*

Isa pushed against Thunder's chest. "Thunder, wait, please stop. We need to slow down."

Thunder wasn't stopping, so Isa pushed harder against him. Finally getting his attention, he stopped kissing her, resting his forehead against hers as his breathing slowed down. Isa punched him on the shoulder. Thunder quickly grabbed her by the upper arms to hold her in place so she wouldn't fall off his lap.

"What the hell, woman? Why did you hit me?" Thunder sounded flabbergasted. "I stopped."

"Thunder, I'm sorry," she broke away from his kiss and turned her head, "I can't do this."

She was afraid she'd gone too far and now he was going to hit or rape her. She felt a tear escape, chased by another and another until she was shaking and sobbing as she tried to escape his grip. *Was this why Asshole Keith had left her or why he would force himself on her?* One minute, she was hot to trot and the next she was cold as ice. *What was wrong with her?*

"Isa, look at me, please." Reaching up with both hands to frame her face, he wiped her tears. He dipped his head to look in to her eyes.

"Isa, honey, please don't cry. I'm so sorry, I…"

At that moment, there was a knock on the door.

"*Wakíyaŋ Hotóŋpi*, it's Sarah. Are you all right? I saw the lady come up here with you, and I didn't know if you needed some help to get the stain off. Thunder, can you hear me?"

The knocking became louder, more like a pounding on his door. He wasn't sure why she was trying to break down the door. This was a small apartment, and Sarah knew he could hear her knocking from anywhere in the apartment. Well, unless he was in the shower with the music on.

Isa pulled away from him and got off his lap while she wiped her eyes.

"I gotta go." She snatched his shirt off the floor. Holding the garment in front of her like a shield, she stared at him like a deer caught in headlights.

"Isa, that's my sister, Sarah. Wait just a second. I will step out and let her know we're okay. We have to talk about what just happened. I don't want you leaving like this," he pleaded with her. "If you want, you can step into the bathroom," he guided her to the bathroom. Once she went in, she locked the door.

"I'm coming, Sarah," he yelled, "hold your horses!" As he turned around to answer the door, he saw Isa run out of the bathroom door with his buckskin shirt on.

"Thunder, I gotta go, I just can't right now, sorry," she reached into her purse and dug for her keys.

"Isa, please look at me. Please talk to me. Let's talk about this."

Isa could barely look at Thunder as he stood by the door, trying to talk to her. She pulled her keys out of her purse and ran to the front door, which was only a few steps away.

"Thunder, let me out or I will scream!" She yelled at him.

He unlocked the door and lifted both hands up.

"Isa, please." She pushed him out of the way and opened the door. In her hurry to get out, she nearly knocked Sarah down.

"Whoa, hey are you alright?" Sarah asked Isa.

Isa didn't answer. She continued running down the stairs. As she ran, she realized that in her rush to leave, she'd left her shoes and bra in the apartment. Well, she wasn't going back, that was for sure. When she reached the bottom, she opened the door and took a peek into the kitchen to see if anyone was around. There was a chef at the stove, but he was busy cooking and didn't notice her. She walked out of the kitchen and into the restaurant. There were six people dining and another few out in the lobby. She knew she had to get out of there fast, but she couldn't run or everyone would notice the crazy lady running through the museum. She had to hurry before Thunder caught up to her. He seemed concerned, and she was certain he would follow her because he's sounded hell bent on talking to her tonight and didn't want her to leave. She didn't want to talk about what happened upstairs. She just wanted to get home, crawl into bed, and hide from her life.

Taking a deep breath, she walked slowly but steadily through the restaurant, trying not to attract too much attention. Isa looked toward the front door and made no eye contact with anyone as she blended in as best she could, even though she was only wearing his shirt and her thong. Surely, she had suffered enough embarrassment and humiliation for one night. Nothing like the walk of shame in nothing but a man's shirt.

Just as she thought it was over, Tommy's dad smiled at her by the door. Isa groaned and fought the urge to roll her eyes. Just her luck.

"Ma'am, are you alright? My son was truly sorry for what he did. I hope your dress will be alright." He looked down and noticed she wasn't in her dress and was barefoot. "Does Thunder have your dress? I will talk to him and if it dries with any stains, I will be more than willing to pay for it."

Just when Isa thought it couldn't get any worse, she heard a voice she hoped to never hear again in her lifetime.

"Isa, is that you? Are you okay?" Keith asked her.

Well shit, Isa thought, *this sucks!* She turned around and smiled a fake smile at Keith.

"Keith, how are you? So nice to see you. Unfortunately, I don't have time to talk." She tried to spin around and leave, but Keith grabbed her arm.

"Wait, it's good to see you. You look great. Maybe we can go back to your place and catch up," he leered at her bare legs.

"Uh, no. Not gonna happen." She tried to pull her arm away from Keith and looked to Grayhorse for help.

"Sir, I don't think the lady wants to talk to you right now." Grayhorse grabbed Keith's wrist and squeezed until Keith let go of her arm.

"Dude, get your hand off me. Isa and I are friends," he told Grayhorse.

"I'm sure you are friends, but grabbing her like that is not what a friend does. Why don't you check out our museum and see our beautiful displays and you can talk to her later?" Grayhorse turned him around and pointed toward the museum entrance.

Keith was not ready to give up. He tried walking around Grayhorse and said, "Isa, I really want to talk to you."

"Not now Keith." Isa saw Grayhorse block Keith so he couldn't get to her.

"Ok, sure. But call me Isa. We need to discuss our future." Keith turned around and spoke over his shoulder as Grayhorse gave him a slight push toward the museum entrance.

Isa looked at Grayhorse with tears in her eyes. *Would this night ever end?*

"Is there anything I can get you? A glass of water maybe?" he moved his arm around her to escort her to the restaurant. Logically, Isa knew he was being nice and just wanted to help her, but she couldn't stop herself from jerking out of his hold.

If Grayhorse only knew, it wasn't about the dress. Seeing Keith just added to her humiliation for the night. She ignored him for two whole years, and now when she reached an ultimate embarrassing low, she ran into him. How dare he approach her and want to talk about a future? What an asshole! Just because she was half naked didn't mean she was a convenient lay. Ugh, she hated Asshole Keith. He just reminded her of her failures and insecurities.

"Here comes Thunder now. Maybe he can help you." Grayhorse's statement broke into her thoughts.

At the mention of Thunder's name, Isa looked up and saw him coming out of the kitchen toward her with a worried look on his face. She quickly pulled away from Grayhorse and walked backward, heading toward the front door as she said, "I gotta go, don't worry about the dress. It's alright really, but thank you for offering to pay for it. Please tell Tommy it wasn't his fault. Also, thank you for your help with Keith." Thunder was closing in on her and she had to get out, so she turned and ran out of the cultural center.

"Isa," Isa heard Thunder's voice call her name.

*** *Thunder* ***

"*Wakíyaŋ Hotóŋpi*, let her go." Grayhorse grabbed Thunder's arm. "She needs time to calm down. She seemed really upset."

Thunder stopped and watched Isa leave.

"Where's Isa?" Sarah caught up to him. "What happened up there? Why aren't you talking to me? Why do I have to chase you through this entire center? Is she still mad at Tommy? He promised not to do it again. And believe me, I think he learned his lesson." Sarah kept rambling as she stopped next to Grayhorse.

Thunder just stared out the door.

"*Wakíyaŋ Hotóŋpi*, did something else happen up there that I should know about? Why are you shirtless? Is she running out of the museum with your buckskin shirt?" Sarah continued to stare at him for answers.

Grayhorse of course, piped in with his commentary, "She was upset when she ran out of the restaurant. Then she ran into some guy that wanted to leave with her." That comment got Thunder's attention.

"What? What do you mean?" Thunder spun around and said through gritted teeth.

"Some guy named Keith stopped her. He grabbed her arm and said he was her friend. She turned him down and looked at me for help. I made him release her arm and told him to go visit the museum. By the time I finished talking to him and turned back to face her, she was crying. This Keith guy freaked her out and became panic-stricken when she saw you heading toward her."

"Thank you for helping her, Grayhorse." Thunder ran a hand over his face, trying to control his temper. "Nothing happened, Sarah." He glanced outside to avoid his sister's accusing eyes. He didn't want to tell her everything that happened upstairs.

"When Isa got her keys out of her purse, she dropped her wallet. I wanted to bring it to her, so I ignored you upstairs and followed her, hoping to catch her before she left. But now she's gone without her wallet. I'm gonna have to call or text her so I can get it to her. She should not be driving without a license."

"Well, it will not be tonight unless you know where she lives. We need to see if we have to do some damage control. See if anyone noticed other than that guy, Keith? Luckily, most of our guests are gone and the tribal council left an hour ago." Grayhorse said as he looked around to see who was in the lobby.

"*Han*, Grayhorse, you're right. I'll text her so she won't worry that she lost it." Thunder had her number and sent her text messages. He knew she wouldn't answer. "Worse comes to worst, I can always take it to her tomorrow at Teramar. Thanks for trying to help. What did the guy look like that you saw trying to talk to Isa?"

"He was white, brown short hair, brown eyes, shorter than us, medium build, and he wore a dark blue business suit with a gray paisley print tie. I'm sure I could point him out if I saw him again. Do you want me to go with you to the museum?"

"No, thanks," Thunder murmured. "I'll look for someone matching that description. Stay at the door and let's not let anyone else in. It's almost 10:00 p.m."

Thunder entered the museum and looked around, noticing a man in a dark blue suit by the back wall. He walked up to him and introduced himself.

"Good evening, my name is Thunder. Are you Keith, Isa's friend?" He asked the man.

"Yes, I know Isa. That little firecracker. She looked pretty hot in that little number, huh?" He elbowed Thunder.

"That little number was my shirt, and I suggest you never talk like that about her again. In the future, please have some respect." Thunder said, trying to keep his temper under control.

"Oh shit, sorry, man. I didn't know she was dating anyone. You're really taking this Indian shit really seriously, huh? Is she your squaw?" Keith smirked.

"Not funny," Thunder grumbled. "Squaw is an offensive word for an American Indian woman. As far as I know, she's Cuban." Thunder crossed his arms and stared at Keith. "And yes, I take my culture and customs seriously."

"Okay, okay, I didn't know, man," Keith raised his hands and backed away from Thunder. "Just don't scalp me," he laughed.

"Again, not funny," Thunder scolded, wishing he could scalp him if that would stop him from saying stupid shit.

"Well, good luck with her. Her mood swings faster than a swinging bar door. She runs hot and cold quickly and it takes a lot to make her run hot. If you know what I mean." Keith smiled smugly at Thunder.

Thunder could feel his blood boiling just from talking to this idiot. If it wasn't for where they were, he would knock this asshole out. However, he had to pretend to be civil and not let his temper have any adverse effects on the opening.

Looking at his watch, Thunder said, "Well, would you look at the time? Our cultural center will close in a couple of minutes. Maybe you can come back another time."

"Ah, sure, I'll be back. This stuff is cool as shit," Keith said as Thunder escorted him out of the museum to the front door.

"Great. Good night," Thunder said as he opened the door for Keith.

"You too, man," Keith answered.

"Asshole," Thunder murmured under his breath when the door shut after Keith.

"Yep," Grayhorse nodded.

"I'm going to check if anyone else is still in any other rooms. The museum is empty."

"Sounds good," Grayhorse said.

Thunder walked into the storytelling room and saw Tommy sleeping on the floor. The rest of the room was empty. He'd tell Sarah where Tommy was. Seeing two women in the gift shop making their last-minute purchases, he waited until they finished and escorted them out. They kept staring at his chest, and he remembered he was shirtless. They told him they loved everything and promised to tell all their friends and family. Sarah walked up to him as he was locking the front door.

"It went well *Wakíyaŋ Hotóŋpi*, except for the Isa incident. Do you want to tell me what really happened now?" Sarah asked.

"It's late *taŋkši*, you've got to get Tommy to bed. He's passed out in the Storytelling Room on the carpet. I'll talk to you in the morning."

"You can't avoid me forever, you know?"

"I know, but for now, can we drop it? Please? It's been a long night," he begged her. His sister was like a dog with a bone when she wanted information.

"Ok, for tonight."

"*Pilámaya, taŋkši*. What would I do without you?" he pulled her into his arms for a hug as he kissed her forehead.

Sarah looked at him and smiled, "*Taŋyáŋ yahípi, tibló*. Let me go get Tommy so we can go home. It's late for a school night."

"Look who I found sleeping on the job in the Storytelling Room," Grayhorse said as he walked toward them, carrying a sleeping Tommy in his arms.

"Ah, *súŋkawakháŋhota cíkala*, you worked so hard today," Thunder whispered as he ran a hand over Tommy's head.

"He sure did," said Grayhorse.

Thunder held the door open for them.

"I will see you guys later. Drive safely."

"Do not forget about family day on Sunday. You are coming over for lunch, right?" Sarah stated before Thunder closed the door.

They had been getting together every Sunday since they'd all moved there for a family lunch and afternoon fun. Something they all made time for. Family was everything.

"I will be there." Thunder waved and stepped back in to set the alarm, turn off the lights, and lock the door. He was tired after a long day and went upstairs to sleep in his apartment instead of driving home. As he made his way into his apartment, he checked his phone and noticed Isa hadn't texted back. Well, at least she knew he had it. When he walked into the bathroom, he found her shoes and bra on the floor.

"Huh, pretty soon I will have her full wardrobe, or at least a full outfit." He smiled.

How could a great day and opening end in such a shitshow? He used the restroom, brushed his teeth, and took off his clothes. He liked to sleep naked. Folding his clothes into a pile, he left them on the bathroom counter along with Isa's bra. It was a nice see-through lacy bra. One that looked better on the floor, giving him full access to her perfect breasts.

Fuck it! Thunder left the bathroom, pulled on a pair of sweatpants and t-shirt he kept in the apartment as backup and decided he was driving to her house and returning her wallet. Grabbing her wallet from the table, he looked inside for her license and read the address. He entered the address on his phone's GPS. It wasn't far from the cultural center. He'd promised Grayhorse he wouldn't go to her and would leave her alone tonight, but he couldn't. He wanted to see her and apologize.

Jogging downstairs, he ran into Rachel in the kitchen, wiping the counter.

"Rachel, what are you still doing here?"

"Just wanted to finish cleaning up. Where are you going? Is there something I can help you with?"

"I need to run an errand," Thunder held up Isa's wallet.

"Now? Isn't it kinda late?"

"Better late than never. See you tomorrow." Thunder didn't wait to hear Rachel's parting words. He strode out of the center, got in his car, and followed his GPS.

On the drive, he rehearsed his apology. Assuring her how awful he felt was his main goal. He made good time, considering it was almost midnight. Everyone talks about New York being the city that never sleeps, but Ft. Lauderdale bars were usually open until three or four in the morning every day of the week. Parking in her apartment complex, he looked at the apartment number and walked to her door. Thunder knocked twice and waited until the door opened.

"Who are you?" a half-naked man answered the door, rubbing his eyes. "What the fuck, man? Do you know what time it is?"

"I'm sorry," Thunder's jaw dropped when a half-naked man opened the door. Had she left him to come sleep with this guy? "I came to bring Isa her wallet. Is she here?" Thunder gritted his teeth and lifted his hand, showing said object.

"Who the fuck is Isa?" half-naked man quirked an eyebrow. "There's no one here named Isa."

"This was the address on her license." Thunder sighed in relief, opened her wallet, and showed him.

"She's hot...but doesn't live here. It must be the previous renter. I've been here for the past six months."

"Okay. I'm so sorry. Thank you for your help." Thunder grimaced.

"No problem. I hope you find her," the half-naked guy gave him a chin lift before slamming the door shut.

Fuck! His apology would have to wait until tomorrow. Thunder was so frustrated he drove around for about an hour until the long day caught up to him and he drove back to the cultural center.

Undressing again, he crawled into bed, and laid down on top of his sheets, he couldn't stop thinking about their little adventure earlier. She looked so hot when she sat on his lap, mostly naked. He relived every moment while he used his hand to relieve the pressure building on his cock. Fuck, he came quicker than ever, letting his cum land on his stomach. When his breathing returned to normal, he cleaned himself up and got back into bed.

Thunder needed her in his life. No other girl had ever affected him so quickly. Everything was going great until he started talking dirty. Maybe she didn't like that, but did she have to punch him? He'd stopped when she pushed him. That question had to be answered, especially after meeting Keith. How could Isa be friends with such an idiot? Had they dated? Did he force himself on her? Was he gonna have to kick his ass? Too many questions to ponder tonight, and he was exhausted. Let the groveling begin tomorrow so he could get to the root of the problem.

Chapter 18

The Grayhorse's Drive Home

SARAH

Grayhorse put Tommy in the back seat and went around to the front to start the car. Tommy was still dead asleep, so Sarah buckled him in, closed the door and sat in the passenger seat.

"What do you think went on up there? With that woman? I'm assuming they had a disagreement. And by the way, Thunder was neither dressed when I went upstairs to check on her nor when he ran to the lobby. I don't think they were just having tea."

"What do you mean?"

"About half an hour after the crash, I noticed that Thunder had not come downstairs again, so I went up to see if there was anything I could do. You know, woman to woman. So, I knocked, and then suddenly, the door swung open, and Isa pushed past me as she ran down the stairs. I walked in to talk to Thunder, and he was standing in the kitchen with no shirt on. I'm pretty sure he didn't get food on his buckskin shirt. Not to mention, as she bolted by me, I noticed her wearing his buckskin shirt," she said wryly.

"You notice everything, don't you?" Grayhorse grinned at her.

"It was hard not to, if you know what I mean."

Grayhorse laughed, "Of course I do. I think you know the answer to what you are thinking. Your brother is reckless with women, but he would never hurt one. He needs someone to help settle him down, like you did for me. Maybe this one will take your brother's heart away. I mean, he chased her after all."

"Well, she already has his shirt, so I guess they will have to see each other. Not to mention he has her wallet and shoes, from what I could see." She smiled.

"She also rattled him, like no other lady has in a long time. He couldn't concentrate on a single conversation all night. But we've got to let him handle this on his own. Do not get involved *mitáwicu*. Do you hear me, woman?"

"Yes, I hear you, loud and clear. He can take care of himself, I guess. I hope someday he finds the right woman if it isn't Isa. I worry about him."

She reached across the seat and placed her hand on Grayhorse's thigh. He took her hand and raised it to his mouth for a kiss.

"*Mitáwicu thečhíhila.* I hope he finds what I have found with you." He laid both their hands on his thigh.

She smiled and laid her head back on the headrest. She felt so blessed, wrapped up in her husband's love, and that was what she wanted for her brother. Sarah had been married for seven years now. It seemed like just yesterday when they'd met and fallen in love.

When Thunder had left for college, Sarah was fourteen years old and getting ready to start high school. Thunder only came home on holidays because he worked at the college tutoring year-round. He needed to work to offset the college costs. Unfortunately, they saw little of each other. They kept in touch via text, face time, and phone calls, but it wasn't the same. Growing up, they had been inseparable even though they were four years apart.

Sarah's mind wandered as she stared out the window. Her eyelids grew heavy, and she allowed her memories to sweep her away.

Sarah was home alone watching a movie when she heard a knock on the door.

"Hi Uncle Spirit," she smiled and gave him a hug, "What are you doing here? I thought you were with mom and dad at the community center playing BINGO?"

"Hau, Sarah," Uncle Spirit looked so sad, "May I come in?"

"Of course. What's going on? You look like you are about ready to cry?"

"Come sit with me on the couch."

"You're really freaking me out, Uncle Spirit. Do you want something to drink?"

"No," Uncle Spirit sat next to Sarah and held her hands, "I have something to tell you, and I want you to know I'm here for you."

"Okay," Sarah said slowly.

"Your mom and dad were driving home from the community center and they had an accident. A couple of drunk teenagers from the reservation crossed the double yellow lines and ran into them head on. There were no survivors." Uncle Spirit gently said, while watching Sarah's reaction.

"No, that can't be. I would have heard." Sarah stood up and paced frantically across her living room. "No one has called me. The police haven't been by. You must be wrong." She glanced down at Uncle Spirit with tears in her eyes.

"Sarah, I was behind them." Uncle Spirit stood up and held her. "I saw the accident. No one has called you because I asked them not to come. I told them I would let you know."

"No! No!" Sarah broke down. Her body shaking so hard she would've collapsed to the ground had Uncle Spirit not held her tightly.

"I'm so sorry, Sarah. By the time I got to them, they had both passed. The police said they had died on impact. At least we know they didn't suffer."

"Uncle Spirit, what am I going to do without them?" she cried into his chest.

"I will always be here for you and your brother. You're family."

"Have you told Thunder?"

"No, I came here first."

"I'll call him now."

Sarah remembered telling Thunder. Thunder made arrangements to come home in time for the funeral. Those had been dark days packing up all of their parents' things. She wanted to stay in their house, but Uncle Spirit thought it was best if she stayed with him and his family.

Sarah loved Uncle Spirit and his wife Morning Sunshine, but she soon realized that their son Joseph had a crush on her. Sarah told Joseph she loved him like a brother, not a boyfriend. It took him a while to understand, but he finally got the message and they became friends.

A boyfriend... Sarah remembered the day she met Grayhorse.

"Sarah," Thunder sat next to her on the couch, "I have a friend that is training horses with me that just broke up with his girlfriend and needs a place to stay. I thought he could stay in your old room since you're in the master bedroom. Is that okay?"

"Who is it?" Sarah frowned at Thunder.

"His name is Jake Grayhorse. He is Lakota but grew up outside of the reservation. I've been teaching him about our culture. He's a really nice guy that had a very shitty girlfriend."

"Okay, if you trust him, that's fine."

The next day, Thunder brought Jake Grayhorse home and helped him move in. Sarah got a big crush on Grayhorse the minute he walked in the door. He was tall and good looking. Grayhorse and Sarah spent a lot of time together and soon fell in love. They got married only four months after they met. Grayhorse moved into the master bedroom with Sarah and they had Tommy nine months later.

Now that she thought about the past and her relationship with Joseph, she found it strange that Joseph came down with the elders for this opening. She thought he might cause trouble for Thunder. Though she never saw him with Thunder. She was in the lobby the entire night and every time she saw him, he was in the storytelling room with Uncle Spirit. Huh.

"What are you thinking about over there? You are so quiet," Grayhorse asked her.

She sighed deeply, "Just thinking about my parents, Thunder, you, the cultural center, world peace," she grinned, looking at him.

"Wow, that's a lot for this late at night. Well, home sweet home. After we put Tommy to bed, can we think about our world peace?" He winked.

"I would love to do world peace with you," she smiled. During the evening, she'd caught Grayhorse watching her several times. A few times, he even walked behind her and pinched her ass. She would world peace him alright. This was going to be a satisfyingly long night.

Chapter 19

Rachel's Adventure in the AICC Kitchen

RACHEL

Rachel watched from the doorway of Thunder's office as he locked up and headed toward his apartment. She knew the *wašicuŋ wíŋyaŋ* had been upstairs with him earlier. She didn't know what had happened, but she'd seen when the woman left with Thunder's shirt and no shoes. Did they fuck? She was going to find out. She was furious that Thunder even paid attention to the woman. Thunder had always chosen Rachel to spend the night with him when his openings were a success. He was always so full of adrenaline after a show and tonight had surpassed all the previous openings. She'd hoped he would be fucking her all night long. She knew he hadn't been seeing anyone. *Maybe he's secretly pining for me and is embarrassed to tell me,* Rachel thought, *I have to show him how much I love him so we can get back together.* He'd been the best lover she ever had, and she always got him off in bed.

Rachel walked into the kitchen and saw there were a few dirty dishes in the sink. She figured she might as well clean them before leaving for the night. Maybe if she made enough noise in the kitchen, Thunder would hear her and come down. Once he saw her, he would take her upstairs to his bed and fuck her.

Shockingly, she turned when she heard Thunder coming down the stairs. Had she dreamed him up? Was he coming to get her? She hoped he wanted her, but she was wrong. She felt deflated when he left to run an errand. Shit, this chick might have already dug her claws into him. She needed to step up her game.

His rejection had her daydreaming about the past when their relationship ended as she finished the dishes.

They had been inseparable those first two years when they ran the center together. Then his sister and her family moved to South Florida, and he spent more time with them. Soon Thunder kept inviting his family to do things together. Rachel didn't hate Sarah. She just wanted more alone time with Thunder. It hadn't helped when Thunder started turning to Sarah and Grayhorse for their advice. Advice she was way more qualified to give since she was his assistant. It grated on her nerves every time he went to them.

It wasn't long before Rachel felt lonely. She turned to other men to fill the gaping hole Thunder left in her life with his incessant visits to 'spend time with his nephew.'

After she slept with Joseph, Thunder became distant. She had a feeling that Thunder suspected her of cheating, and she was surprised he never flat out asked her. Thunder would never forgive her if he knew she cheated on him with Joseph. Then one day, he called her into his office.

"Rachel, we need to talk."

"Sure baby," Rachel walked into his office and kissed him before he closed his door. "What's going on?"

"Have a seat," they both sat down on the couch.

"I really care about you Rachel, but this isn't working out." Thunder held her hands.

"What are you talking about?"

"Us," he pointed to both of them. "I think we both just kind of let this happen since we depend on each other so much and came out here together. We agreed that this wasn't serious, just two lonely people seeking comfort. Now that Sarah, Grayhorse and Tommy are here, I really need to focus on my family. I don't want Tommy getting confused about our relationship. I care about you, but I don't love you the way you should be loved. It isn't fair to either of us to continue this."

Rachel was stunned by his comments. She was in love with him. He just needed to spend more time with her instead of Tommy.

"I don't see why Tommy can't understand that I'm your girlfriend?"

"Well," he rubbed the back of his neck. He always did this when he was nervous.

"I just think we need to just be friends."

"Just like that? The two years of fucking me meant nothing to you?"

"I didn't say that, Rachel," he looked at her angrily, "Don't put words in my mouth. I don't want to hurt you."

"And saying you want to break up with me is not hurting me," Rachel stood up and headed towards the door.

"I'm sorry, Rachel, I treasure your friendship," Thunder stated.

"One day you will regret this Thunder. I am the best thing you'll ever have. I just wanted to spend more time with you, but obviously, your priorities have changed." Rachel stormed out of the office before she said something she would regret. She would do anything she could to show him he made a mistake - she would get him back.

Remembering that conversation was painful, but she had stuck to her plan. She became his confidant and pretended to only love him as a friend. He fell for it and would talk to her about his family and his women. Well, not the specifics of his dates, but she knew where he was sleeping and with whom. The women that followed were like a revolving door of one-night stands. He'd told her he was tired of loving and leaving them. That's when she knew it was time to make her intentions known. He'd taken none of those women home, so they obviously meant nothing to him.

Until now. That *wašícuŋ wíŋyaŋ* was ruining everything! She had to go. Rachel was vigorously scrubbing the remaining plates.

Why had he chosen the *wašícuŋ wíŋyaŋ*? She wasn't as pretty as her. She didn't have long black hair and pretty brown eyes like her. As her thoughts were drifting toward what might have happened upstairs, a man came up behind her and covered her eyes, his lips pressing into her neck.

"*Hau*, Rachel," Joseph whispered in her ear. "I have missed you."

She recognized his voice instantly. She hadn't seen him in almost two years, but she saw him sneak into the Storytelling Room earlier today. Her body stiffened, but then she figured if she couldn't have Thunder, his cousin would be a suitable substitute. They were both tall, but Joseph was thinner compared to Thunder's more muscled body. Thunder was also more attractive than Joseph, with his chiseled jaw and handsome features. Joseph wasn't as good as Thunder in bed, but if she closed her eyes, she could imagine Thunder fucking her instead of Joseph.

She was already horny thinking about Thunder and thoroughly enjoyed the feel of hands roaming over her body. In her mind, they were Thunder's hands, not Joseph's.

"*Tóhaŋ niš hwo?*" she asked Joseph.

"About an hour ago, did you not see me? My father and I were in the Storytelling Room. I stepped out to use the restroom, and I saw the *wašícuŋ wíŋyaŋ* go with Thunder upstairs. I knew you would be upset, so I tried to find you."

"I went into the office to get something," she answered breathlessly. "They weren't up there long. I saw her leave shortly after."

"Yes, I saw her leave as well, but he went upstairs by himself for the night and forgot about you. I would never do that. I know you must be very lonely tonight, so I thought I would make you feel good."

*** *Joseph* ***

Joseph didn't like to play second best for anyone, especially Thunder, but Rachel was an exception. Plus, he needed her for his plan to work. He knew Rachel compared him to Thunder. She had even cried out the wrong name in ecstasy several times. Joseph didn't care. As long as she satisfied his lust, she could cry out anyone's name. Rachel was a toy for him to play with for the moment. Soon he would have everything Thunder owned and then he would discard her. He assumed Thunder just amused himself with her as well. He must have because they'd never wed, and they had been living in this hot, miserable place for over five years now. When they'd broken up, Thunder had told Joseph that he still cared for Rachel, but not as a future wife. Joseph took some pleasure because they'd broken up shortly after he'd fucked Rachel. But he hadn't told Thunder that. Not yet, he wanted to tell him when he was ready. It was one more thing that Thunder had that Joseph had taken. Joseph pretended to like Thunder and kept in touch, but he was just biding his time.

"Joseph, that's very kind of you, but I will be fine. She isn't up there any longer. Maybe I will surprise him," she purred.

Joseph knew she was playing games with him. If Thunder wanted her, he would have taken her upstairs instead of leaving a few minutes ago. But he would go along with her game. She didn't need to know he was hiding out in the warehouse.

Rachel was a woman who was always ready to fuck and loved to tease him. She liked it rough, at least with Joseph. He pushed her against the sink with his body so she could feel his hardened cock on her ass. He roughly tweaked her breasts as he slammed her back against his chest so he could devour her neck. She was wearing a buckskin dress, and he knew she was naked underneath.

He stepped back and turned her around so he could sit her up on the counter next to the sink. He pulled her dress up to her waist while kissing her neck. Slipping his right hand's middle finger inside her, he fingered her until she fucked his hand. He felt her wetness and knew she was ready. Quickly undoing his pants with his left hand, he let them slide to the floor and savagely thrust into her.

Grabbing the counter to hold herself in place, Rachel clamped her legs around his waist and screamed.

"Now Thunder! Give me all you have, love me!" Joseph sensed her orgasm building as her inner muscles clamped onto him. She moaned very loud causing Joseph to cover her mouth with his hand. They continued to pound into each other until they both climaxed.

*** *Rachel* ***

Rachel climaxed quickly. Lucky for her, because Joseph never took part in too much foreplay and didn't take a woman's satisfaction into consideration. That was a major difference between the cousins.

After Joseph came inside her, they both collapsed against the counter. Thank goodness she was on the pill. Yet another difference between them. Thunder took care of his partners, but Joseph just didn't care. Now she had to clean herself up. He slowly withdrew from her and put his pants on. Rachel jumped off the counter and dropped her dress back down.

"Can I give you a ride home, Rachel?"

"Let me use the restroom first."

"I'll wait in the lobby."

"Okay." Rachel quickly wiped the counter and went to the restroom. After cleaning herself up, she stopped by Thunder's office to grab her purse and walked to the lobby to get Joseph. He didn't have neither the code nor key to set the alarm and lock up.

"Okay, I'm ready. Let me undo the alarm code. You walk out and I will reset it before I lock up."

"Sounds good," Joseph said to her and stepped out after she disarmed the alarm.

Once Joseph stepped out, she closed the door. Rearmed the alarm, opened the door, walked out, and relocked it.

"I got a rental." Joseph pointed to the only other car in the lot next to Thunder's truck.

Hoping to spend the night with Thunder, she got a ride to work from Mark earlier that day.

Joseph opened the door for her. So gentlemanly, so not like him. Especially since she'd screamed out Thunder's name right before her orgasm. Oops, it wasn't the first time she'd done that. She always found it surprising that he didn't get mad. His eyes would blaze with a frightening intensity, a terrifying glare that always made her flinch, convinced he was about to strike, though he never did. He hadn't looked at her like that this time. Weird. But she would not bring it up just in case. She'd heard stories about his anger issues. But she wondered if he hit her, would Thunder care and come to her rescue? Would he take care of her? Maybe that was what she needed to do to get Thunder to notice her again.

She could play the damsel in distress. She'd have to think about it. It might be worth the pain of getting hit by Joseph if Thunder would take her back and love and protect her. She thought about it the whole way to her apartment. Maybe she could talk to Joseph once she figured out a plan. Rachel knew she had to act quick before that *wašícuŋ wíŋyaŋ* sank her claws into her man.

Chapter 20

Friday...Day After the Opening

Isa

The next morning, Isa woke up to her alarm ringing. Rolling over to turn off her alarm, she noticed a text and voicemail from Thunder. She read the text first.

> Thunder: Isa, I left you a voicemail. I have your wallet. Please call or text me.

Ugh...she'd been such an idiot last night. Moving on to the voicemail, she hit play and listened.

> Isa, It's Thunder. I'm so sorry about what happened last night. I'm sorry if I hurt you, please call me. I really want to talk to you. Anyway, you dropped your wallet in my apartment and I'm sure you need it. I would have brought it to you last night, but I don't know where you live. Please call me.
> Ok, well hopefully I'll talk to you soon.

He had such a nice, deep, soothing voice she could listen to for hours. She looked up at the ceiling and realized it was time to get up and face the music. When she'd gotten home last night, she'd washed her face, brushed her teeth, and gone straight to bed. She never looked at her phone. Thunder's shirt smelled like him and felt so soft against her skin that she hadn't bothered to take it off. She'd just crawled under her covers and passed out.

As she lay in bed thinking about the coming day, she would stop by the cultural center and make the exchange. His shirt for her stuff. She was hoping to talk to him before she went to work. She knew the cultural center was open today from nine to five. It was 7:30, so by the time she showered and dressed, she could be there when it opened. She would get to work a little later than normal, but she didn't have any meetings scheduled for this morning. Before she got up, she texted Maggie.

Isa: Mags, I need to run an errand this morning and I'll be a few minutes late.

Maggie: okey dokey.

Isa hoped Thunder was alone at work this morning and she'd make the exchange quietly with no fuss. He deserved an apology after she freaked out on him last night. Maintaining a good relationship with him was important, especially since he was a client.

After she got ready, she drove to the cultural center and arrived at nine on the dot. Reaching for the front door, she noticed the lights were on, but couldn't see anyone inside. She attempted to open the door, but it remained locked. She knocked twice before she saw a young American Indian woman walk toward her. Isa hesitated.

"Good morning," the woman said after she opened the door. "Can I help you?"

"Good morning," Isa replied as she shifted the shirt between her hands. "Is Thunder here? I need to speak to him and return this." She told the woman as she held out her hand. Isa had seen her last night but didn't know her name.

"I'm Rachel. Thunder is not here right now, but who, may I say, came to see him? I can leave him a message. I haven't seen you here before. Then again, I lose track of Thunder's ladies," she said as she winked at her. "They are always returning some article of his clothing that he left at their place." She laughed and reached out to take the shirt.

Isa pulled the shirt back against her chest.

"What do you mean?" she furrowed her brow.

"Nothing." Rachel looked at her like she was an idiot. "I'm sure you know how Thunder is. He changes girlfriends, or should I say lovers, like he changes his underwear. I should know, we've been friends for a long time. I was in your shoes not too long ago." She pointed to the shirt she was holding. "Don't look so surprised. Thunder is no saint. You're holding proof of that. He knows how to pleasure women until they don't know how much of their heart and soul they've lost to him. He is what you all call a Romeo Joe."

*** *Rachel* ***

Rachel could see the color draining from Isa's face. Direct hit.

"Why are you saying these things to me?" Isa seemed astonishingly surprised.

"I'm not saying this to be mean. You just seem like a nice person. I'd hate to see you get hurt. Oops, you are holding his shirt, so maybe he already loved you and left you. He can be so cruel sometimes. I keep telling him to be nicer and stop sleeping around." Rachel said with a sympathetic look on her face.

"Well, thank you. But I can take care of myself. I refuse to be manipulated like a starry-eyed bimbo. Besides, nothing happened last night. Not that it's any of your business."

Rachel could tell Isa was straightening her back and jutting out her chin in a false sense of bravado. She could see tears forming in her eyes. Definitely a direct hit.

"Of course," Rachel said, "I'm so sorry. I didn't mean to belittle you. What message can I leave for Thunder?"

Isa cleared her throat and said, "Uh, can you just tell him Isa came by to deliver his shirt? He can drop off my stuff at Teramar Studios later today. I'll let the receptionist know to look for it. Now if you'll excuse me, I'm running very late. Thank you." She handed her the shirt.

"You're welcome."

*** Isa ***

It took all of Isa's courage to hold her head up high as she walked to her car, holding back tears.

Once she got into her car, she started the engine and slammed her hands against the steering wheel. *Dammit,* she thought, *why do I always pick losers, users, and manipulators? How many times do I have to play the fool before I wake up and smell the coffee?* She should have known he was just a player and horny for anyone. Turning him down meant nothing to him. He probably went out and found another girl to fuck. Hell, he probably fucked Rachel. Well, as far as she was concerned, it meant nothing to her either.

Shit, her wallet. She wondered if Rachel knew where it was. Ah, hell, she wasn't going back in there. She would drive carefully to work and hope he dropped it off today before she drove home.

She pulled up to the parking lot exit and looked both ways for oncoming traffic. When she looked to the right, she noticed Thunder jogging back to the center, shirtless in his sweatpants. He must have been out for a run. He walked to the door and Rachel handed him a towel for him to wipe his neck and face as she smiled at him. Then she kissed him on the cheek and put her arms around him as he walked inside.

"Son of a bitch!" Isa screamed then sighed, "I guess I'm just another one of his bimbos after all."

She wished the cultural center did not have a glass front door. Seeing that just ruined her day. She was an idiot. Last night, he'd tried to seduce her and act like he cared. Meanwhile, today, he was all warm and cozy with Rachel—asshole.

"Asshole, he probably slept with her after I left." she said to herself, "Oh no, what if the asshole was planning on doing both of us last night one right after the other!" Rachel had known all about his women, yet she was all over him. Maybe they were friends with benefits. Isa didn't need to see any more. She was not interested in that type of relationship. She gunned her engine and pulled out into traffic.

*** *Thunder* ***

Thunder had finished his morning run when he spotted Rachel at the front door with a towel for him. That was strange. She never waited for him at the door like that.

"Rachel, what's going on? Is everything ok?" Rachel leaned over and wiped his face with the towel. Then she kissed his cheek. Ok, this was getting awkward.

"Nothing *Wakíyaŋ Hotóŋpi*, but it is a gorgeous day, is it not?"

"Sure, but most days are, and you never wait for me at the door with a towel. What's going on?" He frowned at her. What was she up to? Was that his shirt in her hands?

"Rachel, is that my shirt?" he pointed to her hand. "Did Isa stop by? Is she here?" He asked as he stepped inside and scanned the center for Isa.

"She isn't here, but yes, she stopped by. She specifically asked me to drop off her stuff at Teramar today so she wouldn't have to see you because she doesn't want to speak to you again. Her intention is to maintain your relationship on a professional level. She seemed furious when she said if you didn't agree with her decision, she would cancel your account since her agency is big enough and they can pick who they want to work for." Rachel was fidgeting with her hands. "I didn't want her to get angry with us, so I told her you would agree to her terms. That seemed to satisfy her. She said from now on, you need to contact John Cummings directly and leave her out of the equation." Rachel scrunched up her face. "I think that's how she put it."

What the hell? By this point, Thunder was fuming. Leave him out of the equation. The center wasn't an important enough client to keep. Who did she think she was, anyway? Before she ran out last night, he had attempted to talk to her. Leaving her a message, he apologized. He was so dumb-founded, he just stared at Rachel. He couldn't believe Isa said that. That didn't sound like her.

"Did you sleep well last night? It was a great night." Rachel tried to change the subject.

"Actually, I slept like a baby." He lied through his teeth. No one needed to know that thoughts of the high and mighty Princess Isa kept him up all night, especially now.

"Good, today will be a long day since we've got to clean up after last night. Don't forget you told the elders you would meet with them today before they leave town."

"Right. Thanks for reminding me. I'm going to take a shower and change. I'll be down and help clean up when I finish. If Spirit of the Eagle or anyone else comes looking for me, tell them to wait in my office. I won't be long."

"Ok, *Wakíyaŋ Hotóŋpi*, here is your shirt."

"Thanks." He took his shirt and stormed upstairs. Fuck the dry cleaning. Rachel could take her belongings today. He just needed to pack up her shit. As if he was some piece of trash, he didn't need Her Mightiness looking down at him. He was so pissed it was probably best if he stayed away from her before he said something he'd regret, and he didn't want to do business with another agency. Or maybe he needed to man up and go set Princess Isa straight.

Chapter 21

Joseph's Thoughts

JOSEPH

Joseph had convinced Rachel to let him stay with her the night before. They'd fucked again when they got to her apartment. He was awake when Rachel left in the morning, but he pretended to be asleep. She was really pissing him off. Not only did she call him Thunder at the center, but again when he fucked her last night.

After she left, he got dressed and headed to the cultural center. Parking across the street, he waited for Thunder to return from his morning run. Thunder was so predictable in the morning, you could set your clock by him.

As Joseph waited, he noticed Rachel standing at the door speaking to the white woman from last night. What was Rachel up to? She wasn't letting her in. Who was that woman and what was she doing with a buckskin shirt in her hands? She didn't look like the type to wear American Indian clothing, especially dressed in that very sexy business suit and heels. Suddenly, the woman stood up taller and shoved the shirt at Rachel. She seemed angry. As Rachel took the shirt, the woman turned around and walked to her car.

She was inside her car when she slammed her hands against the steering wheel as she stared straight ahead at the center. What had Rachel said to her to piss her off so much? He'd ask Rachel about it later.

For now, he waited until she pulled out into the street. As he saw her stop and wait by the parking lot exit, he noticed she was looking toward the front entrance of the center. Following her gaze to see what she was looking at, he saw Rachel open the door for Thunder with a towel. She even wiped his face and kissed him. *What the fuck!* He thought they had broken up. He heard tires squeal and looked over to see the woman peel out of the parking lot. She must have seen them, too. Well, this was just getting better and better. He whispered to himself, "Soon Cousin, you will pay for all you have taken away from me. I promise."

He followed the woman to see where she was going.

A few miles later, she pulled into a parking lot, parked her car and walked into a building with a "Teramar Studios" sign. He wrote the name. He'd have to google it and find out what kind of place it was.

Chapter 22

Friday @ Teramar Studios

ISA

I sa was fuming as she sped to work, forgetting about her not having her driver's license. Walking into the building later than usual, she waved to Maggie.

"Hey Mags, how was your date?" Isa tried to act happy it wasn't Maggie's fault Thunder had joined the ranks of Asshole Keith. Maggie and Isa always shared information about their dates. Maggie really deserved to date a nice guy, and she hoped her date had gone better than Isa's night at the cultural center opening. Hell, a date with an executioner would have been better than hers.

Maggie held up her finger in the universal signal to wait while she finished on the phone.

"Mr. Jones, Isa is busy on another line. Can she call you back? Great, I'll let her know. Thank you and have a nice day." Maggie hung up the phone and glanced at the clock.

"Isa, where have you been? Is anything wrong? It's almost ten and you're never this late. I was worrying about you?"

"Sorry, Mags, it's a long story, which I'll tell you later. I texted you and told you I would be late this morning."

"I know, but you are NEVER late and I was worried."

"Sorry, I'll tell you at lunch. Was that Mr. Jones, my appointment for 10 a.m. today?"

"Yes, Mr. Jones said he's running late. To expect him around eleven. I told him it was okay."

"Thanks, Mags, this is one time I'm glad he's running late. Do you want to have lunch around one today?"

"That sounds good to me, Let's do Chinese today, if that's okay with," Maggie stopped mid-sentence holding up her finger again as she answered her phone, "Good morning, Teramar Studios, how can I help you?"

Isa nodded to Maggie to let her know she was ready and went to her office. She had to prepare notes and storyboards for her meeting with Mr. Jones, a sales representative for a major department store in the South Florida Region.

The meeting went well and Isa and Maggie walked a city block to their favorite Chinese restaurant when it was over. It was easy to eat a variety of cultural foods when you worked in such a diverse city. There were several restaurants within walking distance and others they could drive to. Maggie and Isa came to this restaurant a lot for their lunch buffet. So much so that all the employees knew them by name. They walked to a table, set their purses down, and headed straight for the buffet. They piled up their plates with Sweet and Sour Chicken, Pork Fried Rice and an egg roll. After they sat down with their plates, their waitress, Kim, served them hot tea. They loved the hot tea from this restaurant.

"So how was your date with Ryan?" Isa asked Maggie before she could grill her about Thunder.

"It was really nice. He took me to dinner at Palatio's and then we went dancing at The Dragon. He drove me home around 2:00am." Isa raised her eyebrow at her. "Well, we were just going to go to dinner, but we didn't want to leave each other's company so soon." Mags smiled dreamily. "When we drove by The Dragon, he asked if I wanted to get a drink, so we went in. He is an excellent dancer, by the way."

Isa could see Maggie's eyes light up as she spoke about Ryan. She wished she could feel the same way about Thunder. "That's awesome, Mags. I'm so happy for you. He really is a nice guy. You know if you ever want to have lunch with him, just say the word. It won't hurt my feelings."

"Don't be ridiculous, you can come along too," Maggie giggled.

"You're crazy Mags. But seriously, I won't get mad if you want to go just with him. I'm so glad you found someone that will treat you right. You deserve better than Tom. He was the lowest of the lows."

"We both deserve better than Tom and Asshole Keith. So now, you tell me about the opening at the cultural center," Maggie asked before she took a bite of her Sweet and Sour Chicken.

"It was really fascinating."

Isa hesitated and looked down at her plate. When she looked up again, Maggie's expression was full of concern.

"There were many exhibits, pottery, paintings, sculptures, clothing, bows & arrows, lances, music, food and superb storytelling. It was really quite interesting and cool. I'm glad I went."

Isa could tell Maggie wasn't buying it.

"If it was so great, Isa, why do you look so sad?"

"Oh Mags, I did it again. I fell for the body and forgot to think with my brain." Isa sighed, not making eye contact and pushing her food around her plate.

"What are you talking about?" Maggie asked curiously.

"I saw Thunder there, and he turned my world upside down."

"Thunder? You mean Johnny Thunderbird? Well, it is his cultural center, of course you would see him there. But how did he turn your world upside down?" Maggie raised her eyebrows.

"Yep, he goes by Thunder. Last night, he dressed in his full regalia and I totally made a fool of myself."

"Isa, you're not making any sense? How did you make a fool out of yourself in one night?"

"It was easy, really. I walked into a little boy carrying a tray of food and wore the honey dipping sauce."

"Oh my God," Maggie put her hand over her mouth, "Did you actually get something spilled on you again? That is not like you. You are not this clumsy."

"I know, right," Isa said wryly. "I guess he brings it out in me. Then he took me upstairs to his apartment. We exchanged shirts and I let things get too far."

"You exchanged shirts again!" Maggie interrupted her.

"Yes, again." Isa rolled her eyes.

"Isa, honey, start at the beginning. I think I'm lost."

"Okay. It all started when I was staring at a lance...," Isa told Maggie everything that happened in a shortened version. Their lunchtime was not long enough to get into all the details. Isa summarized the evening.

"Wow," Maggie said between bites, "that's a crazy night."

"Oh Mags, he looked so handsome and sexy and he really seemed interested in me. I mean, we were talking and getting along so well until I was naked, sitting on his lap and I panicked. All I could think about was how Asshole Keith would use me whenever he wanted sex, whether I wanted to or not, then leave and cheat on me with someone else. Asshole Keith always said I was like a cold fish in bed. I couldn't get the comments out of my head and I pushed Thunder away. When he stopped, I freaked out, and I punched him and started crying, of all things."

"You punched him?" Maggie looked stunned. "In the face?"

"No, on his shoulder. My hormones were all out of wack."

"Oh Isa, I'm so sorry. Stop thinking about Asshole Keith. You know we call him that for a reason and it has nothing to do with you. You are a wonderful, smart, beautiful woman and he is an asshole."

"Thanks Mags," Isa smiled crookedly at Maggie. "I appreciate you."

"Well, I love you, bestie, and you need to stop being so hard on yourself. He was a loser that could not appreciate you. His loss. Now, continue with your story. I'm on pins and needles since you came to work late and looked angry."

"Ok. Well, Thunder tried to apologize, and he left me a text and voicemail. So, this morning I went to the center to return his shirt and get my stuff and it went from bad to worse," she cried.

"What happened this morning?" Maggie asked.

"I drove to the center to make the exchange and this woman, Rachel, was there. She told me he was out of the office. Then she let me know I was one of his many conquests and he had many women. I told her nothing happened, and that I wasn't a bimbo. It was a moot point since I was standing there with his shirt in my hands. I am such an idiot. I made a fool out of myself to a total stranger. So I left quickly. Then, as I was pulling out of the lot as if it couldn't get any worse, I saw him come back in shirtless after his run and SHE handed him a towel along with a kiss. Ugh!!!" Isa groaned into her hands.

"Ouch." Maggie winced. "Well, maybe you never have to see them again." Isa appreciated Maggie trying to cheer her up.

"Really, Mags, did you forget they are one of our clients?"

"Oops, that little detail slipped my mind. Well, just let John deal with him whenever he comes in. That's his contact anyway, isn't it? It figures it was too good to be true. What an asshole! Him and her."

"Yeah, you're right, but why did my hot prince have to turn into a toad so quickly? I mean, at first, he seemed like he was going to force himself on me, and then he touched me so gently while he wiped my tears and couldn't stop apologizing."

"Oh, Isa. I wish I could tell you he is a nice guy, but we really don't know him very well. He probably sleeps around a lot. I mean, look at him. He's drop dead gorgeous. What woman in their right mind wouldn't beg for the chance to spend the night with him?"

"Gee thanks, Mags. I feel better already," Isa remarked sarcastically.

"Sorry, just trying to help," Maggie shrugged, then looked at her watch. "Well, it's time to blow this popsicle stand, ready to roll?"

"Yeah, I'm ready." Isa grumbled. She grabbed her purse and went to grab her wallet. "Shit! Maggie, I totally forgot, I don't have my wallet. I dropped it in Thunder's apartment. I was so frazzled this morning by talking to that woman, I never asked her about it. Can you cover my bill and I'll pay next time?"

"Of course, but what are you going to do about your wallet?"

"I'm hoping he drops it off today. If he does, don't let him know I'm there." Isa grabbed Maggie's hand and pleaded with her.

"Okay, okay. We're back to ghosting." Maggie paid for their food. "You know you will have to talk to him at some point if he keeps calling like he did last time, right? Not to mention you should probably apologize for punching him."

"Yeah, I know. Let's go. Thanks Mags, I owe you one."

They left the restaurant and walked back to work. As they were walking to the office building, Isa saw Thunder getting out of his truck and walking toward them.

"Oh shit Mags, there's Thunder. I guess I can't turn around now. He already saw me."

"Stand tall Isa, you did nothing wrong last night, well other than punching him." Maggie rolled her eyes. "A woman has a right to change her mind. Now hold your head up high and if you need me, holler cause I'm going inside."

Chapter 23

Got My Wallet and License and Apparently a Date

Isa

"Isa," Thunder called out as he approached them, "May I speak with you please?" Thunder turned to Maggie and said, "Hello Maggie, how are you?"

"Hi, Mr. Thunderbird. I'm doing well. So nice to see you. If you'll excuse me, I can hear the phones ringing off the hook from here. See ya' later, Isa."

"Coward," Isa whispered loud enough for Maggie to hear, then turned toward Thunder.

"What can I help you with, Mr. Thunderbird?"

"Why so formal, Isa? You weren't like that last night when I had my tongue down your throat. Or when I was sucking your breasts. Or when I had my hand in your pussy." He spoke loud enough that an elderly couple walking by heard them and gave her an evil look.

"Would you lower your voice? This is not the time or place for this conversation. We are right outside my place of business. What do you want, anyway?"

"Temper, temper, Isa honey. What happened to treating me like a professional client, since you work for me in a matter of speaking?" He smiled that panty dropping smile.

Isa took a deep breath and counted to ten. "Sorry, Mr. Thunderbird, what can I do for you today?" she said through gritted teeth.

"Now that's more like it. Do I get a smile with that?"

He was taunting her, and she was running out of patience, but she gave him a forced smile.

"A little stiff, Isa, but not too bad. See, a little kindness goes a long way."

Was he purposely being a dick or was this a new side to him that Isa had not seen before? She tried another tactic. "Did you get your shirt from your girlfriend, assistant, worker, whatever she is?"

"Do I detect a note of jealousy in your voice, Isa, honey?"

"No, and please stop calling me, honey?"

"Awww, come on Isa honey, don't get riled. I swear I didn't touch another woman after you left last night. Well, I did hug my sister, but that doesn't count, does it?"

"This conversation is ridiculous. Did you come all the way over here just to harass me? Or did you really need the agency's help? I can't stand out here all day with you arguing." Isa tapped her foot and crossed her arms.

"Well, I drove to the address on your license last night, but guess who hasn't updated their driver's license?" Thunder pointed at her.

"I've been busy," Isa squinted and pressed her lips together angrily at him.

"Clearly. So, I wanted to stop by before lunch and return this to you, but I got busy and wasn't able to get here sooner."

She noticed he was holding her wallet and shoes in his hand.

"Do you want to get something to eat, or did you just get back from eating with Maggie?" Thunder asked.

"Sorry, Maggie and I were just coming back from lunch. Maybe next time."

"How about dinner tonight?"

"Sorry, I'm busy." Isa looked down and scraped toes across the concrete.

"Doing your nails or washing your hair? Or am I just beneath you? Just another man to play with," Thunder asked sarcastically.

"What is wrong with you?" Isa stopped fidgeting and her head snapped up to stare at him. "What are you talking about? I'm the one you were messing with, not the other way around. What I'm doing is none of your business. Are you done insulting me yet?" Isa was stunned by his behavior. He was acting so mean. She knew they needed to talk, but now she just wanted to get away from him.

"You're right. I'm sorry that was out of line. I just wanted to bring you your stuff personally."

"Thank you," Isa reached out for her items, but Thunder put them behind his back.

"Aren't you going to kiss me?" Thunder leaned down and presented her with his cheek.

"Of all the nerve...pray tell, what for?" she asked him.

"For bringing you your wallet and shoes" he gave her his best smoldering look as he looked around and saw two women walking toward them. "You left them both in my apartment last night."

Isa turned around to see what he was looking at. The two ladies that worked with Isa smiled at them before entering the office.

"Oh, great. You had to say that just as the office gossips walked by. My day is getting better and better. Can I just have my stuff, please?" She reached out again.

"Nope, where's my thank you kiss?" Thunder leaned down again and placed his cheek toward her.

"Are you serious right now?" Isa balked. "May I have my wallet, please?" She ignored his cheek.

"No kiss?" He turned to her and raised an eyebrow.

"The wallet and shoes, please," she stuck her hand out.

"The wallet and shoes for dinner tonight."

"I don't think so."

He extended his arm to give her the wallet and shoes. When she reached for them, he pulled his arm back again.

"Why not? Aren't you glad I found it?" Thunder's gaze zeroed in on her.

"I didn't realize it was common practice in American Indian culture to steal and blackmail women into dating them." She cocked her head to the side in mock confusion. "Must have left that part out of the exhibit last night."

"Don't bring my culture into this," Thunder crossed his arms, "I'm just asking for a kiss on the cheek and a date."

"Okay, fine," Isa rolled her eyes and gave in.

He finally handed her the wallet and shoes, positively beaming.

"See, that wasn't so hard. I'll call you when I get back to my office."

"Okay, and thanks for bringing it to me," Isa nodded.

"I would have been here sooner, but I had some minor problems this morning."

"I bet you did," Isa murmured under her breath. She still remembered her conversation with Rachel and the way she greeted him when he finished his run. He was such a jerk.

"What did you say?" he asked her with a look of confusion.

"I said, I'll see you later."

"That's not what you said."

"Well, this was fun. But I gotta go," Isa said as she quickly entered the building. Turning around at the last minute to make sure he didn't follow her. She couldn't believe he had the gall to wink at her before he turned around to leave. What a bizarre conversation? She must be crazy to agree to go out with him. Either she was a real idiot or he was definitely a charmer. Guess all players were charmers, otherwise they wouldn't have many girls to play with.

Isa turned back around and walked to Maggie. "Thanks for leaving me out there hanging Mags, you're supposed to be my wing-woman. I'm a fool and I think I just got played."

"What? Is he gone?" Maggie pretended to be shocked.

"As if you didn't know. You can see right out the window." Isa gasped, exasperated, as she pointed out the window to a clear view of the outside.

Maggie grinned at her.

"Yep, and as angry as we both were, he still got me to agree to go out with him tonight. Ugh, what am I going to do, Mags? I am such an idiot." Isa smacked her head.

"Wait a minute. I thought you didn't want to see him again. We just had a conversation about this, like five minutes ago. Are you crazy? Besides, I just talked to Ryan. He's trying to set you up with one of his friends tonight so we can double date."

"Mags, you didn't." Isa looked at her like she wanted to strangle her.

"Isa, I did. I just wanted to cheer you up."

"Buzz his office right now and stop him from making that call, Maggie." Isa raised her voice.

"Okay, okay." Maggie picked up the phone and called Ryan's extension. "Hey Ryan, it's me."

Isa could only hear Maggie's side of the conversation. "You already called him. It's set for tonight," she looked up at her helplessly and shrugged her shoulders, "Yeah, I told Isa. No, she can't wait." She winced as she lied on the phone.

Isa stared at her with her mouth open and whispered angrily, "Maggie, tell him to cancel. Right now!"

"Okay Ryan, listen I gotta go but I'll see you later, bye," she quickly hung up the phone. "Isa I'm sorry, but please do this for me? It's been a while since we've double dated and it will be so much fun. Please. If Thunder calls, tell him you have other plans. Shoot, tell him you have another date. You said he was a player, so give him a little taste of his own medicine. Besides, you said you didn't want to see him again."

Isa couldn't stand to see Maggie beg, but she wanted to see her squirm. It was payback time. Besides, she really didn't want to see Thunder, did she?

"Oh, alright Mags, fine. But if he calls, YOU," Isa pointed at her, "have to come up with an excuse for me and not transfer his call to my office phone." Isa smiled wickedly at her.

"Ugh, I knew there would be a catch to this. I will tell him you are busy or out of the office or going potty," she smiled back.

"You better chose one of the first two excuses if you want me to show up for this double date."

"Fine. You drive a hard bargain. Thanks Isa, you're the best. You won't regret this," Maggie shouted as Isa walked away.

"I'm sure I will," Isa grumbled as she walked toward the staircase to go to her office.

Chapter 24

Friday @ AICC

THUNDER

T hunder couldn't concentrate after seeing Isa. He kept daydreaming about their verbal sparring, and it was seriously turning him on.

"Thunder," Rachel appeared at his office door, "The tribal council is here. They want to discuss the opening before you take them to the airport."

"Ok," Thunder looked up and out into the lobby.

"Where are they?" Thunder didn't see them in the lobby.

"They went into the kitchen to speak to the Grayfeathers."

"Ok, I'll go talk to them. Thank you, Rachel."

Thunder looked over his inventory spreadsheet again and got himself under control. He didn't need the council members seeing him with a hard on. Walking into the kitchen, he said hello and asked them to follow him to his office so he could get their feedback in private.

"How did you all like the exhibit?" Thunder asked.

"It was fantastic!" Swift Antelope exclaimed.

"The stories were a hit," Uncle Spirit commented.

"I think everyone learned a lot. Everyone seemed very interested and kind when they spoke to me," Tall Bear said. "This was definitely a success. We are so proud of you, Thunder. You have really created awareness for our people in such a positive way."

All the tribal members were shaking their heads in agreement with Tall Bear.

"*Pilámaya*, this means a lot coming from all of you." Thunder bowed his head towards them.

"*Wakaŋ Táŋka* has blessed us with this undertaking," Tall Bear looked at Thunder, "we are talking about opening up another cultural center at another location. We will consult with you if we move forward with this venture. For now, we are just grateful for all you have done here."

"*Pilámaya, Mató Háŋska*." Thunder's excitement of Tall Bear's words was inspiring. "I am honored to serve our people."

"Quick question. Why did a young lady run out with your shirt late in the evening?" Uncle Spirit smirked. "Is there something we should know?"

"She had an accident with a food tray and I gave her my shirt while I cleaned her dress." Thunder wasn't sure how they knew, since Grayhorse said they left before Isa ran out.

"Well, that's interesting," Tall Bear gasped. "Was she okay? Is she going to talk bad about us?"

"No," Thunder shook his head, "I will get it all sorted."

They continued to meet and discuss future exhibits while He Who Laughs A lot stepped out to tell stories to our shelter kids while they finished up the meeting.

"Okay, well, it's time to head out. *Wakíyaŋ Hotóŋpi* can you drive us back to the casino?" Tall Bear asked.

"Of course," Thunder replied.

"I would like to try my luck one more time at the roulette table before we leave for the airport tonight." Tall Bear smiled.

"I hope you brought a lot of money," Swift Antelope mumbled.

"What do you mean? I always win at the roulette table." Tall Bear smacked Swift Antelope on the back.

"Since when?" Swift Antelope laughed. "You've lost every time you've played during this entire trip."

Thunder could hear them bickering on their way out of his office. Uncle Spirit stayed behind.

"The woman was beautiful, no?" Uncle Spirit asked

"You saw her?" He asked, "I thought you left before all that happened?"

"*Han, Wakíyaŋ Hotóŋpi*, I saw her go upstairs with you. I noticed you stayed up there for a while, ignoring your responsibilities down here. But I left with the council before she ran out barefoot in your shirt. Joseph told me about that this morning. Do you like this woman?"

"I like her a lot, but our relationship is complicated, to say the least." Uncle Spirit nodded. "Nothing happened, but I think she felt embarrassed. I am taking her to dinner tonight after I drop you all off at the airport."

"*Hiyá, Wakíyaŋ Hotóŋpi*, sounds good. Hear my words and remember them. You and this woman will encounter much over the next several weeks. Listen with your heart and don't let the words of others guide you. Coyote the trickster and Iktomi the spider will sneak up on you. You need to move forward with kindness and a strong heart." Uncle Spirit gave him a hug and said, "Take care of your family."

"*Pilámaya*, Uncle Spirit," Thunder was always grateful for Uncle Spirit's wisdom.

"Have you seen Joseph?"

"No, Uncle Spirit, I have not. I thought I saw him in the storytelling room last night, but I didn't have time to talk to him. I didn't know he was in town."

"He came in on a flight yesterday and rented a car. Last time I saw him, he was talking to Sarah. Bah, you young kids today, you never have time for family. He should have come with us so I could spend more time with him."

"Uncle Spirit, I may be far away, but I always have time for you," Thunder smiled at him and gave him another hug.

"You are a charmer *Wakíyaŋ Hotóŋpi*. Use it to your advantage with your woman. It is one of your many exceptional assets." He smiled at Thunder.

"*Pilámaya*, I think." Uncle Spirit's comment baffled him. "Now, let me drive you to the casino, so Tall Bear has one more time to lose." They both laughed.

"You are so right. I'm ready whenever you are. Please tell my son to call me and I'll see him when he gets home."

"Do you know how long his visit will be?" Thunder asked.

"No, he didn't tell me." Uncle Spirit sighed.

They walked out to the lobby.

Thunder looked around.

"Where's Rachel?" He asked the other tribal council members in the lobby.

"We haven't seen her since before lunch," Tall Bear said.

"Let me look around real quick. If she's not here, I need to lock up and put a sign on the door. Hang on, I'll be right back." Thunder had given Mark the day off because of the late night with the opening. So, it was only Rachel and him today. He searched through the center and could not find her. That was odd. She rarely left without telling him. Not to mention, she never said goodbye to the tribal council. That was not like her. He wrote a quick note apologizing for closing a couple hours early and taped it to the front door. Hopefully, it didn't inconvenience anyone. He had no choice.

Thunder escorted the tribal council members to his truck and drove them to the hotel.

"*Wakíyaŋ Hotóŋpi*," Tall Bear said from the back seat, "While they get the luggage, I'm going to the roulette table for one final spin. Swift Antelope, grab my bag from upstairs."

"This is not a good idea," Swift Antelope murmured and whispered to Thunder when he got out of the truck, "Please go with him *Wakíyaŋ Hotóŋpi* and make sure he only plays one game. He's lost enough."

Thunder nodded.

"*Mató Háŋska*," Thunder hurried to catch up to Tall Bear, "I'll go with you while I wait for them to come back down."

Tall Bear waited for Thunder before heading to a roulette table. He lost, of course.

The traffic at the airport was horrible and by the time he'd gotten the council members' suitcases out and said goodbye, it was late afternoon.

As he glanced at his watch, he felt a wave of surprise wash over him when he realized it was already four. Oh no, he hadn't called Isa. Shit. He slammed his hand against the steering wheel. He should have given her a time. Well, there was nothing he could do about it now.

By the time he got back to the office, someone had taken down the sign and unlocked the door. Rachel must have come back from wherever she had gone. Walking into his office, he picked up his phone and dialed Teramar's number.

"Hello, Teramar Studios, may I help you?"

It was a man's voice, which meant that Maggie was probably gone for the day.

"Yes, hi, I would like to speak with Isabel Gonzalez, please."

"Let me buzz her office, but I think she's gone for the day. Please hold for just a moment."

A few minutes later, the man came back on the phone. "I'm sorry, sir, she's not answering her phone. Would you like to leave a message?"

"No, thank you. I'll call her on Monday."

"Very well. Have a nice evening."

"Thank you, you as well." Yeah, right, like hell, he'd have a nice evening. Maybe if he called her cell, he could reach her. But her phone kept ringing until her voicemail answered, asking him to please leave a message.

> "Isa, I'm so sorry. I was with the tribal council all afternoon and had to give them a ride to the airport. Just got back. I can swing by and get you for dinner. Just text me your address. Or call me. Talk to you soon."

Maybe she was in the shower getting ready for their date and she would call back in a few minutes. Thunder also sent her a text.

> Thunder: Hi, I'm sorry to be texting now. I left you a message on your phone.

> Text me your address and I can come get you for dinner around 5:30-6:00.

Well, damn. He guessed he fucked that up.

Rachel entered his office.

"What's wrong? You look upset. Did the meeting not go well?"

"It went well. They were quite happy with the turnout and all the displays provided by so many tribes. Where did you go? You weren't here to say goodbye." Thunder looked at her with concern.

"Well, I'm glad it went well. I ran home because I left something I needed there. I thought the council was leaving later tonight after we closed. Sorry, I should have told you, but I didn't want to interrupt the meeting," Rachel answered.

*** *Rachel* ***

Rachel was dying to ask him about how it went with Isa when he returned her stuff. She'd told him she would go, but Thunder got all alpha and said he would handle it.

"So, you look sad. What's up?" Rachel prodded.

"Nothing, just thinking about things I need to do." Thunder ran a hand down his face.

"Anything I can do to help." Rachel walked behind Thunder's chair and began massaging his back. She noticed he was frowning at his phone when she walked in.

"No, but thanks for asking." He slowly wheeled his chair back and stood extricating himself from her hands.

"You keep staring at your phone. Are you expecting a call?"

"Yes, I'm expecting a phone call from Isa."

"Who is Isa?" Rachel inquired, even though she knew who Isa was.

"She's the art director at Teramar Studios. We were going to get together tonight, but she hasn't returned my call."

"Since you don't have plans, do you want to get some dinner?" Rachel asked hopefully.

"No, I think I'll catch up on some paperwork and eat when I get home later. I put it all aside to prepare for the opening, and now that it's over, I need to clear my pile. Hold all my calls unless it's Isa Gonzalez from Teramar. If she calls, track me down. If I'm not here, I might be in the warehouse taking inventory."

Rachel was upset that Thunder's attention was not on her. She watched as he grabbed the top file folder and sifted through its contents.

"Are you sure I can't help you?" Rachel asked, lightly rubbing his arm.

"No," he smiled and pulled away, walking toward the warehouse door, "I'm good."

When Thunder built AICC, he added a warehouse to the back that ran the length of the building to house their outgoing and incoming inventory. Thunder installed doors to the warehouse in his office and the Gift Shop for easy access.

"Okay. But I'm taking off in about an hour." Rachel bristled, hiding her anger as she walked away.

So, he expected to hear from that bimbo, Isa. Well, wouldn't he be surprised when she didn't call? Because if Isa called while Rachel was there, she would not be finding Thunder. She would make up an excuse or drop the call. Rachel would be around when Isa turned Thunder down. He might need a shoulder to cry on or a woman to fuck. She would be more than happy to help him out with whatever he needed.

"That's fine. Please lock the door when you leave. If I'm in the warehouse, I can't hear if anyone comes in," Thunder muttered absently.

"Will do." Rachel answered with a sarcastic salute.

Chapter 25

Friday Double Date...NOT

ISA

I sa didn't hear from Thunder before she left the office. Oh well, he must have been kidding about calling her. It had been a strange conversation. And of course, as far as Maggie's double date went, the guy meant to be her date had cancelled at the last minute. So, she came home early to get ready for nothing.

Maggie told her Dan, Isa's date, was sorry, and they were rescheduling for tomorrow night but, she and Ryan were going to dinner if she wanted to join them. Isa gracefully declined, not wanting to be a third wheel. Maggie promised to call her tomorrow to give her the details of their double date. They were talking about going to dinner at an Italian restaurant out at the beach called Giovanni's. She'd never been there, but knew the locals rated it four out of five stars.

Apparently, Dan would be available then. She hoped this date would not be terrible. How bad could dinner and a movie be? Dinner might seem long with the initial let's get to know each other talk, but at least she could relax watching the movie if she wasn't interested. She would drive herself so she could leave right after the movie. No sense in worrying about it now, though. Maggie would call with the details tomorrow, and she would just go along with the plan.

She noticed Thunder left her a message on her cell phone. He must have tried to call her at the office, but she ignored his voicemail and text. She had already showered and put on her comfy pajamas. She was not about to change again. Besides, she was looking forward to sitting on her couch and watching some TV before going to bed.

Chapter 26

Important Artifact...Missing

THUNDER

T hunder heard a noise coming from outside his office. Last night, he had worked late to finish up his inventory list. For a few minutes, he recalled lying down on the couch. He must have been more tired than he thought because morning came and he was still on the couch. Squinting, he tried to open his eyes, not knowing what time it was, but could hear footsteps heading toward his office.

"*Hau, Wakíyaŋ Hotóŋpi*, did you sleep here last night?" Rachel asked him. She leaned over and brushed his hair back from his eyes. He moved to sit up on the couch.

"*Han*, I must have fallen asleep." He stood up and moved behind his desk to sit in his chair. Rachel was acting strange, and he wanted to place some distance between them.

"I saw you laying on the couch, so I brought you some coffee."

"*Pilámaya*, Rachel." He didn't like it when she paid this much attention to him. First, the fingers in his hair and now the coffee. What was she up to? They were just friends. He didn't want to hurt her feelings. He thought they'd both agreed two years ago not to be intimate anymore. They'd confessed to each other when they broke up that they loved each other but were not in love with each other. If she was having second thoughts, he needed to let her know he wasn't. Rachel should not waste her time with him. Maybe she was feeling lonely again since her family was still in South Dakota. Rachel deserved someone who would love and cherish her. He knew he was not that person. He was just her friend. Hell, thoughts of Isa were consuming him.

He massaged his sore neck muscles. He knew he should've taken his paperwork upstairs last night. His bed was much more comfortable than the couch. He was so tall he couldn't even stretch out on the couch.

Rachel moved behind his chair and pushed his hands away. She massaged his sore muscles. He tried to catch her hands to stop her, but she moved them lower. Although he didn't want to hurt her feelings, he really needed her to stop. He spun around in his chair, grabbed Rachel's hands, and pushed them aside.

"Is something going on, Rachel?" he asked her.

"No, I just noticed that you were rubbing your neck, and I wanted to help you out. You know I care about you." She smiled.

"Oh. Uh, thanks. You are a great friend. Thank you for caring." Maybe if he stressed she was his friend, he could distract her. "Was storytelling full yesterday?"

One of the tribal council elders filled in for him yesterday afternoon while he met with the rest of them in his office. He Who Smiles A Lot always enjoyed telling stories. He said he wanted to see the reaction he would get from the children in this area. Thunder told him the children who came after lunch on Friday were runaways from the nearby shelter. They loved to hear about American Indian Folklore and Myths. They had been coming consistently for the past three years. It wasn't always the same children, but the old comers would bring the newcomers. He Who Smiles A Lot gladly volunteered to spend time with them.

"*Han*, He Who Smiles A Lot seemed to really be enjoying himself. I walked in to let him know I was stepping out for a bit. He assured me he was fine and told me to go. According to him, the children were excellent listeners. He went back to telling his story before I left the room. Thunder, everyone who came on Thursday night, was totally blown away by all the exhibits and wanted to hear the stories again. I think they will come back. What did the tribal council say? Are they satisfied with our work here?" Rachel rambled.

"*Han*, they are. But we must remember not to sell any of our ancestral belongings. We can only sell our modern-day paintings, pottery, jewelry, and sculptures by the American Indian Artists who send us their work with their prices. We raised the price as a seller's fee, but we must remember to send the artists their full asking amount."

Thunder mentioned this because this was the first opening which included other Native American Artists from other tribes around the country.

"I assured them that our ancestral belongings have great significance among our people and are cherished. We would never sell them for money, and we would not short change our artists. They commented that some of the white eyes would not understand and reiterated that we must not be offensive when we explain our customs and beliefs."

"Thunder," Rachel interrupted, "we don't do that."

"I know Rachel," Thunder put his hands up, "they just wanted to repeat the importance of what we are doing here. No blame was being placed on us by them. They are happy with our success. They also suggested we let our guests know if it doesn't have a price tag, it is strictly to help us teach our culture and history."

"*Han*, I understand. Which reminds me." Rachel twisted her hands and looked down. Nervously fidgeting with her hands, she said, "You will not be pleased."

Thunder looked at her with a confused look on his face.

"What do you mean? What happened?"

"The knife that was dated back to 1874 during the Indian Wars is missing. I was checking everything yesterday morning before the council members came and I noticed the knife was missing from the glass case. I looked around hoping someone just moved it, but I haven't been able to find it. That's why I ran home yesterday. I thought maybe I had taken it home with the other artifacts that I sometimes take home to clean."

Thunder was furious. That knife was from one of his ancestors. "What do you mean, missing? Do you mean someone stole it? How? Who? Are you sure it's not at your house? Why don't you just clean the artifacts here? Did you or someone else sell it?"

"*Hiyá, Wakíyaŋ Hotóŋpi*, I've always taken items home, but I bring them back the next day. I checked the register, and I didn't see a receipt for the knife from the gift shop, which means Mark didn't sell it." Rachel stared at Thunder wide-eyed. "I respect all our ancestor's artifacts. I would never sell them. Besides, I know how important they are to you. Not to mention, like you just said, our elders would not be pleased if I sold such a precious item." Rachel paced anxiously in Thunder's office.

"I'm sorry for snapping at you. You're right. I know you would never do such a thing. We'll keep looking. Maybe it's somewhere in the warehouse. We might have put the description in the case but forgot to put the knife with it. Highly unlikely, but we were so busy getting everything ready and we're only human. We were moving a lot of items around for the opening." Thunder laid his head back in his chair and ran his hands over his face, feeling defeated and frustrated. Not only had he lost a sacred and important knife, but Isa was not returning his calls—again.

Chapter 27

Saturday in the Park

THUNDER

"*Lekší!*" Tommy hollered loudly as he walked in the front door, "let's go to the park."

Thunder sat up and saw Tommy running toward him from the lobby. He quickly stood up as Tommy leapt into his arms. He caught Tommy mid-air and hugged him tight. It felt good to have someone who loved him unconditionally. Tommy was a kind boy with a pure heart, his love shining in his eyes when he looked at Thunder.

"*Hau, súŋkawakháŋhota cíkala*, how is my favorite *t͡ʰuŋšká* doing today?"

"I'm your only *t͡ʰuŋšká, lekší.*"

"Ah, but even if you were not, you would still be my favorite," he hugged his nephew again.

"Remember, you said that?" Grayhorse pointed a finger at Thunder. "He might remind you of that someday when he has a brother."

Thunder looked up at Grayhorse and smiled, "Nah, your next child will be a little girl. You'll see."

Grayhorse chuckled, "Keep dreaming. So, I haven't talked to you. How was Thursday night, brother?"

"It was good. What brings you here?"

"Sarah threw us out of the house. Her office friends came over for a 'girls' spa day'. Grayhorse added air quotes as he spoke. "So, Tommy and I came to entice you into going with us to the park and throwing some balls around? Are you interested?"

"Rachel, how are you?" Grayhorse turned to look at Rachel.

"Good." Rachel answered.

"Great," Grayhorse responded.

"*Hiyú wo, lekší*, let's go, pleeeeeease," Tommy looked pleadingly at Thunder.

His nephew could melt his heart in an instant with those puppy dog eyes. Besides, he needed a distraction from the stolen knife issue. Maybe when Tommy was distracted on the swings and monkey bars, he could talk to Grayhorse about it.

"Okay, *t͡ʰuŋšká* let me run upstairs and change into shorts and a t-shirt and we'll go," he put Tommy down and smiled at him.

"Woo-hoo," Tommy screamed as he jumped up and down.

"Rachel, could you please stay today and close up for me? I'm not sure when I'll be back," he called on his way out the door.

"Of course." Rachel answered with a forced smile.

"We'll meet you at the car. I'll drive." Grayhorse shouted as he and Tommy walked out the door.

Grayhorse drove them to the park across the street from the beach. They parked in a shady area. It was a beautiful day, but the sun was a scorcher. They grabbed the balls, bats, and mitts out of the car and headed toward a clearing. No one had arrived in the area yet, but soon locals and tourists would fill it up, cooking out. This park was perfect because you could play under the shade of the trees, cook out on the grill, eat at the picnic tables, and use the overpass to walk to the beach whenever you wanted to swim to cool off. They found a shady area near the children's playground.

They set themselves up in a triangle formation to toss the ball to each other. They needed to get warmed up before they started batting. Tommy was pretty good for his age, but they still had to run everywhere to catch his balls. After a few throws, Tommy wanted to bat instead of playing catch. Grayhorse and Thunder took turns pitching the ball to Tommy. One of them would pitch while the other caught whatever he hit. Thunder didn't mind running after the balls. Truth be told, he needed the exercise since he hadn't gone for his run that morning.

"Tommmmyyyyy!" Thunder looked up and saw his Tommy's friend Jaime waving over to him from the swings.

"*Até*, can I go play with Jaime on the swings? You can still see me from here, please?"

"*Han, ciŋkší,*" said Grayhorse.

"*Pilámaya, Até!*" Tommy screamed as he ran toward Jaime.

Grayhorse and Thunder gathered all the baseball equipment, and Thunder walked it to the car. Thunder came back and joined Grayhorse at a picnic table, which gave them a good view of Tommy on the playground. They were pretty sure Tommy was done with the baseball equipment once he saw Jaime.

"Thank you for taking that stuff to the car," Grayhorse said.

"No problem. He's such a wonderful son. You and Sarah are very lucky to have him. You've done such a good job of being his parents." Thunder sat down on top of the picnic table next to Grayhorse and watched Tommy on the swings.

"*Pilámaya.* He is a handful, but he is good. Well, as curious as an inquisitively active little boy can be." Grayhorse smiled at his son.

"Well, he gets that from you. You know, like father like son."

"Ha, you're funny. Pretty sure he gets that from his *lekší.*" Grayhorse smirked at him. "So, what was the serious conversation that Tommy and I had walked in on? You looked very frustrated. Is it Rachel again?"

"Rachel informed me this morning that my great grandfather's 1874 knife was missing. I asked her if she sold it. She said no. But her behavior has been strange lately. If she sold it, I can't figure out why? If we don't find it, the council will be so angry they might fire me."

"First, the council would not fire you," Grayhorse shoved Thunder with his hand. "They might be upset and disappointed, but they love you. Second, did either of you check the warehouse?"

"I asked her if she had checked the warehouse and she said no, she would check there today."

"Could someone else have sold it?"

"I had Mark working the register since he was aware of all our inventory. He knows which items can be sold and which are priceless. Rachel said she checked the receipts from the register in the Gift Shop and she could not find one for a knife. I can ask Mark on Monday. I told him to take yesterday and today off since he put in so much overtime to set up for the opening." Thunder answered as he watched Tommy on the monkey bars.

"Why is she just telling you now?" Grayhorse seems stunned.

"I think she was scared to tell me, but realized she had no choice. She probably thought she would find it. Had she misplaced it, I'm sure she would've put it in the display case and not told me."

"Do the elders know?" Grayhorse asked.

"Not yet. I'm going to wait a few more days and see if it turns up. We'll keep looking for it. Do you have any idea who might have taken it? Did you see anything strange Thursday Night since you were at the door?" Thunder looked at Grayhorse.

"You mean other than a beautiful woman running away from you barefoot with your shirt on?" Grayhorse laughed at him.

"Asshole." Thunder punched him on the arm. "Yes, other than that."

The conversation stalled as they both thought back to that night, absently watching Tommy with his friend. Oh, to be young and not have a care in the world.

Grayhorse broke the silence when he said, "*Tibló*, could it have been Rachel, just to get your attention? I got the feeling she really wanted to spend the day with you. Maybe she hid it and wanted you to help her find it today? Remember, she was asking Sarah about anyone you were dating when they put up the flyers. She didn't like the way you were looking at the *wašícuŋ wíŋyaŋ*."

"You mean Isa?" He asked Grayhorse. Grayhorse nodded at him.

"It is my belief that Rachel wouldn't lie to me about not taking it. I know she has been acting strange, but that would take it too far. I can't imagine she's vying for my attention. She knows we're just friends."

"Then why do you have a confused look on your face when you say that?" Grayhorse questioned him.

"Because lately she's been acting very loving toward me. She keeps flirting with me, and I catch her watching me all the time at work. Yesterday, she greeted me at the door with a towel after my run. Then she kissed me on the cheek. She hasn't done that since we broke up. Last night I worked too late and fell asleep on the couch in my office. When I woke up this morning, she was in my office bringing me coffee. Before I could sit up, she sat on the couch, a little too close for my comfort, as she brushed my hair away from my face. I took the coffee and got up before she got any other ideas and sat behind my desk. My biggest mistake was rubbing my sore neck. Before you guys arrived today, she was trying to give me a massage. We haven't been together in over two years. I always thought she was involved with someone while we were dating. It's one reason I broke it off. I wasn't interested anymore, and it seemed like she had found someone else. I wanted her to explore her options without me in her way. Although now that I think about it, she has brought no one to the center. I really don't pay attention to her love life, though. Besides, I told you I asked her, and she said she didn't know where it was. Do you think she's lying to me?"

"Well, it seems to me she has lied to you before if she was seeing someone while you guys were dating. I'll keep thinking about it and I'll ask Sarah if she saw anything suspicious. She watches everything like a hawk. Now, on a lighter note, how is Isa with the long brown curls?" Grayhorse shoulder bumped him.

Thunder let out a sigh and looked at him with a troubled stare.

"I fucked up again. I was supposed to call her yesterday so we could go to dinner. The council members kept me busy between the meeting and the drive to the airport. By the time I got back, I called her office, but she'd already left for the day. I left her a message on her cell, but I didn't hear from her."

"She will think you forgot about her."

"Yep, but I hope she understands." Thunder exhaled his breath as he bent down and placed his elbows on his knees.

"So do I, for your sake."

"Let's get Tommy and get some grub. Seeing all these people grilling is making me hungry." Thunder looked across the park, watching a dad grilling, and rubbed his stomach.

"Sounds good to me," Grayhorse got down from the table, but before he could whistle to call Tommy, he saw Isa at the playground with a little girl.

Chapter 28

A Pleasant Surprise

THUNDER

"Oh Brother, *Wakan Tanka* is blessing you today." Grayhorse slapped Thunder on the back.

"What are you talking about?" Thunder asked and looked up at Grayhorse.

"I believe he granted you a wish." Grayhorse pointed toward the playground. "Look who's here."

Thunder looked toward the playground, and his heart dropped. He saw Isa pushing a little girl on the swing while she talked to Tommy. The little girl looked to be younger than Tommy.

"I need to go talk to her."

"Well, let's go then." Grayhorse smirked as they headed toward Isa.

"Wish me luck." Thunder whispered to Grayhorse.

"You got this, *tibló*." Grayhorse patted Thunder on the shoulder.

Thunder walked around to the front of the swing.

"Hi Isa, good to see you."

"*Lekší*, look who I found? Remember Isa?" Tommy yelled before turning around and running back to Jaime on the monkey bars.

"I sure do *tʿuŋšká*." Thunder smiled and did a slight wave with his hand.

"Hi Thunder," Isa looked surprise to see him, "What are you doing here?"

"Grayhorse and I brought Tommy to the park for the day," Thunder swung his arm out in Grayhorse's direction.

"I saw Tommy, but I wasn't sure who he came here with," she grinned at Tommy.

"This is Jake Grayhorse, my brother-in-law, and Tommy's dad," he rambled. Of course, she knew that from the food accident during the opening. "I guess you already met him."

"Hi Isa, it's nice to formally meet you."

Isa stopped the swing while she was talking to them. Grayhorse put his hand out and shook her hand.

"It's nice to meet you, Grayhorse." She smiled brightly at him.

"Are you here with your family?" Thunder asked Isa.

"Yes, this is Lucy she's five," Isa ran her hand over the head of the little girl on the swing, "and that is Emmy," she pointed toward the play equipment, "over by the monkey bars with Tommy, she's seven."

"Lucy, can you say hello to Mr. Thunderbird and Mr. Grayhorse?"

"Hi," Lucy said with a huge smile on her face, "I love your hair! Can I braid it?" Lucy asked enthusiastically, while looking from Thunder to Grayhorse.

"Lucy!" Isa said, shocked by Lucy's request.

"It's ok," Thunder laughed, "Yes, you can braid it. But let's make a deal."

"What kind of deal?" Lucy warily looked at Thunder. Thunder squatted down in front of her to be at her eye level.

"Nothing terrible. Just that you call me Thunder and him Grayhorse." Thunder turned to Grayhorse, and he nodded to Lucy. "You don't need to call us, mister. Our friends don't call us mister. Can we shake on it?" He smiled at Lucy and put out his hand.

"Deal." Lucy smiled and shook his hand. "So can I braid your hair now, Thunder and Grayhorse!" Lucy asked loudly as she got off the swing, jumping up and down while clapping her hands.

Thunder and Grayhorse both laughed at her antics.

"Lucy, maybe later." Isa stepped in with a mumbled apology.

"Isa, can I talk to you for a minute?" Thunder asked her.

"Um," Isa looked from Thunder to Lucy.

"Lucy, you can braid my hair while Thunder talks to your aunt. We can go sit over by that picnic table." Grayhorse volunteered, pointing to a table that was close to the swings.

"*Tia*, can I?" Lucy begged.

"Sure, if it is okay with Grayhorse, it's ok with me." Isa looked at Grayhorse and he nodded. "But stay with Grayhorse. Don't run off."

"I won't, *Tia*."

Grayhorse held out his hand to Lucy. They walked hand in hand to the table.

"Grayhorse will take good care of her. Can we talk over there?" Thunder pointed toward the picnic table he and Grayhorse had just abandoned.

"Sure."

Thunder put his hand behind Isa to guide her. Once there, Isa sat on the bench and held her hands in her lap. Thunder sat next to her and turned to her. He reached out to hold her hands.

"Isa, I'm so sorry about opening night and not calling yesterday. I..."

"Thunder, I'm sorry I..." Isa interrupted him.

"Isa, please let me finish," Thunder stopped her. He shook his head and gazed into her eyes.

"The night of the opening, I was out of line. Without realizing you wanted to stop, I ran full speed ahead, only noticing when your body froze up and I felt your tears on my face. I never want to do anything to make you cry and I deeply regret what happened. I've never forced myself on a woman and I shouldn't have made you feel bad."

"Thunder, I'm sorry I punched you," Isa tried to interrupt again.

Thunder held up his hand. "No, Isa, whatever you are going to say. I was wrong. It was my fault. When I went to see you on Friday, what you told Rachel hurt me." Thunder raised his hand and noticed the confused look on Isa's face, but continued. "When I saw you, I was rude and mean because I felt like you had just belittled me and my center. But I was going to call you on a date that night. I just got busy with work. Then I had to take the Tribal Council to the airport. By the time I called you at the office, you had left. But I left you messages. Why didn't you answer me?"

"Opening night wasn't all your fault." Isa said as she looked down at their hands. "I had an ex that said some pretty demeaning things to me about my sexual behavior. He always called me a tease and said I was like a cold fish in bed. I got scared that I wouldn't satisfy you. That I wasn't pretty enough or good enough. Then all I could think about was my embarrassment over stopping."

"Isa, stop please," Thunder raised their joined hands to his lips. "Before you continue, you need to know that you didn't feel like a cold fish in my arms. You felt great and very responsive. That is why I had a hard time stopping. But you are not a tease, you have the right to want to stop at any moment."

"Thank you," Isa sighed and looked at Thunder. "I'm confused about Friday, though. What did you mean by what Rachel said?"

"Rachel told me you came by to give me my shirt. She said you wanted her to bring your stuff to Teramar because you never wanted to see me again." Thunder moved his gaze from Isa's eyes to over her shoulder. "That if I contacted you, you'd cancel my account with Teramar. I couldn't believe that you hated me so much that you would mix business with pleasure. I felt like you didn't understand how much the center meant to me and the community. You were willing to dump the account, and it made me furious. Me and my center are not something you can just discard, like trash. So, I went to confront you. And to be honest, to piss you off." Thunder blinked and looked down.

"Thunder," Isa tugged at his hands. She continued until he looked at her. "I never said that."

"What do you mean? Are you saying Rachel lied to me?"

"Yes, I am, because I never said that. I know how much of yourself you put into the center. It's obvious how special it is to you. I loved working on your ad campaign. I would never do that to you or the center."

Thunder looked confused. "So, you were mad at me," he sighed.

"No, well yes. But I went over to talk to you and to get my stuff. I realized I needed to apologize. Then Rachel opened the door and took your shirt. She made sure I knew you slept around and had a lot of women who were constantly returning your clothes from previous one-night stands. I felt so embarrassed and humiliated. I felt like such a slut."

"Isa, that's not true. I'll admit I used to sleep around in my younger days, but I don't anymore. Rachel has been acting strange lately, but I didn't realize she was so jealous."

"Are you sleeping with her?" Isa asked.

"No! Absolutely not," Thunder adamantly shook his head.

"When we moved here, we depended on each other and that lead to us having sex for comfort. I ended it about two years ago because I didn't have any deep feelings for her."

"Then why was she waiting for you when you got back from your run with a towel and a kiss?"

"You saw that?" Thunder was avoiding eye contact.

"Yes," she said angrily, "I was just pulling out of the parking lot."

"I'm sorry." Thunder squeezed her hand. "I don't know what that was. She's never greeted me like that before, I swear."

Isa didn't look like she believed him.

"Look," Thunder said, "Once you get to know me, you will learn I don't play games."

"Thunder, I get Rachel was lying to both of us, but I'm not sure us dating is a good idea. We're kind of explosive and both jump to conclusions."

"Why do you think that? We haven't even gone out on our first date. Let me take you out tonight. I'll make it up to you," Thunder pleaded.

"Uh, how do I put this gently?" Isa winced.

"Just say it." Thunder grumbled.

"I have a date tonight."

"You what? Well, you move fast." Thunder said through gritted teeth.

"What the fuck did you just say to me? Did you call me a slut?" Isa seethed, releasing his hand and stood up to leave.

"No!" Thunder tried to grab her hand. "I just thought you would have settled your issues with me before agreeing to a date with another man."

"Well, not that it is any of your business, but I promised Maggie to go on a double date with her and her boyfriend, Ryan. We were supposed to go out Friday night, when I was still mad at you, by the way," she said as she poked him in the chest with her pointer finger, "but he cancelled and rescheduled for tonight."

"Well," he said, holding her finger, "now that you are not angry with me, you can cancel."

"What makes you think I'm not angry with you?" She pulled her hand away.

"I just explained everything to you. We fixed our issues. You are my woman. I will not allow you to go on a date with another man." Thunder could see the anger rising on her face. Uh-oh, he might have gone too far. She looked like she was about ready to blow.

"Are you shitting me right now? You don't own me. We are not even dating. What century are you living in? I am going on this date, and you can't stop me!" Isa crossed her arms and stared at him, standing with her hip cocked and rapidly tapping her foot.

"Isa," Thunder attempted to calm her down by placing his hands on her arms, "let me explain what I meant to say."

"Don't touch me, you neanderthal." Isa gasped when he touched her.

"Okay," Thunder raised his hands, "I just mean that you don't need to see anyone since we are together and you belong to me." Oh Shit, that came out wrong too.

"Asshole, trying to tell me what to do." Isa pushed him aside and walked back to Grayhorse and Lucy, mumbling under her breath. "Ugh, and I thought he was so nice. Damn Dr. Jekyll and Mr. Hyde."

"Dammit, Isa," Thunder caught up to her, spun her around and held her hands while he faced her. "That came out wrong, but we are together, and I want us to be monogamous. Please do not go on that date."

"This is what I mean by we are explosive. We can't even talk without one of us getting mad. No, Thunder. I am going on this date. But I will not cancel your account and we can remain friends."

"No," Thunder was shifting his weight from side to side, "I want more with you." Thunder released her hands and pinched the bridge of his nose.

"You know what, fine keep your promise and go on your date." Gazing back into Isa's eyes, he said, "But you must go on a date with me next week? I'll call you, you will answer, and we will go."

"Fine," Isa muttered angrily. "Now let me go. I need to get my nieces back to their mom."

"Fine." He spoke under his breath as they both walked back to Grayhorse.

Thunder was stunned speechless to see all the braids in Grayhorse's hair. Lucy was a quick hair braider. Braids were sticking out from totally different directions. Lucy had even tied some together at the top of his head with his hair tie. Grayhorse didn't have even one piece of hair that survived Lucy's braiding technique.

"Lucy, how many braids did you put in Grayhorse's hair?" Isa asked as she covered her mouth so she would not laugh out loud.

"Tons, *Tía*," she said happily as she clapped her hands.

"Well, you were gone quite a while," Grayhorse quirked his eyebrow.

"*Abuela, mira*," Lucy yelled when she saw her grandmother, Aurora, walking toward her.

"Wow, *qué lindo*," Aurora said, her eyes widening when she saw Lucy's multiple braids in Grayhorse's hair. "Can I meet your new friend Lucy?" She said with a sparkle in her eyes.

"This is Grayhorse, *Abuela*." Lucy pointed proudly at Grayhorse. "And that's Thunder, *Tia Isa's* new friend," Lucy pointed at Thunder.

"Nice to meet you, ma'am," Grayhorse said, shaking her hand.

"Nice to meet you too," she smiled at him. "I see you have entered Lucy's Hair Salon."

"I sure have. How do I look?" Grayhorse held his hands out and spun around, waiting to be told he looked great.

Tommy chose that moment to walk over with Emmy.

"Wow, *até*. That's a lot of braids." He looked stunned.

"You can thank Lucy for my new style," Grayhorse looked at Lucy and she giggled.

"Mrs. Gonzalez, it's a pleasure to meet you," he said, extending a hand to Aurora. "I'm Thunder."

"Hi Thunder, please call me Aurora. How did you escape Lucy's Hair Salon?" She chuckled at Thunder.

"I was speaking to Isa while I waited for my turn."

Isa groaned, rolled her eyes and mumbled, "Yeah, right."

"Isa," Aurora scolded her. "*¿Qué pasa?*"

"Well, this has been fun, but we need to go. Grayhorse, thank you for entertaining Lucy." Isa hugged Grayhorse. "Tommy, it was great to see you again." She hugged Tommy.

Thunder was waiting for his hug.

"Thunder, it's been real," she looked at him with a forced smile.

Oh, hell no!

"Isa, it was a pleasure, as always. I'll see you next week," he said and pulled her into a hug. He whispered in her ear. "Hug me back or your mom will wonder what's going on."

Isa hugged him back and responded, "I hate you right now."

"I love it when you whisper sweet nothings in my ear, honey," he said quickly before releasing her.

"Ok, well, we gotta go. Lucy, thank Grayhorse for being a good patient, I mean customer."

"Thank you, Grayhorse," Lucy said as she gave him a big hug.

"You're welcome, Lucy. Anytime." Grayhorse hugged her back and smiled.

"Now you've done it," Aurora said at the same time as Lucy said, "Really?"

"Yes, it was fun hanging out with you, Lucy," Grayhorse squatted down to her level, "My wife will be jealous when she sees my new style."

"You are so cool, Grayhorse," Lucy beamed at him.

"Alright, come on, Lucy and Emmy, let's get you guys home0. Bye everyone." Isa said as she grabbed each girl's hand and walked away.

"Nice to meet you all. Hopefully, we will see you soon," Aurora smiled as she waved goodbye.

"Well, that was interesting," mumbled Grayhorse.

"*Até*, are you really going to show mom your new hairstyle?" Tommy laughed.

"Huh, nope. You will take it out in the car while I sit in the back and your uncle drives my truck." Grayhorse reached up and felt his hair, "I think I need your help."

"I'm positive you need my help, *até*."

Grayhorse looked at Thunder and said, "What took you so long? It didn't look like she was all in with you."

As Grayhorse was talking to Thunder, Tommy took out his phone and took photos of his dad's braids.

"Uh, Tommy, what are you doing?" Grayhorse looked at Tommy. "Let me see your phone."

"Nope, I'm saving this to show mom," he said, "since you're taking them out before we get home. She's gonna love that you had a spa day too," Tommy laughed and ran toward the car.

"See what you've done," Grayhorse said to Thunder, "I will never live this down with your sister. You owe me big time *tibló*." He said as he ran to catch Tommy. "Wait Tommy, let's talk about this."

Thunder ran after them, thinking this day hadn't gone to plan, but at least he'd cleared the air with Isa about opening night. Now he had to stop acting like a caveman and remember to call her on Monday for their date.

Chapter 29

Saturday Night Fiasco

THUNDER

T hunder dropped himself off at the center after the park and went into the warehouse to look for the knife. Checking the time, he realized it was six, and he still hadn't found the knife. *Time flies when you're having fun*, he thought, as his stomach grumbled. He hadn't had lunch after the fiasco with Isa at the park. Now it was dinnertime, and he didn't feel like cooking. He just wanted to go home and sleep in his own bed tonight. Once he arrived home, he showered and placed a takeout order at Giovanni's, a local Italian restaurant. He ordered from them several times and week. Sometimes he picked it up, sometimes he had it delivered, and sometimes he ate it there. Today was a pickup day. He wanted to go for a quick walk after all the bending and heavy lifting he did in the warehouse looking for the knife. Giovanni's was only two blocks from his house and he knew he could call in his order and it would be ready by the time he arrived.

Tonight, he ordered their Prime Rib Dinner with a baked potato and vegetables instead of a pasta dish. He'd worked up an appetite. It was a beautiful night with a light breeze coming from the ocean. He loved living near the beach.

Thunder walked into Giovanni's and saw George working behind the bar. George looked up as Thunder was walking toward him and waved him over.

"Hi George, how are you tonight?"

"Good, Thunder. How are you?"

"Good, but starving," Thunder smiled at him and sat down on a nearby stool. "I phoned in a Prime Rib Dinner order. Do you know if it's ready?"

"No one has brought it to me, but I'll go check on it. Here," George smiled as he slid a soda in front of Thunder, "have a soda on me." George knew he didn't drink alcoholic beverages.

"Thanks, George."

Thunder looked around to see who was working tonight. He came here often and knew several of the employees. From a table behind him, he heard some laughter. He was glad someone was having a good time. When he turned around to see who was laughing, he felt like someone sucker punched him in the stomach. There at the table sat Isa, with a man who had his arm draped behind her chair. They were with another couple. The female in that couple was Maggie. The foursome seemed quite cozy. Of all the places for her to be on her date, why this one? He couldn't believe his eyes. That was his girl. He kept staring at her, hoping she would look up at him.

*** *Isa* ***

After the park, Isa was so angry at Thunder. What gave him the right to order her around? Filled with adrenaline, she'd done her laundry and cleaned her entire apartment.

Maggie called her after lunch to give her the details of their double date. According to Ryan, his friend Dan was a lot of fun and he'd felt bad about canceling last night. Maggie told Isa to go to her apartment around five so they could get ready together. The guys were coming to pick them up at six. An hour was plenty of time to do their hair and makeup. Isa would already be dressed by the time she got to Maggie's.

The guys were on time. They looked nice in their dress pants and sports coats. Dan was attractive, approximately 6 feet, with blonde hair and blue eyes. He was very polite and nice, but Isa couldn't get a certain dark-haired, dark eyed domineering man out of her mind. Maggie informed them she had already made a reservation at six-thirty for the four of them at Giovanni's on the beach.

As soon as they arrived, someone seated them. Dinner was going well, except Dan's chair and body kept getting closer and closer to Isa. He was so close, his arm behind her chair touched her back. It was making Isa very uncomfortable.

"So, Dan, did your team win the baseball game last night?" Ryan asked as he took a sip of wine.

"Yep, sure did," he boasted, then looked at her. "That's why I had to cancel our date last night. It was a last-minute game. The opposing team's coach had to leave for the weekend on some emergency and the team didn't want to forfeit the game, so we played last night."

"Dan, I didn't know you played baseball," Mags said. "Isa loves baseball. Don't you Isa?"

Isa looked up from her plate and looked at Dan. "Yes, I do."

"Well, you'll have to come see me at one of my games." Dan said as he dropped his arm from the back of the chair onto her shoulder and started massaging her neck.

"Dan is quite good. He's the pitcher," commented Ryan.

Maggie sighed. "I know nothing about baseball. I only know when someone scores a point, they run past the catcher and get a goal."

They all laughed at Maggie. "What's so funny?" She asked, confused by their reaction.

"Actually Mags, you don't even know that," Isa was still laughing, "you score a goal in football and a home run in baseball."

"Oh," Maggie laughed, "well, I guess I know nothing about football either."

They all laughed and Dan took that moment to slip his arm around her shoulder and pull her toward him. Isa started fidgeting with her fork and glanced around the room, looking for the restroom or any excuse to get away from Dan. As she scanned the bar area, she froze when she saw a pair of anger filled black eyes staring at her.

Oh shit, it was Thunder. Of all the places. What was he doing here? Meeting some female for dinner and drinks? Why was he angry at her? He knew she would be on a date.

*** *Thunder* ***

Thunder was fuming. How dare she go out with another guy when he'd specifically told her not to do that? He knew he'd said it was fine for her to go, but he really didn't think she would go through with it. He realized right then and there how mad she really was. Except she was looking at him like a deer caught in headlights, so maybe she was feeling guilty and regretting her decision. You didn't see him with another woman. Hell, that would have been sitting with his arm around her if she had agreed to go on a date with him tonight.

George came back over to him. "Here you go Thunder, sorry to keep you waiting."

Thunder broke his stare and looked at George with a forced smile. "That's alright George. I'll see you soon."

"Sure, hey are you alright?" Thunder nodded with a tight smile and George shrugged. Thunder turned to leave, but George stopped him. "Stick around. Guess who just walked in the door?"

Thunder turned and watched as Joseph walked toward him. "Joseph, I heard you were in town. Where have you been?"

"*Hau*, Thunder, I'm good. How are you?"

"Good, I was just picking up my dinner and going home." Thunder motioned with his Styrofoam box in his hands toward the door.

"Why don't we sit at a table?" Joseph suggested, "I haven't talked to you in a while and I'm starving."

"Sure, why not? George, can you send a waitress over to that table over there?" Thunder pointed to a table across from Isa. He wanted to see how far things would go with this guy who had his arm around his girl.

"Of course, go have a seat and I'll send Kelly right over."

"Thanks George."

"So, where have you been hiding these past few days? Your father said you were in town, but I haven't seen you. Were you at the opening the entire night? Was I that busy and distracted that I didn't see you at all?" Thunder was surprised that Joseph hadn't come by to talk to him. He could understand the night of the opening because it was so chaotic, but usually if Joseph was in town, he would come into the center to say hello.

"Not really. I showed up for a little while. They told me you were upstairs helping a lady who ran into Tommy. I hung out in the Storytelling room and left soon after," Joseph said.

*** *Joseph* ***

Joseph didn't want to tell Thunder that he had come back and fucked Rachel in his kitchen. He didn't want Thunder connecting him with Rachel, not just yet. He didn't want any kinks in his plan. The less Thunder knew and suspected, the better.

Joseph had discovered the lady's name from the opening was Isa. He'd followed her to Teramar Studios yesterday. He tried to set up an appointment with her on some phony ad consultation, but she was too busy. They told him someone else would be happy to assist him, but he wanted her. Once he found out she was the one Thunder had taken an interest in, he'd followed her around for the last two days. She was easy to follow, because she never really went anywhere except from work to her apartment and vice versa.

While following her tonight to her friend's apartment, he watched those guys escort the ladies out to their car. He figured he would follow them to see where they were going. While he waited outside, he saw Thunder go in. Now that was an interesting turn of events. He decided, what the hell, he was hungry. He would see what was going on inside. Now there he sat with a furious Thunder, who kept staring at Isa while she sat with her date.

"Are you okay, Thunder?" Joseph asked, knowing full well the answer.

"Yes," Thunder said through gritted teeth. He then looked down and ate another bite of his food. "I'm fine. Why do you ask?"

"Because you keep staring at that table behind me. Do you know them?"

"Yes, I know the two ladies. They work for the ad agency that did the brochures for the Red Path Exhibit."

"Do you want to say hello?" Joseph asked, but Kelly, the waitress, interrupted.

"Hello boys. Can I take your order?" Kelly was a blonde, skinny but full-figured pretty girl.

"Hello Kelly," Thunder greeted her with a smile, "my cousin, Joseph, would like to order something. I'm going to eat what I ordered for takeout."

"Well, Joseph, what can I get you tonight?" Joseph watched as Kelly leaned down behind Thunder, pushing her breasts against his cheek as she placed a menu across the table for him.

"May I suggest the Chicken Parmigiana," Kelly said as she pointed over at the entry on Joseph's menu.

Watching Kelly rub her body all over Thunder was entertaining Joseph. She could have easily walked over to his side of the table. Suddenly, Joseph noticed Thunder's eyes widen. Something must have happened at the table behind him with Isa because now Thunder smiled that charming smile of his and muttered into Kelly's tits, "Kelly, that is an excellent choice."

Joseph caught on and played along for now. "Actually, I'll have what Thunder's having." Joseph knew Thunder didn't realize he meant Isa. Clapping his hands together and rubbing them back and forth like he was going to have a tasty meal.

"Prime Rib?" Kelly clarified. Joseph smirked and nodded.

"It's delicious," Thunder said. *It will be*, Joseph thought.

"Well, of course it is, Thunder," Kelly smiled and bumped him in the shoulder with her hip, "I'll get your order in right away, Joseph."

"Thanks Kelly," Thunder said with a smile. Then Kelly winked at him and walked away, swaying her hips seductively for Thunder's benefit.

"What was that all about? Are you two dating?" Joseph said, making sure he spoke loud enough for Thunder's new woman to hear.

Thunder turned back around and saw Isa's raised eyebrow at him. He smiled at her in return and said, "No Joseph, I'm not seeing anyone. Although, I would like to remedy that matter and I plan to, soon."

*** *Isa* ***

Thunder flirting with the waitress utterly shocked Isa. Had he kissed her breasts in front of her? What a dick! And he said he didn't play any games. Of all people, he flirted with the sleazy waitress with the huge breasts that were on display for everyone. Was he trying to piss her off? He was living up to his scoundrel ways. Well, two could play at that game.

"Isa, are you okay?" Mags asked as she turned around to see what Isa was looking at. Her eyes widened when she realized it was Johnny Thunderbird. He smiled at her, and she turned back around quickly.

"Hey Isa," Mags kicked Isa under the table, "Dan asked you a question?" Maggie said, not so sweetly to her.

"Ouch, yeah," she stared at Mags. Why had she kicked her? What was wrong with her? Isa looked at Dan and saw he was waiting for her answer. What was the question?

"So, Isa, how about it?" Dan asked.

"I'm sorry. How about what?"

Mags answered, "Dan wants to take us out on his boat tomorrow? Doesn't that sound like fun?"

"Oh, that's very nice but I'm afraid I can't go I...," Isa was about to finish her answer when the flirty blonde served Thunder's friend his dinner. Now why did she have to keep rubbing up against Thunder when she was serving the other guy across the table? And Thunder, the asshole, couldn't keep his eyes off her very large breasts. Well, she would give him a dose of his own medicine. She leaned over to Dan and gave him a quick kiss on the cheek and said, "I would love to go tomorrow. Aren't you a dear to invite us? I haven't been on a boat in ages." She giggled. Now there was a stellar and convincing performance.

She looked over at Thunder out of the corner of her eye and saw his jaw drop. He looked stunned and ready to kill her. Good, her plan was working, except she had to let Dan down easily because she had plans with her family tomorrow. She was so stupid playing this game with Thunder. Now she was hurting Dan, and he seemed like a nice guy. Damn Thunder. This was a dangerous game, and she was playing with fire.

Isa put her hand on Dan's chest and batted her eyelashes at him when she said, "Oh wait, Dan, I forgot. I promised my nieces that we would watch movies tomorrow at their house. I'm sorry."

Dan patted her hand on his chest. "Maybe another time then?" Dan looked confused and disappointed.

Isa looked at Maggie apologetically and said, "Sure, another time." Maggie was shooting daggers at her with her eyes.

Dan told Ryan and Maggie they were still welcome to come. Isa totally ignored the conversation, trying to gather her wits. The threesome agreed to meet tomorrow in the morning at the marina so they could go down to the intracoastal waterway.

Thunder had apparently had enough. Isa spotted him walking over to their table, his expression full of murderous intent.

"Good evening, everyone. May I have a word with you, Isa, please?"

Oh, shitty shit, here it comes, Isa thought. She smiled sweetly at Dan, "Please excuse me, I'll be right back." As she got up, Thunder grabbed her arm and led her to the hallway near the bathrooms. He spun her around to face him once they were standing by the back wall.

"Would you mind telling me what the fuck you are doing over there?" he asked her through gritted teeth.

"I was having a very pleasant dinner with friends until you showed up." Isa mentioned nonchalantly, looking at her nails.

"Until I showed up, you were all over that guy." Thunder pointed in Dan's direction, "Somehow, I didn't take you for a tease, Isa. I thought I meant something to you. You kissed him and rubbed his chest. What the hell?"

"Like when you rubbed your face in that waitress's tits." Isa squinted up at him.

"I guess you come on to all the men you are around like a hussy." Thunder hissed and placed his arms on his hips, staring at her.

Isa slapped Thunder hard across the face. All she could see was Asshole Keith calling her a slutty bitch and a tease.

"Don't you ever call me that again. I opened up to you and told you how my ex would throw that in my face. That was a low blow," her voice quivered as Thunder reached out to hold her, "And I do not have to answer to you. Why don't you go fuck that blonde waitress. She seemed to enjoy putting her breasts in your mouth. What the hell was that?" She pulled out of his grasp.

"You pissed me off," Thunder looked down and rubbed the back of his neck before looking up at her, "Isa, honey, I deserved that. I'm sorry." He gently tried to take her hand. "I seem to say that a lot to you lately. I didn't mean what I said. You just made me so angry when you kissed that guy. You wouldn't even give me a kiss on the cheek yesterday." Thunder ran his hand over his face.

"Look," Thunder fixed his gaze on her, "let's start over. Let me take you home. We need to talk."

"There is absolutely nothing I want to say to you, Thunder." Isa was still livid from his comments.

"Well, there's something I want to say to you." His voice got low and raspy as he reached over and kissed her gently on the lips. At first, he nibbled on her bottom lip. He waited for her to push him away, but when she didn't, he gave her little kisses over her lips. She finally opened her mouth, and he slipped his tongue inside. Isa couldn't stop her moan. He was such a good kisser.

"Isa, honey, please let me take you home."

"I can't," she said breathlessly. "I'm supposed to be on a date. This isn't right."

"Awww, honey, this is more than right. Do you not feel the chemistry between us? I feel like I'm going to burn up if I don't touch you."

"Thunder, we've got to stop. This is crazy."

"Isa, you drive me crazy," he whispered into her ear before kissing her earlobe and trailing kisses down her neck. Thunder had her pinned up against the wall with his body. She could feel his cock pressing against her.

"Oh, excuse me. I'll come back later to use the restroom." Kelly said.

Isa stiffened in his arms. He held her steady by her hips as he raised his head and looked into her eyes.

"Honey, please let me take you home," he pleaded with her.

"I...I...can't. It wouldn't be right. He's a nice guy and doesn't deserve this. Besides, my car is at Maggie's." Isa was breathing heavily and having a hard time saying no to Thunder when he was pleading with her and looking at her with such sad longing in his eyes. "I gotta go." She put her hands on Thunder's chest and pushed him away.

Thunder stepped back and lifted his hands up in the air as if he surrendered. He cleared his throat and said,

"Fine, Isa, have it your way for now. Can I call you tomorrow? Will you answer the phone?"

"I'm busy tomorrow."

"Another date?" He asked angrily.

"No, if you must know, I'm visiting my family. Thunder, you don't own me. Hell, we haven't even dated!" Isa got mad and walked away.

"Isa, wait," she heard him say from behind her. She turned around and looked at him. "This will not work. We're always fighting."

"We're always fighting because you will not listen to me and give me a chance." He ran his hand over his face.

"All right Thunder, I'll give you a chance."

"A chance for a date, a proper date?" He asked suspiciously, "promise me."

"Yes, a proper date, I promise. You can even come and pick me up. Call me at work on Monday and we'll set something up. I told my brother I would babysit tomorrow. That's why I can't see you."

"Okay. I won't jump to any more conclusions," he grinned at her, "and I will call you on Monday."

"Good, now I really have to get back before they come looking for me."

When she turned to walk away, Thunder grabbed her arm and spun her around. He kissed her until her stomach started doing somersaults. They were always arguing, but she had to admit their chemistry was off the charts.

"I'll see you later, honey." He whispered and walked out of the hallway and back to his table.

Isa held her stomach and leaned up against the wall to gather herself. That man could kiss her senseless. Whoa, time to get a hold of herself and go back to the table. Maggie was probably beginning to worry.

Isa walked back to the table and scooted her chair away from Dan before she sat down. She looked over at Thunder and he winked at her. She could feel herself blushing. He was such a devilish man.

"Is everything alright, Isa?" asked Maggie.

"Yes, fine. That's Mr. Thunderbird," she explained to Dan. "He has an account with us. He runs the American Indian Cultural Center out by the Sawgrass Mall. We just needed to discuss some business. Sorry I took so long."

They finished dinner and ended the evening, deciding to skip the movie. Dan drove them back to Maggie's house. Isa told Maggie she didn't feel well and left quickly so Maggie could have some alone time with Ryan. Dan was a gentleman and walked Isa to her car.

Isa felt Dan squeezing her shoulder, and she looked up at him.

"It was a pleasure meeting you, Isa. I hope we can get together again soon." Then he kissed her, but she didn't feel any sparks.

"It was very nice meeting you, Dan. You're a nice person, but I just don't know if I want to get involved with anyone right now."

"Well, I think you are interested in getting involved with someone, just not me." He smiled.

Isa was going to say something, but Dan held up his finger to interrupt her.

"That's alright. But maybe you could give me another chance sometime. Especially if you want to make him jealous, like you were doing earlier this evening."

Now she felt lower than low. It was a mean thing to do to him during their date. "I'm so sorry to pull you into my problems, Dan."

"Like I said before, it's alright. Sometimes certain people make us do crazy things. But keep my number and call me if you change your mind. No matter what, I would still like to be friends."

"That sounds great, and thanks for being such a good sport about this whole thing. I have a feeling I would very much like to have you as my friend." Isa gave him a quick hug.

"Have a good night, Dan. I hope you guys have fun boating tomorrow. Just for the record, I really have plans with my nieces tomorrow." Isa knew she didn't owe him an explanation, but he deserved one.

"You don't need to explain." He took her hand and gave it a squeeze. He was such a nice guy. Why wasn't she attracted to him like she was to Thunder? Dan was attractive, but he didn't make her heart flutter or get her hot and bothered like Thunder.

Dan leaned over and placed a kiss on her cheek. "Good night, Isa. I'll talk to you soon."

"Good night, Dan."

Isa got in her car and drove home.

Chapter 30

Sunday...Babysitting

ISA

Sunday morning was another gloriously sunny day and Isa felt miserable. She hadn't gotten an ounce of sleep last night. She kept tossing and turning, not being able to sleep because she kept thinking about Thunder. By the time she finally dozed off, it was after midnight. In her dreams, he said he loved her, and they made wild, passionate love. It seemed so real, but when she woke up, her bed was empty, and she craved him. They had to get their issues sorted because he was turning her life upside down.

After lying in bed for an hour thinking about Thunder, she got up and showered. She told her mom she would go to her house for breakfast before they went to babysit her nieces. After her shower, she dressed and texted her mom.

Isa: I'm leaving my house now, mami.

Aurora: Ok mija.

Aurora planned it just right. She had breakfast plated and in the oven to stay warm when Isa arrived.

"*Hola, mami. ¿Cómo estás?*"

"*Hola, mija, bien, y tú?*"

Isa walked into the kitchen and gave her mom a hug and kiss on the cheek, "I'm good *mami*. It smells good."

"I see you are hungry as usual," Aurora said in her heavy Cuban accent. "Take a seat at the table. I'll bring you your plate."

"I'm always hungry for your cooking, *mami*." Isa sat down. Aurora was an excellent cook. Isa tried to learn from her mom. She was ok, but didn't practice enough to be as good as her mom. Aurora walked to the table and set a plate of eggs, ham, and toast in front of Isa and another across the table for herself.

"Mmm, *mami* it tastes as good as it smells and looks."

Her mom smiled at her. It was so nice when they could have these moments together on Sunday. They would eat early, go to church, and then go shopping. However, today they'd promised Matteo, her brother, their babysitting services. Matteo wanted to take his wife, Gaby, out to lunch and a movie.

"Did you find the badminton rackets and birdies so we can play with them in the backyard?" Isa asked her mom. Growing up, Matteo and Isa loved to play badminton with or without a net. It kept them busy and out of their mom's hair for hours.

"*Sí*, they were in the garage. I also wanted to take a jump rope. I want to tire them out before your brother comes home."

"Sounds good to me. If we tire them out during the day, maybe they'll go to sleep better for their parents tonight. Those two little girls have more energy than I've ever seen before."

"I'm sure your brother would agree with you." Aurora pointed her fork at Isa. "You and your brother were like that when you were young. Why do you think we bought the badminton set and sent you outside all the time?"

They finished their food, did the dishes, and went to Sunday mass. After church, they drove to Matteo's house for a movie and playtime with the girls. Matteo and Gaby rushed out of the house so they could make their lunch reservation on time.

For lunch, they all had the girl's favorite lunch: PB&J sandwiches, chips, grapes, and water. Emmy and Lucy watched a princess animated movie while they ate lunch. When the movie ended, they all went outside to play badminton and jump rope. The girls were getting hot outside, so Isa told them to put on their bathing suits and come to the front yard. While Isa set up the sprinkler in the front yard, Aurora went inside to cook dinner for them. The girls ran around in the sprinkler until their parents came home right before dinner.

The girls were barely awake as they ate dinner. They were exhausted.

"Mom, can we go to bed?" Emmy yawned.

"Yes, go ahead. I'll be right up."

"Gaby, I got this." Isa said as she got up to follow the girls, "I'll take them up. I'll make sure they shower, brush their teeth, and then I'll read them a story."

"Thank you, Isa. I'll start working on the dishes."

"No, *mija*," Aurora said to Gaby, "Matteo, pour your wife a glass of wine and take her to the couch. You guys relax. I'll take care of the dishes. Go," Aurora shooed them, "go."

"*Mami*, are you sure?" Matteo asked. "You guys have done so much for us today already." Matteo and Gaby were so grateful to Isa and Aurora for tiring out the girls and making *Fricase de Pollo y Arroz Blanco* for dinner.

"I'm sure. You guys go finish your date. We'll take care of everything."

Aurora kissed Matteo on the cheek and started clearing the table.

"*Gracias Mami. Te quiero*," Matteo said and hugged his mom.

Matteo got a glass of wine for Gaby and himself and headed toward the couch. Gaby was already searching through movies for them to watch.

After reading to the girls and tucking them in, Isa went downstairs to get her mom so they could leave.

Gaby was lying on Matteo as they watched a movie. They looked so cute together. If only she and Thunder could get to that point in their relationship.

"Hey, sorry to interrupt," Isa announced as Matteo hit pause on the remote.

"Do you need us to go up?" Gaby got up and turned to Isa.

"Nope, they are sound asleep. You can relax and keep watching your movie. I'll get *mami* so we can get going."

"Thank you so much Isa," Gaby said.

"Yeah, thanks sis," Matteo looked at Gaby. "We really needed this."

"No problem, anytime. It was a lot of fun." Isa walked to the kitchen to get her mother. Aurora finished cleaning up. Their work was done. They both said their goodbyes. She wondered how her brother and Gaby did this every day.

Matteo was an attorney which monetarily allowed Gaby to be a stay-at-home mom. She guessed it was easier for Gaby now that the girls went to school during the day. However, Gaby volunteered at their school and worked freelance jobs for Isa. Isa met Gaby when they both worked as graphic designers for Asshole Keith. Gaby warned her about Keith, but Isa didn't listen. Instead, she succumbed to Keith's charms. She should've listened. Working with Keith resulted in at least one good thing. Isa met Gaby and introduced her to Matteo. They hit it off from their first date. The rest, as they say, is history.

"Isa," Aurora interrupted Isa's thoughts, "What was going on with that handsome young man at the park?"

"Grayhorse?" Isa pretended not to understand her mom. "He's nice, right?"

"Isa don't pretend you don't know who I mean," Aurora looked sternly at Isa. "While Grayhorse is a very nice man, I meant Thunder, the other one. You know, the one you were being rude to."

"*Ay, mami,* he wants to go out with me, but we are always arguing." Isa sighs.

"Well, you know there is a fine line between love and hate," she looked amused.

"*Mami*, I don't know him well enough to love or hate him."

"Then I think you should date him and find out. He seemed nice, respectful, and interested in you." Aurora continued, "Besides, when was the last time you went out on a date, *mija*?"

"Since Keith," Isa mumbled.

"That's what I thought. He was no good for you, *mija*," Aurora shook her head no.

"I know *mami*, but how could I have been so wrong about him? Maybe I just can't pick nice guys." Isa groaned.

"*Mija*, I could have told you from day one that Keith was no good. He was too, *ingenioso*."

"What does that mean, *mami*?" Isa was not familiar with that word.

"It means he was clever, but not honest. You are a good, kind, caring, person, *mija*. You try to see the good in everyone, but Keith was always belittling you for your kindness. He bullied you all the time, and you didn't even see it."

"How do you know that *mami*?" Isa asked curiously.

"Because we saw him doing it. I can't tell you how many times I had to stop Matteo from stepping in and hitting him. But I was afraid you would stop talking to us and take Keith's side. Keith was slowly brainwashing you and driving you away from us," Aurora said as a single tear ran down her cheek.

"Why didn't you say anything?"

"I was afraid of losing you, *mija*." Aurora turned to Isa and touched her arm. "I kept praying that one day you would see him for the domineering man he was. It was great when he also turned out to be a cheater. I knew you wouldn't put up with that."

"*Ay, mami*," Isa sighed, "I'm so sorry I put all of you through that. I truly didn't see it. He just kept telling me what a horrible person I was and I kept trying to change for him. Well, until I caught him having sex with an employee and he couldn't deny it since I walked in on them."

"Well, I'm glad he did that." Aurora huffed.

"*Mami*, why would you say that?" Isa was stunned.

"Because," Aurora said, "I have my little girl back. I couldn't be happier. *Te quiero mucho mija.*"

"*Gracias mami, te quiero mucho también.*" Isa smiled at her mom.

Chapter 31

Sunday...Family Lunch and Fun in the Sun Day

THUNDER

Thunder finally had a decent night's sleep, knowing he'd given Isa something to think about. That kiss against the wall had been so hot. This time he would call her tomorrow morning and not late in the day. He got up and went for his six-mile run and prayer time.

When he got home, he headed for the shower. On his way, he heard his cell phone ringing.

"Hello?"

"Good morning, big brother," Sarah said.

"Híŋhaŋni wašté, taŋkši."

"What time are you coming over?"

"In about an hour. I need to shower and change. Did you need me to bring anything?"

"Yes. I wanted you to stop by Skip's place on your way here. Minnie said she had some fresh cow's milk for me."

Skip was one of Sarah's neighbors. Thunder met Skip and Minnie when he first moved there. They had a ranch in Davie with livestock and they stabled horses. When Thunder moved here, he'd driven his truck from South Dakota and pulled his horse in his trailer. He needed somewhere to stable him, and that's how he found Skip and Minnie. At first, Thunder had little money while he was building the cultural center, so he worked out a trade with them. They would stable *Sapa*, his stallion, and he would train their horses and help around the ranch. It was a good trade because they owned a lot of land and needed his help. Skip and Minnie were in their late fifties and it was hard for them to keep the ranch running. Once Grayhorse, Sarah, and Tommy moved down, Grayhorse took over most of his duties at their ranch. Skip sold them some land, and they could build a small home on the property. Thunder tried to go over and help.

"Sure, I'll stop by on my way there."

"Pilámaya."

"Anything for you, my favorite sister." Thunder hung up before she could give him shit. It was shower time and then... he was ready for Family Lunch and Sun in the Fun Day as Tommy liked to call it.

*** *Sarah* ***

"So, are you going to tell Thunder about the baby today?" Grayhorse asked Sarah as she finished getting dressed in their bedroom.

"*Han*, today, if he has not already guessed. I asked him to go pick up some fresh cow's milk from Skip's. But he sounded preoccupied, so he probably doesn't remember that I craved it when I was pregnant with Tommy."

Grayhorse came up behind her and hugged her tight. He gently placed a kiss on her temple.

"Your brother has a lot on his mind. Someone stole his 1874 knife."

Sarah was stunned that anyone would steal from the cultural center. That had never happened before. "Does he have any idea who might have taken it?"

"He was thinking Rachel or Joseph."

Sarah turned around in Grayhorse's arms and stared at him. "Are you serious?" She gasped.

"Yep. What do you think?"

"On the night of the opening, my conversation with Joseph was strange. I thought he was just drunk." Sarah squinted at Grayhorse.

"Strange, how?"

"Well, he said he needed money and everyone should help him, since he was just down on his luck. I told him to go see Skip and ask for a job. Then he started rambling about why he had to drop out of community college. Something about him being smarter than his professors. Stupid stuff." Sarah said.

"Did he say anything specific about the knife?" Grayhorse questioned.

"Not that I remember. He saw his dad and went into the storytelling room." Sarah sighed, "Next time I saw him, Uncle Spirit was giving him some money. He probably gave him all the cash he had in his wallet."

"I'll talk to Thunder about it, but on top of the knife incident, he is trying to woo Isa." Grayhorse wiggled his eyebrows at her.

"I can't believe my brother has fallen this hard for a woman so soon." Sarah wrapped her arms tighter around Grayhorse's neck, leaning against his body.

"I talked to her the night of the opening and at the park. She seemed like a nice person," Grayhorse mumbled as he rained kisses her neck.

"She is beautiful." Sarah moaned.

"Not as beautiful as you, *mitáwicu*."

"I wasn't fishing for a compliment. I was just making an observation." Sarah's eyes and hands roaming over Grayhorse's bare chest. "Do you think she is the one for Thunder? He hasn't been the same since that girl in college broke his heart. I know he dated Rachel, but he was never really into her. Do you think this Isa person could hurt him?"

"I don't know, but I think your brother means to find out." Grayhorse continued to trail kisses down her neck and cupped her breasts with his hands. Soon her breasts would fill with milk for Grayhorse's son or daughter, and Sarah knew from her previous pregnancy how much that turned him on. He loved to lavish her breasts tenderly when she was pregnant, especially when every once in a while a little milk would leak out.

"Did you talk to her when you saw her in the park?" Sarah groaned.

"No, I mostly got my hair braided by her niece." Grayhorse said as he pulled off Sarah's nightgown.

"I'm glad your son took photos for me. You looked very sexy." Sarah smirked at him.

Grayhorse remained focused on his mission to have sex with his wife this morning. Slowly, he began walking her backwards toward the bed while sucking on her breasts.

"Well, I will have to meet this Isa soon. I wish to speak to her." Sarah announced while pushing Grayhorse's sweatpants down.

"Hush woman and make love to your husband, who cannot wait any longer," Grayhorse moaned hoarsely as he laid Sarah down on their bed.

Tommy, being a late riser on Sunday mornings, would still be asleep for at least another hour, so they made love. They locked the door, making Tommy think they were asleep, too.

*** Thunder ***

Thunder arrived at 11:30 as promised. "So, what's for lunch?" he shouted as he entered the house. He set the milk down on the foyer table because he knew Tommy was coming soon. Just as he thought, Tommy came running out of his room.

"*Lekší*, you came," he cried and jumped up as usual.

"Well, of course. If I didn't, your mother would tan my hide," he wiggled his eyebrows, "literally."

"That's right, I would, so count your blessings that you're here." Sarah walked into the hallway, wiping her hands on a dishtowel.

Thunder put Tommy down and walked to his sister for a hug. He picked her up, swung her around, and gave her a big kiss on the cheek. "Oh, I missed you too, *taŋkší.*"

"Put me down, you big ox. Grab the milk and come into the kitchen. Lunch is on the table. Grayhorse will be right in. He just went to wash up."

Thunder grabbed Tommy and threw him over his shoulder like a sack of potatoes. Tommy was laughing hysterically when they entered the kitchen.

"*Lekší*, put me down."

"If you say so," Thunder pretended to put Tommy upside down in the chair.

"*Hiyá*, not upside down," Tommy giggled.

Thunder flipped him right side up and plopped him in the chair.

Grayhorse entered the kitchen, saw the milk, and gave his wife a wink.

"*Hau*, Thunder, it's nice to see your sister can work her wiles on you too and make you run errands for her."

Thunder smirked and Tommy asked, "What are wiles, *iná?*"

Sarah stared at Grayhorse with a stern look. He shrugged at her, then she looked at Tommy and answered, "Nothing *ciŋkší*, ignore your *até*. Did you wash your hands?"

Tommy nodded, and they piled food onto their plates. Thunder enjoyed having his family together on Sunday. Some weeks it was the only day he got to spend time with them, depending on their schedules. It all started when they'd all lived together in their parents' house. Sarah loved to cook, and Sunday was a good day for them to sit around the table and talk about what was going on in their lives. It had changed when Thunder moved, but they'd started it again as soon as Sarah, Grayhorse and Tommy moved there.

"*Iná*," Tommy said, "Jaime and Cody didn't believe I got paid cash. So I showed them one of my ten-dollar bills."

"Tommy," Sarah stopped chewing, "You can't take money to school. What if you lose it?"

"I know *iná* but they didn't believe me," Tommy whined, "they asked to see proof. How else am I supposed to do that?"

"Well, some companies pay you with a check and we had a paystub, but since *lekší* pays you cash, I'm not sure." Sarah looked at Thunder.

"*Lekší* can you help me?"

"*Hanťuŋšká*, I don't have a paystub since I paid you in cash. But I can make up an invoice that says paid for you to take to school. It will list your services."

Tommy's eyes lit up. "*Pilámaya lekší.* That will work. Can you sign it, so it looks official? Oh, and put it on American Indian Cultural Center paper. I saw some in your desk drawer." Tommy got up to help his mom clear the dishes.

"Of course you did. It will definitely look official," Thunder grimaced at Tommy.

Grayhorse watched in amusement as Tommy wrapped his uncle around his finger.

"You spoil him, you know," Grayhorse said to Thunder as he grabbed his plate and walked to the sink. "Let's sit on the porch for a while."

As they both went outside and sat down, Grayhorse asked, "Thunder, do you think maybe Joseph took the knife?"

"What makes you say that?"

"I don't know. Sarah said he was acting strange and bummed some money from his dad."

"I didn't know that. Uncle Spirit said he talked to him briefly. He didn't tell me Joseph asked him for money. It's not like Uncle Spirit has a lot to give. Why do you think Joseph would take the knife? Do you think he would sell it?" Thunder shook his head. "It makes little sense."

"I don't know. Unless he needed a lot more money than Uncle Spirit had on him. It's just a thought. I'm sure when he's at home, he's always borrowing money from Uncle Spirit, and we just don't know it. Especially since every time he comes down here, he seems to need money. I think he feels like you owe him, since you are doing so well."

"Yeah, but I work damn hard for my money. He just pisses his away. Last night when I saw him at dinner, he asked me to pay. Said he was down on his luck."

"Wait a minute, you saw him last night?"

Thunder sighed, "I ordered take out and when I went to pick it up, I ran into him. I also ran into Isa while she was on a double date."

"Wait, wait, wait, hold up," Grayhorse held up his hand, stopping Thunder from continuing. "Isa was on a double date? I thought she was your girl, and you had worked it out."

"We are working it out. Anyway, I saw her there, and I sat near her, long story short. I talked to her, and I had dinner with Joseph. Fucking weird and exhausting night. I'm gonna see Isa tomorrow and I will definitely monitor

Joseph. I'll look through the center again tomorrow and if I can't find it, then I'll ask Joseph. It's hard for me to accept that my cousin could betray our culture and beliefs for money."

"Yeah," Grayhorse sighed. "I get that."

Sarah and Tommy walked out just then. "Hey, you two, what are you so serious about?" Sarah asked as Tommy ran toward the horses.

Their house was in the middle of their acreage. To the right of their front porch was a fence around their stable and yard for their horses to run free. Thunder could watch the horses all day from their front porch. He always felt overcome with serenity as he observed the horses.

"We were discussing Joseph and the missing knife." Grayhorse answered.

"*Wakíyaŋ Hotóŋpi*, what do you think? Joseph hasn't been the same since he lost his job last year on the rez. I think he is drinking more, and that's why he still hasn't finished his degree at the community college. Anytime I talk to him, he is always complaining about not having any money. That's what we were talking about the night of the opening. I told him if he was staying here longer, he should talk to Skip about a job. Do you think he would sabotage your exhibit? Is he that jealous of you? Was anything else missing?" Sarah asked as she went to sit on Grayhorse's lap.

"If only I had the answer to all those questions, but unfortunately, I don't have a clue. I'll ask Rachel. She's the one who noticed it was missing. The night after the exhibit, I inventoried everything in the warehouse and accounted for all of those items. As for sabotaging the exhibit, I don't think so. Every time he wants to come down to help me, Uncle Spirit pays for his ticket. Of course, once he gets here, he never works, just goes out drinking and causing trouble. But he's done nothing to hurt the center." Thunder couldn't figure out Joseph's angle. If Joseph had stolen the knife, he'd have to tell the tribal council. He'd covered up Joseph's behavior for too long. However, if his suspicions were correct, it would kill Uncle Spirit. Maybe he'd talk to Uncle Spirit before he set up a meeting with the tribal council.

Sarah looked at Thunder and said, "You know, if Joseph works for Skip, that means that you don't have to go over there twice a week and even my cute hubby can take some time off. Then you can both help me with the baby."

"Sarah," Thunder mumbled, still thinking about how to tell Uncle Spirit, "Tommy is not a baby."

Sarah and Grayhorse busted out laughing.

"What's so funny?" Thunder looked at them, questioning their behavior. What had he missed? "He's not a baby. I mean, Tommy can't train horses yet, but he can feed them and muck out the stalls." He said, looking at them, confused.

"*Tibló*, you are going to be an uncle, again," she stood up from Grayhorse's lap and screamed, "I'm pregnant!"

Thunder was stunned by his sister's announcement. He jumped out of his chair and stepped over to her. He picked her up and swung her around before he put her down and gave her a great big hug.

Tommy must have heard his mom scream she was pregnant because he came running over to them.

"*Lekší*, I'm going to have a little sister or brother. Isn't that great? I can't wait to be the big brother." Tommy was jumping up and down with excitement.

"*Súŋkawakháŋhota cíkala*, you knew and didn't tell me. How did you keep this secret so well hidden from me?" Thunder asked Tommy as he let go of his sister and started tickling Tommy.

Tommy was screeching from being tickled.

"*Iná*, only told me before we came out here. She told me to go check on the horses so I wouldn't slip up and tell you before she did. Tell him *iná*, tell *lekší* that I didn't keep it from him for very long," Tommy laughed so hard tears rolled down his face.

Sarah and Grayhorse smiled at their antics.

"Stop Thunder or you're going to make him pee his pants. He's right. I just told him and asked him to check on the horses because I knew he would blurt it out before I had time to tell you. I thought for sure you would figure it out when I asked you to bring me fresh cow's milk from Skip."

"How long have you known? I can't believe I didn't catch that."

"Well, you have had other things on your mind," smirked Grayhorse.

"We found out a couple of weeks before the opening, but we knew how busy you were with everything. We figured we'd tell you after the opening at our weekly lunch." Sarah was glowing.

"Do you know if it is a boy or girl?" Thunder sat, setting Tommy on his lap.

"Not yet, but we want it to be a surprise. We'll be happy as long as the baby is healthy." Sarah said as Grayhorse stood behind her and wrapped his arms around her.

"I couldn't be happier for you guys. I will be an uncle again," Thunder beamed at them and said, "it's turning out to be a good day after all."

They sat on the porch talking about boy's and girl's names for hours after that. When they really started coming up with crazy ones, Thunder knew it was time for him to go home. After hearing the news, he felt a little lonely. He really wanted to talk to Isa and share his news, but he'd promised to call her tomorrow at work. Besides, she was with her family. He didn't want to interrupt.

He waved goodbye and got in his truck. On his way home, he couldn't stop thinking about the knife, Joseph, and Rachel. He decided to do something productive and find Joseph by heading to his favorite bar.

When he got to the bar, he noticed the place was pretty empty for a Sunday night. He saw his buddy Alan tending the bar, though. He walked over to talk to him.

"Thunder, how's it going, man?"

"Good Alan, how are you?"

"Can't complain. Wish it was busier, though. Can I get you something to drink?" Alan asked.

"No, thanks. I'm actually looking for Joseph?"

"I haven't seen Joe in over two months. Is he in town?" Alan asked.

"He just got in on Thursday. I thought for sure he would be here shooting the shit with you." Thunder frowned.

"Nope, haven't seen him," Alan looked down and wiped the bar, "but if I do, I'll tell him you were looking for him."

"Thanks Alan, I appreciate that. Have a good night." Thunder nodded.

"No problem, man, see ya' around." Alan nodded back.

Thunder walked out of the bar and headed home. Joseph could be anywhere in this town. He'd talk to Rachel tomorrow at work and see if she knew where he was staying. He also had to talk to Rachel about what she'd said to Isa.

Chapter 32

Monday Mixup

THUNDER

By Monday, Thunder was going crazy. He couldn't wait to talk to Isa. He got up and did his morning run and ritual. Then he went back to his house to shower and change for work. Thoughts of Isa consumed him on his drive to work. He'd call her as soon as he got to his office. She said they were going on a date. He hoped it was tonight. He'd pick her up at six and she could pick the restaurant.

When he arrived at work, he headed straight for his office, nodding at Rachel as he walked by, not wanting to get sidetracked before he called Isa. Maggie answered when he called and told him she was in a meeting. Because she had specifically said to call, he didn't text her. He was not fucking up this time. He walked out to the "Red Path Exhibit" and started double checking the inventory in the museum while he looked for the knife, making sure it wasn't in another display case. Noticing nothing unusual, he walked into the lobby to find Rachel.

"Rachel, any luck?" Thunder asked her.

"No, Thunder, I've looked everywhere."

"Did you know Joseph was in town?"

"Yes, I saw him for a few minutes the night of the opening. He was flirting with me," she batted her eyes at Thunder. Interesting, Grayhorse had said he was talking to Sarah, not Rachel.

"Oh, okay. Well, if you see him, can you let him know I'm looking for him?"

"Of course." Rachel answered sweetly. Something was up, but he couldn't put his finger on it.

"Ok, on a different topic. I spoke to Isa, and she said you told her I was a womanizer?" Thunder stood feet apart with his arms crossed over his chest, staring Rachel down.

"I don't know what you're talking about." Rachel's eyes widened, and she sounded innocent.

"She said you told her that a lot of women come here to return my clothes." Thunder gave her an accusatory glare.

"She must've misunderstood me, Thunder. I know you've been really busy and haven't had time to sleep around."

"She also said she didn't tell you I should stay away."

"I told her that so she would leave you alone. After she ran out of the exhibit half naked, I didn't want her to speak badly about us."

"Rachel," Thunder stated firmly as he pointed at her, "you had no right to say that to her." Thunder shifted his stance, placing his hands on his hips, scolding her like a misbehaving child.

"I know," Rachel looked down, "I'm sorry Thunder. I realize now that you like her. I was just trying to save you from making a big mistake. She didn't seem nice."

"What, well of course she wasn't nice. She was upset!" Thunder screamed at Rachel, "you made her think she was just another conquest. Which she is not!"

"Ok, Thunder. I'm sorry," she reached out and touched his arm, "I promise I will not get involved. I just wanted to make you happy."

Thunder pulled his arm away when Rachel rubbed it.

"Rachel, I'm happy you are my friend, but that's it. You are my past and Isa is my future." Thunder internally winced. That seemed a little harsh. "Rachel, I'm sorry too. I count on you, so please don't lie to me and make up stories. I really don't appreciate it. If Isa and I have an issue, I will handle it. Promise me you will stay out of it."

"Of course," Rachel took a couple steps back and glance around the room, "again I'm sorry."

"Ok, let's move past this. Did you have time to finish the inventory in the exhibit?"

"I did, but you can double check me. Four eyes are better than two," she scrutinized Thunder's reaction.

"Okay. I've already done it once, but I'll just do another quick run through. Thanks."

Rachel's behavior still confused Thunder. It was necessary for him to keep an eye on her. He stayed busy throughout the day, but by 3:30, he was fuming because he had now called Isa at work twice and she never answered. Finally, he broke down and texted her after lunch. She still hadn't answered. Snatching his phone and keys from his desk, he stormed out of his office. Until he laid eyes on her, he had no plans of leaving Teramar.

He yelled, "Rachel, I'm going out and I'm not coming back today. Can you please close up for me?" He neither paused in his stride nor listened to her response.

Thunder kept walking out the door to his truck. If Isa was going to turn him down, he wanted her to do it to his face. He was done playing games. He drove to Teramar and made it there in record time. She would not get away with avoiding him again. What had gotten into her now? When they'd left each other on Saturday, they had an agreement.

Having arrived at Teramar, he stepped out of his truck and forcefully closed the door. Leaning against his truck, he inhaled deeply twice. He was going into a place of business. He needed to calm down. With a few deep breaths, he propelled himself away from his car and went directly to the lobby. Maggie was sitting at the receptionist's desk.

"Hi Maggie, I'm here to see Isa, could you please tell her I'm here?" He asked nicely. Apparently, he still had an angry look on his face because Maggie looked startled and scared.

"Sure, Mr. Thunderbird, let me buzz her office and see if she's in."

"Thank you," he forced a smile.

Maggie picked up the phone and dialed Isa's extension.

"Melanie, is Isa in her office. Johnny Thunderbird is here to see her?"

"Hi Maggie, Isa's in a meeting, but I can leave a message for her." Melanie answered.

"Thanks Melanie, that would be great. I'll let Mr. Thunderbird know." Maggie said as she hung up the phone:

"Mr. Thunderbird, Isa's in a meeting in her office, but her secretary is leaving a message for you on her desk."

"Great," Thunder smiled wryly. "May I use your restroom?"

"Absolutely. Do you remember where it is?" Maggie smirked.

"Yes Maggie," Thunder smiled, "I sure do."

Thunder walked past the restroom and up the stairs to the second floor. He would check every room on that floor until he found her, starting with the office she was coming out of on the day of the coffee incident.

As he rounded the corner, he walked straight to that office and opened the door.

"Why are you avoiding me again?" he said as he stormed into the room and slammed the door closed.

"Ah, Mr. Thunderbird," Isa stood up from behind her desk, "This is my boss Eric Marshall. Eric, this is one of our clients. He owns the American Indian Cultural Center."

"Nice to meet you, Mr. Thunderbird." Eric stood up, turned around, and held out his hand.

"Nice to meet you as well, Mr. Marshall," Thunder quickly recovered from his blunder.

"What is this about Isa avoiding you?" Eric asked, looking between Isa and Thunder.

"Uh, no, I was just joking with her." Thunder pretended to laugh it off, but Isa was staring daggers at him behind Eric's back.

"Isa," Thunder swallowed hard, "is a wonderful art director, so creative with our account." Thunder could feel the sweat pouring off his body. Now he had to get himself out of this and keep Isa's reputation and job intact.

"Well, I'm glad to hear that. Isa is the best art director we've ever had." Eric turned and smiled at Isa.

Thunder mouthed "I'm sorry".

"Mr. Marshall," Thunder said, getting his attention again.

"I'm so sorry for the interruption." Thunder pulled his phone out and pretended to look at it.

"Would you look at that?" Thunder turned it around to show them, "I was wrong. She wasn't avoiding me. I hadn't checked my messages. Busy day at the cultural center." Thunder was rambling as he walked backwards toward the door, fumbling behind him to find the doorknob. "Isa, I will talk to you tomorrow. Mr. Marshall, it was a pleasure to meet you." Thunder said as he ambled backwards out the door.

"Thank you, Mr. Thunderbird. I will call you tomorrow to set up a meeting. Have a nice day." Isa said a little too happily.

Thunder knew he was in trouble now.

"That sounds great, bye." Thunder held up his hand right before he closed the door.

Shit! He'd fucked up AGAIN! He didn't believe Maggie, and he almost got Isa in trouble. *Fuck!* More groveling ahead.

"Goodbye Mr. Thunderbird, have a nice day." Maggie said on his way out.

"You too," he mumbled as he waved and continued to walk out the door, not breaking his stride.

Oh Fuck Me!!! Thunder screamed when he got in the car. He was going to have to wait for her so he could follow her to her house. He knew it was a stalker ish move, but he had to apologize and he didn't know where she lived. It was his only option because she sure as shit wasn't going to answer his calls after this fiasco.

*** *Isa* ***

"Isa, is Mr. Thunderbird okay?" Eric sat back down. "That was a really strange conversation."

"Aren't they all?" Isa mumbled under her breath.

"You've had trouble with him before?" Eric looked surprised.

"No, Eric," Isa sat down and rested her hands on her desk. His busy schedule with the latest exhibit has made him quite temperamental. One of our most recent clients, he is still familiarizing himself with our company. He's genuinely kind and an exceptional client. John is his contact, but every once in a while he likes reassurance from the art director. It's nothing to worry about."

"Ok, well, as long as you have it under control." Eric stood up to leave. "I'll leave you to it."

"Thank you Eric." Isa replied and sunk into her chair after he closed her office door. Leaning her head back, she exhaled her breath and thought about killing Thunder. He almost got her fired if he had continued with his tirade. Eric did not accept any of his workers ignoring clients. For now, Thunder was lucky he'd started rambling and seemed apologetic. It had been funny to watch him backpedaling, trying to get his foot out of his mouth. Isa called Maggie to see if he was still in the building, otherwise she'd call him tomorrow.

"Mags, is Thunder gone?" she asked.

"Hey Isa, the coast is clear," then Maggie whispered, "what the fuck is going on between you two? He said he was going to the bathroom and then he disappeared. When he reappeared, he looked furious."

"He interrupted my meeting with Eric," Isa grumbled angrily. "That's what's going on."

"Ouch," Maggie winced, "he probably thought we were lying to him again."

"Oh, I'm aware. I don't know what to do. I really like him when we are together. He's such a sweet talker. But then when we're apart, I over analyze everything in my head. I'm afraid that once he sleeps with me, he'll hightail it out of my life so fast I'll just see the skid marks. What if I fall for him and he breaks my heart? I know he's going to call me. He looked so confused when he saw I really was in a meeting."

"Isa, if you like him, you need to give him a chance. Not everyone is like Asshole Keith. Besides, he said Rachel lied to you and you agreed to date him this week."

"Why would she lie Mags? She doesn't know me?"

"Who knows, maybe she likes him and got jealous. I mean, she only kissed him on the cheek. It's not like they had a full make-out session at the door. Aahhh, I would love to continue this conversation, but I have a call coming in. Please consider giving him the benefit of the doubt. He might be worth it." With that advice, Maggie hung up.

Isa hung up and grabbed her stuff and go home. She was only leaving a few minutes early. Grabbing her purse, she made her way downstairs.

"Bye Mags," Isa waved to Maggie on her way out. "I'll think about what you said. See ya' tomorrow."

Maggie waved back and said, "Sure Isa, goodnight."

After diving home, Isa just wanted to change her clothes and relax before she made dinner. After stepping into her bedroom, she took off her work clothes and bra. To unwind, she changed into a t-shirt and sweatpants. Walking into her kitchen, she poured a glass of white wine for herself. Just as she settled on the couch, the doorbell rang. She wasn't expecting anyone. Not knowing who it could be, she walked over to the door and said, "Who is it?" as she looked through the peephole. *Oh, shit.* It was Thunder.

She turned around with her back to the door.

"Isa, I know you can see me through your peephole. Please let me in, we need to talk," Thunder said nicely.

Isa gulped. "Okay, give me a minute." She unlocked all the locks and opened the door.

Thunder was standing outside her door, leaning both hands on either side of her doorframe, waiting for her to let him in.

"Hi," Isa froze.

"Hi, may I come in please?" he asked quietly.

"Yes, come in." Isa stepped aside, then closed the door. He walked past the kitchen and into a living room.

"Can I get you something to drink?" Isa glanced around nervously.

"No, thank you," Thunder responded as he turned to face her. He shoved his hands in his pockets.

"What's going on Isa? Why have you ignored me today? You said we would talk today and set everything straight. You promised me."

She turned to look at Thunder. Not knowing what to say, she looked down at the floor, bidding her time.

"Isa, look at me. Answer me," he spoke sharply and startled her.

Isa's head jerked up at the sound of his voice.

"What do you want, Thunder? How dare you come into my apartment and start ordering me around? You almost got me in trouble with my boss. Go away and leave me alone," she snapped at him.

"Well, if you had answered any of my calls or texts, I wouldn't have gone to your office and made a complete and utter fool of myself!" he yelled.

"Wait, a minute. How do you know where I live? Oh no, tell me you didn't follow me home from work?" Isa's voice was getting louder and more irate by the moment.

*** *Thunder* ***

Thunder closed his eyes and counted to ten. This was not going well. Once again, they were fighting. All he wanted to do was reach out and kiss her so they could start this conversation all over again. He opened his eyes and looked at her. His temper was intact for the moment.

"Yes, I followed you," he tried to say calmly, "because I wanted to talk to you in private and you keep ignoring me. I just want to clear the air between us. Are you going to continue to go out with that guy? Is he your boyfriend now? You lead me to believe that you were going to hear me out and we could start again."

"Boyfriend?" Isa looked confused. "What are you talking about? I told you it was just a friendly date."

"No Isa, you never explained who he was and what was going on. All I know is that you would not leave with me because you had to go back to him and your promise to Maggie."

"Nothing happened," Isa screamed at him. "Not that it's any of your business. As for today, I was busy. Where do you get off questioning me about who I see and when?" Isa was getting worked up again.

"Fine, you don't owe me a damn thing. At least you could have told me the truth. That you are dating someone instead of ignoring me?" He was losing his patience fast. She was squirming, but he didn't know why.

"I..I'm sorry. I should have called you back today, or at the very least talked to you when you came to the office. It was a busy day, and I really lost track of time. Then Eric came in and I asked Melanie to hold all my calls." Isa explained.

"I need to refill my wine." She walked away from him and went into the kitchen. From the kitchen she said loudly, "As far as Dan is concerned, I already told him I wasn't interested in dating him. That we could be friends."

Thunder thought the words coming out of her mouth sounded reasonable. He had once again gotten possessive and flown off the handle? Did she really tell that guy no? Dammit, she needed to talk to him face to face, not room to room. He followed her into the kitchen and stood behind her as she took a sip of wine.

"So, who is this Dan person, then?" His voice sounded raspy and filled with emotion.

Startled by hearing his voice so close to her ear, Isa jumped, splashing her wine onto her light pink t-shirt and the counter.

"What are you doing coming up behind me so quietly, you startled me?" Isa tried to dry her shirt with a kitchen towel. It was no use. Then she wiped the counter.

Thunder was fed up with her antics by this point. He grabbed her by the arm and spun her around to face him. Oh shit. Her shirt was wet and plastered to her breasts and she wasn't wearing a bra. Fuck me. Her tits were every man's wet dream. He cleared his throat and looked up into her eyes. He needed to stay focused on this conversation.

"If I startled you, it's because you are acting skittish. What is the problem, Isa? I'm not gonna hurt you. The night of my opening, you were into me just as much as I was into you. Then you panicked, which is fine. I understand. We were moving way too fast. You told me about your ex-boyfriend and I explained to you that you were not a cold fish to me. Then you ignored me and went out on a date with another man. I think we're done with that little adventure and now you are ignoring me again. I feel like I'm on a fucking roller coaster with you." He'd trapped her in place between his body and the counter. He didn't want her running from him again.

She looked up into his eyes and bit her bottom lip.

That did it. He wanted a taste of that lip again. So he bent down slowly, giving her time to stop him. He looked into her eyes right before he ran his tongue over her bottom lip. Isa moaned into his mouth.

"Isa, which is it? Do you want me or not?" he asked her between kisses to her lips.

His hand caressed her breast, and his lips were leaving a trail down her neck to her breasts.

"Thunder, I can't do this," she whispered.

Those words froze him in his tracks like a bucket of cold water thrown over his head, and he took a step back. This was a puzzle he wanted to solve because her body was saying yes, but her head was saying no.

He looked into her eyes, "Isa, look at me. What do you mean?" he asked her with a raised eyebrow. "You don't want to fuck me or you don't want to date me? Be specific."

"That night at the opening was a mistake. We got out of hand. We went too far too fast. I'm not like that. I can't think when you kiss me." Isa slipped out from between Thunder and the counter.

Thunder's head was spinning. What did she mean it was a mistake? How could it be a mistake when she said she couldn't think when he kissed her? If it was a mistake, it was the sweetest one he'd ever made. Thunder leaned down against the counter. Why couldn't she just give him a chance? He could hold off on sleeping with her. Couldn't they get to know each other with some kissing and holding? He just wanted to seek comfort and intimacy with her and carry on a conversation without fighting. She was driving him crazy.

Thunder pushed off the counter and turned around. Crossing his arms, he leaned back against it and looked at her.

He asked her calmly, "What do you mean, it was a mistake?"

"I shouldn't have been naked sitting on your lap on our first date!" She screamed at him, "Now you probably think I'm a slut. Then I stopped you, so now I'm a tease or a bitch."

He reached out to hold both of her hands, widened his stance, and pulled her toward him.

"Honey, I don't think you are a slut, tease, or a bitch. If I thought that, why would I be chasing you?"

"Duh," she looked at him like he was stupid, "to get laid."

"Honey, we didn't get that far."

"Yeah, but not for your lack of trying." She was getting hysterical.

"Honey, what do you expect me to do? You're a beautiful woman who was sitting on my lap in only her underwear. I'm only human. You looked sexy as shit. If you recall, I went slow and even asked for your permission while you had your clothes on."

"I know, but I was confused. It had been a while since my last date, and I had three glasses of wine. Your whispered intentions scared and overwhelmed me. I've never experienced someone talking dirty to me, so I was unsure how to react. Suddenly, I heard a knock on your door, followed by a woman's voice. I knew I had to get out of there. I was so embarrassed to get caught half naked with you!" Isa screamed her confession and looked down at their intertwined hands.

"Isa, are you trying to say that fucking me was embarrassing for you? You don't want to be seen with me? Is that why you have been avoiding me? I did not expect this from you," Thunder dropped her hands and strode angrily around her, waving his arms around as he got madder.

"Was I just some savage fantasy that you considered while you were drunk? Did you get what you wanted? Was it all you ever dreamed?" Thunder's voice grew louder as his anger rose. He turned around and stared at Isa.

"Well? Answer me. I think I deserve that much from you." He couldn't believe he was hearing this again. He'd heard it all his life. Some white women just loved to play games with the Indians. They drank too much and became daring. The moment they realized it would be embarrassing to fuck an Indian and bring them home to mom, they pretended nothing happened. He'd never thought Isa would do that since she was a minority as well. Yet there she stood, doing what other white women had done to him in the past. Coming from her, it really hurt because he thought they shared a strong connection. She had callously thrown his heart back at him after he foolishly gave it to her. He couldn't stop staring at her in disbelief. It never crossed his mind that she felt ashamed to be seen with him.

Isa stood rooted to the floor, staring at Thunder with a very confused look on her face.

Thunder took her silence to mean that he had hit the nail on the head. He could not be in the same room with her any longer. He stormed out of the kitchen and headed toward the front door.

"Thunder, wait," Isa shouted and tried to grab his arm but he was quicker than her and he slipped out the door. "Thunder, please." Isa screamed again.

Thunder could hear her running after him. But he was so damn angry his tires screeched as he backed out of the parking spot and peeled out. Dammit, why now? He had protected himself from this for years. Never getting too close so he would not get hurt, especially by white women. Apparently, he had learned nothing from his past relationship with Jennifer. How did Isa get under his skin so damn fast? He had only known her for a month. If he didn't know better, he would believe in love at first sight. He'd just realized he was falling in love with her. How could he, though? He didn't know her that well. She wouldn't give him the time of day, and they were always fighting. Now, if they brought that frustration into the bedroom, they would be explosive.

He still faced racism daily, but he figured people just didn't understand what they didn't know. That was his mission for the cultural center to teach everyone about his people. With understanding came kindness, awareness, and acceptance. She was supposed to be different. She had seemed so interested in his culture.

Rachel was calling him. Perfect. Could his night get any better?

"Rachel, what's going on?"

"Hi Thunder, Isa is here, and she's flirting with Joseph," she whispered. "I just thought you should know."

"What! Are you shitting me? I just left her house a little while ago? How could she already be there?" He screamed into the phone, "Wait, why is Joseph there?" Thunder had been on his way home, so he made a u-turn and headed towards AICC.

"He's staying with me and he's my ride home. Maybe you can stop her. She acting drunk."

"I'm on my way. I should be there in ten minutes."

Thunder was furious. What the hell was she doing? She just told him he embarrassed her, and she was going after Joseph? What did Rachel mean by she was acting drunk? He'd just left her and he swore she only had one glass of wine. After she'd refilled, she'd spilled most of it. There was no way she could have drunk several glasses of wine before she got to the cultural center. Maybe she had shots? Who the hell knew?

"What the hell are you playing at, Isa?" he muttered as he drove like a bat out of hell to his center.

*** Joseph ***

"Rachel, she is heading for the cultural center. Looks like they had a fight. She will fall right into your hands. Do everything like we planned. I know we thought this encounter would happen later, but we've got to take this opportunity and use it to our advantage," Joseph said as he followed Isa to the center and parked around the back of the building. Rachel had left the back door open for him to enter. Over the weekend, he included Rachel in his plans. After all, she would do anything to get rid of Isa and keep Thunder to herself. What he hadn't told Rachel was that Thunder might not be around by the time Joseph finished with him. He led Rachel to believe that he was only getting rid of Isa.

Chapter 33

Monday Night Misunderstanding

Isa

I sa pulled into the cultural center's parking lot. She didn't see Thunder's car, but the lights were on inside. When she tried the door, it was open, so she walked in.

"Hello, is anybody here?" She asked. Isa stayed by the door in case she needed to leave.

A gentleman came out from Thunder's office. It was the same man she'd seen Thunder eating dinner with at Giovanni's.

"*Hau*, Can I help you, miss?" Joseph asked as he left Thunder's office and walked toward her.

"Yes, hi. I'm looking for Johnny Thunderbird. Have you seen him? Is he here?"

"No, Thunder is not here. But if you want to wait in his office, I can call him. Please follow me." Joseph pointed toward a glass enclosed area between the storytelling room and the gift shop. "My name is Joseph. Thunder is my cousin. I saw you at Giovanni's the other night. What's your name?" Joseph was slowly guiding her to the office.

"Uh, I can come back tomorrow." Isa remembered him from the opening and the restaurant.

"Nonsense. Thunder said he was coming in tonight to do inventory. He's just not here yet."

"Okay. My name is Isa. I'm a friend of Thunder. Do you know what time he was coming in?"

"No, I haven't seen him since this morning when he came by my house."

"Oh, well, if you know he's coming, and you don't mind me waiting a little longer?" Isa hedged.

"Not at all. Make yourself comfortable."

Joseph was staring at her, and it was making her very uncomfortable.

"Am I stopping you from working, Joseph? You don't need to entertain me. I'll just wait here quietly and not interrupt you." Isa was fidgeting with her hands as she looked around the room.

"Please have a seat," Joseph pointed to the couch.

"Thank you." Isa sat on the edge of the couch.

"I need to look at something, so if you'll excuse me," he said, then walked out.

*** *Joseph* ***

"Have you called him?" Joseph walked into the restaurant and whispered into his cellphone.

"No," Rachel answered.

"Well, call him, dammit! I need to know where he is. Timing is crucial to our plan."

"Fine. Don't yell at me. I'll call him right now."

Joseph hung up the phone and put it in his pocket, wandering around the center, acting as if he was checking things. Plan A was for Rachel to tell Thunder Isa was drunk and he needed to come get her. Of course, Thunder would catch Isa and Joseph in a compromising situation. But if Rachel couldn't convince Thunder, then Plan B was for Rachel to call him back a few minutes later and tell Thunder she saw an intruder in the cultural center warehouse and she hiding in the gift shop. Thunder, being the overprotective male that he was, would come to her rescue. Rachel would park in the parking lot and text Joseph the word HERE the moment Thunder pulled in and parked. That would give Joseph plenty of time to set up his plan.

Instead of texting Joseph, Rachel called him.

"You were supposed to text," Joseph retorted. *Could she not do anything right?*

"He said he would be here in ten minutes."

"Good. What did you tell him?" Joseph asked so he could plan his scheme.

"I went with Plan A."

"Perfect ten minutes is all the time I need. He'll be here just in time for the fireworks. Get in here and be ready to delay him until I give you the sign to let him go into his office." Joseph was excited to hurt Thunder.

"Fine, I'll be right there. This better work. I don't want him seeing her anymore. He should be with me, not her." Rachel grumbled.

"Just get in here and stop whining. This will work." Joseph hung up the phone and walked into Thunder's office.

Joseph was so excited to piss off Thunder that his adrenaline was skyrocketing. He needed to calm down before facing Isa. Stopping outside of Thunder's office, he took a few deep breaths before he walked in.

"Isa, was it?" Joseph said from the doorway, smiling at her.

Isa turned and nodded.

"Thunder just called. He said he's on his way. He got hung up in traffic and should be here soon. Can I get you something to drink? I just made some coffee."

"Some water would be nice, thank you."

"Of course, I will be right back." Joseph went to the coffee machine and poured some coffee into a mug. Coffee would be easier to spill on her than a bottle of water. He only had a couple of minutes left. This better be good. He looked toward the entrance and saw Rachel talking to Thunder. Rachel ensured that Thunder's back was turned until Joseph nodded to her, signaling for him to turn around. Joseph was not sure what she was telling him, but it looked convincing. This would be awesome. Since Thunder's office was all glass, he could see everything that was going on in his office between him and Isa.

Show time, Joseph nodded to Rachel and Thunder walked through the front door. It was perfect that Isa was sitting on the couch with her back to the front of the center. She never saw Thunder standing out there with Rachel.

"Here you go Isa," Joseph said as he held the mug just out of her reach so she would have to stand up to come and get it.

"Oh sorry, I actually asked for water," she asked confused as she looked into the mug and saw coffee instead of water.

At that moment, Joseph bumped into Isa and spilled the hot coffee all over her t-shirt. Isa looked down in shock and pain at her shirt with her mouth open, attempting to pull it away from her breasts. Joseph trapped her hands between their bodies, slamming his mouth onto hers and reaching his left hand under her t-shirt, heading toward her breast. Isa's eyes widened, and she tried to push him away.

"What the fuck is going on here?" Thunder roared.

Joseph finally released Isa. She jumped back, away from Joseph, wiping her hand on her mouth and turned toward Thunder.

"Thunder, I came by to...," Isa tried to finish but Joseph cut her off.

"She came here looking for you, but I accidentally spilled coffee on her t-shirt. I was going to switch shirts with her and clean it up." Joseph smiled and winked at Isa.

"That's enough out of you two. It would seem that you make a habit of this Isa. Well, carry your party somewhere else. I'm tired and I'm closing up, so leave. All of you!" Thunder turned his back on them and walked toward the front door.

"Go, NOW!" he shouted once he reached the front door.

Joseph and Rachel walked out first.

Isa walked toward Thunder.

"Thunder, I...It's not...," she stuttered.

"I said leave," Thunder growled through clenched teeth.

Joseph watched out of the corner of his eye. He'd never seen Thunder so angry. This was fucking perfect. Thunder kept the door open and stared out into the street. He wouldn't even look at her. After Isa walked out the door, he slammed it shut in her face, locked it, set the alarm, turned off the lights and stormed away.

Joseph watched Isa stare at Thunder as he locked her out and walked away before he headed toward the parking lot, smiling.

"You," Joseph heard her yell as she pointed to him, "What the hell was that all about? You lied to him and led him to believe there was something going on between us. Why?"

Joseph smirked at Isa, "I don't know what you're talking about?" Joseph knew he needed to get out of there quick. Unfortunately, he'd parked in the back. Rachel had parked by the front and was long gone. This was just a small part of his plan. He had to throw Isa off his trail. "I told him it was an accident that I spilled the coffee on you."

"Yeah, but why the hell did you kiss me? You led him to believe there was something going on with us. That we were exchanging clothes, really?"

"Well, you are a beautiful woman and I wanted to get your mind off of the hot coffee on your breasts."

"Whatever," she mumbled. "Men are such assholes," Isa added as she walked to her car.

"Bye Isa, have a good night," Joseph said as he walked away.

*** *Isa* ***

Talking to Joseph was like talking to a brick wall. Was he really that dense? Isa had to talk to Thunder. She realized now it was her turn to chase him down and make him understand.

Fuck it. She was not leaving without him hearing her out. Turning on the flashlight on her phone, she began searching for a rock to throw at his apartment window. A simple task, since the parking lot was made of gravel. She hurled several, but they were too tiny to do anything. A couple hit the window but most barely reached. She continued searching until she discovered a larger one. It was about the size of her palm and probably too big, but what the hell? It came as no shock when she threw the rock and it smashed his window, creating a loud crash and a large hole in the glass.

"Oops." Isa winced. "At least I got his attention."

She watched Thunder walk over to the window and stare down at her in disbelief. He had one hand on his hip and the other holding the rock. His eyes were fuming with anger, but all she could focus on was his beautiful, broad, naked chest that went down into a v-shape at his waist. He was so lean that his jeans rode low on his hips. She snapped out of her trance when he walked away. She ran to the front door, hoping he was heading down to confront her. He must have run down the stairs because it wasn't even a full minute before he appeared at the front door. He disarmed the alarm, unlocked the door, and yanked it open.

"What the fuck is wrong with you? What the hell do you think you're doing, woman? Have you lost your mind? I told you to leave and now you throw a fucking rock through my window. Are you crazy? Was Joseph not enough for you? Are you ready for round two with me? Your bravery at night is incredible compared to your shyness and indifference during the day!"

He finally stopped yelling and waving his arms around. Great, now it was her turn and he damn well better listen.

"No, I'm not crazy. You are!" she yelled back and jabbed her finger into his chest.

"I beg your pardon? You are the one that just placed a hole in my window upstairs. What the hell?" He added as she pushed past him so he could not lock her out again.

"I need you to listen to me, and I'm not leaving until you do." With that said, she stomped through the lobby, restaurant, kitchen, and headed up the stairs while he locked up. She didn't stop until she was waiting for him in his apartment.

*** *Thunder* ***

Thunder could not believe her gall to walk up to his apartment and wait for him there. After he locked up, yet again, he followed her.

"Fine, Isa, talk," he was running out of patience as he stood with his hands on his hips in front of her. He had been naked in bed when he'd heard the rocks. He was going to ignore them until the last one broke his window.

"I came by here to talk to you because I think you misunderstood what I was trying to tell you at my apartment. Everything you said earlier is not true." Isa was glaring at Thunder.

Thunder raised his eyebrows and kept staring at her. He nodded his head and said, "Go on."

Thunder followed her gaze and noticed she was staring at his abs and then his cock. His jeans were zipped but not buttoned.

"My eyes are up here, Isa," he said as he pointed to his face.

"Sorry," she looked at his eyes and continued, "I didn't set out to tease you like you accused me of. I haven't been with anyone in two years." She looked down at the floor. "After we went as far as we did, I felt sleazy and stupid. I figured you'd forget about me, that you just said you'd call because all men say that. Not because you were interested in me as someone to date. Besides, I told you about Asshole Keith. How he cheated on me, said I was a cold fish in bed, and that I would never hold on to a real man. He said it was my fault he cheated. That was why I felt embarrassed." Taking a deep breath between her rambling, she looked into Thunder's eyes with sincerity, "not because you are an American Indian. I am not ashamed to be seen with you."

"Keith really did a number on you?" Thunder interjected.

"Yes, he was not only my ex-boyfriend, but my ex-fiancé. We were almost married when I caught him with another woman fucking in his office. Besides, I know you must date a lot of women. Why would you want to call me again? I thought you called me out of friendly concern, lust, or you felt sorry for me. At Giovanni's, I promised you I would go out with you, but I chickened out, okay?" Isa threw her arms up in frustration. "I'm sorry. I was insecure about myself, not you. When you came over tonight to talk, it seemed as if you really were interested in me. I realized you might care for me. I tried to find the right words, but I was too slow in trying to explain my thoughts. You misunderstood me and stormed out. I would never feel ashamed to be seen with you. I thought you'd be ashamed to be seen with me," Isa confessed, pointing at herself.

Thunder watched her in silent fascination. Did she care about him, too? "So, let me get this straight. You ignored me because you thought I did not care for you? Isa, if you were a cold fish, asshole's words, not mine," Isa nodded and Thunder continued, "then why do you melt in my arms every time I kiss you? If I only wanted to sleep with you, would I have put myself through these last four days of hell?"

"Yes, that's what he called me and no, you would not." Isa mumbled.

Thunder let out a sigh and walked over to her, gripping her arms. He then positioned her between his legs and cupped her ass with his hands.

"Do you feel that?" he whispered.

Isa shook her head yes.

"Isa," he whispered, "are these the actions of a man who thinks you are cold?" He kissed her, ravishing her mouth with his tongue. "Woman, talk to me and stop driving me crazy. A few minutes ago, I thought I wasn't enough for you and that you wanted my cousin."

"Thunder, I'm sorry. You are all that I want. I just couldn't accept the fact that you would want me," she whispered into his mouth and wound her arms around his neck. "As far as Joseph, I don't know what that was. One minute he'd spilled coffee on me and the next he kissed me."

"I'll deal with Joseph tomorrow," he spoke hoarsely, "just promise me I am enough. I want you so much it hurts. But we'll slow it down if that is what you want. I just want to be with you."

"You are enough Thunder. I promise. Please let me show you," she smiled saucily at him and lowered his zipper.

"What about Dan?" He groaned.

"Dan Who?" She pushed her hands into his pants and cupped his ass.

"The Saturday night date," Thunder moaned as he caressed her head with his fingers.

"He was a blind date that did not work out because I was thinking about a sexy, tall, long-haired brown-eyed man at another table who was staring at me." Isa slid his jeans over his ass and licked her lips when his cock sprung out ready for action.

"He means nothing to me. I told him that night after the date that we can only be friends." She trailed kisses down Thunder's neck to his belly and over his hips as she got down on her knees and pushed his pants to the ground so he could step out of them. He was staring down at her, waiting to see what she was going to do next. Isa looked up into his eyes as she licked his cock and sucked it into her mouth. Thunder held her head to his cock and slid in and out of her mouth.

"Oh Fuck, Isa," he moaned and pulled her up. He slipped his arm under her knees and carried her to his bed. He let her body slide against his until she was standing by the bed.

He was staring into her eyes, "Isa are you sure about this? I've wanted you so much these past few days. All I could think about was kissing every delectable inch of your body. I burn for you, honey. If you don't want this, please tell me now."

"I want you Thunder. I am sure this time."

Thunder peeled off her clothes. First her shirt, then her sweatpants.

"You are so fucking beautiful," he said as he placed her on the bed. He pulled her thong off her legs and threw it on the floor. Lying on top of her, he raised her hands above her head and held them in place. He liked this position. It raised her breasts closer to him.

They kissed for a while, their tongues chasing each other in their mouths. He sucked and bit on her lower lip before he moved down to her neck. Isa moaned when he found her favorite spot. He then continued to travel down to her breasts.

"Thunder, please suck them," Isa said breathlessly.

"My pleasure honey, leave your hands up here," he said as he put her arms over her head, "while I play."

He licked around her nipples while he pinched them.

"You are such a tease, suck them," she groaned.

He chuckled right before he took one into his mouth and sucked hard.

"Like that," he groaned.

"Just like that. Now do the other one." Isa was moaning and writhing all over the bed.

Thunder suckled one breast while his hand tweaked and pulled the other nipple. Her breasts were so sensitive and she was so responsive in her body language, showing him exactly what she liked. By sucking and playing with her breasts, he was confident he could make her orgasm. He lavished each one until her nipples grew swollen and hard. Continuing down her body, he licked and sucked all the way to her pussy. He spread her legs nice and wide and slipped his tongue inside her folds. She stiffened and tried to push him away while she sat up, resting on her elbows.

"Isa, please don't stop me," he whispered hoarsely as he gazed into her eyes, "I want to taste every inch of your body. I want to know everything that pleasures you. There should be no shyness or secrets between us."

"Thunder, I've never done this before." She looked embarrassed to be laying there so exposed to him.

"So I'll be your first," he smiled. "Trust me. Just lay back and relax. I promise to give you pleasure so deep that you will soar to the heavens."

She laid back down on the bed, and he got to work pleasuring her.

Thunder felt her muscles relax as he continued to lick and suck her.

"Oh Thunder, that feels so good," she moaned.

Thunder swirled his tongue around her clit and pushed two fingers inside her.

"Oh baby, you are so wet for me," he groaned.

Thunder found her g-spot with his fingers and stroked it. He sped up his pace. He was now going faster and harder until he felt her tighten around his fingers. Isa screamed out his name as she reached her climax. He removed his fingers and licked her dry.

While she was recovering, Thunder licked his way back up to her breasts. He loved her breasts. After sucking each one once, he stopped and waited for her to look at him. They were now both looking into each other's eyes as Thunder licked his fingers.

"Yum, you taste so sweet."

"Thunder, please," Isa gasped, trying to catch her breath. "I need to touch you."

Thunder heard her plea and rolled onto his back to give her free access to his body. He took her face in his hands and kissed her mouth savagely.

After Thunder kissed her, he let go of her face and stretched his hands over his head and said hoarsely, "Go ahead *wíŋyaŋ mitáwa*, touch away. I'm all yours," he grinned at her.

"Can I? I can touch you anywhere I want?" Isa's cheeks were a rosy pink.

"Yep, do anything you want," Thunder answered, loving her shyness. She looked so cute when she blushed.

Isa smiled devilishly at him and ran her hands over his sexy abs and down to his narrow waist. She looked up at Thunder, making sure she could keep going. He nodded and kept watching her. She bent down and licked her way down his chest while she reached down with her hand and stroked his cock. He was leaking out of the top and Isa wanted to taste him. She continued licking him until she reached for his cock. Gripping him and stroking his penis, she licked the top, getting a taste of him before sucking the top into her mouth.

"Good lord, woman, you are killing me," he groaned.

She sucked the head of his cock like a lollipop.

"Fuck woman," Thunder mumbled, "that feels so good."

Then she reached round to his ass and pulled him into her mouth so far back he could feel her throat. Thunder didn't want to cum in her mouth their first time, so he gently pulled her off.

"Did I do that wrong?" Thunder noticed the concern and worry on Isa's face.

"No, baby," he groaned, "you did everything right. I just want to be inside you the first time I cum." He pulled her up his body and sat her down on his stomach.

"Guide me in baby," Thunder whispered, "whenever you're ready for me."

Isa raised herself up and guided him into her warm, wet body. When he was all the way in, she started rolling onto him. Thunder held her hands while she raised herself up and rammed down on him, fucking him harder while she set the rhythm. He wanted her to have full control in case she changed her mind. He didn't want to be on her asshole list.

"Thunder, help me, please." Isa's body was trembling with desire. "I'm almost there, please."

Thunder released her hand and reached down to her clit. He stroked and pinched it until he felt her tighten around him as she screamed and threw her head back, arching into him. It was such a fucking beautiful sight. He couldn't hold out any longer. He grasped her hips to hold her in place and pumped hard into her twice until he climaxed. Isa collapsed onto his chest as they tried to steady their breathing.

"*Wiŋyaŋ mitáwa*, are you okay?"

"Never felt better," she mumbled into his chest right before she kissed him.

Sweat covered their bodies. They were both breathing as if they had just run a marathon. Isa was stroking his abs, and he could feel himself hardening again inside her. Thunder usually needed a few more minutes, but apparently not with her.

She leaned up and gazed into his eyes with a look of surprise. Pulling her down to kiss her, he rolled them over so she was under him. He was now hard as a rock again and ready for round two. What was this woman doing to him? He had never felt like this before? What kind of power did she have over him? He couldn't seem to get enough of her.

Thunder set a slow rhythm for this round of lovemaking. He wanted her to understand that she was important to him. This was not a one-night stand. He looked lovingly into her eyes as he slid into her slowly and said, "Isa, I want you to know that I am yours, and you are mine now," his voice came out raspy and full of emotions.

"I'd like that," she smiled at him.

He thrust harder into her again. She wrapped her legs around his waist and followed his movements. They climaxed together this time. Thunder rolled off her and spooned her. He brushed the hair away from her face and said, "Do I need to set an alarm for you for tomorrow?"

"7 a.m. please," she murmured, half asleep, "and Thunder, thank you."

"For finally letting you sleep?" Thunder chuckled.

"No, and yes. Thank you for everything and for letting me sleep." She backed up into his body and got comfy before she drifted off to sleep.

"You're welcome, *wíŋyaŋ mitáwa*, sleep well, honey." Thunder knew Isa was already out. He kissed the back of her head and held her tightly to his chest. After three long, sleepless nights, he fell asleep.

In the middle of the night, he woke up hard as a rock with his hand holding her breast. He could not get enough of her. He wanted to wake her up nice and slow and savor every moan and moment.

Slowly, he ran his other hand over her waist and hip, pulling her leg back over his thigh as he glided his hand down between her legs. He caressed her until she became wet and rocked into him as she moaned his name. He then rolled her over and kissed her awake.

"Isa, *wíŋyaŋ mitáwa*, are you awake?" He asked between kisses to her neck.

Isa squinted at him. "Hi," she said breathlessly.

"Hi yourself."

"Is it time to get up?"

"Not quite, but I'm ready for round two, or is it three? Are you?" He laid on top of her, kissing her neck. This was a great way to wake up his woman. She ran her hand through his hair, which was loose and falling onto her.

"Your hair feels so silky smooth."

"Do you like my hair long? It is the way of our warriors," he whispered into her neck between kisses.

"Very much so. It's very sexy. Can I braid it?" she chuckled.

"As long as you don't make me look like Grayhorse," he mumbled into her neck.

"Why not? Uh, I think Lucy gave him an exceptional hairstyle," she moaned as she continued to run her hands through his hair from his head and down his back.

"Umm, smartass," he gently bit her neck. "We'll talk about braiding and hairstyles later."

Isa reached for his ass with her hands and pushed him into her.

"Does my woman want me as much as I want her again?" He heard Isa moan as he caressed the sides of her breasts nerd moved his hands between them so he could feel her whole breasts in his hands. He captured her nipples between his thumbs and forefingers and continued to tweak her breasts until they become hard nubs poking at his chest. "*Aahhh, wíŋyaŋ mitáwa*, you feel so good."

Isa reached down between their bodies and stroked his dick. After a few minutes, he reached down and helped her guide his cock into her pussy. He knew she needed to get up in a few hours, so he quickly entered her, and they made love slowly this time. He loved being inside her. It was a euphoric feeling he wanted to enjoy for the rest of his life. After climaxing and coming down off their high, Thunder rolled over and pulled her into his arms. Isa fell asleep wrapped around Thunder with her head on his chest. Thunder was barely conscious when it occurred to him. They had not used protection. *He would have to talk to Isa about it tomorrow*, he thought as he drifted off to sleep.

Chapter 34

Tuesday...The Morning After

THUNDER

T hunder's morning wood woke him up before the alarm went off. He wanted her again, but he knew she would be sore from last night and earlier this morning. He couldn't find it in himself to wake her up. She felt so good curled up in his arms.

When the alarm finally went off, he grabbed his phone and turned it off. He kissed her on her forehead and whispered, "*Kiktáyo, wíŋyaŋ mitáwa*, wake up, my woman."

"Uhhnn, already?"

"*Han*," he kissed her again.

"Will I see you later today?" She snuggling closer to him.

"You can count on it. Call me when you get home from work or come by here. We'll go to dinner."

"Ok, I will," Isa placed her hand on his chest and climbed over him to get out of bed. Thunder helped her.

"Ahh, *wíŋyaŋ mitáwa*, you are so lucky I am letting you go to work," he told her as she rubbed her body over him.

"What does that mean?"

"What?" he said as he sat up and watched her grab her clothes from the floor.

"What you called me?" After she grabbed her clothes, she stood up and turned to him in all her naked glory to look at him. She was so damn beautiful.

"*Wíŋyaŋ mitáwa?*" He asked, staring at her body.

"Yes."

"It means my woman," he answered as he dragged his eyes from her body to her face to see her reaction.

Isa smiled brightly and said, "I like that," –she then pointed her finger at him and said– "and don't you ever forget that."

He smiled back. "Highly unlikely," he stated.

With that parting comment, she turned around and sashayed her beautiful, naked ass into the bathroom. Collapsing onto the bed, he thought, *she will be the death of me*. After a few deep breaths, he got up and put his jeans on before she came out of the bathroom. He boiled some water for tea. She had left the door cracked, so he figured he could talk to her while she got dressed. He didn't have to talk too loud, since the kitchen was right next to the bathroom.

"Maybe later you will tell me exactly what you do at Teramar, or do you just sit in on meetings?" He knew she did more, but wanted to get her riled.

Isa came walking out of the bathroom and looked at him.

"Funny," she smirked at him. "I, sir," she pointed a finger at herself and said in an overly dramatic tone of voice, "am an artist. Well, a graphic designer, to be exact. Although since I got the Art Director job at Teramar, I really don't get to execute my ideas as much anymore. But since American Indian culture fascinates me. I worked on a design for your ad campaign," she grinned at him. "It was my design that you picked out. I wasn't supposed to work on it, but I just couldn't help myself."

He walked over to her and held her in his arms as he listened to the rest of her story.

"So, I stayed up late a couple of nights and worked on my idea. I put it together with the other two and hoped you would pick mine." She smiled brightly at him. "I didn't want to tell you one of them was mine."

He kissed her, "Unh, I didn't know. But I loved it. Can you stay longer? I like you better naked and in my bed," he told her between kisses.

Isa moaned. "I wish I didn't have to go. What about your window? I'm sorry. I just wanted to get your attention." She gave him a quick kiss on the lips and pulled away.

"Honey, you got that tenfold." He grinned at her.

"I guess I did, maybe threefold." Her smile lit up her eyes. Well, they had done it three times and her smile let him know she was not complaining.

"Don't worry about my window. Do you want some tea before you go? Or you can take it with you. I have disposable to-go cups." He turned toward the whistling teakettle.

"I can pay to have it replaced." She followed him to the stove. "If you have to-go cups, that would be great."

Thunder reached into the counter and pulled down the selection of teas and a to-go cup with a lid.

"Make your tea how you like it," He poured the water in the cup and pointed next to the stove, "there's the sugar. Oh, and don't forget the honey."

"Smartass," Isa shoved him playfully.

"Make sure you put the lid on it." He smiled wickedly at her.

"Stop," she smacked him in the arm, "that's not funny. Besides, if you had a lid on your coffee at my work place we would've never met and exchanged clothes." She kissed him and said, "And we're going to forget about the coffee spill last night...never happened."

"Sounds good. I'll take care of the window," he kissed her cheek. "You wouldn't have broken it if I hadn't wrongly accused you of being a tease. I'm sorry, I sometimes jump to conclusions."

Isa interrupted him, "Sometimes?" She rolled her eyes.

"Okay, smarty pants, I seem to lose my temper around you a lot. Now quit your grinning. I'll walk you down to your car. I need to lock up behind us since we don't open until nine."

"Lazy, what are you gonna do until then? Sleep?" She shot him a crooked grin as she headed for the stairs.

He smacked her ass as she walked by him.

"Hey," she said as she rubbed where he'd smacked, "you almost made me spill my tea."

"No, wiseass," he exclaimed. "I'm going home to do my morning workout, shower, and change. A few times a week, I visit a nearby elementary school. I'm their guest reader and I either read one of their books or they listen to my storytelling. I try to go in every grade level class at least once a month."

Isa was laughing all the way downstairs. It brought him joy to hear her so carefree. He wanted to make her feel that way all the time. He walked her to her car and waited while she unlocked her door. Thunder grabbed her by her hips and turned her around. Pushing her up against her car, he gave her one last sensual kiss. He felt her knees buckling. "*Wíŋyaŋ mitáwa*, leave before I take you back upstairs and chain you to my bed as my sex slave." He looked at Isa and saw her eyes darken with desire.

"You like that huh, being tied up?"

"I think I would like that with you," she whispered.

"Go now before I change my mind. I will miss you, so hurry back to me after work." He growled and kissed her one more time.

"I will miss you too," Isa gave him another quick kiss before she turned around. Opening her door, she got in and started the car. He stepped back and waved while she backed up and pulled out of the parking lot. He walked to his car and drove home.

*** *Joseph* ***

Neither Thunder nor Isa noticed Joseph sitting in his car across the street. When he was leaving the center last night, he saw Isa throwing rocks at Thunder's window through his rear-view mirror. He wasn't sure what was happening, but he didn't have to wait long to see Thunder come storming to the front door. They were arguing by the door before they headed up to his apartment. This was not turning out the way he wanted it to. Joseph was mad, but Rachel would be furious. He'd made a copy of Rachel's key to the back door when she wasn't paying attention.

So, he drove back to the center and parked around the back. After Thunder and Isa went upstairs, he sneaked in through the back door. He knew the code since he'd watched Rachel lock and unlock the alarm now several times. He wanted to see if Thunder and Isa would make up or continue to fight. Once he got in, he slipped upstairs to listen outside the apartment door. Their fighting was winding down and then it got quiet. Suddenly, he heard moaning. That was not good. He walked back downstairs and went out the back door, resetting the alarm. Once he was outside, he lit a cigarette and stood in the back corner of the building.

He had to come up with another plan to take Isa and the center away from Thunder. His two plans hadn't worked so far. The first one was to steal the knife. Thunder would tell the council he lost it and be humiliated when they ordered him home to meet with them. They would relieve him of his center and Joseph could jump right in and volunteer to run it. He knew he could run it better than Thunder. But Thunder threw a monkey wrench into that plan by not notifying the elders yet. Rachel told him Thunder was still looking for the knife. What an idiot. He would not find it. That's ok, it would be more humiliating for Thunder if he waited a while before he told the council he had lost the knife. Not only would he have to admit to his own failure, but he would have to explain why he waited so long to tell them. Joseph could break the news to his father, but he really wanted it to be Thunder that had to grovel with the elders. However, if they didn't replace Thunder, Joseph would steal more artifacts. No one, not even Rachel, knew he had the knife or a key to the center.

His second plan was for Thunder to lose Isa, or vice versa. He would love to get rid of Thunder without killing him. A prison term was not how he wanted to spend the rest of his life. So, the next best thing was for him to steal Isa away from Thunder. That would hurt him so much more if he was falling for her. Joseph was still standing outside smoking when he heard some loud noises coming from Thunder's apartment. He walked around the corner and stood just under the broken window.

As he got closer, her cries of passion got louder. That just added insult to injury. He had to grit his teeth to not shout something at them. *So, I guess they made up*, he thought bitterly. His stunt had not worked. Now, not only did he have to come up with another plan, but he'd have to deal with Rachel as well. The slut would be livid when she heard they'd worked it out. He now realized he should have taken Isa somewhere "to talk" after Thunder threw them out. He never thought she would throw rocks at his window or that Thunder would've been so damn quick to respond.

"Damn," he mumbled angrily as he put out his cigarette and got in his car. "I should've stopped her when I saw what she was doing from my rear-view mirror. He can NOT have everything he wants. First, he takes my father, then the center and Rachel, and now he has this desirable woman that he met through the center. She should be mine! If I can't have her, then no one can." He said as he slammed his hand on his steering wheel.

"The elders love Thunder because he's like a woman and listens to everything they say. Well, I am better than he is. I will prove it. I will run that center and fuck his girl soon."

Joseph pulled out of the parking lot. He wanted to follow Isa when she left. Eventually, he'd fallen asleep.

Now it was morning, and he'd had a miserable night. Rachel tried calling him, but he'd put his phone on silent. He was delaying telling her what happened. He would feel her wrath soon enough.

Joseph scooted up in his seat and rubbed the sleep from his eyes, worried he'd missed Isa. But when he looked across the street, her car was still in the parking lot. He needed coffee to wake up, but he didn't want to leave until Isa left. Finally, he saw Thunder walk Isa to her car. They shared a steamy kiss, and she drove away.

Joseph followed her home, letting her get a head start since he already knew where she lived. An hour later, he watched her get into her car again, dressed for work. He figured she was going to Teramar, but followed her anyway just to make sure.

"Well, well, well, babe. Soon I will know your daily schedule. Then we can finally be together. And if I say so myself, I am looking forward to fucking you in front of Thunder and seeking my revenge. That body is quite delectable. I intend to enjoy it for a long time. I know I can make you happier than Thunder in bed. Imagine his surprise when you pick me over him after we've been together. You'll moan more for me than you did for him."

Joseph watched Isa pull into Teramar's parking lot. He knew he didn't have to stay there all day because Isa never left until after four-thirty, he could come back then. Although, after watching her that morning with Thunder by her car, he was sure she would see him tonight. Thunder was not one to stay away from his woman when it was getting serious. And it sure looked and sounded like it was getting serious.

Decision made, he drove to Rachel's apartment to catch her before she left for work. Rachel was unpredictable, especially since she didn't know the outcome of their scheme. He was positive she was waiting for him to find out before seeing Thunder.

Rachel was waiting for him by the door with her arms crossed over her chest and tapping her foot on the floor. She must have been pacing by the window and saw when he pulled up.

"Where did you go last night? Did you leave with Isa? You never answered your phone or called me to tell me what happened after I left! I wanted to go comfort Thunder. Or did you forget about that part of our plan?" She screamed at him.

"No, I did not forget. Thunder threw us out and before I could think of what to do, Isa began giving me the third degree because I kissed her. I tried to avoid the questions by walking away, and I thought she was going to do the same. Then I noticed her picking up rocks and throwing them at his apartment window. I couldn't believe it. She was acting crazy. Next thing I know, one of her rocks breaks his window and he comes storming downstairs yelling at her. She yelled back, and they ended up going into his apartment." He rubbed the back of his neck. It still hurt from sleeping in a car all night. "I'm pretty sure they made up."

"How do you know they made up? Why are you so sure? Maybe they were fighting."

"All night, Rachel?" He glared at her. "Besides, when I went to snoop, I could hear her screaming out his name, and she wasn't angry with him. If you know what I mean," he stared at her wryly.

"Aaahhhhhhh," she screamed loudly. "Yeah, I know what you mean!" She started pacing, biting her nails. "I thought this would work. What are we going to do now?"

"I'll think about it some more. Just go get dressed and go to work and act as if you know nothing after you left."

"Fine, Joseph, but I won't wait much longer. If you don't find a way for Thunder to be mine, then I will tell him you took the knife." She threatened him before she twirled around.

Joseph grabbed her arm and spun her toward him, pushing her up against the wall and holding her there by her throat.

"How do you know I have the knife?"

"Well, I don't have it and I know we didn't sell it." She struggled as he blocked her airway.

"Don't you EVER threaten me again! Do you hear me? I could break your neck in two seconds and get rid of you in the everglades. No one would ever know and after the gators ate your body parts, no one could find you," he said menacingly while angrily staring into her eyes, "stupid bitch."

"Joseph, I can't breathe," she was gasping for air. "Please, let me go. I'm sorry, I won't do it again."

"Fine," he pushed her head into the wall before he released her. "See that you don't."

Rachel stepped away quickly and held her hand to her neck while she took some deep breaths.

"Don't cross me Rachel," he pointed at her, "I'm warning you. Just stick to my plans and it will all work out."

"Okay, Joseph. I got the message loud and clear. I'm sorry." Rachel mumbled, then walked into the bedroom to change. She didn't want to anger Joseph, she just wanted Thunder. She would have to be patient. Once Joseph took Isa, Thunder would be devastated, and she could comfort him and tell him about Joseph. They could have him arrested for robbery. The tribal council would be so unhappy with Joseph, they would send him back home to serve his punishment. Then everything would be as it was when Thunder and her first got there before she was stupid enough to cheat on Thunder and realized the grass wasn't always greener on the other side. She thought Thunder would fight for her, but he never did. Thunder just thought their relationship had run its course. She loved it here and didn't want to disappoint the tribal council, especially Spirit of the Eagle. Maybe this time, Thunder would finally marry her and they would have children.

Rachel was finally smiling as she finished getting ready for work, picturing them with their kids at his beach house. Everything would work out all right in due time. She put some make-up on her neck to cover the bruises from Joseph's hands. By the time she left, Joseph was asleep on the couch. She walked out slowly and quietly so she wouldn't wake him.

Chapter 35

Tuesday...Prepping for School Field Trip

THUNDER

After Thunder's volunteer time at the elementary school, he went back to work. He changed into his summer hunting warrior Lakota clothing because he had middle schoolers coming in and he wanted them to listen and focus on his teachings. Previous field trips from that age group taught him to look realistic in order to engage their attention. In the old days, black paint was created by mixing powdered charred wood and black earth with buffalo fat. Using a charcoal stick, he applied black paint to his chest in the shape of a thunderbird, along with two diagonal stripes to his arms and cheeks. He wore his loincloth without leggings but, for modesty reasons, put on a black speedo bathing suit underneath. He wanted nothing hanging out in the middle of a lesson. That would not be good.

He saw Rachel in the lobby with some guests, so he headed to his office to get some paperwork done. After lunch, Mark came into his office and told him he had to run an errand. He hadn't seen Rachel and there were some guests in the lobby that wanted a personal tour.

As he was talking to the guests and answering all their questions, he heard his phone ringing in his office.

"Excuse me for a moment. I need to answer that. Would you all like to visit our Red Path Exhibit? I will join you there shortly."

"Yes, of course," they said excitedly and walked to the exhibit.

He ran to his office and answered his phone. "American Indian Cultural Center, can I help you?"

"Hi Thunder, it's Isa."

He smiled as soon as he heard her voice.

"*Hau, wíŋyaŋ mitáwa*, it is good to hear your voice. I miss you. Are you done at work already?" he looked at his watch. "It's only 2:00."

"No, but I wanted to know if you wanted to have dinner with two of my friends tonight. Just the four of us."

"Can we do that tomorrow? I have middle schoolers coming for a field trip and then I am expecting my runaway kids from the local shelter. My kids just called an hour ago to ask if they could come today and I said yes because I don't like to disappoint them. I hope to be done by 5:30, but sometimes I run a little late. I would hate to put out your friends. Besides, all I want to do is feed you a quick dinner and take you to bed."

He could hear the smile in her voice when she responded, "Okay, that sounds wonderful. Maybe we could go to dinner with them tomorrow night."

"What makes you think that tomorrow night I won't want you all to myself?" He asked her sexily.

"I don't know."

"I was hoping you would agree with me, *wíŋyaŋ mitáwa*," he chuckled. "I have to go now. Some guests have arrived and are waiting for me and I can't find Rachel. Can I pick you up after work, or do you want to meet me at my house?"

"Can I meet you at your house? I still haven't seen where you live."

"Absolutely," he said. "I'll text you my address as soon as we hang up."

"I can't wait to see you," she whispered.

"I can't either." They both said goodbye and hung up.

Thunder quickly texted his address so she could GPS it later. Then he went in search of his guests in the exhibit room. The tour only lasted about an hour, which gave him enough time to sit behind the lobby desk and wait for his middle schoolers. Glancing toward the restaurant, he noticed Rachel speaking to Mary.

The children arrived on schedule from Bair Middle School. Thunder looked up as the bus pulled up and turned into their parking lot. He got up and waved to Rachel to come over.

"Rachel, the children are here. Did Grayfeather make enough fry bread?"

"*Han, Wakíyaŋ Hotóŋpi*, he made enough for fifty. They told us they had forty-four kids, one teacher, and two chaperones."

"Good, let's introduce ourselves and take them back to the storytelling room so they can get comfortable before our presentation."

Rachel wore a long buckskin dress and moccasins.

As the teacher approached Thunder, he noticed her staring at his chest. Maybe he should have worn a shirt and leggings with his loincloth and moccasins. While planning his outfit for the middle schoolers, he didn't take the teachers and chaperones into consideration. Oops, big mistake. This was going to get awkward if they kept staring at him. The kids were bound to notice.

Chapter 36

Tuesday...School Field Trip

THUNDER

"Hello, I'm Angie Hardrew. You must be Mr. Thunderbird?" She inquired.

Thunder noticed how she stressed the Miss part of her name so he knew she was single.

"Yes, *Hau*, you can call me Thunder. Ms. Hardrew," he answered and stuck out his hand to shake hers.

"Well then," she blushed and said, "you can call me Angie."

"Very well, Angie. But for the sake of professionalism in front of your students, I will still refer to you as Ms. Hardrew. If that is okay with you?"

"Sure," she said breathlessly.

"Is this your entire class?" he asked, trying to change the subject. He could always charm the ladies, even though he wasn't trying to charm this one.

"Yes, there are forty-one here today. Three are absent."

"Well then, let's get started. Your bus driver may leave the bus parked in our parking lot. He's more than welcome to come inside and join us."

Ms. Hardew walked to the bus and talked to the bus driver. She then reminded the kids to behave and advised them to walk toward Rachel at the front door. Rachel told them to go to Mr. Thunderbird standing by the tree and make a semi-circle around him.

Thunder waved them toward him and waited until all the kids got off the bus and waited with him.

"*Hau*," Thunder said as he held his hand up, "My name is *Zintkála Wakíyaŋ Hotóŋpi*, which translates to Johnny Thunderbird, but you can all call me Thunder. I will be your guide today as you learn about my Lakota culture and other American Indian cultures. Hello and welcome in our language is *Hau*. Can you all say that?" He asked them.

They all said, "*Hau*."

"Awesome," he smiled encouragingly at them. "*Hau*, Bair Middle."

Several said, "*Hau*, Thunder."

He smiled at them and pointed toward the front door to introduce Rachel. "The beautiful lady at the door is my assistant and also from my Lakota Tribe, *Tingleska Ista*, Rachel Doe Eyes."

"*Hau*," Rachel said, smiling as she walked toward them.

"*Hau*," the kids repeated.

"Doe Eyes will escort you to the storytelling room, where we will give you a brief presentation and tell you a story from our Lakota Nation. We will then visit the 'Red Path Exhibit' and finish in the restaurant where you can have a bottle of water and try our Indian Fry Bread. I will be with you in a minute. Please follow Doe Eyes."

The children excitedly followed Rachel into the room. Thunder could see all the dream catchers hanging from the ceiling in the Storytelling room mesmerized them. He waited a few minutes for them to get seated. The chaperones went in with the kids, but Ms. Hardrew stayed behind by his side.

"Can I help you with anything?"

"Not at this time, but thank you." Thunder kindly smiled and answered her.

Thunder held the door open for her and walked into the room after her. He walked to the front of the room and stood on the stage, facing the students. He didn't want any mishaps with his loincloth while he spoke to them.

Thunder raised his hands straight up into the air and tossed his head back and said one of his Lakota prayers. When he finished, he looked at the students and noticed he'd caught their attention. He explained to them how he just prayed to *Wakan Tanka*, his people's great spirit. He repeated his prayer in English so they would understand.

He explained his culture and why he dressed the way he was.

"In our culture, Wakan Tanka is the same as God is to some of you. He is our great spirit and in our culture we pray to *Wakan Tanka* every morning, evening, when we hunt and at other times in our lives. We believe that all animals and plants in this world are our brothers and sisters. Doe Eyes and I dressed like our ancestors would have dressed back in the 1800s. On the plains, it was cold in the winter, so the men would add a buckskin shirt, leggings, and a buffalo robe to this ensemble. Women would add leggings, taller moccasins, and a buffalo robe. If the family did not have a buffalo robe, other animal furs or hides could be used." You could hear a pin drop as he told them about his Lakota heritage.

"We never just killed the animals needlessly. We tried to kill them with mercy, and we always said a prayer for them. The animal's body parts were all used for the specific needs of our people. For example, the bones were used for cooking utensils and tools." Rachel handed him some of those items as he spoke so he could show the students. He let them pass it around if they wanted to hold them. "The tendons or sinew were the thread used for sewing. The stomach or liver were used to boil food for cooking or carry water. Then, of course, the hides were used for clothing. Other parts of the animals were eaten raw, boiled, or dried. You all know this as beef jerky." He could tell they were listening because some grimaced at the thought of raw food. Rachel stepped out to change into her Jingle Dress while he did the storytelling.

"Today, I will tell you one of our Lakota legendary stories, as it was told to me by my father when I was a young child."

He then sat down carefully on the bench on stage and told them about the Lakota Legend of the Dream catcher.

Long ago when the world was young, an old Lakota spiritual leader was on a high mountain and had a vision. In his vision, Iktomi, the great trickster and teacher of wisdom, appeared in the form of a spider. Iktomi spoke to him in a sacred language that only the spiritual leaders of the Lakota could understand. As he spoke Iktomi, the spider, took the elder's willow hoop which had feathers, horsehair, beads and offerings on it and began to spin a web. He spoke to the elder about the cycles of life...and how we begin our lives as infants and we move on to childhood, and then to adulthood. Finally, we go to old age where we must be taken care of as infants, completing the cycle.

"But," Iktomi said as he continued to spin his web, "in each time of life there are many forces – some good and some bad. If you listen to the good forces, they will steer you in the right direction. But if you listen to the bad forces, they will hurt you and steer you in the wrong direction. There are many forces and different directions that can help or interfere with the harmony of nature, and also with the great spirit and all of his wonderful teachings."

All the while the spider spoke, he continued to weave his web starting from the outside and working toward the center. When Iktomi finished speaking, he gave the Lakota elder the web and said, "See, the web is a perfect circle but there is a hole in the center of the circle. Use the web to help yourself and your people to reach your goals and make good use of your people's ideas, dreams and visions. If you believe in the great spirit, the web will catch your good ideas – the bad ones will go through the hole."

The Lakota passed on his vision to his people and now the Sioux Indians use the dream catcher as the web of their life. It is hung above their beds or in their home to sift their dreams and visions. The good in their dreams are captured in the web of life and carried with them...but the evil in their dreams escapes through the hole in the center of the web and are no longer a part of them. We believe the dream catcher holds the destiny of our lives.

"Do you all know what a dream catcher looks like?" he asked the kids.

Some said yes and nodded their heads, while others said no. A few pointed up to the ceiling.

Thunder pointed to the ceiling and said, "Those are some dream catchers that my people made for us for this cultural center. They will catch all your good dreams and thoughts as you sit here and release the bad ones for you."

He could hear the kids sigh and say wow. He saw Rachel was ready when she came back into the room dressed.

"Everyone, please stand up," he said. "Doe Eyes and I will show you a dance." He knew they needed to stand up and move around for a bit.

"At Powwows, you will usually see these two dances that Doe Eyes and I are about to teach you. The boy's dance is called 'Men's Fancy Dance'." He moved to the side of the room and said, "All the boys come over here with me. The girls will follow Doe Eyes on the other side of the room. Doe Eyes will teach you the 'Jingle Dress Dance'. This won't take long. Then we will head out and form a circle around the lobby desk and tree and we'll dance around like they do in pow-wows." Thunder smiled. There were mixed feelings around the room. He saw excitement, embarrassment, and dread on their faces.

While Thunder simplified the steps for the boys, he heard Rachel explaining the significance of the Jingle Dress dance. How every silver cone shaped bell was sewn on the dress and placed there with good thoughts and well wishes. No one could think bad and unpleasant thoughts when making a Jingle Dress.

Out of the corner of his eye, he could see Rachel teaching them the steps. She accentuated her footwork, so the girls heard as many jingle sounds as possible.

After about fifteen minutes, Thunder called Doe Eyes to come over. "Are my Indian Princesses ready to dance for my strong Indian Warriors?" he asked, knowing the kids would get a kick out of playing pretend. The boys all hooted while the girls blushed.

"Yes, my chief, they are ready." Rachel smiled at him.

"Then let us all walk out to the lobby and form two circles around the desk and the tree. A circle in my culture represents the never-ending circle of life. We will perform a Circle Dance. The desk and tree will represent a fire pit. Make sure you are facing the tree. The boys will make an inner circle and the girls will make an outer circle. Make sure you spread out your circle. Normally, these two dances are not performed together like this, but I have combined them for this purpose. Focus on yourselves and your steps. Remember, we are here to learn not to make fun of others if they misstep."

When everyone was in a circle, Rachel and Thunder included, he said, "Now boys, turn to your right. You will dance clockwise in this direction. Follow the person in front of you and stay in your circle. Girls, turn to your left. You will dance counter-clockwise. Again, make sure you follow the person in front of you and stay in your circle. When the music starts, follow Doe Eyes and me and dance the steps you learned." Mark was sitting at the Lobby Desk. "Mark, can you please turn on the music for us? Okay, students, here we go."

The students danced as soon as the music started. In the beginning, they tried doing the correct steps. But as some stumbled, they made up their own steps. Thunder would not correct them as long as they were enjoying themselves. When the first song ended, Thunder stopped everyone.

"Do you all want to do that again?" he shouted.

"Yes!" they all shouted.

"Okay. I'm gonna step out to get your food ready, but keep doing what you're doing. You all look great." He motioned over to Mark to start the music again.

"Mark, turn the music off when this song is over." Thunder told him before he walked toward the restaurant. As the kids were all dancing again and having fun, he went to check on Mary and Grayfeather. They were in the kitchen putting all the indian fry bread on trays.

"How is it going?"

"Great, we are done." Mary smiled at him. "Rachel said she would clean up, so we are going to head out."

"*Pilámaya*, for staying late to do this for me." Thunder hugged Mary.

"*Taŋyáŋ yahípi*," Mary said and the Grayfeathers left.

Thunder carried the tray out to the restaurant and set it down on a table. He went back into the kitchen to grab a couple of cases of water from the refrigerator. As he turned around, he bumped into Ms. Hardrew.

"Sorry, Ms. Hardrew, are you okay? I didn't see you."

"I came to see if you needed any help," she said and rubbed the spot on his arm where he bumped her.

"Uh, no I'm good." Thunder said quickly and walked out of the kitchen to place the first case of water on another table. He needed to distract her so he could go get the second case out of the refrigerator. He didn't want her following him. "On second thought, could you get these waters out of the packaging and ready for your students? I would really appreciate that."

"Of course," she smiled brightly at him. He hurried into the kitchen to grab the second case before she came looking for him again. He came out and set this case on another table and asked her to open those for him as well. Then he went to the hostess stand and grabbed several napkins.

As soon as Ms. Hardrew finished, she stood next to him again. He saw Rachel directing some kids to the restaurant. He heard Rachel give them a choice of snack first or museum.

"Ms. Hardrew, would you mind serving your students? They would probably be more comfortable accepting food from you than me."

"Yes, of course," she winked at him before she walked away.

Whew, women. He knew Ms. Hardrew wanted a piece of him, but he was a taken man. Besides, he liked the thrill of the chase and he'd had to chase Isa, though she was hard to tame. He'd learned that when Isa wanted to talk to him, and threw the rock through his window. His woman had fire in her veins.

Thunder wandered around talking to the students and tried to stay away from Ms. Hardrew as much as he could. He got lucky when he saw his shelter kids pulling into the parking lot. He excused himself from his current conversation with Ms. Hardrew and welcomed his kids.

"*Hau*," Thunder greeted them cheerily at the door.

"*Hau*, Thunder. Uhh, why are you dressed like that?" Tim asked. Thunder never dressed like this for them. He wore this only when he had elementary or middle school field trips.

"Middle School field trip," he said and pointed toward the restaurant. "Why don't you guys start in the exhibit today while I finish up with the field trip? Look around. I'll be there in a few minutes."

There were only six of them today. It broke his heart that these kids didn't feel loved and felt it was better to run away and live on the streets than to stay at home. They were all from broken families and their parents were prostitutes, pimps, drug addicts, alcoholics, gang bangers or prisoners.

The shelter had brought them every time he had a new exhibit. All were between the ages of fourteen and eighteen. Some worked at local grocery stores and tried to stay out of trouble. Others came to see him, so he put them to work. He always paid them minimum wage for their time and tried to mentor them along the way. Many he never saw again after they turned eighteen.

He saw Rachel come out of the restaurant.

"Rachel," he called out. "Our kids are here. Did the Grayfeather's make enough fry bread?" They always referred to the shelter kids as their kids. They just wanted to embrace them as family, since their family didn't seem to care.

"*Han, Wakíyaŋ Hotóŋpi*, yes, I told him our kids were coming. He left another batch in a large-sealed container in the kitchen."

"Thank you Rachel, I totally forgot to ask Mary and George. Let's say our goodbyes to the middle schoolers and then focus on our kids."

Thunder and Rachel walked over to the restaurant. Their teacher and chaperones were telling the kids to throw away their trash while they wiped down the tables. This was a good considerate group. Well, besides the flirtatious teacher.

RED PATH

"Now class, let's say thank you to Thunder and Doe Eyes for their wonderful stories, teaching you those remarkable dances, and feeding you an authentic American Indian dish."

"Thank you, Thunder and Doe Eyes," they all cried out at different times.

"You're welcome. Your steel horse awaits you my friends," Thunder said smiling, "I hope you all had a great time. I know you didn't get time to really see the exhibit or visit our gift shop. But tell your parents about us and hopefully I'll see you again soon. This exhibit will be here for the next three months."

"Alright kids, walk in a single file line towards the bus. Our bus driver is already there waiting for us." Ms. Hardrew stayed behind to talk to him, but some kids were asking him questions on their way out. Finally, as the last child walked out with the chaperones, Ms. Hardrew turned toward him and said, "Thank you Thunder for such an interesting afternoon. I'm sure the kids will talk about this for days to come. You really made them feel very special."

Thunder walked outside as they were talking. Waving to the kids as they waved back to him.

"It was my pleasure. They can come back anytime. Just call me and we'll set up another field trip." He stepped back so she would not reach out and touch him again.

"That would be great," she said as she pulled out a piece of paper and a pen. "Here is my direct line at the school and my personal number, in case you need a friend." She wrote her name and both numbers on the piece of paper and handed it to him.

He took the piece of paper carefully so he wouldn't touch her hand. He wanted to be nice, but he didn't want to lead her on. "Thank you. That was very thoughtful of you."

"Call me anytime. And thanks again." She stuck out her hand to shake his.

"Sure," he said as he shook her hand quickly. "If you'll excuse me, I have another group of kids waiting for me in the exhibit room. Have a great day." Before he turned around, he saw Isa heading toward him.

*** *Isa* ***

Isa had been in meetings all afternoon with clients. When she finally looked up, it was already 4:30. "Time to go. I better text Thunder and see if he's done and on his way home."

Isa: Leaving now. Are you home?

Thunder: Not yet. This field trip is taking longer than I thought.

Isa: K, I'll come to you.

Thunder: Ok.

Isa: ⊠

Isa drove to the center and pulled into the parking lot just as the last of the school kids were piling into the school bus. When she got out of her car, she heard their excited voices over what they had learned today. Thunder was obviously an excellent teacher. She started walking toward him, smiling. The teacher he was talking to was blushing and staring at him like she wanted to eat him up. Isa felt jealous again.

Well, hell. Of course, the teacher was flirting, who wouldn't when all he was wearing was a scrap of clothing to cover his penis. *What the hell? He must dress in these clothes when he is teaching the children from the local schools. Hell, he should dress like that for me. He is so drool worthy right now. My man was some serious eye candy, yum.* He'd painted his chest with a black Thunderbird, painted two black stripes on his arms and face and wore a beautifully beaded armband on his right arm adorned with an eagle feather hanging down. His buckskin loincloth was down to his knees and yet it barely covered his privates. The wind blew just as she was thinking about that, and she noticed he had a black speedo underneath. Thank goodness. He was wearing different moccasins than the ones she saw on opening night. They weren't as elegantly decorated as his other pair.

Isa couldn't stop staring and licking her lips as she walked toward him. What a beautiful man and he had chosen her. At that moment, Thunder turned and saw her. His smile widened, and he held his hand out to her. The teacher must have noticed that Thunder was looking and smiling at someone over her shoulder. She turned around and sighed as her eyes met Isa's. Yeah, Thunder would not be calling her. Isa hid her smirk as she reveled in Thunder's undivided attention.

The teacher looked back at Thunder and said, "Thank you, Thunder, Doe Eyes," Rachel stood next to Thunder to wave to the kids as well. "It was an excellent field trip. We will do this yearly, if not twice a year."

"Well, I hope so. Maybe they will convince their parents to come in and learn about my people."

Isa finally reached Thunder. She didn't want to interrupt, so she took his hand and stayed quiet as she smiled at Ms. Hardrew. Thunder pulled her into his side, wrapped his arm around her waist and gave her a peck on the forehead and he continued to speak to Ms. Hardrew, "If we can begin with the children, then our future in this world will be filled with much happiness."

"Well, I will definitely mention our experience here and list your hours in my weekly email."

"I would appreciate that," Thunder said.

The students sat on the bus waiting for Ms. Hardrew for a head count. All the kids were opening their windows to wave at Thunder.

Thunder grinned and waved to the kids as the school bus closed its doors and pulled out of the parking lot. The children were still waving and screaming, "Bye Thunder, Bye Doe Eyes."

Isa laughed when she saw the kids on the bus pushing each other aside so each one could wave and scream out the window to Thunder and Rachel. "Seems like you guys made an impression on them."

Thunder and Rachel waved until the bus pulled out of the parking lot. He then turned and looked at Isa, pulling her into his arms and whispered in her ear, "Oh, but I want to make an impression on you, *wíŋyaŋ mitáwa*." He kissed her soundly while backing her up against the center's wall.

"Uh, Thunder, your assistant is watching."

Isa noticed Rachel glaring at them.

"I don't care," he said between kisses. "I missed you today."

When he finally let her up for air, Isa said, "Are you hungry for dinner?"

"I am hungry for you first, then dinner, and some more of you." Thunder smiled, grabbed her hand, and pulled her along toward the door. "Rachel, this is Isa, my woman. Isa, this is Rachel, my assistant. I think you already met."

"Briefly." Isa forced a smile. She'd barely spoken to her at the opening, but clearly remembered her from the day she spewed all those horrible things about Thunder. Isa pushed those thoughts away. She was too happy right now to get into a fight with Rachel in front of Thunder. Not when he'd just called her his woman. "It's good to see you again."

"Good to see you as well."

"Rachel, I'm going to go talk to our kids."

Rachel nodded her head and said, "They are still in the exhibit room. I'm gonna take off. See you tomorrow."

"Ok. See you tomorrow," Thunder then turned to Isa. She had a very puzzled look on her face.

"What? Why are you looking at me like that?"

"Our kids?" She asked him.

"Our kids from the shelter," he smirked and explained, "I don't like to call them shelter kids, so Rachel and I say 'our kids'. We try to make them feel like family when they are here. Come with me and I'll introduce you to them." They held hands, and he pulled her along.

"Oooooo, Thunder has a girlfriend! And she's hot too!" Some kids starting singing, "Thunder and his girl sitting in a tree, k-i-s-s-i-n-g."

"Alright, settle down," Thunder said with a smile on his face. Isa was blushing.

Then he pointed at one boy. "Don't be checking out my woman, dude. Do you have a death wish?" He pretended to threaten him.

"Ha, like you would hurt us. We're family, remember?" he wiggled his eyebrows.

"Yeah, Yeah, Yeah, little brother." Thunder laughed and side hugged him.

Isa could see how much they loved each other. The three older ones were the ones joking with Thunder. The three younger ones looked a little wary and were quiet during the verbal exchange. They must be new and not know Thunder as well as the others.

"Anyway, Isa, these are my little brothers. Guys, this is Isa, my woman."

They exchanged hi's all around. They seemed nice.

"Sorry I couldn't be in here when you guys got here, but now that you've looked around, do you have questions for me about this exhibit?" Thunder asked them.

"Yeah, do you have a few minutes to explain these particular weapons over here? They look really old. We were curious about their history and use."

"Sure," Thunder turned to Isa and said, "You can stay with me or meet me in my office. Whichever you prefer. Or if you want to head to my house, I can give you my key."

"Oooooo, he's giving her his key," one boy said and started making kissing sounds.

"Alright lover boy, go toward the weapons in question and give me a minute to speak to my woman...alone," Thunder said wryly.

Isa was laughing at their antics. "I'll stay with you so I can learn about them as well."

"Great," Thunder headed to the case and explained all the weapons. The kids had a lot of questions and Thunder was very patient with them.

"Hey little brothers, I have a surprise for you," Thunder said as he led them to the lobby.

"You mean our surprise wasn't Isa?" Tim said, and they all giggled.

"Isa, this is Tim," Thunder motioned towards him, "he is the oldest in this group and sometimes works for me. As you can see, his favorite pastime is busting my chops."

"So true," Tim announced, as they all laughed.

"No Tim, Isa is my surprise, not yours." Thunder winked at Isa.

"Ohhhh, we see how it is." Tim grabbed his heart as if he was hurt.

Thunder laughed and kept walking.

"Follow me to the restaurant. The Grayfeather's knew you guys were coming, and they left you all a treat."

"Oh shit, did he leave us fry bread?" Tim asked.

"Language," Thunder scolded, "Yes, he left you fry bread to take back with you. Let me go get it."

"Oh man, that is so awesome," Tim said to the group. "You guys will love this shit." He told the three younger ones.

Thunder came out of the back carrying a large, covered container.

"He made all of that for us?" One of the younger kids asked as his eyes got wide.

"He sure did, little brother. Take it all. It's for you." Thunder smiled.

"Wow, this is awesome."

Tim took the container and looked at Thunder with tears in his eyes. "Thank you, big brother. We really appreciate it. We'll see you next week?"

"Of course, we're family. I always look forward to your visits. Let me know if you need anything. Just call me." Thunder squeezed his shoulder.

"Will do. It was nice meeting you, Isa." Tim nodded.

"You too," Isa responded.

Thunder hugged all the boys before they left. He then turned off the lights.

"Step outside. I'm going to set the alarm." Thunder set the alarm and locked the door.

"Now, do you want to follow me or drive with me?"

"I'll follow since I have work tomorrow."

Thunder walked Isa to her car and gave her a quick kiss. "Okay, put the address in your GPS in case we get separated. I'll see you there. We have pressing matters to attend to," he said as he winked at her.

Chapter 37

Date Night at Thunder's

ISA

Isa got in her car, put in the address, and followed Thunder. His house was a beautiful two-story Spanish-style home. He parked in the garage, and Isa parked in his driveway. He got out of his car and waited for her.

"Your house is beautiful," Isa said as she walked toward him. "What pressing matters do we have to discuss?" She looked at him mischievously as he pushed the button to close the garage door.

He opened the door to the house and pulled Isa in front of him. He started kissing her neck. "It would be the matter pressing against your lovely back at the moment."

Isa laughed and walked into his house. He kicked the door shut after them and locked it.

"My, my, that matter is certainly pressing," she giggled.

"You have no idea. But you will in about two seconds." He turned her around and grinned wickedly. Bending down, he picked her up behind her knees and threw her over his shoulders, firefighter style.

"Thunder, put me down!" Isa screamed while she laughed. She was slapping his ass.

"I see your kink is spanking."

"Well, maybe," she said seductively, "I've never done it before, but I trust you."

"Uhn," Thunder groaned. "Maybe later, for now you are my captive and until I've had enough of you," he stopped in the bedroom and slid her down his body, looking into her eyes as he said, "you are not going anywhere." With that said, he undressed her, not stopping until she stood before him in her small scrap of underwear. Isa couldn't wait to undress Thunder, but she'd never undressed a man in a loincloth before. Where did she start? Then she got an idea.

"Thunder?"

"Yes, honey," Thunder said as he stared at her breasts.

"Can you take off that speedo and stay in your loincloth so I can get the full warrior experience?" Her eyes twinkled with excitement as she looked at him.

"For you," Thunder gazed into her eyes, "yes," he whispered as he dropped his speedo and stepped out of it.

"Wow, can you turn around in a circle for me?"

"Yes." Thunder said as he held up his hands and slowly turned in a full circle. When he faced her, he placed his hands on his hip.

"Well?" he asked as she stared at his tented loincloth. "How do I look?"

"Uh," she gulped and was breathing heavily, with her nipples pointing at attention.

"I've left you speechless, *wíŋyaŋ mitáwa*," he said as he closed the gap between them. "Is that a good thing or a bad thing?"

"Oh, it's good," Isa said as she licked her lips and dropped to her knees. She ran her hands under the leather waistband, trying to find a clasp.

"Can I help you?" Thunder groaned, watching her efforts.

"Nope, please let me," she looked pleadingly up at him. She had an idea. Thunder nodded and moved his hands back to his waist.

"Isa, you are killing me. Do what you want to do but do it quick before I run out of patience and throw you on my bed to fuck you," he taking a deep breath and staring at the ceiling.

Isa ran her hands under the loincloth, pulling the flap up onto his chest. She held it there with one hand while she sucked his cock.

"Fuck," Thunder growled.

She released the loincloth and let it drape over her head. One of her hands grabbed his ass, pulling him closer while the other played with his balls.

"Shit woman, that feels so good," Thunder moaned and dropped his hands to hold her head tighter to his body.

Isa continued to take him deeper into her throat while stroking his cock. She wanted him to cum in her mouth. He hadn't let her do that yet, and she was looking forward to it. Isa took him as far back as she could without gagging.

"Fuck, Isa, Isa," he gently tapped the back of her head, "Baby, I'm going to cum in your mouth if you don't release me."

Thunder was panting and holding her as close to his cock as he could. Isa sucked harder and got into a stroking rhythm.

"Fuck! Isa!" He screamed as he released his cum into her mouth.

Isa swallowed and licked him up while he got his breathing under control. When she finished, she pulled the loincloth down and looked up at Thunder, grinning like a Cheshire cat at her achievement.

"Come up here, honey," he said as he helped her stand up and hugged her. "That was fucking fantastic. Thank you," he said before he ravished her mouth.

"You look so hot. But I still don't know how to take off your loincloth," she said when he released her mouth.

"Oh yeah," he smiled at her, "well you look sexy in your thong with your beautiful breasts calling out to me," he said while he roamed his hands around her body to cup her breasts. "Tell me, are you wet below?" His hand traveled down her body and into her thong.

"Oh," she said breathlessly, "are you going to show me how to take it off?"

"Yes, after I eat you for my appetizer."

Thunder latched onto her breast with his mouth while he ripped her thong off her body. Then he licked his way to her pussy. She was drenched.

"Spread your legs, baby, I got you." Thunder draped one of her legs over his shoulder and held her up with his hands on her ass. He licked, sucked, and bit her until she screamed his name and orgasmed in his mouth.

He stood up and carried her to his bed. She gazed at him as he dropped his loincloth.

"That's it," she groaned. "You just drop them down like underwear?"

"I do with this one," he chuckled. "I made it like this, but others are more complicated," he said as he got in bed with her and began caressing her body. He was driving her crazy.

"Thunder please, I can't wait another minute." Isa grabbed his cock and guided him inside her. They savagely thrust into each other. Isa wrapped her legs tightly around Thunder as he tilted her ass and sunk deeper into her until he felt her orgasm building and explode. But Thunder wasn't done yet. He turned her around and pulled her back onto her hands and knees, entering her from behind while she was still in her orgasm.

"Oh my God, Thunder," Isa screamed.

Thunder held her in place with one hand on her hip while playing with her clit with the other as he pounded into her.

"Fuck, Isa," Thunder claimed her like an animal rutting against his mate.

"Oh, Oh, Aahhh," Isa hollered loudly.

"Fuuuckkk!" Thunder screamed simultaneously as they both climaxed and dropped on the bed in a hot, sweaty mess.

Thunder rolled off her, laying on his back panting.

"Now that we have controlled my pressing matter, for the moment," he turned his head to look at her, "What do you want for dinner?"

"How about pizza?" Isa mumbled into the bed. "We can order in and stay naked in bed because I can't move."

"Mmmm," Thunder mumbled as he rained kisses on her back and began massaging her ass, "I like the way you think *wíŋyaŋ mitáwa*. Pizza it is. What kind do you like?"

"Pepperoni and mushroom. What do you like?"

"I'll eat anything. Let me put in the order now, since it will take at least thirty minutes for delivery." Thunder rolled off her and grabbed his phone. He sat up against the headboard as he put the order in online.

As he was doing that, Isa rolled over and closed her eyes. "What will we do for the next thirty minutes?"

He finished and put his phone aside. He smiled wickedly and said, "*Wíŋyaŋ mitáwa*, let's work up an appetite in the shower. I need to wash off this war paint on me and you," he said as he pointed to her breasts. They were smeared with black charcoal.

"Ok my warrior, lead the way." Isa raised her hands when he stood in front of her. Thunder grabbed Isa's hands, pulled her up and led her to his bathroom. He turned on the water and waited until it was hot.

"Ladies first," he said and opened the shower curtain for her. The shower was not too big, but they both fit. Of course, it helped they were plastered to each other the entire time, kissing and touching each other. After they finished washing off the war paint from their bodies, Thunder washed her hair and put the conditioner in it. He was too tall for her to wash him, so she just watched and drooled. After he rinsed his hair, while his eyes were still closed, she dropped to her knees and sucked him.

"Oh shit," he said as he put both hands against the wall of the shower.

She was ready for round two. He looked so sexy standing before her, she couldn't help herself. She kept sucking while she stroked his cock and played with his balls. She could feel him getting harder.

"Oh fuck, that feels so good. Isa, honey, if you don't want to swallow again, pull off because I'm getting ready to blow, baby." He moaned loudly. Isa grabbed his ass with both hands and pulled him into her mouth. Since she couldn't see his face last time because of the loincloth, she now wanted to watch. Wanting to swallow his release, she pulled him as far as she could into her mouth. He braced himself with both hands on the tile wall of the shower. The minute she felt him touch her throat, he moved one of his hands to the back of her head and screamed out in ecstasy. She could feel him pulsing in her mouth and his juices flowing down her throat. She held him tight until he stopped cuming in her mouth. He kept his hand on the back of her head, playing with her hair. He leaned his head on his other arm, braced against the wall while she licked him dry. His breathing was returning to normal when she finally stopped licking him. He pulled her up and just held her tight.

"Honey, that was incredible. Thank you," he said into her hair. Then he rained kisses over her as he held her face with both hands. He then looked into her eyes and said, "You are incredible," and kissed the living daylights out of her.

Five minutes later, they rinsed off, got out of the shower, and got dressed. Thunder said they should get dressed until after the pizza was delivered. Then, all clothes were coming off. She agreed and borrowed one of his t-shirts and sweatpants.

"By the way," he walked out of his closet holding two items on hangers from the dry cleaners. "Here is your shirt and dress." It was the shirt that he had spilled coffee on and the dress from the accident with Tommy.

"Awww, the shirt that started it all," she smiled.

"Maybe I should keep it and put it in a display case. Enshrined forever." He gazed dreamily at her, and she smacked him on his arm.

"Uh, where's my bra that went with that dress?"

"You were wearing a bra?" He looked at her, dramatically confused.

"Yes, you pervert," she laughed.

"Huh," he said as he opened his underwear drawer and pulled out her bra. "Could this be it?"

"That's it," Isa reached up to grab it, but he lifted his arm up too high. She jumped up to get it, but it was just out of reach.

"Are you going to give it to me?" she jumped again.

"Not really. I'm enjoying the show too much to stop it." He pointed to her tits as they jiggled with every jump.

"You are crazy."

"Crazy for you, yes." he winked at her, "I think I'll keep it." He walked back into his closet, hung up the shirt and dress, and put her bra on his top shelf.

"What are you doing?"

He walked out smiling. "Keeping it. I like you better in my clothes or naked." He wiggled his eyebrows. "Besides, I'm always up for another show. Literally," he laughed as he ran out of the closet. Isa chased him into the kitchen. She was just about to catch him when the doorbell rang. Their pizza was there.

"Come on, now that we're presentable, we may as well eat it in the kitchen," he said over his shoulder. "I'll get the door. Can you get the plates?"

"On it," she said while she opened every cabinet door, looking for the plates.

Thunder headed to the front door, tipped the driver, and placed the pizza on the counter.

They talked while they ate their pizza. Isa told him about her childhood with Matteo, and Thunder told her about his with Sarah. When their bellies were full, Thunder started cleaning up.

"I'll meet you in the bedroom, *wíŋyaŋ mitáwa*, get naked," he said while he put the last couple of slices in the fridge. Isa looked at him sassily as she walked by him with her sexy walk. She knew he wouldn't be able to resist slapping her ass.

"See you there," she said over her shoulder, "I expect you to be naked too."

"You don't have to ask me twice," he grumbled.

When Thunder finished in the kitchen, he must have stripped because he was naked as the day he was born when he entered the bedroom. Isa was under the covers. He pulled up the sheet and peaked.

"You are so sexy," he said as he got under the covers and pulled her into his arms.

Cuddling with Thunder felt so right. He was running his hands over her hair and playing with her curls. She loved when he did that. It was so soothing. "Since you are such a wonderful storyteller, or so it seems by the way those kids were in awe of you today. Tell me a story," she muttered.

"Well, *wówaštelaka mitáwa*, I will tell you a story I usually tell the children at the elementary school. It is one that is told from generation to generation. It is about how the Lakota were created and placed on Mother Earth," Thunder said as he continued to stroke her hair and spoke in his soft, gravelly voice. Isa could lie like that and listen to him for hours.

"You see there were people living on mother earth, but they had done things that Wakan Tanka, the Great Spirit, did not approve of. The men did not provide for their families and the women had no sense of family. They were acting very careless. So, Wakan Tanka sent a water monster to create a terrible rainstorm. As a result, it rained for many days. People were desperate and began to climb rocks in order to escape the floods. Their effort was futile because soon all the rocks were covered with water and all the people died, except for one woman. She was carried by the great spotted eagle, Wanblee Galeshka, to the highest point of Paha Sapa, the black hills. There, the young woman and Wanblee had children together. When the flood began to dry up, Wanblee helped the woman and her children down off Paha Sapa. He told them to become Lakota Oyate. And they did, by doing so they prospered into a great nation."

"It's kind of like our Noah's Ark, but in our story, Noah saves one of every animal."

"Yes, I have heard of Noah's Ark," Thunder whispered. "I have compared and contrasted the two stories with the students."

"Oh, look at you with the teaching lingo." Isa snuggled closer.

"Well, I was a teacher on the reservation before I came here," he said wryly as Isa chuckled.

"Thunder, I'm sure you were a wonderful teacher, and that was a beautiful story. No wonder the children love you. You are a superb storyteller."

"*Pilámaya, wíŋyaŋ mitáwa*. It means so much to me that you are so interested in hearing my stories.

"What does *pilámaya* mean?" Isa asked.

"It means thank you." Thunder kissed her on her forehead.

"You're welcome. I enjoy having you as my teacher," she kissed his chest. After having a full stomach and hearing such a wonderful story, Isa relaxed in Thunder's arms and soon they were both asleep.

Chapter 38

Dinner @ Giovanni's, The Right Date This Time

THUNDER

A few nights later, Isa went to Thunder's house after work. It was becoming a routine for them. Thunder's house was bigger than her apartment and they loved taking walks along the beach and talking. Tonight, they walked to Giovanni's. It was a short walk, and they spotted George behind the bar, so they sat at the bar for a drink while they waited for a table.

"Hey, Thunder, how are you?"

"Hi George, doing good. This is Isa, my woman. Isa, I'd like you to meet George, one of my little brothers."

"Hi Isa," George greeted her with a handshake, "What can I get ya'?"

"A glass of white wine would be great." Isa smiled.

"Coming right up," he turned to Thunder and asked, "the usual?"

Thunder nodded. George walked to the other side of the bar to get their drinks.

"What's the usual?" Isa asks him.

"Soda," he smiled at her. "I don't drink."

"Is it because American Indians have a lower tolerance level for alcoholic beverages? I read that somewhere. I also read that at some powwows, alcohol is not served. Have you ever tried it?"

"When I was younger and in high school, I tried beer and whiskey. It took little to get me wasted," he said wryly. "I came home quite drunk many times. My father would sit me down the next morning and reprimand me for the error of my ways. I always had a hangover and would attempt to listen, but it didn't sink in until later when my parents were killed in a drunk driving car accident. I stopped drinking altogether."

"What happened?" Isa was shocked.

"They were driving home one night from playing BINGO at the community center on the rez when two drunk teenage kids crossed the lines on the road and crashed head on into their car." Thunder looked lost in thought as he was thinking back to that day. It felt good to tell Isa, but the hurt was still there, as if it were yesterday. "Ironic isn't it? My father always told me not to drink and drive and then years later he's killed by someone whose father probably told him the same thing."

"Thunder, I'm so sorry." Isa reached out and rubbed his back.

"So am I. They were great parents. I wish you could have met them. They would have loved you," He smiled at Isa.

"How old were you?" Isa asked.

"I was in my last year of college. The hardest part was hearing it from my sister Sarah over the phone. It was hard not being there with her. Luckily, my Uncle Spirit was there and held her while she told me. I flew home the next day."

Thunder looked up as George placed their drinks on the bar and asked, "Are you guys eating at the bar or waiting for a table?"

Thunder turned to answer George and Isa noticed him blink the sadness away and force a smile. "At a table, sorry, little brother. Maybe next time."

"No worries. If I had such a pretty lady by my side, I wouldn't want to share her either."

Isa blushed at his comment and said, "Thank you."

"No problem. I call it as I see it."

The hostess chose that moment to come over to seat them. "Right this way, Thunder."

Thunder turned to George. "Thanks, little brother. See ya' later," he said as he paid cash for the drinks and left George a large tip.

George grinned and winked at Isa.

Thunder got up and placed his hand low on her back, guiding her after the hostess to their table. He pulled her chair out for her before sitting down.

"Here's your menu," the hostess handed them out after they'd sat down, "Susan will be with you shortly."

"Thanks, Jane," Thunder said.

"Sure thing, Thunder," Jane replied.

"You come here a lot, don't you?" Isa inquired.

"Yes, I guess I do. I love their steaks. They're always cooked to perfection." Thunder smacked his lips.

"Well, what kind of steak do you suggest?" Isa asked him as she opened her menu.

"Their prime rib is my favorite. That's what I had the night I saw you here with Dan." He quirked an eyebrow at her.

"Oh. That was a terrible night, don't remind me. He kept getting closer and closer to me every minute. Maggie wanted me to go out with him because he's a friend of Ryan's. She figured the four of us would get along great. I wasn't interested in him even before I saw you here. I can't blame her for trying, though. We haven't seen each other as much since she's been with Ryan and I've been with you. I probably would have done the same thing in her shoes."

"Yes, I had the pleasure of watching him inching closer and closer to you. I wanted to throttle him. As far as Maggie goes, I know she's your friend. I could tell by how she kept giving me the runaround every time I called or came to see you. We should reschedule our double date with them soon."

"I'm sorry. Please don't blame her. I kept asking her to do that for me. Besides, she thinks you're really hot."

"She does, huh? Well, now I know her weak spot. So, if I flirt, I can get to your office easier when I come visit," he smiled charmingly at Isa.

"Don't even think about it. No flirting except with me. I don't like you using your panty dropping smile on anyone else. Unless, of course, it's okay for me to flirt with other men?" she asked innocently.

"Yeah, that's a hard NO, absolutely not."

"Okay, my warrior, I get the message. Anyway, Maggie was just trying to cheer me up by setting me up on a date."

"Why did you need cheering up? We were supposed to get together that night, remember?" Thunder looked confused.

"Since you never called on Friday, I thought I was the last number on your list of women. I figured it would take you days to reach my name in your little black book. Honestly, I went out with Dan to get my mind off you."

"My little black book." he looked at her quizzically and searched his pockets. "Nope, don't have one of those."

"Well, according to Rachel, you did," she mumbled.

"Rachel was wrong. To appease your mind, I do not have a little black book. I can assure you, so," he looked expectantly at Isa, "did it work?"

"Did what work?" Isa asked.

"Dating that guy instead of me."

"Yes, and no."

"What do you mean yes and no?" Thunder grumbled.

"Yes, because his hands kept wandering. I was too busy focusing on where his hands would end up next to think about anything else. No, because you were here. Once you got here, all I could think about was you." Isa reached out and grabbed his hand.

"That's it?"

"What do you mean, 'that's it'? You want me to tell you I was thinking about you every waking moment?" Isa chuckled and batted her eyelashes at him.

"I'm serious, Isa. I thought about you night and day. Did you think about me at all? Other than to think about me with other women and while you were with other men. Were you comparing me to them?" Thunder spoke through gritted teeth.

"Yes, Thunder, I thought about you all the time. But no, I wasn't comparing you," Isa noticed his jaw muscles relax. "Especially after I saw you here. You looked angry to see me with another man. By the time I got over the shock of seeing you, I was going to go talk to you. Then you sat at the table with Joseph and looked at me like I was a piece of trash. That hurt. As if that wasn't enough, you started flirting with the waitress. I was devastated." Isa sighed.

"I'm sorry I hurt you. I was not pleased with you at that moment, but what I did was out of line," he murmured and rubbed his thumb over the top of her hand. He could see her nipples hardening.

"As for the waitress," Thunder continued, "I was trying to make you jealous. And if I say so myself, it worked. But now," he flashed her his panty dropping smile, "I only want to flirt with you."

Isa blushed, then looked at their waitress and her eyes widened.

"Hey handsome, what'll it be tonight?"

Thunder looked up when he heard her voice. Oh shit. It was Kelly, the waitress from that night. Thunder thought, *I better make some introductions fast.*

"Kelly, this is Isa, my girlfriend." He squeezed Isa's hand. "Isa...Kelly."

"Nice to meet ya," Kelly rolled her eyes and said sarcastically while she looked at Isa, "What do you want?"

"Hi Kelly. Nice to meet you too. I'll have the prime rib, medium please. Thunder says it's excellent." She tried to make small talk.

"Well, he should know. He eats it at least twice a week, right, big guy?" Kelly said as she bumped Thunder with her hip. "I guess he needs it to keep those great bulging muscles of his in such good shape, right, honey?" She winked at him.

Can anyone say awkward? Thunder forced a smile and said, "Ah, thanks, Kelly. I'll have the same. Please."

"Sure thing, big guy, coming right up," she wrote the order down on her pad and walked away.

Thunder stayed focused on Isa, and she looked mad. Maybe they should have gone somewhere else.

"You both seem to know each other well." She snapped and withdrew her hand from his, looking around the room, not making eye contact with him.

"*Wiŋyaŋ mitáwa*, look at me please," he pleaded with her, "I am sorry if I upset you. Kelly and I know each other because I do come here a lot. Usually, I sit at the bar and talk to George. She has approached me several times, but nothing has ever happened between us. I know George has a crush on her. He's my little brother, so I would never go after her." Thunder's voice softened. "Isa, look at me, honey." Finally, Isa looked up into his eyes. "I only want you in my life. Why else would I have bent over backwards to get a date with you?" Thunder could see her face softening as her anger melted away.

"No other woman has ever meant as much to me as you do. It is you and only you who I want." He placed his left hand on the table and turned it upside down.

Isa couldn't resist the plea in his eyes and placed her hand in his. "No, I'm sorry. I guess I get a little jealous. It won't happen again."

"It's okay, honey, just know that I am yours and you are mine. There's no one else."

"Ok," Isa sighs and changed the topic. "Tell me about George? You keep referring to him as your little brother."

"George was one of the runaway teens from the shelter who used to come in on Friday for storytelling. While he worked for me, we became close and I became his mentor. After he turned eighteen, he had to leave the shelter and had nowhere to go, so he came to live with me. When he wasn't working for me, he was busing tables or washing dishes here. When he turned twenty-one, I helped him pay for bartending school and he became one of their full-time bartenders. A few months ago, after working a lot of hours, he could finally get his own apartment."

"Wow, what a great young man." Isa mumbled, "Did he live with you all that time?"

"He did. It was nice to have a roommate, though I rarely saw him since he worked all the time. I also never charged him rent so he could save up his money." Thunder sipped his soda and looked at George.

"That was very generous of you."

"George is a runaway teen success story. Not all teens at the runaway shelter get out of their situations like George. He worked hard to achieve his goals every step of the way. He just needed a little extra support. I'm glad I was there to give it to him." Thunder stated, "Now, during the day, he mentors the kids that are currently living at the shelter and at night he tends bar."

"Tell me about your family." Thunder wanted to know more about Isa.

"Well, I only have one brother, Matteo. He is married to Gaby and they have two little girls, Emmy and Lucy. Which you have already met?" Isa grinned, "Which, by the way, Lucy still remembers that you said she could do your hair."

"I agreed to that, didn't I?" Thunder said wryly.

"Yup, and she is still waiting for you to make your hair appointment." Isa said seriously.

"Has she asked about that?" Thunder was surprised.

"She absolutely has. Every time I talk to her, she asks about the man with the long, pretty hair she wants to braid."

"Well," Thunder sighs, "I guess you will have to bring me to her for my hairdo. It's all good as long as she doesn't cut it." Thunder winced.

"I promise, we won't let her near any scissors and I'll stay with you the whole time." she winked.

"Ok, so I've met your mom, but what about your dad?"

"My dad died from cancer a few years ago." Isa looked vacantly at her plate.

"I'm so sorry," Thunder squeezed her hand.

"He had smoked cigarettes since he was sixteen. He tried to quit several times, but just couldn't do it."

"It is a hard habit to break," Thunder sighed. "Many of my friends on the rez smoke. It never interested me."

"Tell me about your sister? She seems like a wonderful mom. I mean, Tommy is such a great kid," Isa stated.

"Order's up," Kelly announced as she placed Thunder's plate in front of him and slid Isa's to her. Had Isa not put her hand up to stop the plate, it would've wound up on her lap. Thunder glared at Kelly, but she just shrugged it off and walked away.

"Sorry about that," Thunder apologized for Kelly's behavior.

"Don't worry," Isa lifted her shoulder, "she's just jealous because I get to take you home."

"My sister Sarah is like my mom, very caring and loving. I was so happy when she moved her family here. It was hard when I was living here without them. It would be great to take you to her house so you could officially meet her. Sarah, Grayhorse, and Tommy live in Davie on a few acres on land where they raise cattle and train horses. You've met and talked to Grayhorse and Tommy."

"I like Tommy." Isa nodded. "When I saw him at the park, I apologized again. He is such a sweet boy. Then he met Emmy, and they both went to play on the monkey bars with his friend Jaime."

"Tommy is a good kid. His parents have done a good job with him. He'll be a great big brother."

"Oh, is your sister pregnant?"

"Yes," he beamed, "She's three months pregnant. I'm hoping for a sweet little girl just like her momma."

Isa smiled, "Little girls are so cute, but they can be clever and sneaky sometimes, too. Some days, Emmy and Lucy give me a run for my money. Emmy is seven and Lucy is five. They can be quite a handful sometimes. But they have their sweet moments. As Grayhorse found out when Lucy wrapped him around her little finger with 'Lucy's Hair Salon'," she laughed, "Was he really mad?"

"Grayhorse? No, he loves kids. But he said I was going to the salon next time." He grinned. "He made me drive home so he could take out all the braids before Sarah saw him. Didn't matter though, cause Tommy took photos and a video so his mom could see his dad's spa experience."

"Oh my God, that's funny," Isa said as she covered her mouth to not laugh too loud.

"Yep, Sarah will give him shit for a long time," Thunder chuckled.

"You must be very close to your sister?"

"I am. She's all I've got left of my immediate family," Thunder thought, "Well, then I count her family, Uncle Spirit's family, and my shelter kids."

"That's great. I'm so happy for you all. Family means everything, whether it's immediate or adoptive." Isa smiled.

"I agree."

"So, about my dress in your closet. I should probably take it home?" Isa inquired.

"Why do you want to take it home? You spend a lot of time at my house, you might need it one day to go to work. It's been dry cleaned, and the stains came out." He acted put out as he placed his hand over his heart and said, "Woman, you wound me. Besides, it looks good in my closet next to my clothes. Your clothes are the only women's clothes I need in my closet."

"Ha, ha, ha," Isa said sarcastically. "I'm sure you've had other women's clothes in your closet." Isa put her hand up as she watched Thunder shaking his head no. "Don't deny it, but I don't want to talk about it. Let me get through a pleasant evening imagining you by yourself pining for me alone in your bedroom for...How old are you, anyway?"

"Thirty-two."

"Pining for me alone in your room for thirty-two years." Isa sighed.

He chuckled at her dramatic flair. "Isa, honey, that's a long time to be pining. I must have been a very smart baby to know to wait for you. Besides, I've never had other women's clothes in my closet because the only woman I've brought to my house is you."

"Really, not Rachel?"

"Nope, my house is sacred. I went to her apartment or the fully furnished apartment I rented before I bought my house. And before you ask, no one has slept in my bed other than you. That includes the bed in my house and the apartment above the center."

"Really?"

"Yep, really."

"I'm glad. And just so you know, no one has slept in my bed except you. When I dumped Keith, I also dumped that bed and bought myself a new one." She smiled at him.

"Well, glad that's settled. I would like to take you to Sarah's house sometime, maybe this weekend."

"Sure, I'd love to see them again."

Thunder and Isa relaxed and continued to talk about each other's families. The dinner was absolutely delicious and after Kelly accepted the fact that Isa was his girlfriend—she left them alone and stopped flirting with Thunder. When they finished their meal, Thunder paid and left a generous tip. They waved bye to George and walked back to Thunder's house. It was a beautiful clear night with a light breeze coming off the ocean.

Thunder noticed Isa crossed her arms and thought she might be cold. He put his arm around her shoulder and pulled her closer to his body heat as they strolled along the busy sidewalk.

Fort Lauderdale at night always seemed crowded, especially now that they'd renovated the entire beachfront area. Every corner had either a restaurant, bar, or dance club. The city had collectively decided it was time to clean up the beach area, since they no longer advertised specifically for the room bashing college student spring breakers. In order to compete with South Beach in Miami, home of the rich and famous, Fort Lauderdale had to up their game and showcase their beautiful hotels and beaches while focusing more on attracting families looking for a peaceful, yet fun vacation spot.

Chapter 39

Time to Think about the Knife Later

THUNDER

W hen Thunder and Isa reached his house, she went to the bedroom while he locked up the house and set the alarm.

Every time he set the alarm here or at the center, he thought about the missing knife. He knew he had locked up and set the alarm that night. It was a ritual he always performed daily. Meaning the knife had to have been stolen during the event. But that wasn't possible. He did inventory the next day, and the knife was there.

That meant someone stole it after the opening, either a guest or someone who knew the alarm code or could override it because they didn't break any windows. Only a handful of people knew the alarm code: Sarah, Grayhorse, Rachel, Mark, and himself.

He knew Sarah and Grayhorse would never steal from him. That left the Grayfeathers, Rachel and Mark. George and Mary only worked from eleven to two, so they never opened or closed the center plus, he never gave them the alarm code.

He asked Rachel and Mark, and they had seen nothing. Could one of them be lying to him? When he'd asked Rachel if she was in trouble and needed money, she looked severely offended. She'd told him she would never take it and sell it. She looked at him like he had lost his mind. So, if they didn't take it, then who did?

That left either someone who attended the opening and came back or someone who broke in. A professional thief would have taken some of the jewelry, which he could easily slip into his pockets. Whoever took it was after that piece specifically because nothing else was taken. But why? The only name that kept popping up in his head was Joseph. He always needed money, and he came into town the same day as the robbery.

Thunder was tossing all these thoughts around in his mind as he headed toward his bedroom. Stepping into his bedroom, he came to a complete stop. His beautiful *wíŋyaŋ mitáwa* was draped on his bed, barely clothed in a see-through black teddy. His throat went dry. He had to take a couple of deep breaths. *Holy shit.*

"Well, are you coming over here, or do you need an invitation?" She smiled seductively at him. The wine she drank at dinner must have helped to relax her.

He still had not moved from his spot by the door. He couldn't stop staring at her. She was offering herself to him, and that was so special. He must've waited too long because Isa got up. He put his hands up to stop her.

"No, *wíŋyaŋ mitáwa*, no need to get up. I'm on my way. I just wanted to remember this moment forever. You look so fucking beautiful." He groaned. His pants became very uncomfortable as he felt himself hardening. Her teddy had done its job effectively.

Isa smiled at him and said, "I can see that. You're so hard, it must hurt. Why don't you bring it over here so I can kiss it and make it better?"

"Isa, keep talking like that and I will not make it to the bed." He grumbled as he watched her bite her lip and lower her left strap.

He walked toward her and ran a finger under the right strap of her teddy.

"This is quite nice. Did you have it on all day?" He ran his finger over her nipple. He stroked it in a circular motion until it became hard. Then ran his finger down to her pussy. She was already wet for him.

"I did," she said breathlessly.

He looked back up at her face. "I see you are ready for me."

She moaned when he unsnapped the buttons on the bottom and inserted the tip of his finger in her pussy, "I am ready. I thought of you all day while I wore this."

He put one knee on the bed while placing the palm of his right hand against her clit and sliding his fingers all the way into her pussy to feel her wetness.

Isa arched up and closed her eyes. Thunder's touch was pure sweet torture. She moaned and Thunder caught it in his mouth. Their kiss started out tender but quickly became explosive. Isa soon climaxed. Thunder felt her muscles tighten round his fingers and felt her release.

"That was one, *wíŋyaŋ mitáwa*. I promise to give you many more before the night is over," Thunder spoke huskily against her mouth.

He raised himself up, leaving one knee still on the bed, and he brought his hand over her belly to her breasts.

"You look so sexy in this black teddy, but I want to see you naked."

Isa was having a hard time catching her breath. No other man had ever made her climax so quickly.

Thunder got on the bed and straddled her. Both his hands were squeezing and rubbing her breasts through the material. Her nipples getting instantly hard from the abrasiveness of the material. Thunder knew he was driving her crazy from the sounds coming out of her mouth and her body movements. He slowly slipped his hands under the straps and brought them down past her shoulders, elbows, and finally, her hands. His mouth only leaving her breast long enough for the lace to be removed. He then voraciously licked and sucked each breast while she held his head in place and gyrated against him.

Thunder released her breasts and trailed wet kisses down her belly. He kissed every inch of her that was revealed to him as he stripped her of the teddy. When he reached the spot between her legs, he licked her pussy, but continued down her legs. He fully intended to return to her pussy, but first he had to get rid of the teddy. He scooted down the bed and kissed her thighs, knees, and calves before he tossed her teddy onto the floor.

When he finished, he sat up straight and looked at Isa. She was writhing on the bed and looked fully aroused. He smirked to himself, thinking, *Let the games begin.*

He grabbed her thighs and put them over his shoulders. Clasping her hips as he ravaged her pussy with his tongue. She couldn't move away from his mouth because he held her tightly so he could devour her. Isa was so out of control she squeezed her hands into fists, gathering the bed sheet.

She screamed, "Thunder now, please.".

Her wish was his command. He knew she was close to climaxing, so he drove his tongue deeper into her passage and moved his right hand just enough to pinch her clit. She exploded into his mouth. He licked her up and slowly laid her legs back down onto the mattress and kissed his way up to her neck.

"That was two, *wíŋyaŋ mitáwa*, but I can't control myself any longer," he whispered against her neck. "You are driving me wild. I love the way your body responds to my touch," he said as he slowly slid inside her, "AAhhh Isa, you feel so warm, good and tight."

Thunder thrusted wildly. Isa wrapped her legs around him and followed his lead. He felt her muscles tighten again, and they both climaxed together.

"Unh, Isa, they always say the third time is the charm," he said before he dropped on top of her.

Realizing he must be crushing her, he shifted his weight onto his elbows. He kissed her neck and looked into her eyes, then gently kissed her lips and smirked before saying, "*wíŋyaŋ mitáwa*, I liked your teddy bear. You can wear it for me anytime. It is an enjoyable diversion from my problems."

"I'm glad you liked it. I was nervous about wearing it."

"Never be nervous with me. You have a beautiful body."

"So do you."

Thunder laughed throatily and rolled over, taking her with him. "Thank you. Now let's get some sleep. Suddenly, I'm very exhausted." He slid behind her and held her tight.

Isa pulled the covers over them and backed up into Thunder. She loved when he spooned her.

"What problems?" Isa asked, remembering what Thunder said earlier.

"Huh?"

"What problems? You said I distracted you from your problems?" Isa repeated.

"Oh, that. I have lost the knife my grandfather gave me, which dates back to the 1800s. No one seems to know what happened to it. Rachel says she hasn't seen it since the night of the opening," he sighed heavily.

"Was it for sale? Could someone have bought it?"

"No, it wasn't for sale. Someone would've had to take it out of the display case. We hoped maybe they took it out to look at it and placed it down somewhere else. But now we've looked everywhere and still no knife. I even checked in the warehouse."

"Have you filed a police report and declared it stolen?"

"I suppose I should have. I just kept hoping it would turn up. We've been so busy I really thought one of us misplaced it. I don't enjoy thinking that someone purposely stole it from me. I also need to tell the tribal council. They will be very disappointed and upset with me. I'm going to keep looking for it this week. But if it doesn't turn up, then I will have to call Uncle Spirit and set up a meeting with the tribal council, as well as file a police report."

"I can't believe anyone would steal from the cultural center."

"I suppose theft is not uncommon anywhere."

"Yeah, I guess," Isa yawned.

"Don't worry. Go to sleep, it's getting late," he kissed her neck.

"Goodnight, Thunder."

"Goodnight, *wíŋyaŋ mitáwa.*"

Thunder wanted to tell her he loved her, but he didn't want to frighten her away. She had said she wanted to go slow. If he told her now that he loved her and wanted to spend the rest of his life with her, she might run from him and that was a risk he wasn't willing to take. Not now when everything in their relationship was so perfect. He felt content every moment he spent with her.

She filled his days and nights with so much happiness, he couldn't risk losing her. When the time was right and he felt she was ready to hear the words, he would tell her. For now, he would show her with his actions, but keep the words to himself.

Chapter 40

Save a Horse, Ride a Cowboy...Well, Ride a Horse Anyway

THUNDER

The rest of the week passed by quickly. Thunder and Isa went to work during the day, ate dinner together and slept in each other's arms every night.

On Saturday, Thunder wanted to do something special for Isa. He sat up on his elbow and looked at her as she was waking up.

"Good morning," he murmured as he kissed her neck.

"Good morning."

"What do you want to do today? I want to spend the day with you." He grinned. "Outside of bed, that is. So, if you could do anything you wanted, what would it be?"

Isa closed her eyes and said, "Horseback riding. I've been wanting to do that for a while now. When I was young, my friend Shelly's mom used to take us a few times a year. My mom wasn't too thrilled because she was afraid I would get hurt, so when Shelly moved away, I could never go again."

"*Han, wíŋyaŋ mitáwa*," He looked at her delightedly, "I can certainly do that for you. When was the last time you rode a horse?"

"When I was ten," Isa winced. "I really don't remember how to sit on one now."

He kissed her one more time, then got off the bed and pulled her up with him.

"*Úwo*, we will shower together," he said as they walked into his bathroom. "My sister has a ranch and some horses, but her horses have a lot more spirit than my friend Skip's horses. So, we'll go to Skip's ranch. Then we can ride over to Sarah's and you can meet her. I'll have Grayhorse, my brother-in-law, drop off *Sapa*, my stallion, over there for me."

"Won't that be an inconvenience to take your horse over there?"

"No," he said over his shoulder as he tested the temperature of the water, "they are next-door neighbors."

Isa followed Thunder into the shower. They bathed each other and made love again. They could hardly keep their hands off each other.

"I will leave you to finish while I go call Skip about going over there." He kissed her gently on the lips and walked out of the shower.

Thunder grabbed a towel and began drying off. Feeling as if he was being watched, he turned around and saw Isa staring at his body.

"Isa honey, if you don't stop staring, we will never leave." Thunder growled at her as his cock rose from her attention.

"Sorry," Isa jumped, "okay, I'm working on it."

Thunder chuckled and wrapped the towel around his waist. Leaving the door partially open as he walked out to the bedroom to get his phone.

Thunder watched Isa step out of the shower and dry herself off. Her bottle of lotion was sitting on the counter and she rubbed it on her body slowly, not knowing the effect she was having on Thunder.

Thunder was in the bedroom, watching her through the bathroom mirror. He was really loving mirrors. Who knew mirrors could be so enjoyable to watch? He had a clear view of her rubbing lotion on her soft, beautiful body. She placed her foot on the counter and was applying it to her legs.

Skip had just answered the phone when he saw what she was doing. "Skip, *hau*, I will stop by with my woman to do some riding. Can you saddle up a horse for her? Can you also call Grayhorse and ask him to bring *Sapa* to you?"

"Thunder, hi, sure. I'll call Grayhorse and saddle up Annabelle for the lady. How was your openin'? Sorry I couldn't make it. Minnie wasn't feelin' too good."

Thunder missed most of Skip's reply. He was too busy watching Isa. He thought Skip said something about Minnie being sick. "Is she okay?"

"Yeah, just a headache. When are ya' comin'?"

"In about twe...," he stopped mid sentence. Isa had applied the lotion to her stomach. "Make that an hour."

Isa looked up into the mirror and saw Thunder watching her from the bedroom, licking his lips. He was on the phone, but it didn't seem as if he was listening to whoever was on the other end. As his eyes darkened with desire as he watched her.

"Thunder, ya' there?" asked Skip.

"*Haŋ*, I'll see you in about an hour. I have to go."

Thunder barely heard Skip say goodbye when he hung up his phone and dropped it on the bed. He walked over to Isa, never taking his eyes off her as he came up behind her and cupped her breasts. Isa released a heavy sigh.

"*Wíŋyaŋ mitáwa*, at the rate we are going, you'll be riding me, not a horse," he murmured into her neck.

Thunder spun her around and sat her up on the counter. He pulled her to the edge and felt her to see if she was wet. She was soaked. He entered her quickly, and they rode into ecstasy together. Each time they made love, he felt himself losing more of his independence and becoming one. When they both finally relaxed their breathing, he held her head in his hands and looked into her eyes. He gave her a gentle kiss, and in that moment, he knew she had taken his heart.

"You can borrow my buckskin shirt. I will follow you to your house so you can change. You will need to be wearing some jeans instead of my shirt or your work clothes to ride a horse," he said as he helped her off the counter. Then he grinned and walked away, saying over his shoulder. "Oh, and stay away from that lotion or lock the door behind me, woman, or else we will never leave."

Isa shut the door behind him. Hanging on the back of the door was his shirt. He put it there when she was taking a shower. She hugged it against herself for a few minutes before she put it on.

"Ready whenever you are," she said as she walked out of the bedroom. Thunder was sitting on the couch. He got up and walked over to her.

"Let's go then." He smiled. He never tired of seeing her in his clothes, especially that shirt.

As she walked by Thunder, he ran his hand down her back and squeezed her bottom.

"Are you naked under my shirt?" Thunder growled.

Thunder startled her, and she jumped. "Yes, remember I wore the teddy all day. I didn't want to put it back on, so I'll put on underwear when we get to my house."

"Oh, honey," Thunder moaned, running his hands up her ass and trying to pull her against him.

"None of that, mister," Isa turned around and wagged her finger at him, "you promised me a horse ride and I intend to get one."

"You would get a horse. A fine tall dark stallion who would be more than happy to service you." He winked at her as he dove towards her.

Isa swerved out of his reach and ran out the door yelling, "I bet you would, but you'd have to catch me first."

He stood up straight and watched her run outside. Grinning, he decided not to catch her. He mumbled to himself, "Oh Isa, it's a good thing you really want to ride a horse today. What was I thinking when we could have stayed in bed?"

Thunder followed her home. She didn't live very far from the center. He waited for her in the living room while she walked into her bedroom to change. She must've remembered his earlier warning about closing doors, because as soon as she entered her bedroom, she closed the door.

Thunder chuckled to himself and looked around for something to keep his mind occupied. All his thoughts kept turning towards her naked in the other room. *What had she done to him?* He was like a horny teenage boy who couldn't control himself enough to keep his hands off her. All he could concentrate on was pleasuring her until she screamed his name as she climaxed. Needing a distraction, he walked around the living room and saw some black and white photos of old looking buildings. He assumed they were of some place in Cuba. One photo looked intriguingly like our U.S. Capitol building, but in a different setting.

Fifteen minutes later, when she opened the door, he was sprawled out on her couch drinking a glass of water.

"I hope you don't mind that I got something to drink?" Thunder lifted the glass toward her.

"Nope, I'm glad you made yourself at home." Isa answered, "it was rude of me not to ask if you were thirsty."

"No worries. Are you ready?" he stood.

"Yep, as ready as I'll ever be."

He walked over to the wall with the photos and pointed at them. "Are these photos of Cuba?"

"Yes, as you can see, our capitol building is a replica of the one here."

"Do you wish you could go there?" Thunder asked curiously.

"Yes, very much. And I will someday when it is not communistic. I hope."

He noticed Isa's eyes becoming sad at her last comment, so he changed the subject. Today was about her doing something fun for herself.

"Come, let's enjoy our day together. I told Skip we would be there in an hour and we're running late." He walked toward her and kissed her forehead.

"And whose fault is that?" she smirked at him.

"Ahh, well, you could have stopped me."

"Right," she laughed, "but I didn't really want to."

"I'm glad you didn't," he said as he guided her out the door.

They drove to the city of Davie. The one place in Broward County that still had cowboys, ranches, and rodeos. They turned at the entrance to the 'Double M Horse Ranch', then continued down a long driveway. Thunder pulled up to a modest ranch style home with a front porch and parked his truck.

"You'll like Skip and Minnie. They're really nice," he said as he got out, walked around to Isa's door, and opened it for her. He helped her down from his truck.

"Thank you." Isa looked up and saw a man and woman coming from the house.

"You're welcome." He turned around and guided her to the front porch.

Chapter 41

Horseback Riding Lesson

THUNDER

"Hey Thunder, bin waitin' fer ya', got Sapa n' Annabelle saddl'd n'ready. Who's the purdy li'l lady?"

"*Hau* Skip, this is Isa Gonzalez, my woman. Isa this is Skip Morris and his wife Minnie. They own this horse ranch."

Skip came down from the porch to shake hands with Isa. Minnie waved hello and said, "I'll see you two later. I have something in the oven, and I don't want it to burn. It was nice meeting you, Isa. Come up into the house after your ride."

Isa smiled and said, "Nice meeting you as well."

"So, what made ya' decide ta' com' out 'ere today? Ya' don' usually com' by on Saturdays 'nless yur trainin' a horse." Skip glanced between Isa and Thunder.

"Isa wanted to go horseback riding, so I thought to bring her here, since I'm familiar with all the horses. Besides, you have more tame ones than Sarah."

"Well, seein' as ya' broke 'em all in, I reckon it makes sense," Skip said as he walked them toward the stables.

Thunder grabbed Isa's hand and gave it a squeeze. She pulled him toward her and he bent down.

"What does he mean by, since you broke them all in?" Isa whispered in his ear,

"Lakota's are good with horses. On Saturdays and Mondays, I come by and train Skip's horses. I have been doing it for about two years now. But he is exaggerating. I have not broken them all in. Grayhorse has been doing it lately."

Isa looked at the two horses that were saddled outside the stable and they looked huge.

Isa looked at him strangely and stopped walking, pulling him back.

"Ahh, Thunder, I haven't ridden a horse since I was ten. Maybe this wasn't such a good idea."

Thunder shot her that roguish grin she loved.

"*Wíŋyaŋ mitáwa*, I would let nothing happen to you. Don't worry, I have ridden all these horses. I will protect you from any danger. I promise. You will ride Annabelle. She's very tame."

Thunder was still challenging her with his gaze when Skip hollered, "Are ya'll gonna stare at each other all day or ride a horse?"

They both laughed and walked over to Skip.

"Go anywhere ya' want," he said, "ya' know where all the waterin' holes are. Have fun, kids." Skip handed the reins over to Thunder.

Thunder nodded and turned to Isa.

"Isa, meet Annabelle," Thunder said as he smiled at Annabelle and ran his hand from her mane to her neck.

"I'm riding my horse, *Sapa*. They are friends, so she will follow him wherever he goes. Here are a few important tips to remember. Always approach a horse from the left side and from the front, if possible. Speak softly when approaching, especially from behind, to let them know of your presence. It is best to approach at an angle, never directly from the rear. You don't want to startle them and get kicked. Now come over here and pet Annabelle so she can see you and get to know you before you get on. You might also want to whisper some kind words to her."

"Okay," Isa said as she moved closer to Annabelle and stroked her mane, "Hi Annabelle, I'm Isa. I hope you will be ok with me riding you today. You are so strong and beautiful." Isa laughed when Annabelle neighed at her.

"That's good." Thunder complemented her, "She's responding to your voice and touch. Now let me explain how you will get on. Stay on the left side of Annabelle. Take the reins in your left hand and put your left foot in the stirrup. Lay your right hand on the saddle for support and stand up in the left stirrup. Then swing your right leg over the horse and gently sit down on the saddle. After you are seated, put your right foot in the stirrup on the right side of the horse. You can hold the pummel," he pointed to the pummel, "to adjust yourself on the saddle and hold the reins with both hands. Let's try it so I can help you."

Isa did as he instructed. Thunder put his hand on her waist after giving her a boost onto Annabelle. She felt a little strange being so high above the ground, but was comfortable.

"How are you doing up there?" he asked her.

"Fine, so far, but what about when Annabelle moves?"

"Don't worry, *wówaštelaka mitáwa*, I won't let you fall," Thunder chuckled.

Isa noticed Thunder had called her something different in Lakota. It wasn't what he usually called her. She was about to ask him what it meant, but then he started giving her instructions about riding.

"If you want to stop, pull the reins back gently and say 'whoa'. Don't pull back on the reins too hard because the bit in Annabelle's mouth will hurt her and she will get angry. Now, hold on to the reins like this, and try to relax. If you pull the reins to the left, Annabelle will turn left, and likewise if you pull the reins to the right, she'll go right. There are four different gaits for a horse. They can walk, trot, canter, and gallop. First, we'll start with the walk so you can get accustomed to her." Thunder walked over to *Sapa* and stroked his mane, neck, and nose as he whispered something to him before he gracefully mounted him with little to no effort and gathered the reins.

Isa watched Thunder. He looked so perfect sitting on top of his horse. She didn't know why he called him *Sapa*. Sapo in Spanish meant toad. She would have to ask him later. Thunder maneuvered *Sapa* in front of Annabelle.

"Isa, try moving the reins slowly to the right. Just like that. See how Annabelle responds?" Annabelle moved to the right.

"Yes," Isa cheered, "it just seems too easy."

"It is. Since you haven't been on a horse in a long time, the fastest we will go is a trot. We will save the cantering and galloping for another time. I don't want you to get scared or hurt yourself." Thunder kept turning around to watch her. She was smiling and seemed to have a good time.

"Just relax because a horse can always sense what their rider is feeling. If you are tense, then they will be tense. Also, don't squeeze Annabelle with your legs too hard or she'll come to a stop. Try to follow the rhythm of your horse and the ride will go smoothly. If you resist Annabelle's motions, then your bottom will be very sore tomorrow. Relaxing your thighs allows your heels to become aligned with your hips and you will have better stability. It is best to sit up straight with your chest out and maintain some of your weight on your legs, not just your behind. Keep your ankles in and your toes out and grip Annabelle with your lower leg, like this. I know that's a lot. Are you ready to leave this yard and go on a trail?"

"Alright, let's go. I'm as ready as I'll ever be," Isa announced excitedly.

"You're doing great. Continue to relax and breathe. Look around you. It is a beautiful day for a ride. We'll continue to walk at this pace since you haven't been on a horse for a long time. Annabelle is very gentle. She won't burst into a gallop."

Thunder led the way on a path into the woods. *Sapa* was a beautiful black stallion. Thunder looked absolutely sexy and powerful while he rode. He rode as if he was one with the stallion. His hair was wild and blowing back in the wind. He rode *Sapa* with such grace and strength, like a Lakota warrior. He then slowed down and let Annabelle catch up to him. Isa had a very wide smile on her face.

"Well, how does it feel, *wówaštelaka mitáwa*?"

"I feel like I could ride forever." Isa was beaming. "I feel so free and alive. I'm still a little scared, but it's so much fun. The last time I was on a horse with my friend, we were on a trail. When the guide told us to stop at a nearby pond, I stayed on the horse. The horse leaned so far down to drink, I almost fell into the pond."

"You were probably too small to fit on the horse."

"Yes, you're right," Isa laughed, "I weighed maybe fifty lbs."

Thunder looked tenderly at her and nodded at what she had said. Now that she was more comfortable on Annabelle, they rode side by side. They rode in silence for a long time. Thunder thinking about how lovely her facial expressions were every time she saw something that caught her attention. Whether it was a beautiful flower or a bird flying overhead.

"I can't believe we are still in Broward County."

"Yep, this is the only area around here that I know of that has this much land and ranches." Thunder said.

"It is so beautiful and peaceful here," she gaped in awe at the landscape.

"*Han*, are you not glad you got to do something for yourself today? Especially with such a strong, sexy guide?" He grinned at her.

"Well, the riding is fun and worth it. But the guide," she sighed, "I don't know," she shrugged her shoulders.

Thunder rode over to her and with one quick pull, he lifted her right off her horse and settled her onto his lap, facing him.

"Ah, what are you doing?" Isa screamed, "Oh my god? Don't drop me!"

"I won't drop you," Thunder laughed. "What was it you said about that guide?" He raised an eyebrow at her.

"Well, I know he can ride slow, a little boring, but can he gallop?" She challenged.

"You want to gallop, huh," he smiled at her, "Honey, your guide can do anything with you. Hold tight!" Thunder said right before he kicked *Sapa* in his hand quarters and they took off.

"Oh my God, Thunder, don't let me fall!" Isa screamed as Thunder laughed. She had plastered her body to his until there was no space between them. He held her tightly against him with one hand while he held the reins with the other. Isa's bouncing body was causing his cock to stiffen quickly.

"Ah, Thunder," she whispered. "Maybe this wasn't such a good idea." She groaned, and he felt her mouth on his neck while she licked and sucked. He was so turned on. Thunder slowed down *Sapa*.

"So, what was that you said about your guide?" he growled.

"Oh, I said he was wonderful, intelligent, handsome, strong, sexy. Did I say wonderful yet?" Isa asked as she looked into his eyes. Thunder smiled at her, showing all his perfectly white teeth.

"That is what I thought you said. Never forget that woman." Thunder grinned.

Thunder slowed *Sapa* to a walk and kissed her tenderly. Isa returned his kisses. Her tongue doing a very seductive dance with his.

He stopped kissing Isa and groaned, "Woman, what you do to me? How about we go get something to eat, then we'll stop by Sarah's?"

"That sounds like a wonderful idea," said Isa as he heard her stomach grumble. "I guess I hadn't thought of food until right now. I am a little hungry."

"*Han*, I am hungry also but for something else," he groaned in a husky voice and wrapped the reins around the pummel. He'd ridden *Sapa* many times without reins. When they rode together, it was as if they were one. He could guide him with just his legs. *Sapa* was a magnificent horse. Thunder's mouth traveled to her lips and his hands to her breasts. He quickly realized he'd better stop. Having sex on a horse was a lot harder than just groping each other. He released her breasts and hugged her tight. Then reached past her to unwrap and grab the reins as they rode back to the ranch. Annabelle followed *Sapa*.

"Why do you call him *Sapa*?"

"His full name is *Paha Sapa* which means Black Hills. But over the years, I've shortened it to *Sapa*."

"Well, that makes sense," she laughed, "I couldn't figure it out because in spanish 'sapa' means a female toad and clearly he is not female or a toad."

"No," Thunder chuckled, "I just wanted reminders of my home and culture. I miss seeing the Black Hills and Badlands."

When they reached the ranch, Thunder got down first and put his hands on Isa's waist to help her down. He made sure her body slid slowly against his all the way down. When her feet touched the ground, he braced himself with his legs apart so he could tuck her between his legs. Thunder bent down and kissed her as his hands cupped her bottom and they were both moving together as one.

"Thunder, somebody's going to catch us," Isa murmured against his lips.

"Only Skip, or one of his ranch hands, and they know better than to stick around and watch. But you are right, I can wait until I get you home, naked under me." Isa blushed.

Thunder led the horses back into the stable and handed the reins to one of the local teenage boys Skip had hired to help with the horses. He turned around and led her toward the house.

"Let's say goodbye to Skip and Minnie and we will be on our way." Thunder knocked on the door and stepped in. "Skip, Minnie?" He called out, "we're leaving now."

Minnie poked her head out of the kitchen door.

"Oh, you can't leave just yet. I will finish making my apple pie and lunch in two minutes. Isa, come, sit in the kitchen with me until it's ready. Thunder, you can go get Skip for me. He's in the barn." Minnie went back into the kitchen.

"*Han*, I'll go find him. Is this okay with you?" He asked Isa quietly.

"Yeah." Isa gave him a quick kiss on the lips. "I'll be in the kitchen. Besides, I'm starving and I haven't had homemade apple pie in ages."

Thunder gave her another quick peck on the lips and patted her on the ass before she turned to walk to the kitchen. Thunder left the house and walked to the barn.

"Skip, are you in here? Minnie wants you to come to the house. She made us lunch and an apple pie. Pie's almost ready. You know how fussy she is about her hot out of the oven apple pies."

"Yeah, ya' don' ave ta' tell me 'bout it. How's yur ride? She's a mighty purty lady. Where'd ya' meet 'er?"

Thunder smiled at Skip's choice of words. "She designed some brochures for the opening. She is quite a woman."

"Seems nice too. Seems ta' 've caught yur attention."

"You could say that. Let's go up to the house. I don't want Minnie filling Isa's head with all of my adventures. If you know what I mean."

"Hah, I sure do. But my Minnie likes ya'. Sh'll paint ya' 'n such a good light. Heck, Isa prably won't b'lieve 'er", Skip grinned at him and slapped him on the back. Skip loved Thunder like a son and just wanted to see him happy.

*** *Isa* ***

"Have a seat, Isa. Would you like some water?" Minnie asked.

"Yes, please. Can I help you with anything?"

"No, Isa, you are a guest in my home." Minnie admonished and gave her a glass of water.

"So, how long have you known Thunder?" Minnie asked inquisitively.

"A few weeks. I met him when he came to the ad agency where I work. He needed some brochures and an ad campaign for his Red Path Exhibit. We didn't hit it off well at first, but then he kept coming around and finally wore me down. He is a wonderful man," Isa said.

"Yes, he is, which amazes me since he has lived with prejudices all his life. You would think he would hate the white man, but he believes in teaching them his ways. That's why he said yes when they asked him to come here. He also visits the local schools and teaches children all about the plight of the American Indian. Bringing the Lakota and other American Indian cultures to the diverse cultures in this area brings him so much joy. If he could do that here with so many immigrants, then anything was possible around the country. The tribal council helps him get artifacts from other tribes and, in return, he works with the people in the community."

Isa listened intently as Minnie continued to rave about Thunder.

"The restaurant in the cultural center only serves authentic food so tourists can truly learn about their way of life. Have you eaten there yet?" Minnie inquired.

"At the opening I had some Indian Fry Bread," Isa nodded. "It was fantastic."

"I'm sure. George Grayfeather makes the best fry bread, according to Thunder." Minnie agreed while she filled the sub rolls with sliced roast beef. "Then at the end of July he returns to South Dakota for the Powwow on his reservation. From what his sister tells me, he's an excellent dancer." Minnie smiled at Isa.

"I didn't know that," Isa said in awe. Learning all this about Thunder made her feel good to know she was with someone who was proud of his culture, because she was proud of hers. It was good that he wanted to teach others about his traditions. It was a great way to save your heritage.

"What did you not know?" Thunder startled Isa as he bent down and spoke next to her ear while he looked at Minnie with a questioning stare.

Isa didn't hear him sneak up behind her because he entered so quietly.

"Don't do that," she turned and smacked him in the chest, "you scared me."

"Sorry honey," Thunder kissed her quickly and wrapped his arm around her back.

"Nothing," Minnie said, "we were just talking girl talk. Oh, would you look at that? Both the lunch I fixed for us and the pie I made are ready. Isa, would you be a dear and get the plates from that cabinet over there on your right? I'll get the food and the silverware. You are both staying for lunch and dessert, right?"

"Sure, Minnie. We will stay and have lunch with you guys. Besides, who could turn down your apple pie for dessert?" He smiled at Minnie.

Isa grabbed the plates and set the table. Skip went to wash his hands and Thunder helped Isa with the glasses.

The next few hours went by much too fast for Isa, as she learned about horses from Skip, who also filled her in on several funny stories about Thunder's falls from the horses. Thunder called Sarah, but she wasn't home. However, one of her employees said she was running errands in town and would be back after dinner. After they finished the pie, Skip wanted Thunder to look at a couple of horses he had just bought. Isa remained in the kitchen with Minnie, to help her clean up.

Chapter 42

After Dinner Coffee

THUNDER

Thunder texted Sarah as he walked with Skip to see the horses.

> Thunder: Where are you?

> Sarah: Feed Store. Why?

> Thunder: I'm with Isa at Skip's and I was going to bring her over to meet you.

> Sarah: Can you hang out there for another hour? We're almost done.

> Thunder: Sure, text me when you get home.

> Sarah: Will do.

After Thunder helped Skip with the horses, they came back to the house. Minnie had made coffee for everyone.

"Glad you boys are back. I made some coffee so we can sit on the porch for a few minutes and digest our food. Come get a cup."

Everyone grabbed their cup and headed out. Thunder and Isa sat on the porch swing while Minnie and Skip sat on their rockers.

"Isa, are you from around here?" Minnie asked.

"Yes," she answered, "I am now. I was born in Cuba, but moved to Miami when I was two. Then in elementary school we moved to Ft. Lauderdale and have been there ever since."

Thunder was listening, but checked his phone when he received a text:

Thunder noticed Isa looking at him when he was texting.

"My sister is home," he held up his phone, "I told her we would be there in twenty minutes."

"Well, then we can continue this story later," Minnie got up from her chair, "Just bring your cups into the kitchen."

"I'll take them." Thunder finished his coffee and took his and Isa's.

"Thanks," Isa smiled up at him, "I'll go get my purse."

"Stay here, I'll get it for you. I'm going in anyway."

After returning with her purse, he came back and helped Isa out of the swing.

"Thank you for everything today," Isa said as she hugged Minnie and Skip.

"You are very welcome. Come back anytime," Minnie answered.

"Thunder, again I'm sorry 'bout missin' yur openin'. We'll stop by soon. I wanna git a look at those Lakota weapons. I'd luv to see 'em."

Thunder turned to Skip after he hugged Minnie. "Anytime you want to come by the center, let me know. I will show you the weapons along with anything else you want to see." He then hugged Skip.

"Luv ya' son, see ya' soon," Skip said as he patted his back. He then hugged Isa, "Luv'd seein' ya' li'l lady. Come back soon."

"I will. Thank you again," Isa smiled at them.

They got in the car and waved goodbye as they pulled out of the driveway.

"Is it ok that I told my sister we were coming over?"

"I was wondering who you were texting. Yes, I would love to go over there and see Tommy," she smiled brightly, "well and officially meet your, sister."

"Great. I think you will love Sarah," he winked.

"I'm sure I will," Isa agreed.

"Did you have a good time?" Thunder asked Isa.

"I had a great time. They are really something. How long have you known them?"

"About two years. It was my lucky day. As I arrived in town with my trailer, I entered the feed store to ask about horse stables for boarding *Sapa*. I overheard Skip say that he needed someone to help train his horses. His need for a horse trainer implied he has a stable. So I introduced myself and told him I was qualified. He agreed to stable *Sapa* while I trained his horses. Once Sarah and Grayhorse bought the property next door, I moved *Sapa* to their stable. But I still go by to help Skip when he needs me to train a horse. Mostly it's training them so people can ride them on his trail rides. We also train them to handle cattle drives, then sell them to cattle ranchers in central Florida. Some we've even sold to cattle ranchers as far as Montana and Wyoming." He kept glancing at her to make sure she was still listening. She was so quiet as she looked out the window at the scenery.

"How did you learn to train horses?" Isa asked.

"We had some horses on the rez and I was crazy enough to learn. I fell a lot, but I started getting better because I wouldn't give up. Skip doesn't get many wild horses that need breaking, but it's a lot of fun when you see a horse you trained doing well. I've also trained horses for different rodeo events, such as barrel racing and calf roping. Working with horses makes me feel free, like my ancestors must have felt when they rode all over the plains."

Chapter 43

Isa Formally Meets Her Future in Laws

THUNDER

"Here we are." Thunder exclaimed as he pulled into Sarah's driveway.

"That was fast."

"I told you they were neighbors," Thunder chuckled.

"I guess I didn't realize how close."

Thunder stepped out of the truck and went around to help Isa.

"*Lekší!*" Tommy screamed.

"Oh Shit," he made sure Isa was out of the truck before spinning around to catch Tommy.

"Ah, my favorite *ťuŋšká*," Thunder spun Tommy around.

"Not for long," Tommy smiled.

"Yes, for long," he whispered in Tommy's ear, "I think your momma will have a little girl."

He saw Isa smirking at him.

"How do you know?" Tommy leaned back in Thunder's arms and asked with a puzzled look on his face.

"Just a hunch."

"What does hunch mean?" Tommy inquired.

"It means a feeling." Thunder put Tommy down.

"Oh," Tommy then turned to Isa, "Hi Isa. Come with me. Let me show you my room." Tommy grabbed Isa's hand and began dragging her towards the house.

"I think he likes you," Thunder whispered, keeping up with them as Isa laughed.

When they made it to the front door, Sarah was waiting for them.

"*Iná*, look who came to visit me." Tommy exclaimed excitedly.

"Hi, I'm this crazy little boy's mom, Sarah. It's nice to see you again." Sarah extended her hand.

"It's nice to see you, I'm Isa," Isa shook hands with Sarah.

"*Iná*, I'm going to show Isa my room," Tommy said as he grabbed her hand again and ran past the kitchen toward his room. Sarah and Grayhorse lived in a four-bedroom, open concept, one-story ranch-style house.

"It's good to see you, Isa. Tommy, not so fast," Grayhorse scolded from the kitchen island. "Slow down!"

"Nice to see you too, Grayhorse," Isa waved back with her free hand.

Thunder hugged Sarah, and they walked into the house.

"I guess I'm not the only one vying for her attention." Thunder grumbled.

"Nope," Grayhorse came over to hug Thunder, "you have some competition," he slapped him on the back.

"Do you want something to drink?" Sarah walked to the fridge.

"I'll take some water or coffee," Thunder answered.

"I'll make you some coffee," Grayhorse commented. "Go sit with your sister. I'm sure she has a lot of questions." He chuckled, and Sarah smacked him on the shoulder.

"What?" he raised his eyebrows at her. "You know you do."

"Of course I do." she shooed him with her hands. "Now go make us some coffee."

"Women," he mumbled as he walked by Thunder.

"Hey, you deserve that after throwing me under the bus," Thunder mumbled back.

"So *tibló*, come sit with me." Sarah motioned Thunder over to the couch for his interrogation.

"How is it going with Isa?" Sarah quirked her eyebrow.

"We had a rocky start, but it's been going really well the past few weeks," Thunder nodded. "We've worked out the misunderstandings."

"I haven't seen you look at a woman like you look at her before. Do you love her?"

"I think so. I know it's really soon, but I can't imagine my life without her." Thunder stared at Sarah.

"Please be careful and get to know her before you fall too hard."

"Too late, I've already fallen." Thunder confessed.

"Have you told her?" Sarah asked.

"No. I don't want to scare her off. She wanted to take this slow," he sighed, "I haven't found the right moment."

"Just know that I'm here for you. I love you." Sarah hugged Thunder.

"I know *taŋkši*," Thunder mumbled, "*pilámaya*, I love you too."

"Here is your coffee Thunder. Do we need to save Isa?" Grayhorse wondered, looking around the living room. "She's been gone quite a while."

"I'll go." Sarah got up from the couch and walked to Tommy's room.

Sarah stood by the door and watched Tommy pointing to a photo of him and Thunder dressed in their regalia dancing at the Powwow at their reservation.

"That's really cool Tommy," Isa commented. "I didn't know you could dance. You look great!"

"I'm really good," Tommy puffed out his chest, "*lekší* and *até* taught me when I was young."

"Tommy, have you shown Isa everything in your room?" Sarah interrupted, covering her mouth so Tommy wouldn't see her laughing at him.

"Not yet." Tommy scrambled over to his toy bin, ready to open it.

"Ok *ciŋkší*, let's leave some things for her next visit," Sarah giggled. "Isa, would you like something to drink?"

"That would be great." Isa replied to Sarah then squatted down to Tommy, "Thank you Tommy for sharing your stories with me."

"You're welcome," Tommy grinned. "Will you come back again and play with me?"

"Of course," Isa hugged Tommy. "Maybe next time I can bring my nieces, Emmy and Lucy. Do you remember them from the park?"

"Yes!" Tommy laughed. "Emmy was really cool and Lucy was funny how she did my dad's hair."

"Lucy's Hair Salon strikes again," Isa laughed with him.

"I saw that remarkable hairstyle my husband had. Well, the photos and video, thanks to my son," Sarah pointed toward Tommy, "Grayhorse had taken it down by the time he made it home. I like that little girl. She has style."

"Lucy is very serious about her hairstyles," Isa nodded. "She keeps asking me when she can do Thunder's."

"Oh well, definitely bring her over." Sarah stated, "I've got to see that."

They all laughed as they walked into the living room. Thunder and Grayhorse looked at each other. This does not look good. What did they have up their sleeves?

"Uh, what's so funny?" Thunder looked scared.

"Isa was just telling me you need to make a hair style appointment at Lucy's Hair Salon and I want to host it here so Tommy can play with Emmy." Sarah commented.

"Um," Thunder looked worried as he stared at Grayhorse.

"Don't look at me." Grayhorse held his hands up. "I already went to that salon and paid my dues."

"Thunder," Isa grabbed his attention, "It's your turn. Lucy's been asking about you. You don't want to disappoint her, do you?"

Thunder watched as Isa gave him her puppy dog eyes and best pout ever. He loved kids. What could go wrong?

"Of course," Thunder nodded, "Let's set up a day and time and I'll do it."

"Yay!" Tommy jumped up and down. "I can't wait. What about tomorrow? *Iná* can make some food and we can do that as our fun for the day." Tommy pleaded with his mom with his puppy dog eyes.

"Ha," Thunder laughed, "Yes, *iná* you can make food while we play."

"Funny," Sarah smirked at Thunder. Sarah then turned to Tommy and said, "Of course Tommy, it's fine with me, but let's make sure Isa and her nieces can come over first before we plan our day. They might already have plans for tomorrow. How about next Sunday?"

"Okay," Tommy clapped his hands, "Isa, can you ask Emmy and Lucy?"

"Yes Tommy," Isa chuckled at his antics, "I'll find out this week and get back to you."

"Great!" Tommy exclaimed. "I'm so excited. We are going to have so much fun!"

"Ok, now that we've settled that, Tommy, why don't you go to your room to play? We need to talk to Uncle Thunder." Grayhorse asked.

"Ok," Tommy looked at Isa, "Don't forget to come say goodbye before you leave, Isa."

"I won't," Isa said, "I promise."

"What am I, chopped liver?" Thunder said as he approached Tommy and started tickling him.

"No *lekší!*" Tommy started hollering, "I want you to say good night too."

"Ok," Thunder stopped tickling him, "I'll come see you too."

Tommy then turned and took off, running toward his room.

"What did you want to talk to me about?" Thunder looked seriously at Grayhorse.

"Before we get started," Sarah looked at Isa, "Isa what can I get you to drink?"

"Water would be great," Isa answered.

"Ok, I'll be right back."

"What's this about?" Thunder asked again.

"We were wondering if you found the knife?" Grayhorse inquired.

"No," Thunder sighed, "Rachel and I have looked everywhere. If I can't find it by the end of this week, I will have to call Uncle Spirit."

"And file a police report," Isa said as she took the water from Sarah. "Thank you, Sarah."

"Yes, Isa suggested I file a police report," Thunder agreed.

"That's a good idea," Sarah nodded. "I would file the report as soon as possible."

"You don't think I should talk to Uncle Spirit before I file the report?" Thunder asked Sarah.

"No, I think you need to do that now." Sarah mentioned, "Although, it might be too late for them to get any prints since you didn't call them right away."

"Sarah's right," Isa piped in. "You can file the report and let them do their jobs. Tell them everything you know. Then call the tribal council, but don't mention you suspect Joseph. Let them know you are still looking for it."

"I like the filing the report," Grayhorse agreed, "but I wouldn't call the tribal council until you hear from the police."

"Why not?" Isa asked.

"Because the tribal council will ask about the police's findings and could ultimately fire me from my job." Thunder frowned.

"What?" Isa stared shockingly at Thunder. "That's kind of harsh."

"Thunder," Sarah admonished Thunder, "that council loves you. Granted, they won't be happy about the circumstances, but they will forgive you and not fire you. Look at all you've done for them."

"I hope you're right," Thunder exhaled loudly, "because this mystery is driving me crazy. There's just something I'm missing and I can't quite put my finger on it."

"We'll figure it out," Grayhorse interjected.

"I appreciate all your help," Thunder murmured. "I'll call the police tomorrow and file that report."

"Sounds good," Sarah nodded. "Do you want me to call Uncle Spirit?"

"No," Thunder groaned and stood up, "It's my job and my responsibility. I'll call him tomorrow. But thank you. Isa, we should get home."

They all stood up and walked to the door.

"Wait," Isa cried out, "Thunder, we need to say goodbye to Tommy. We promised."

"You're right," Thunder guided Isa to Tommy's room and knocked on his door.

"Come in," Tommy yelled.

"Hey *lekši*," Thunder announced, "We were leaving and wanted to say goodbye."

Tommy got up from the floor. He had been playing with his legos.

"Bye Isa," Tommy said as he hugged Isa.

"Bye *lekší*," Tommy then hugged Thunder.

"Bye *t'uŋšká*, I love you," Thunder held Tommy, "I'll see you tomorrow."

"Ok," Tommy answered and went back to play with his legos.

Thunder chuckled and led Isa back to the living room.

"Bye, Sarah," Thunder gave her a kiss on the cheek.

"Bye Grayhorse," Thunder patted him on the back.

"Bye," Isa said, hugging Sarah and Grayhorse. "It was really nice to get together."

"I agree. Don't be a stranger." Sarah held the door open for them. "Isa, we'll do a girls' night or something soon. Also, check with your nieces about a playdate next Sunday."

"I will," Isa responded.

Thunder held Isa's hand while they walked to the truck. After helping her up, he got in the driver's side and saw Sarah and Grayhorse with their arms wrapped around each other at the front door. He started the truck and waved goodbye before backing out of the driveway.

"They are really nice," Isa said as she waved goodbye.

"I think they really liked you too," Thunder confirmed.

"I hope so."

Thunder reached over and grasped her hand.

"Do you want to stay at your place or my house?"

"Do you have to work tomorrow?" Isa asked.

"No, it's Sunday. We're closed. Rachel said she had to go in and do some work. I wasn't planning on going in. Although if I'm going to file a report, then I'll have to go in for a little while. It probably would be best to do it when we are closed and we don't have any guests."

Thunder felt Isa's hand twitch when he said Rachel's name.

"Isa, is something wrong? Do you want to come with me?"

"No, nothing's wrong. Depending on what time you go tomorrow, I might go with you," Isa thought it over and decided she didn't want her time to end with him and she didn't want to ruin it with talk about Rachel. "Let's go to my apartment if that's okay with you?"

"Of course, *wówaštelaka mitáwa*, it's fine with me." he brought her hand up to his lips and kissed her palm.

That night, Thunder was restless and couldn't sleep. His tossing and turning finally woke up Isa.

"Thunder, what's wrong? It's two in the morning?" she mumbled.

"Sorry honey, I can't sleep thinking about that damn knife," he whispered.

**** Isa ****

Isa wanted to relax Thunder so he could get a few hours of sleep. She rolled onto her other side so she could face him. He was lying on his back with his right hand under his head and his left hand resting on his chest. The sheet was down below his belly, barely covering him. His left leg was lying over the top of the sheet.

Isa waited until her eyes adjusted to the dark before she scooted closer. His breathing was even, but his eyes were closed.

She reached out her hand and lightly ran it down his chest. He was so beautiful. His body was so well defined and sexy. She licked her lips as she watched her hand glide over him.

With one eye open, he observed Isa's hand caressing him, as though committing his body to memory. He lifted his gaze and focused on her face. Witnessing her lick her lips made him moan.

She looked up just as he closed his eyes and moaned again. His breathing increased, and she looked down towards his cock. It was now peeking out of the sheet, greeting her. She reached her finger out and touched the tip, eliciting a sharp intake of breath and another moan. His cock was now further out of the sheet and fully erect. She moved her finger in a circular motion over the tip.

Thunder didn't move. He opened his eyes and caught Isa looking at his cock. He watched as her finger wiped a drop of cum and brought it to her mouth and sucked her finger.

He groaned and said hoarsely, "Isa, please. Finish what you started."

Isa looked up into his eyes and straddled him.

"You know, I think this has become my new favorite toy." Isa smiled salaciously at him as she bent down and licked her way down to his cock. Cupping him with one hand as she guided and stroked him into her mouth with the other.

Thunder's hips jolted upward, and he gritted his teeth, "Aaaahhhh, Isa. You're killing me," he reached down and pushed Isa's head toward him. It didn't take him long to lose himself in her mouth.

Isa swallowed and licked him dry. She waited until his body stilled and kissed his belly, chest, and neck. She then stretched out on top of him. Thunder wrapped his arms around her as she sunk into his relaxed body.

"*Pilámaya, wíŋyaŋ mitáwa, thečhíhila,*" he murmured to the top of her head and kissed her.

Isa heard him murmur something, and he soon fell asleep. She rolled off him and turned to her side. His body followed her into his sleep, and he spooned her from behind.

Isa was pleased she enjoyed going down on him. His cock was her new favorite toy. She loved pleasuring him and seeing him lose control. Surely, he would now realize that she would do anything for him. She was in tune with his feelings. She loved him. But why hadn't he told her he loved her? And what did he say before he fell asleep? She really had to learn the Lakota language. Maybe Thunder could give her lessons after work or on the weekends. If he was too busy, then she would have to meet Sarah. Maybe she could help her. She couldn't imagine his sister not teaching his girlfriend about the language and some customs. She'd get Sarah's number from Thunder and call her for a girls' day.

Chapter 44

Police Scrutiny

THUNDER

Sunday morning, Thunder and Isa drove to the cultural center to file the police report. Rachel was there when they arrived.

"Rachel, I'm glad you're here," Thunder said when he found Rachel in his office.

"Thunder," Rachel looked surprised, "What are you doing here?"

"I came in to call the police and file a report on the missing knife. It's time since we can't seem to find it anywhere. Please stay so you can give them a statement."

"Of course," Rachel looked at Isa, "How are you?"

"I'm good, thank you," Isa stayed outside his office, "Thunder, I can sit at the lobby desk so I'm not in your way."

"Honey," he said as he gave her a kiss on her forehead, "You are never in my way, but let's go use that phone while Rachel finishes up in here."

"Thunder," Rachel interrupted him, "I can leave your office and use the computer on the lobby desk."

"No, it's fine," he nodded. "We'll use that phone."

Thunder guided Isa to the desk, pulled out the chair for her to sit and dialed the police department.

"Good morning, Sunrise Police Department. May I help you?"

"I hope so," Thunder spoke. "I would like to report a theft."

"Ok. Tell me your name, number and address and I will dispatch an officer right away."

"That would be great, thank you." Thunder preceded to give her the required information. She informed him someone would be there within the hour.

"What did they say?" Isa inquired.

"They will send an officer within the hour." Thunder hung up the phone and looked at Isa. "Want to raid the refrigerator with me?"

"Sure," Isa answered when Thunder grabbed her hand and led her to the kitchen. "What do you think we will find?"

"I'm hoping for some fry bread," Thunder answered. "Mary sometimes will keep a stash for me in the fridge."

"Yum, that sounds good."

Thunder opened the fridge and found his stash in a clear plastic container. He pulled out a few pieces for them to share and grabbed a couple of bottles of water. Thunder put the waters under his arms and grabbed the plate.

"Let's go sit out there so we can see when the police arrive." Thunder nodded his head toward the lobby.

"Sounds good," Isa agreed. "You know I can carry something for you."

"Nope, honey. I got this. Just grab a couple of paper towels from over there by the sink." Thunder led them to a table at the edge of the restaurant where he had a perfect view of the front door.

"This is wonderful, even cold," Isa mumbled while she chewed.

"Yep, George makes the best fry bread." Thunder said while devouring his piece.

They continued to eat in silence until Thunder looked up and saw the two police officers enter the lobby.

"Isa, the police are here. You can stay here and finish the fry bread," he said as he wiped his hands and mouth. "I'll be back."

Thunder stood and walked over to the police officer.

"Hello officers."

"Sir, did you phone in a theft?"

"Yes," Thunder answered, "A couple weeks ago on Thursday night we had our opening for a new exhibit and on Friday we realized that one of my knives from our artifacts display case was missing. I asked my assistant Rachel if she had sold it and she had not."

"Is Rachel here? Is that her over there?" one officer pointed toward Isa.

"No, that's my girlfriend Isa," Thunder answered. "Let me get Rachel."

Thunder walked toward his office.

"Rachel, the police are here and they would like to speak to both of us."

"Ok," Rachel stood up and walked around the desk.

"Are you Rachel?" the officer asked.

"Yes."

"Can you both show us where the knife was located?" the officer requested.

"Of course," Thunder replied, "right this way."

Thunder walked with them into the exhibit room and pointed to the empty space.

"We had it right here. It would have been sitting next to that description card." Thunder pointed out.

"Why are you just reporting this now?" the officer sounded dumbfounded.

"That's my fault," Thunder explained. "I really thought we had misplaced it. So, I asked Rachel to double check her apartment, and I checked my house and our warehouse. We had been so busy setting up for that opening and I thought maybe we placed the description card, but got sidetracked before placing the knife next to it."

"Ok," the officer sighed, "How do you open this case?"

Thunder reached in his pocket, took out his keys, and unlocked the display case. Then he lifted the front glass upward like you would open a refrigerated display case.

"Who else has a key to this display case?" the officer asked.

"I do." Rachel answered.

"No one else?"

"No sir," Thunder and Rachel answered.

"Ok," the officer sighed, "It doesn't look like it was tampered with. "Are you both sure it was locked?"

"We," Thunder looked at Rachel, "always lock it, but I suppose if we forgot to put the knife in, then we could have forgotten to lock it."

"I'm going to have someone come and dust for prints from this case and all your doors. We noticed a security system on your front door. We'll have them check that, too. Do you have any cameras?" the officer was looking around.

"Unfortunately, no." Thunder shook his head. "We've never had a theft problem."

"I would highly suggest you get some. You have some pretty pricey items in here."

"I'll call a company tomorrow and get working on that." Thunder pulled down the front glass from the display case and relocked it.

"I'm gonna be honest with you," the officer rubbed the back of his neck, "If you had many people here for the opening and since then, there might not be much that we can do."

"I understand," Thunder mumbled.

"I'm also gonna need you both to come down to the station and give us your prints and give your statements."

"Of course, we can follow you there."

"Great, let me take some quick photos on my phone and we'll meet you there," the officer mentioned.

"Rachel, do you need a ride to the station?" Thunder asked.

"No," she answered, "I have my car today."

"Ok, let me talk to Isa and we'll lock up and follow the officers."

Thunder walked over to Isa and told her he needed to go down to the police station. She agreed to go with him. When the officers finished with their photos, Thunder locked up and they all headed down to the station.

Chapter 45

So Many Viewpoints as the Plot Thickens

THUNDER

With each passing day, Thunder and Isa grew even closer, and Thunder realized he wanted to spend his life with her - she was his soulmate. This morning while Isa was finishing in the shower, he opened his dresser drawer and took out a wooden box that contained his mother's silver and turquoise diamond ring, quickly pocketing it before she came out of the bathroom. Hand in hand, he walked Isa to her car, and they agreed to meet at her apartment. Several heated kisses later, she left for work, and he ran back inside to grab his suit and tie. Thunder didn't want her to see him nicely dressed because she would start asking questions. He would change his clothes at work in his apartment before he left to pick her up.

Tonight after work, he'd buy her a nice bouquet of flowers before he picked her up at her apartment and take her to a nice dinner. When they got to the dessert portion of their meal, he would get down on one knee professing his undying love to Isa and ask her to marry him. He hadn't been this happy in a long time, and he hoped tonight would go smoothly. He knew they hadn't known each other for very long, but he hoped Isa had fallen for him just as quickly as he fell for her. She hadn't told him she loved him, but actions were louder than words and he had been very observant.

Shortly after he got to work, the forensic investigators from the police department arrived and dusted for prints, letting him know they would get back to him if they found anything suspicious.

Since they were closed to the public today and Thunder had a lot of nervous energy due to his impending proposal, he cleaned the cultural center to stay busy. When he finished cleaning the downstairs, he moved into his apartment upstairs since it was still too early to call it a day. Once he had cleaned everything he could think of, he looked at his watch and realized he only had forty-five minutes to shower and change before leaving to get Isa.

"Rachel!" Thunder looked around the lobby until he found her in his office, "can you please close up for me today?"

"Wow," Rachel whistled, "Don't you look nice? Where are you going all dressed up?"

"I'm going to pick up Isa at her apartment and take her to dinner."

"*Han, Wakíyaŋ Hotóŋpi*, I can close for you. But Isa called a few minutes ago and said she had an afternoon meeting she had to attend. She said for you to wait for her at her apartment."

"Did she say what time her meeting started?"

"No, just that it might run late."

"Oh, okay, then I'm on my way to her place. Please let her know if she calls. I'll see you tomorrow."

Rachel waited until Thunder walked out and called Joseph. "It's all set on this end. He's on his way to Isa's apartment, and she called and said she was on her way here. When can you get here?"

"I'm on my way. Rachel, remember to delay her if I'm not there by the time she gets there."

"Got it."

*** *Isa* ***

Isa planned to confess her love to Thunder tonight. Although they hadn't expressed it yet, she was confident that he loved her, too. She couldn't contain her excitement and anxiety, so she left work early and contacted the cultural center.

"Good afternoon, American Indian Cultural Center, may I help you?"

"Hi Rachel," Isa recognized her voice. "Is Thunder there?"

"He's in the warehouse," Rachel lied.

"Can you let him know that I'm on my way to him? He doesn't have to come get me at my apartment."

"Of course," Rachel answered, "I'll let him know."

"Thank you." Isa said, but Rachel hung up the phone.

Isa pulled into the parking lot a few minutes later, but didn't bother to look for his car. She was in a hurry to see him and talk to him. Walking in the door, she spotted Rachel in his office, so she walked toward her.

"Hi Rachel," Isa held the doorframe to his office and peaked inside, "is Thunder down here or upstairs?" Rachel still made her nervous. They hadn't talked since that crazy morning.

Rachel turned toward the door, looking away from the computer.

"He stepped out but said to tell you to wait for him here in his office. You can have a seat on the couch. He should be back soon." Rachel's smile seemed forced.

"Are you sure? If you're working, I can walk around the exhibit or wait upstairs? I don't want to disturb you."

"Not at all. Make yourself at home. I'm almost done writing this letter. Please have a seat." Rachel pointed toward the couch and turned back to the computer.

*** *Rachel* ***

After Isa sat down on the couch, Rachel pretended to write a letter on the computer, but in reality she was daydreaming about what was to come.

Joseph was still staying with Rachel. She was nice to him after the night he almost strangled her to death. She pretended he was Thunder because he expected her to be his fuck buddy. Now it was finally ending. She could finally be free from Joseph's presence. With anticipation, she knew Joseph had plans to eliminate Isa tonight. Because of his habit of talking to himself when he believed he was alone, she only had limited knowledge of his plan.

She'd heard him several times over the past few weeks. His voice filled with so much hate for Thunder. She figured he wanted to humiliate Thunder in front of Isa and then kill her while Thunder watched. Thunder would then kill Joseph because he would be crazy with anger. Nothing short of death would stop him from avenging Isa.

She, of course, would be there to comfort Thunder and convince him that the best thing for them would be to return home. They would soon marry and put all of this behind them. For a while, she wanted them to run the center together, but now she just wanted to go home. She didn't want any memories of Isa, which Thunder would have if he stayed here.

Rachel's phone beeped with a text message snapping her out of her thoughts as she read it.

Joseph: I'm here. I'll be right in.

Rachel: okay.

"Will you excuse me, Isa? I have something I need to attend to." Rachel got up and walked out of Thunder's office, smiling happily.

"Sure," Isa nodded.

*** *Joseph* ***

Joseph saw Rachel exit the office and ran into the room. "Isa, I'm so glad you're here," Joseph was huffing and puffing out of breath. "There has been an accident and Thunder needs your help. His sister is having problems with her pregnancy and Thunder thinks another woman might calm her down until the doctor arrives. He sent me here to come get you. Hurry, Sarah is in terrible shape."

Joseph grabbed Isa's hand and pulled her off the couch as he spoke to her hurriedly running toward the parking lot. He had to do this quickly so she wouldn't have time to think about what he was saying or doing. Once he got her in his car, he could make up answers to her questions.

"Joseph, not so fast." Isa was being pulled by Joseph at a punishing pace. "I'll do what I can, but I'm not a doctor. I know nothing about mental health." Isa suddenly stopped when Joseph opened the door to leave. "Wait Joseph! What about Rachel? Aren't they friends?"

"No," Joseph whispered as he pushed her out the door toward his rental car, "they don't really get along. Besides, I think Thunder wants you by his side.

He feels another woman's presence will have a calming effect on Sarah. In her condition, she shouldn't be getting alarmed. Stress is bad for the baby."

"My car is over here." Isa attempted to turn around, but Joseph would not let her. "Why don't you come with me so you can come back with Thunder, and you won't have to drive two cars later?"

*** *Isa* ***

Isa felt a sense of urgency as Joseph's hands pushed her into his car. As soon as Joseph got behind the wheel, he locked the doors and sped off. Isa buckled in and held onto the 'oh shit' bar above her door. Joseph was driving like a wild man. *It must really be bad*, she thought and hoped Sarah was okay. Sarah and her new baby were so important to Thunder, he would be devasted if anything happened to them. Isa didn't know how to help Sarah, but she would do whatever she could for Thunder's sister.

Isa didn't recognize the drive to Sarah's because last time she went with Thunder, they had gone to Skip and Minnie's house first. For all she knew, there was another way to Sarah's.

They approached a shack in the middle of nowhere. This was not Sarah's house. *Maybe this was a shack on the outskirts of their property and Sarah had come out to clean it*, she thought, although that seemed weird. However, as they got closer to it, Isa didn't see any cars or horses anywhere. Isa was fidgeting and looking around for anything that looked familiar. Maybe she shouldn't have trusted Joseph. After all, the last time she was in a room with him, he'd forced himself on her, and she'd ended up in a fight with Thunder. This was not good.

Joseph stopped in front of the shack.

"Where are their cars? This isn't Sarah's house," she asked nervously as she kept looking from Joseph to the shack.

"This is a shack on their property. Sarah comes here to think. They rode over on their horses and hitched them to a post off the back porch," he answered, "come on, hurry."

Isa got out of the car and ran into the house.

"Thunder, where are you? It's me, I'm here. Where's Sarah?" She searched every room, but there was nobody to be found. A strange feeling was forming in the pit of her stomach. Did Joseph kidnap her? She was aware of him entering the house and locking the door. Turning swiftly, she met his gaze with a fierce glare.

"Where are they, Joseph? I thought you said they were here!" she screamed at him.

"Not quite but make yourself comfortable because you will be my guest until I drive Thunder crazy with worry over you."

"I will not stay here, get out of my way," Isa tried to run past him to the front door, but he grabbed her hair and swung her against the kitchen table. She crashed headfirst into the table before sliding to the floor. Seconds later, she opened her eyes and saw multiple Josephs standing in front of her, laughing. Raising up on her elbow, she held her head and felt something wet. Pulling her hand away from her head, she saw blood on her fingers and started shaking.

"Are you crazy? Thunder will kill you! Let me go. You're his cousin!" She cried hysterically at him.

"I will get him before he gets me, so sit tight. Or I will beat you into submission," he said with a crazed look on his face.

"Don't you dare lay a hand on me!" she swayed, trying to stand up.

"Is that a threat?" Joseph growled. "I thought you liked to play with Indians. I have given pleasure and pain, which do you prefer?" he asked, prowling toward her.

Isa took a step back and picked up a chair in front of her as if she was taming a lion.

"You stay away from me!" she pushed the chair at him in quick jabs.

Joseph grabbed the chair by the legs and threw it across the room. It crashed against the wall and split into multiple pieces. Isa could see so much evil reflecting in his eyes, but before she could move away from him, she felt a hard punch to her face. Isa didn't expect that. She fell to the floor, and it was lights out.

*** *Joseph* ***

Joseph hated hitting women, but in this case, it was Thunder's woman and he didn't care. The slut deserved it. She would spread her legs for him soon enough and once he fucked her, she wouldn't want to go back to Thunder. He was better at fucking than Thunder. He was making himself hard just thinking about when Thunder saw her bruises.

"Maybe I could hit her a few more times to really irritate Thunder. Nah, I'll wait." Joseph muttered to himself, "After I beat him within an inch of his life and tie him up, I'll make him watch as I hit her a few more times before I rape her and kill her. I will exact my revenge by witnessing his last moments of despair. He will die knowing he could not protect his woman. I'll bury them both in the back. I already dug the hole. I'll go home and lie low for a while at dad's house. After a couple of months, I'll suggest to dad to place me here to run this cultural center. I'll tell him how much I helped Thunder and Rachel. If Rachel doesn't keep quiet, I'll kill her, too. I'm beginning to really like Florida."

Joseph got busy undressing Isa and carrying her to the bed. He tied her hands and feet to the four-poster bed. He wanted her to feel helpless and humiliated when she woke up. Not to mention the sense of desperation when she realized she can't escape.

*** *Thunder* ***

Thunder waited for Isa in his car for over an hour. She was never this late. He was really getting worried something had happened to her. If she was running late, she would always text him. *Where was she?* Maybe they'd gotten their wires crossed. Damn, he never got Aurora's or Matteo's number. As Thunder was debating googling their names, a car pulled up next to his and Aurora got out and walked to Isa's door and knocked. Thunder looked up at the sky and thanked *Wakan Tanka* for answering his prayers. Thunder got out of the car and walked toward Aurora.

"Hello, ma'am. Do you remember me from the park? Johnny Thunderbird. I was supposed to meet Isa here, but she hasn't shown up or called me. Have you seen her?" Thunder didn't want to tell her how long he had really been waiting for Isa.

"*Sí*, I remember you and your friend Grayhorse. You and Isa are dating, No?" Aurora answered.

"Yes ma'am."

"Please call me Aurora, especially since you are dating my Isa."

"Then, please call me Thunder."

"Now what is this about Isa making a date to be home and not being here? I just got back from a business trip and was stopping by to say hi. I have a key if you would like to wait with me inside. We can call her brother and see if she stopped by his house to see the girls."

"That would be great, thank you." Thunder followed her.

After walking in, Aurora said, "Would you like something to drink?"

"Yes, please. A glass of water would be great." Thunder knew where everything was since he'd spent many nights there with Isa, but he didn't know if Aurora knew how serious their relationship was.

"I'll be right back." Aurora walked to the kitchen to get his water, then came back and handed it to Thunder. She walked to her purse and got out her cell phone. She called Matteo, Isa's brother, and asked if she was there. He had not heard from her since the previous Sunday. Aurora hung up and called Maggie.

"Maggie said she left at five, Thunder. Where could she be? It's not like Isa to do this." Aurora was wringing her hands as she stared at Thunder. Thunder needed to calm her down and go looking for Isa.

"Maybe she's been waiting for me at my office. I probably just misunderstood her about where to meet. After all, it is strange that she would want to meet me at her apartment." He smiled kindly at her.

"Really, Thunder," Aurora smirked at him, "I know you and my daughter are sleeping together. You don't have to sugarcoat it for me."

"Sorry, Aurora," Thunder nodded, "But you need to know that I love your daughter and I plan to have a future with her. I'm not just sowing some wild oats with her."

"I believe you. Does she know you love her?"

"Ah, I haven't told her yet because she wanted to take it slow after her last relationship and I didn't want to scare her away." Thunder rubbed the back of his neck. "I know it's really soon. We've only been dating for a few weeks." Thunder shifted his stance nervously. "But she is my soulmate. I want to wake up and go to sleep every day seeing her beautiful face next to me."

"Thunder, you need to tell her how you feel. I think you will find that she returns your love," she said with a twinkle in her eyes. "Of course, you didn't hear that from me."

Thunder breathed a sigh of relief. Isa must have spoken to her mother about their relationship. His heart lightened, knowing Isa might love him and he had her mother's blessing. Now he just had to find Isa and tell her how he felt.

"Of course," Thunder smiled brightly. "I will go to my office and if you give me your number, I'll call you as soon as I see her. Or I'll have her call you."

"That sounds great."

Aurora told him her number as he entered it into his phone. He gave her a quick hug and promised to call her.

Thunder hurried to the center, hoping she was there. As he pulled into the parking lot, he saw her car and exhaled a huge breath he didn't realize he was holding. Unlocking and opening the door, he ran into the center.

"Isa, *wíŋyaŋ mitáwa*. I am so sorry I was waiting for you at your apartment...Isa?" Thunder was speaking, but no one was around. The center was empty. Ah, maybe Rachel let her into his apartment. Thunder ran upstairs.

"Isa, honey, are you here?" He walked into his apartment. No sign of her. Where was she? He went back downstairs and looked everywhere. Frustration and worry set in as he walked over to his desk. Maybe she'd left him a note. He didn't see any messages from her on his desk. He covered his face with his hands. *Where are you, Isa?* He thought as panic set in. At that moment, his cell phone rang, when he looked at the screen and noticed it was Sarah. He answered it quickly.

"Sarah, is Isa with you?"

"No, have you misplaced your woman?" Sarah asked, giggling.

"*Hau, taŋkši*, now is not a good time. Can I call you back later?"

"*Wakíyaŋ Hotóŋpi* are you okay? You sound strange."

"Isa is missing and I'm going out of my mind." Thunder sighed heavily.

"What do you mean, she's missing?"

"*Han, taŋkši*...wait my office line is ringing, maybe it's Isa." Thunder put his cell down on his desk and answered his desk phone. "Good evening, American Indian Cultural Center, can I help you?"

"Why, yes Thunder, you can. Or maybe I can help you. I believe we have a trade of some sort." Thunder recognized Joseph's voice.

"Joseph, this isn't a good time. Can I call you tomorrow?"

"Oh, I think you will want to make time for this. You see, I have something you want, and you have something I want. So, I figure we fight it out and the winner gets both. What do you say?"

Thunder had a sinking feeling in the pit of his stomach. "Joseph, what the hell are you talking about? What could you possibly have that I would want? Unless you're the one who took my grandfather's knife!" he screamed into the phone.

"Tsk, tsk, don't be so grouchy. Now that you mention it. I have two things that belong to you. You've guessed the first. Let's see if you can guess the second?"

"Get away from me!" Isa screamed right before Thunder heard a loud slap. Did he slap her? Thunder was livid. He could hear every sound over the phone.

"Joseph, if you harm her, I swear I will kill you," Thunder roared into the phone. "Your problems are with me, not her." Thunder heard another slap and Isa's whimper. "Let her go Joseph. Isa, *wíŋyaŋ mitáwa*, can you hear me?"

Joseph put the phone on speaker so Isa could hear Thunder's pleas.

"I believe she heard you, Thunder. I mean, she is crying," Joseph laughed.

Thunder could hear Isa crying. This was killing him. "Joseph let her go. It's me you want to hurt, not her. She has nothing to do with this. Let me talk to her? Where are you?"

"Not so soon. I haven't even begun to torture you. My, my, your woman certainly must work out. She is thin but curvy in all the right places. She has the most beautiful breasts with rosy pink nipples that I can't wait to suck."

Thunder could hear Isa whimpering. He was quickly losing his patience. "Joseph, you wouldn't dare."

"I wouldn't, huh? Isa dear, please tell Thunder what I have in my hand."

Isa was still whimpering. "My breast," she murmured.

"A little louder dear, he can't hear you," he said as he suddenly squeezed her breast painfully hard.

"Ouch," she screamed out in pain and shouted, "My breast!"

"Fuck! Stop, Joseph!" Thunder was so angry he swept everything off his desk since he couldn't reach through the phone and ring Joseph's neck.

"Very good Isa. I think he heard you this time."

"You've made your point. Leave her alone. Tell me where you are." Thunder pinched the bridge of his nose.

"Well, it's hard for me to leave her alone when I see everything she offers me clearly. Go ahead, Isa, tell Thunder what you're wearing." He squeezed her breast again.

"Nothing."

Thunder could hear the anger in her voice. Isa was trying to keep her emotions under control. He would find her and he would kill Joseph. Oh *Wakan Tanka*, keep her safe.

"Ah, Thunder as I run my hand over her body and I see why you like to fuck her." Joseph whispered into the phone.

"Joseph," Thunder screamed into the phone, trying to divert his attention, "Joseph, where do you want to meet me?" Suddenly, he heard another woman's voice in the background. Was that Rachel's voice? What the fuck was going on?

"Joseph, did you..." Rachel stopped mid-sentence as she walked into the room. "Well, that answers my question. You got her, and she is tied up nicely, if I may add. What are you going to do with her?"

Thunder could hear Rachel's betrayal.

"I'm going to make Thunder worry all night about her. Then tomorrow night when we meet at nine at night, I'm going to take her with me. After I beat the shit out of Thunder, I will make him watch me ride his woman. I want that to be the last thing he sees before I kill him." He laughed maniacally loud enough for Thunder to hear.

"I thought you just wanted to humiliate Thunder, not kill him. You promised me you were just going to tie him up, rape her, and kill her! You were supposed to leave Thunder to me. That was the deal!" Rachel screamed at Joseph.

"Now, now Rachel. Do you really think he will want you after I've been fucking you for years? Does he know I was the man between your legs when you guys were dating? Why would he want you when you cheated on him with me in the first place?" Joseph spewed their secret to Thunder.

Thunder couldn't believe what he was hearing. "Rachel, damn you! What have you done!" He screamed into the phone.

"Joseph, was that Thunder's voice? What are you holding behind your back?" Rachel yelled and Thunder heard a scuffle.

"I don't think he wants you anymore, Rachel, not after what he just heard. Don't look so pale sweetheart, I'm sure he never wanted you back," Joseph sneered.

"If that really is Thunder, let me talk to him. I need to explain." Thunder heard more rustling. "Thunder! I had nothing to do with the kidnapping and I never cheated on you with Joseph. He's just making up shit! Give me the phone. Don't place it on the bitch's stomach. I need to talk to Thunder. Give me the damn phone!" Thunder heard Joseph laugh and Rachel scream. "Don't you dare touch me, Joseph!"

"Well, my dear, it seems you are in a rather terrible predicament and you are a liar to boot. Let's see, Thunder doesn't want you and neither do I."

"You stole the knife? You asshole. I knew it!" Rachel screamed.

"Rachel, stop, he's not in his right mind," Thunder screamed through the phone, "you're going to get hurt."

"You are useless to me now, Rachel. I'm afraid you'll have to say goodbye." Joseph sighed.

Thunder had a feeling that Joseph was going to hurt Rachel and he didn't want Isa to see that.

"Isa," Thunder whispered, "I know you can see what's happening. Honey close your eyes, please don't cry, shhh."

"Joseph," Rachel scolded, "you don't want to do this. I helped you remember. Think of all the nights we spent together. All the time I spent loving you, didn't that mean anything to you?"

"You mean like it meant to you. Your pet name for me must have been Thunder, since you called me that every time you climaxed! And now you finally confess you were sleeping with me, so I don't kill you. You're a whore, Rachel, and now I'm done with you, bitch! Goodbye, *mitákcola*. Burn in hell!"

Isa screamed. Thunder could hear the terror in her voice.

Chapter 46

Play-by-Play Terror

THUNDER

"Joseph, what did you do?" Thunder desperately asked.

"Well, you want the play-by-play," Joseph giggled, "Ok, so Rachel wanted to talk to you. I said no. The bitch wouldn't shut up, so I stabbed her with the knife. Oh, and I twisted it in her stomach so it did the most damage. She slid to the ground and her eyes and mouth were wide open. Looking at me in horror, because I killed her so fast she never had time to scream. Dirty whore, that will teach her to ever call me Thunder again. So," Joseph laughed, "the wicked witch is dead. Which is alright since Isa on the other side of the room is screaming her head off. Now I'm wiping my knife off on Rachel's clothes. Gotta clean it up before I slice up your woman. I must say, I like this play-by-play, especially since it's driving you crazy. Isa, shut the fuck up, bitch, or I'll open up your stomach as well!" Joseph shouted.

Thunder closed his fist and pounded it on his desk. He just needed Isa to calm down and listen to him.

"Isa, Isa, stop. *Wiŋyaŋ mitáwa*, please be quiet." He tried to tell her. He didn't know how far the phone was from her, but he prayed she could hear him. Clearly, Joseph had lost his mind. He'd already killed one person. It would be easy for him to kill another.

"Joseph, can you hear me? Please, pick up the phone." He was trying to be sound calm.

"Yes, my dear cousin, I hear you. Now you know what a traitor your assistant was. Not only did she fuck me, but she wanted to get rid of your girlfriend." Joseph was hooting and hollering as Isa screamed in the background. "Will you shut up, bitch!"

"Joseph, let me talk to Isa. Please, I can calm her down. She won't be any more trouble for you. Please." Thunder begged.

"Fine, talk to your bitch, but get her to shut up or I'll knock her unconscious again until tomorrow night." Joseph put the phone next to Isa's ear.

"Here bitch, talk to your boyfriend. It might be the last time you hear his voice."

"Isa, *wiŋyaŋ mitáwa*, are you there? Honey, please stop screaming and listen to me."

"Thunder?" she whimpered into the phone. "I'm so scared. He just killed her."

"I know honey, shhh, listen to me," Thunder said as he raked a hand through his hair. He had to keep his voice low and soothing. "*Wíŋyaŋ mitáwa*, stay calm and do what he says. I will find you. I promise. Just hold on tight and do nothing to anger him."

"No Thunder," she screamed, "you can't come here. He'll kill you. Don't come to the sha...aaahhhh!"

"Isaaa," Thunder heard a crunch like a punch. Then it was dead quiet. She had said something that sounded like a shack. "Joseph!" Thunder yelled, "What the hell have you done?"

"Kept her from telling you everything. She's quiet for now. Maybe when she becomes conscious again, she'll be a good girl. I can't wait to fuck her." He laughed.

"Joseph, if you even touch her, you are a dead man. There will be no place where you can hide from me. I will find you!" Thunder hollered into the phone.

"Tsk, tsk, Thunder, temper, temper. If you want your precious Isa, then you have to play by my rules."

"Fine. Name the place and time and I will be there."

"We will meet tomorrow night at that deserted land between Skip's property and the crooked creek. Oh, and Thunder, bring war weapons because we are playing to the death. In memory of our ancestors, there will be only one standing warrior. I hope that my sleeping with your woman all night tonight will not bring me bad luck tomorrow. But it's a chance I'm willing to take. She is a beauty. Maybe I'll suck her tits until she wakes up."

"No, Joseph. Leave her alone. You said you wanted me to watch. That would hurt me more," Thunder tried saying to get him to leave Isa alone until he could find them. Thunder continued, "How about we do it tonight? I can meet you there tonight."

"Tonight isn't good for me. My schedule is already booked with kidnapping, murder, and rape. But look for me by the fire tomorrow night at 9 p.m. May the best warrior win, *Hoka Hey!*" and with those parting words, the line went dead.

"Nooooooo Joseph," Thunder howled into his phone at the dial tone. He forgot he still had his sister on his cell phone. Hanging up the office phone, he picked up his cell and said, "Sarah, is Grayhorse home?"

"*Wakíyaŋ Hotóŋpi*, what's going on?" Sarah shouted freaking out, "Who were you talking to? I could only hear your side and the panic in your voice is heart wrenching. Are you okay?"

"*Taŋkší*, shit, I was talking to Joseph. He kidnapped Isa and just killed Rachel."

"Grayhorse," Sarah shrieked, "Come here for a minute, hurry."

"What's wrong, are you okay?" Thunder could hear Grayhorse in the background.

"Yes, but Thunder needs us." Sarah put the phone on speaker and said, "Okay, Grayhorse is here. Tell us what you know."

"Okay, so Joseph has taken Isa and he won't tell me where his is. He wants to seek revenge on me with her. I've got to find him, but I don't know where to look. He's hit her multiple times, and he killed Rachel in front of her. He instructed me to meet him tomorrow night at the empty area between Skip's land and the twisted creek. Oh, and the motherfucker instructed me to bring weapons for a fight to the death. Fuck! Then he knocked her out and said he was going to rape her all night long. Fucker!" Thunder screamed into the phone.

"Do either of you know where he might have taken her?" Sarah asked.

"Thunder, where are you?" Grayhorse asked.

"I'm in my office at the center and no, I don't know where he is."

"Ok, hang tight. I'm on my way." Thunder heard Grayhorse kiss Sarah and say, "I love you."

"I love you too. Be careful."

"*Wakíyaŋ Hotóŋpi*, please be careful. Joseph has always wanted what you have. Grayhorse just left with a couple of knives. Please wait for him?"

"*Han*, I could use his help."

Thunder hung up and headed back into his office. He wanted to make a list of all the places where Joseph hung out.

Oh shit, first he had to call Aurora. What should he say? He promised to call her. He dialed her number and waited for her to answer. Should he lie or tell her the truth? Maybe a partial truth.

"*Hola*," Aurora answered, "Thunder, is this you? I didn't recognize the number."

"Yes, Aurora, it's me."

"Is Isa with you?"

"No," shit, this was going to be hard. He squeezed the bridge of his nose and ran his hand over his face before he said, "She was kidnapped by my cousin, Joseph."

"*¡Qué! Ay*, no, no, not my Isa!" Aurora wailed.

"*Mami. ¿Que paso?*"

"Aurora," Thunder heard a man's voice right before Aurora started crying.

"Who is this?" The man's voice came on the phone.

"Hi this is Thunder, Isa's boyfriend."

"Why is my mother hysterical on the floor of my kitchen?"

"Hi Matteo, I just found out my cousin kidnapped Isa to hurt me."

"What the hell are you talking about? Who is this asshole that has my sister? Where is she? I'm gonna fucking kick your ass if anything happens to her!" Matteo sounded furious.

"I'm kicking my ass, trust me. His name is Joseph. I don't know where he has her. He wants me to meet him tomorrow night, but my brother-in-law and I are going to look for him tonight. Can you please call the police and let them know? If you give me your phone number, I will call you with updates every hour."

"Fuck! Can I trust you?"

"Yes, I love your sister and I want to marry her." Thunder stated.

"Okay, I'll call the police, but you better call me with updates."

"Absolutely."

Thunder put him on speakerphone and added his number to his contacts. He gave Matteo all the information he had about the meeting tomorrow night. Just in case he didn't find Joseph by then. After promising to call with updates again, he hung up and started thinking about where Joseph might have gone.

Joseph drank too much, which caused him to talk too much. Someone might have overheard what he was up to. He and Grayhorse could split up and hit all his favorite bars before they closed at midnight. He hated to think that he would have to wait until tomorrow night.

"*Wakan Tanka*, please look after my woman. Please do not let any harm come to her." Thunder spoke aloud.

Grayhorse arrived twenty minutes later. He ran into Thunder's office. "Ok, start from the beginning. What the hell happened?"

Thunder took a deep breath, stood up, and began pacing while he told Grayhorse everything he knew.

"Shit, okay. Did Isa or Joseph give you any clues to where they might be? Any sounds, noises?"

"After I tried to calm Isa down so he wouldn't hurt her, she said, don't come to the 'sha' or something like that. Then he punched her. I think she was trying to say shack. But what shack?"

"We'll find her, brother, I promise. First, let's call her mom and tell her Isa is with you."

"I already called and told her Joseph kidnapped Isa and to put out a missing person's report."

"Oh shit, how did she take it?"

"Not good. She collapsed on the floor of Isa's brother's kitchen."

"Well, at least she wasn't alone."

"Then her brother basically told me he was going to kick my ass. As well as he should. I told him to call the cops and that I would call him with updates every hour. Now, can we please leave and start checking out Joseph's usual hangouts?"

"Abso-fucking-lutely."

"I have them all written here," he pointed to a pad on his desk. He tore off the sheet and handed it to Grayhorse.

"Okay," Grayhorse tore the sheet in half, "you take the first two and I'll take the last two. We'll meet back here in two hours or sooner and exchange notes. Remember, he won't kill her if he wants to torture you."

Thunder looked scared. "I know, but he threatened to rape her all night long. I'm afraid of her mental state when we find her."

Grayhorse saw the fear in Thunder's eyes. "That will not happen. We will find her before he hurts her any further. I promise you."

Thunder knew Grayhorse couldn't keep that promise, but he still hoped. Two hours later, Grayhorse and Thunder met back at the cultural center. They'd questioned everyone who knew Joseph at those locations. No one seemed to know where he was. They hadn't seen him in a couple of days. Probably the two days Joseph needed to set up his scheme.

Suddenly, Grayhorse snapped his fingers.

"Thunder, if Rachel was involved, then let's go to her apartment. See if we find anything."

"Good idea. I have a key to her apartment somewhere in this drawer." Thunder opened his top drawer and moved a few things around. "Here it is. Let's go."

"How did she get involved with Joseph? Do you know?" Grayhorse asked Thunder, confusion written all over his face.

"Apparently, they've been fucking each other for a while now. He's the man she was cheating on me with when we were dating. She wanted me back, so she teamed up with Joseph to get rid of Isa and be with me. So fucked up because even without Isa, I would not be turning to her. I could only hear bits and pieces of the argument between Joseph and Rachel before he killed her."

"How do you know he killed her?"

"Because the fucker described everything he did to Rachel on the phone to me." Thunder pointed at his desk phone.

"Has he gone mad?" Grayhorse was stunned.

"It would seem like it. I don't give a damn, except he has my woman. Wait here, I'll be right back." Thunder ran upstairs to grab his American Indian clothes along with a couple knives and a lance he kept in his apartment. If he found Joseph tonight, he wanted to be dressed and ready to bring the fight to him. Running back downstairs, he headed straight for the front door.

"Ok, let's go."

"Lead the way, brother. But I'm driving." Grayhorse firmly stated.

"Fine."

"I see you grabbed some weapons as well." Grayhorse looked down at Thunder's hands.

"Yes, But Fuck!!!" Thunder roared, "I don't want to use them."

Grayhorse drove Thunder the short distance to Rachel's apartment complex like a bat out of hell. Time was of the essence.

Chapter 47

Joseph's Demented Games

Isa

Isa woke up but could barely open her eyes. Her head was pounding and her eyes would not fully open. They felt swollen from being punched in the face twice. The last thing she remembered was talking to Thunder and trying to tell him about the abandoned shack. Then Joseph punched her in the face again. She was so thirsty she tried to wet her lips with her tongue and immediately winced when she tasted blood. She knew Thunder would try to find her, but how long before he got here?

Joseph must've heard her moan because when she turned her head, he was staring down at her. Joseph was looking at Isa with deadly intent. Isa's body shook uncontrollably as she swallowed her fear and kept her mouth shut and not provoke him. She saw how maniacal he looked when he killed Rachel. She wasn't ready to die.

"Now, sweetheart, it's just you, me, and Thunder." He wiped the blood from his hands on her stomach. "You don't mind a little blood, do you? I know you and Rachel didn't get along very well."

"What are you talking about?" she whispered.

"Well, I just had to bury Rachel. That's her blood on your stomach," Joseph said as he pointed towards her stomach. "Hope you don't mind."

Isa's body convulsed, bile rising to the surface as she stared in horror at the crimson smear across her stomach. She remained still and stayed quiet. He was acting like a madman.

"Discarding a body is tiring work. I'm going to take a nap and then me and you can play a little game called, 'Let's put a smile on Cousin Joseph's face', he sneered before slinking out of the room."

Isa guessed he would take his nap on the couch in the living room since she was taking up the entire bed and there was only one bedroom in this shack.

She didn't know what he was ranting about, but she was grateful that she didn't have to keep looking at Rachel's death stare. She would never forget it. After Joseph stabbed Rachel and twisted the knife, he'd pushed her against the wall right before she slid down to the floor with her mouth open in shock. Isa was sure she'd have nightmares for years to come.

She tried to undo the ropes while he slept, wanting to escape before he woke up. But the more she tried, the knot just got tighter. The rope was cutting into her skin, blood running around her wrists and down her arms. *Oh Thunder, where are you?* Quietly, she turned her head and cried into the pillow, not wanting to wake Joseph. She hoped he would continue sleeping until morning. What was she going to do? What if Thunder didn't win tomorrow night? She'd never seen Thunder fight. Hell, what if Joseph raped and killed her?

Her poor mother. How would she feel having lost a husband and a child? No, she had to stop thinking negatively and try to think of a way to get out. She couldn't give up. Maybe Thunder would find her tonight and this would all be just a bad dream.

With a quick burst of energy, Isa pulled her hands and feet, attempting to slide out of the ropes. After experiencing a few minutes of excruciating pain, she gave up and cried herself to sleep.

*** *Thunder* ***

Thunder and Grayhorse entered Rachel's apartment. They searched around for any sign of something that might give them a clue to where Joseph might be. They were growing desperate and searched through drawers for any scraps of paper.

Grayhorse was looking through Rachel's nightstand when he spotted an envelope.

"Thunder," he screamed, "look over here."

Thunder hurried over to him and picked up the envelope, which had a note written on it and it wasn't Rachel's handwriting. The note said to call the phone company and transfer calls to the following number. When he flipped the envelope, he saw it was for Joseph Eagle at a familiar address.

"This address is near Skip's place," Thunder said as he looked at Grayhorse. "As a matter of fact, it's that abandoned shack that sits about a mile from the edge of his land near the crooked creek. Joseph said to meet him tomorrow night at nine at the crooked creek. Do you think he's there now? She said something about a shack."

"It's worth a shot. If he is not there, we can set a trap for tomorrow," Grayhorse advised.

"Let's go, then."

They both hurried to the shack hoping Isa was there and safe.

*** *Joseph* ***

It was still dark outside when Joseph slammed the door as he came inside after moving his car behind the shack so no one would see it. Joseph walked into the bedroom and shined his flashlight on her face.

"So my little white whore is finally awake?"

He put the flashlight on the nightstand, pointing it towards her. With the knife in his hand, he ran it down her body. The blade was to the side, so he wasn't cutting her...yet.

Isa tried to move away from the knife, but the rope binding her hands and feet was too tight. Joseph knew she was terrified by the way she trembled and breathed erratically.

"I thought you were going to wait to do this in front of Thunder," she reminded him timidly, watching the movement of the knife on her body from beneath her lashes.

"I was, but seeing you look so delectable laying there all naked and spread out for me like this...is so very tempting. Besides, I know you're not a virgin. You've already slept with Thunder, I heard you. So why shouldn't I get to enjoy your body also? I already told Thunder I would fuck you all night long, so why disappoint him?" he grinned wickedly. "I would hate to be called a liar," he laughed.

Isa knew she was no match for his strength on a good day, but tied to the bed, she was utterly defenseless. Maybe if she could just keep him talking, she could buy herself some more time.

"Why are you doing this, Joseph?" She tried to keep her voice to a whisper.

"Because I hate him." Joseph snarled.

"What did he do to you? Please tell me. I would like to understand."

Joseph stopped in his tracks. He withdrew the knife and paced the room like a caged tiger.

"Well, let's see, where should I start? I guess it doesn't matter since we have the rest of the night and all day tomorrow to talk and fuck." He glanced at her. "It started when I was little. Thunder always got everything. Everyone liked him more than me. They said he was nicer, smarter, more social, easier to get along with, and the list goes on and on. Then, as I got older, even my girlfriends liked him more than me. Some would go out with me to double date with Thunder. I was glad when he went away to college. I didn't have any competition. But then he became a hero, since he got a scholarship and was going to become a big shot architect."

He stopped and suddenly smiled.

"Then it happened. By some twist of fate, something bad finally happened to him. He lost his parents in a car accident and had to leave college. But that soon ended in another happy ending when my father told him to continue, that he would care for Sarah and help him."

His expression turned solemn as he stared out the bedroom window.

"Sarah, she's another story. Why couldn't she be my girlfriend? I cared for her and looked after her while Thunder was away. But she didn't care for me like that. She said she loved me like family. It was always Thunder this... and Thunder that...," he said as he continued to pace the room. "Then Thunder finishes college and comes back and... BOOM... she leaves to go back with Thunder and live in their parent's home. To make matters worse, he brings his friend Grayhorse to live with them. Sarah turned away from me and began dating Grayhorse. That center should have been mine and Sarah's. I'm the one who stayed on the reservation and took up his slack. He's the one who left and didn't care about anyone, least of all his people." He grew angry again. Isa thought he had a warped sense of what happened, but she kept quiet.

"Now everyone talks about how brave a warrior he is. And how good he's doing with the center. Well, dammit! It should have been mine!" Joseph roared and stopped mid stride and pointed towards himself.

Isa noticed he was getting worked up and tried to talk him down. "Joseph, I'm sure Sarah loves you and she would not want either you or Thunder to be hurt."

"What do you know? You're just his whore for now. Do you realize how many women he's slept with? Giving them pleasure and then dumping them. You are so stupid if you think you are special and have a future with him. I'm doing you a favor." Joseph walked to the bed again with the knife and poised it over her body.

"Okay, Joseph, forget about me." She got scared again. She needed to distract him. "Think about Sarah, sweet Sarah, the woman you love. How could you do this to her?"

"Sarah will get over it. Besides, she rarely speaks to me anymore. She'll never know what happened. I will fuck you, kill you, then kill Thunder. I will bury the bodies in the same grave I dug for Rachel. There will be no witnesses." He moved the knife down toward her breasts. "You have beautiful breasts, white whore. They're so nice and round and they peak at just the right time." He had drawn circles around her nipple with the tip of the knife. He was not drawing blood. But her body was responding to the sensation of an object skimming over her breast and nipple. She was terrified, trying not to shake so he wouldn't accidentally cut her.

"No wonder Thunder was interested."

Isa became still. He straddled her on the bed and held the knife to her throat. "Now that we've gotten to know each other, do you promise to be a good girl?"

Isa stared at him. Joseph leaned down and kissed her, trying to force his tongue into her mouth. Isa kept her teeth clenched, not wanting to give him access to her mouth.

"Open your mouth, whore!" Joseph shouted at her and pressed the blade of the knife against her throat.

Isa immediately opened her mouth and Joseph thrust his tongue inside, roughly biting and sucking her tongue. Joseph opened his eyes and watched Isa's tears rolling down her face. He got so turned on by her resistance and distress, he kept his clothes on while riding her and painfully squeezing her breast.

*** *Thunder* ***

Thunder and Grayhorse arrived at the abandoned shack. Taking the lead, Thunder motioned to Grayhorse to take the front. He would look around the back. Thunder peered in every window, trying to see inside. When he reached the bedroom window, he saw Joseph straddling Isa with a knife to her throat while he dry humped her.

Quickly running to the front door, Thunder whispered to Grayhorse that he was going in.

"They're in the bedroom. I'm going in," Thunder quickly whispered to Grayhorse, "stay out here and call Matteo. Tell him where we are and ask him to call the police, then come inside."

Thunder quietly tried to open the door. He didn't want to make too much noise because Joseph had a knife to Isa's throat. Unfortunately, the door creaked as it opened, but he was hoping Joseph had not heard it.

When Thunder walked into the bedroom, what he saw would forever be etched in his mind. Isa was on her knees, naked in front of Joseph, with blood smeared on her stomach. Her head was resting back on Joseph's shoulder so the knife would not cut into her throat. His other hand held a rope that had been tied around her wrists.

"Joseph, get your hands off my woman, NOW!" He screamed. He couldn't help it. He saw tears coming down her eyes as she tried not to move.

Suddenly, Joseph applied pressure to the knife at her throat. Thunder saw a drop of blood trail down her neck and heard her whimpering.

"Take one more step," Joseph snarled, "and I will slice her head off."

"Joseph, let her go, it's me you want." Thunder stopped walking and put up his hands, begging. "Please let her go." Thunder saw so much hatred in Joseph's eyes. This was the missing link to everything, and he had been so oblivious.

"Joseph, listen to me," Thunder spoke calmly. He could see Isa was having a hard time breathing. "Let her walk out of this room and we will settle this man to man."

Grayhorse walked into the room, holding a blanket he'd gotten from the truck.

"How can we be man to man when you bring him with you?" Joseph yelled.

"Grayhorse will not get involved in our fight. He just came to take care of Isa. You don't need her anymore now that you have me."

"You're right. What difference does it make if it's tomorrow night or now? We'll go outside now and fight to the death."

"You want to go outside? Why?" Thunder didn't want to go outside. Isa was naked and she would be cold.

"We will fight like we planned. Do I have your word?" Joseph pushed Isa's head back with the edge of the knife. "I know if you give me your word, you will keep it. Do you promise to fight me now? The winner gets the white whore."

"Yes, Joseph, just let her go to Grayhorse. I will fight you."

"I have your word?" Joseph asked.

"Yes, you have my word."

"To the death?" Joseph enunciated.

"Fine Joseph, to the death. Just let her go."

Joseph pushed Isa toward him and walked out of the shack. Thunder caught Isa and held her tight while he watched Joseph.

"Isa *wíŋyaŋ mitáwa*, are you okay?"

Grayhorse stepped forward and gave Thunder the blanket. Grayhorse watched Joseph gather his clothing and weapons so Thunder could have a few minutes with Isa. Thunder wrapped Isa in the blanket as she cried into his chest while he held her. Then he brushed his hand over her head.

"Ah, *wíŋyaŋ mitáwa*, I was so worried when you didn't show up." He gently lifted her face up so he could get a good look at her. His body grew still. While

Joseph was holding her captive in front of him with her head back, Thunder had not gotten a good look at her face. Now Thunder could see the split lip, bruises, and black eyes.

"I will kill him," Thunder murmured.

She held the blanket with one hand and grabbed his forearm with the other. She looked pleadingly into his eyes.

"No, Thunder, it's over. Please do not fight him. I can't bear to lose you. Haven't I been through enough?"

Thunder shrugged out of his shirt and gave it to Grayhorse.

"Isa, please put on my shirt and wrap yourself up in the blanket. Grayhorse will take the ropes off your hands and feet and take care of you. I have a score to settle." He looked at Isa and whispered, *"Mitáwicu caŋté thečhíhila."* He then gave her a kiss on her forehead and handed her over to Grayhorse. It was time to prepare for the fight. He nodded at Grayhorse and in that moment, they made an unspoken agreement for Grayhorse to take care of Isa if anything happened to Thunder.

"Thunder," Isa grabbed Thunder, "please don't go out there."

"Isa, I must fight him. My word is my bond. I would've done anything to get you away from him. Besides, after what he did to you," he gently ran the back of his hand down her cheek, "I owe him a few bruises."

Thunder turned around and stormed out of the shack screaming, "Joseph, where are you? I'm going to kill you!" Thunder ran to his car and took out some clothing and weapons. He needed to go to the place in the woods by the crooked creek.

*** *Isa* ***

Isa turned to Grayhorse and asked, "What did he say to me?"

"Isa, I will turn around. Please put on Thunder's shirt."

"Fine," she said. She dropped the blanket and put on Thunder's shirt. "You can turn around. Now what did he say?"

Grayhorse looked confused. "He said he had a score to settle…"

Isa interrupted him, "No, the part he said in Lakota. What did he say to me?" She was getting hysterical again. "Please, tell me."

Grayhorse looked at her kindly. "Ah, he said, 'I love you, my heart'." He didn't want to tell her that Thunder already considered her his wife. That was not his place.

Isa turned and bolted out of the shack. She had to catch him before it was too late. "Thunder!" She screamed at the top of her lungs.

"Isa," Grayhorse was yelling at her, "come back. You can't be a distraction for Thunder."

She heard Grayhorse, but needed to tell Thunder that she loved him, too.

Chapter 48

A Score to Settle

THUNDER

T hunder reached the creek and changed into his loincloth and moccasins, painting black streaks on his cheeks and chest. There was no doubt in his mind that Joseph had gone crazy if he wanted to fight to the death, like in the old days.

Dropping to his knees, he raised his hands up in the air and prayed to *Wakan Tanka* for Joseph to realize his mistake and stop this foolish mission. Thunder wanted to defeat him so Isa would be safe, but he didn't want to kill Uncle Spirit's son. However, if it turned out badly for him and Joseph took his life, he asked *Wakan Tanka* to look after Isa until they meet again in the spirit world.

After he finished his prayers, he walked into the forest to find twigs and rocks so he could build a fire, since Joseph wasn't there yet. After collecting as many as would be necessary, he selected a spot far away from the forest and closer to the river. He then placed the twigs down and arranged rocks around them to contain the fire in a circle. He lit a match and placed it on the twigs. After building the fire, he sat in front of it with his legs crossed, his hands on his knees, and waited. He thought he heard Isa scream his name, but it must have been his imagination because she was with safe with Grayhorse. Where was Joseph?

*** *Isa* ***

Isa blindly ran through the trees, calling out to Thunder when someone suddenly yanked her by the hair.

"OW!" she screamed, trying to raise her hands to her head to relieve the pain.

"Shut up, bitch." Joseph spat as he wrapped one hand tightly around her hair while his other hand held the knife against her throat. One wrong move or even if she tripped, he would cut her neck.

"Well, it seems your warrior is already here. He must be ready to die," Joseph mumbled into her ear as he dragged her towards Thunder.

Isa prayed to God she would come out of this alive. What had she done? Grayhorse had warned her to stay away, but she hadn't listened. Instead, she ran away from Grayhorse to find Thunder like an idiot. She was like one of those stupid females in horror movies that ran to the murderer. Closing her eyes, she prayed Thunder would be okay. He was going to be livid when he saw Joseph had her again. She didn't wish to see anyone die, but if this asshole didn't stop pulling her by the hair, then her vote was for Thunder to kill him.

Thunder must have heard them because he jumped up and spun around just in time to see Joseph pulling her toward him. Thunder clenched his hands into fists. *Well, at least she wasn't naked*, Isa thought, *but being barefoot in the woods was not one of her brightest ideas.*

"Joseph, why are you holding her again? You have my word, you don't have to cheat. I told you I would fight you. Let her go. Isa, are you okay?" *Stupid question Thunder.* Isa thought *of course she wasn't ok. A psycho was holding her by her hair.*

"Yes," her voice quivered as tears rolled down her face. She hadn't thought his grip could get any tighter in her hair—she was wrong.

"Let her go Joseph, again it's me you want and I'm right here and ready." Thunder held up his hands and dropped them in frustration.

"You are right, cousin," Joseph pushed Isa to the ground and went running toward Thunder with his knife up in the air, ready to plunge it into his heart. Thunder ducked, but Joseph's legs tripped him.

Isa scurried back until she bumped into a tree and sat down. While watching Thunder, she attempted to remove the remaining rope around her wrists and ankles. The blood was drying and clotting, but she continued to tug and pull, making it worse. If anything happened to Thunder, she needed to be totally free to run as fast as possible. She'd run away from Grayhorse, and she didn't know where he was.

She watched Thunder jump up off the ground. He was balancing his weight on the balls of his feet, ready for a fight. Circling each other. Their knives glowing from the light of the fire. Joseph lunged, but Thunder moved out of the way. They were both so evenly matched. Each one would take a chance and the other would move out of the way. Isa was so scared her heart was pounding a mile a minute. Suddenly, she heard a noise directly behind her. As she screamed, a hand came over her mouth and she froze, not knowing what to do.

"Do not move, little sister, it's Grayhorse. I came with Thunder remember, in the cabin I gave you his shirt before you ran from me?"

Isa nodded, and he removed his hand from her mouth. "I was calling out to you. You should not be here to see this. Thunder wanted me to take you to Sarah until this was over. You didn't even give me a chance to unbind the rope from your hands and feet. Stay still. Let me undo those knots. Do not make a sound. I don't want you to distract Thunder."

Isa shook her head yes and whispered, "Thank you. I'm sorry I should have listened, but I just wanted to reach Thunder so badly. I wanted to tell him I loved him."

Grayhorse nodded and released her hands from the rope. He had grabbed some salve out of his truck when he got the blanket for Isa. He applied it to her wrists and ankles.

"I will put this on now. It will soothe the cuts and chafing. However, when we get you home, you'll need to shower to really clean it out and reapply."

"Thank you," Isa whispered.

"Any chance you will leave here with me now?"

"I'm sorry, but no."

Grayhorse sighed, "I didn't think so, but if, by some miracle, things go south for Thunder, you must come with me quickly. Agreed?"

"Agreed," she murmured.

They both watched as Thunder punched Joseph so hard he fell to the ground. Joseph tripped Thunder again, and they began rolling on the ground as they traded punches. They were really close to the fire and Joseph was on top of Thunder. Joseph had the knife and was about to nick Thunder's neck when Thunder punched Joseph in his kidneys and pushed Joseph's hand with the knife into the fire. Joseph screamed and rolled away from the fire. Thunder jumped up onto his feet and crouched down, ready to fight.

"Joseph, it doesn't have to end this way. Why did you do this? We can stop this now."

"Because you always get everything. The cultural center should have been mine! The elders should have given it to me, not you. Spirit of the Eagle is my father, not yours! Yet he appoints you over me, his own son!" He howled.

"So I waited for the right time. Recognize this knife, cousin?" Joseph said bitterly. "I stole it right from under your fucking nose. It also should have been mine, not yours. I was going to take you down piece by piece and set you up so the elders would think that you were selling the merchandise to the customers - condemning you in their eyes. But then Rachel told me about how much you liked that bitch. And I decided I wanted her too. So I stole her from you, just like I stole Rachel so many years ago. Now, it's just you and me, winner take all. But then you had to sleep with her. Well, I don't want your leftovers, so she has to die. But not before I hurt you, make you watch me fuck her in front of you."

Isa gasped when she heard what Joseph said.

"Shhh," Grayhorse whispered in Isa's ear. He hugged her tighter and said, "That will never happen as long as Thunder and I are breathing."

"Okay, thank you," she murmured. Isa noticed Grayhorse texting someone.

"Who are you texting?"

"Your brother. I'm letting him know where we are. He's bringing the police, but I want to make sure they don't distract Thunder when they arrive."

"Then I would kill you both!" Joseph screamed.

"You will never take Isa. Do you hear me? I love her and I will fight for her to my death," Thunder kept circling around Joseph.

"Well, that was exactly what I had in mind. Because I mean to kill you tonight!"

"Oh Thunder, I love you so. Please make it out of this alive so we can spend the rest of our lives together." Isa mumbled.

Grayhorse leaned over and whispered in her ear, "Isa if anything happens to Thunder, you need to run to my truck and lock the doors until the police get here. I will protect you with my life little sister. You do not need to worry about your safety."

Isa tried to remain calm. Oh, would this fight ever end? She couldn't take it anymore. And then it happened so quickly. Thunder swiped Joseph's feet out from under him, causing him to drop the knife when he tried to catch himself.

Thunder kicked the knife away and climbed on top of Joseph, holding his knife to Joseph's neck like he had done to Isa.

"Joseph, it's over," Thunder was panting as he spoke, "Do you concede defeat?"

"No!" Joseph screamed and spit in Thunder's face.

"Joseph, don't make me kill you!" Thunder yelled at Joseph, "We can still work something out. Can we call a truce?"

"Fine," Joseph gritted his teeth, "Get off me. Truce"

"Okay." Thunder groaned, getting off Joseph, "Truce it is. I refuse to be accused of being a murderer to one of my people. You will go before the tribal council and they will decide your fate. Prepare an explanation for your father."

Thunder turned around and walked towards Isa. He saw Isa's eyes widen right before she screamed, "Lookout!"

Thunder heard Joseph's war cry. In a matter of seconds, he bent down, grabbed a small knife from his moccasin, spun around, and, with incredible accuracy, threw it at Joseph. It landed in Joseph's heart, ending his war cry as he toppled forward, pushing it further in and dying instantly.

Isa stood up and ran to Thunder, who hugged her tightly. "Isa, *wówaštelaka mitáwa*, are you okay? You're not supposed to be here to see this. Why did you follow me?" He looked over at Grayhorse.

"She didn't listen to me." Grayhorse shrugged. "She ran through the woods like a banshee wanting to get to you."

Thunder ran his hands over her body. Then he cupped her face with both hands and looked into her eyes. "I could kill him all over again for hurting you."

"Oh Thunder, I was so worried. He told me you were with Sarah and there was something wrong with her pregnancy. He said you wanted me to come right away. That's why I went with him. Rachel was in on it, too. And when Rachel arrived, he told her he was going to kill you. Rachel confronted him and that's when he killed her." Isa was rambling and started shaking.

"*Wówaštelaka mitáwa*, it's okay now. None of this is your fault. I didn't realize he held so much hatred toward me. Everything will be alright now. Come on, let's go home."

"*Wakíyaŋ Hotóŋpi*, you go ahead." Grayhorse motioned toward the road. "Matteo is on his way with the police. I will take care of everything here. Then I'll go home. Your sister will probably question me until the sun rises."

Thunder smiled at Grayhorse and reached his hand out. Grayhorse grasped it.

"*Pilámaya, Súŋkawakháŋhota* for all your help tonight."

"What are brothers for?" Grayhorse replied. "Bye Isa, next time let's hang out over Sunday lunch."

"I agree," Isa muttered. "This was enough excitement to last a lifetime."

Isa turned with Thunder to walk back to the truck when they halted. Several police officers were running towards them with their guns drawn. Leading the pack was Matteo.

"Freeze, put your hands up!" one officer screamed.

Isa and Thunder immediately stopped and raised their hands.

"That's my sister," Matteo shouted as he kept running toward Isa.

"Ma'am are you okay?" another officer asked Isa.

"Officer, this man," —Isa pointed at Thunder— "Is my boyfriend and he just saved my life."

"Isa, honey, stay with your brother. I need to talk to the police. I'll be right back," Thunder said and kissed her forehead.

"Isa, oh my God, are you okay?" Matteo couldn't stop hugging her. "You scared the shit out of us."

"Matteo, I'm okay now. Thunder came and saved me."

"Well, you wouldn't be in this mess if it wasn't for him." Matteo rolled his eyes and placed his hands on his hips.

"I know you think that. But Thunder didn't know how psychotic Joseph was. If he knew, he would have protected me better. Please don't hate him. I love him," Isa said with tears in her eyes.

"Ok, I'll give him a chance," Matteo sighed, "for now."

"Come on, I'll take you home. What the hell happened to your face? *Mami* will freak out when she sees you like this." Matteo wrapped his arm around Isa, guiding her to his car.

"No," Isa stopped walking. "I want to wait for Thunder," Isa pulled away from Matteo. "Besides, I might need to talk to the officers."

"Okay, I'll wait with you."

"No Matteo, it's okay. Go home and tell *mami* I'm okay. I can even talk to her later if she wants to hear my voice. I'm going home with Thunder."

"Okay. But let me call *mami* so you can talk to her."

Matteo called Aurora. Isa cried on the phone when she spoke with her mom. She reassured her mom that Joseph was dead, and the police were here. She was safe and going to stay with Thunder, but she promised to go see her later that day.

The officers had a lot of questions for Isa, Thunder, and Grayhorse. A couple of hours later, they had all given their versions of the story and let them know that Rachel's body was buried somewhere on the property. Some officers went in search of and found the dug out grave with Rachel's body dumped inside behind the shack. Since the ground had not been covered, the officers suspected Joseph was planning to dump more bodies in the grave before the day was over.

After finding the grave, seeing Isa's face and Rachel's dead body, the police believed them and told them all to come down to the station the next day to give their statements. They said after the coroner finished the autopsies, they could take the bodies of Joseph and Rachel back to the reservation. The police wrapped up their questions just as the sun came up.

Thunder picked up Isa and carried her to Grayhorse's truck. He sat in the back, holding her while Grayhorse drove them to the center so Thunder could get his truck. Thunder carried her from Grayhorse's truck to his and drove to his house. Isa was silent on the way home, staring out the window. After he parked, he came around to get Isa out of his truck. He opened her door and whispered, "*Wówaštelaka mitáwa*, we are home."

Isa just stared at Thunder like a lost child. He picked her up and carried her to his bedroom. He undressed her and started a bath for her. She probably needed to relax and rinse away anything that would remind her of Joseph. When the tub was filled, he helped her in and washed her.

"Isa, I know you don't want to talk about this, but did Joseph touch you? Do I need to take you to a doctor? Are you hurt?" Thunder asked her gently.

Isa looked at him and whispered, "No Thunder, he wanted to wait until you were on your last breath to violate me in front of you. He wanted it to be the last thing you saw. But he must have changed his mind. He got angry and was going to do it, but that's when you showed up," Isa shivered.

Thunder cursed, stripped out of his clothes and got in the tub behind her, clinging onto her. Isa closed her eyes and rested her head on Thunder's chest, hearing his heartbeat was relaxing her. After a while, the water became cold and Isa shivered. Thunder washed himself quickly, got out of the tub, and grabbed some towels. He gave Isa a hand out of the tub, dried her off, and put his bathrobe on her. Then he dried himself off and wrapped a towel around his waist. He carried her into his bed and tucked her in.

"I'm going to bring you some hot tea. I'll be right back."

Isa snuggled into Thunder's bathrobe. It smelled like him. She knew it was morning and she would have to call Maggie, but she didn't have the energy to look for her phone and send the message. She would take a nap and then call. Besides, it was still early. She turned onto her side and got comfy.

"Isa," Thunder brushed her hair back and whispered in her ear, "I found your phone in your purse and texted Maggie. Honey, you really should change your phone code from 1111," he chuckled. "I told her you were sick and wouldn't be in for a couple of days. I figured you can explain everything that happened to her later."

"Okay," Isa murmured.

"Honey, do you want your tea?" Thunder asked, but she never answered.

She was fast asleep. Thunder placed the tea on the nightstand, dropped his towel and crawled in bed spooning her. It didn't take him long to fall asleep. It had been a long night.

Chapter 49

Afternoon After the Shit Storm

THUNDER

I sa was still sleeping, but Thunder needed to call Aurora. He slowly untangled himself from Isa and went to the kitchen for privacy.

"*Hola*, Thunder. *¿Cómo está Isa?*"

"Isa is good. She's still sleeping," he told her, "but I wanted a moment to speak to you privately. I love Isa and I wanted to ask you for permission for her hand in marriage."

"*Oh, Dios mío*. You want to marry my Isa?"

"Yes ma'am, I mean Aurora."

"Matteo told me about everything that happened last night, and I know you will do everything in your power to take care of my little girl. You have my blessing."

"I will love her with all my heart. I can't wait to build a family and start a future with her."

"Thank you for asking Thunder."

"You're welcome. I respect you and I know Isa loves her family. I'm looking forward to being a part of it." Thunder felt relief knowing he had her mother's blessing.

"You're a good boy, Thunder. Now you take care of my Isa and tell her to call me when she gets a moment."

"I will," Thunder chuckled. He hadn't been called a boy in a long time.

"*Adios*, talk to you soon."

"*Adios*, Aurora."

Thunder was heating water for a fresh cup of tea for Isa while he spoke with Aurora. As soon as he hung up the phone, the teakettle whistled. Perfect timing. He prepared her tea with some honey, just the way she liked it. When he walked into his bedroom, he noticed she was sitting up in bed, staring at nothing. He was so worried about her. He set her tea on his nightstand.

"*Wówaštelaka mitáwa*, please look at me." Isa heard him and looked into his eyes. "Are you okay?" Isa did not move or say anything. She just kept staring at him.

"Isa, I love you and I don't want to lose you. Please, if are listening to me, talk to me."

"You love me Thunder, really?" She asked so softly, as if it was incredible for anyone to love her.

"*Han, wówaštelaka mitáwa*, I love you with all my heart and I want to marry you. I know we have not known each other long, but my heart can't live without you. I knew that from the moment I spilled that cup of coffee on you. Then at the opening, you looked like an angel with your long, beautiful curly hair. I knew then I belonged to you and you to me. That we were one heartbeat, one soul, one being."

Isa had tears streaming down her cheeks. "Thunder, I love you too. I thought I would never get to tell you. That you would die right before my eyes, and I would want to die with you."

"*Wówaštelaka mitáwa*, I am right here with you."

Thunder slid off the bed and got down on one knee as he held her hand and said, "Isabel Emelina Gonzalez, will you marry me?"

"*Han*, Johnny *Zintkála Wakíyaŋ Hotóŋpi*, it would be my pleasure."

He was so happy he jumped up onto the bed, straddled her, and started raining kisses on her face.

"Under one condition," Isa put her finger between their lips.

Thunder stopped and looked at her confused, "Name it?"

"You promise to love me forever because I can't live without you." Isa whispered as tears streamed down her face.

"Done." Thunder held her head and wiped her tears. "That is a simple thing to do because I can't live without you, either. Stay here, don't move. I'll be right back," he said and stretched over to his nightstand and opened the top drawer. "I have something for you," he winked at her. He took out the box with his mother's ring and handed it to her.

She opened it and covered her mouth with her hand.

"Oh, wow. This is beautiful."

"That was my mother's wedding ring. I hope it can be yours. But if you don't like it, I will get you another one."

"No, I love this one."

He took out the ring and placed it on her finger. "Now, woman, let us seal the deal."

Isa nodded, and they made love. Neither one leaving an inch of the other's body untouched. Both giving and receiving all that each offered.

Chapter 50

Epilogue - Happily Ever After

THUNDER

It was a little rough after the incident with Joseph. Thunder had called Uncle Spirit and told him everything that had happened. Uncle Spirit was upset that his child would do something so extreme. In the end, Thunder bought caskets for Joseph and Rachel and had them shipped to the reservation for a proper burial. He paid for all the expenses and flew to the burial ceremony by himself. Isa was still recovering, and he didn't want her to have any further stress. However, he felt like he had to be there for Uncle Spirit.

Several months later, Thunder and Isa's wedding comprised family and very close friends, because neither side wanted to wait too long to get married. They went to South Dakota on their honeymoon, so Isa could see where Thunder grew up. Thunder could tell she was fascinated with the Black Hills, Badlands, and Bear Butte.

While there, Thunder asked Spirit of the Eagle to perform a traditional Lakota wedding ceremony so they would be married in both cultures. Isa was once again a radiant bride in a white doeskin dress adorned with turquoise beads. She loved the Lakota ceremony. She found it to be very spiritual, peaceful, and full of love. Thunder's people crowded around the lodge where the ceremony was performed. She knew how well-respected Thunder was among his people by the number of guests that arrived to congratulate them.

Their honeymoon was cut short when Grayhorse called to tell them Sarah had gone into labor. They caught the next flight home and hoped to beat the baby's arrival. Sarah was having a hard time dilating, so she was in labor for over fourteen hours.

They arrived at the hospital just as Sarah pushed for the last time and Lilly entered the world. Grayhorse gave Sarah a kiss as the doctor placed their baby girl onto her chest. The hospital staff took the mother and daughter to a private room.

Grayhorse entered the room, puffing his chest out with pride. Thunder looked around, noticing how his family had grown since he married Isa. Not only was he here with Isa in the waiting room, but so were Aurora, Matteo, Gaby, Emmy, and Lucy. The two girls were playing cards with Tommy. Everyone looked up as Grayhorse entered the room.

"It is a beautiful baby girl. Her name is Lilly because Lilly's are such delicately unique and beautiful flowers that make you smile when you gaze at them." He beamed.

"It is a beautiful name, *Súŋkawakháŋhota*," Thunder stood up and moved toward Grayhorse to embrace him.

"Congratulations, Grayhorse. When can we see Sarah and Lilly?" Isa asked as she hugged him.

"Thank you, little sister. They are taking them to a private room and will notify me as soon as they have her settled in."

Tommy came running to his father to give him a hug.

"*Até*," Grayhorse bent down and picked him up. "I will be a good big brother and friend to my sister."

Grayhorse smiled and kissed Tommy on the cheek. "I know you will *ciŋkší*. That is why *Wakan Tanka* blessed us with you first and Lilly second. He knew you would be very gentle, patient, and caring toward your little sister." He put Tommy down.

Tommy stood up straight and tall, puffing his chest out, when he heard his father's words. He walked over to the girls to continue his card game until they could go see his mother and sister.

Thunder came up behind Isa and held her in his arms while everyone else congratulated Grayhorse.

"As soon as we see Sarah and Lilly, we will go home and continue our honeymoon." He whispered in her ear as he trailed kisses down her neck.

*** *Isa* ***

Thunder made her feel so special, beautiful, and feminine. He was always looking at her with love and want in his eyes. No one had ever looked at her that way before and she vowed to make him happy for the rest of his life. Starting tonight when she told him it wouldn't be long before he was walking into a waiting room filled with a family like today. She smiled to herself. She twirled around in his arms and placed her arms around his neck as she kissed him.

"Promises, promises," she whispered between kisses.

"Hey, you two, do you think you can stop your honeymoon so we can see Sarah and Lilly?" Matteo said as he tapped Thunder on the shoulder.

They had totally forgotten where they were until Matteo interrupted them. As a matter of fact, they hadn't even heard or saw the nurse enter the waiting room and tell Grayhorse that Sarah was in room 202 and asking to see her family.

"Sorry, we got a little carried away," Thunder grinned as he released Isa. He gave her a quick kiss on the lips and grabbed her hand. He then bent down and picked up Tommy.

"Well, *tᶜuŋšká*, are you ready to meet Lilly?"

"*Han, lekší*, I can't wait to see *iná* and Lilly." Tommy smiled at Thunder.

They all headed towards room 202. Sarah looked tired, but happy. Lilly, well, she was absolutely beautiful. She had a full head of black hair, as dark as midnight. And when she opened her eyes, they matched her mom and dad's beautiful brown eyes. She looked like a Lakota. Isa hoped their child would look just like Thunder with the same dark features and beautiful face.

After everyone saw the baby, the nurse asked them to leave because mother and child needed to eat and rest. They all said goodbye and promised to come back tomorrow.

Thunder and Isa drove home. They were now living in Thunder's house. Isa's lease had ended, and they moved all her belongings to Thunder's house before the wedding. It had been a wonderful day and was about to get better by the minute. Isa couldn't wait to tell Thunder her news.

They pulled into their driveway. Thunder came around to hold the door open for Isa. She smiled at him. He put his hand out to help her out of the truck.

"I'm glad we are home *wówaštelaka mitáwa*. I have waited all day for us to be alone."

"Me too," Isa reached up and hugged him as he closed the door.

"So, you missed my kisses?"

"Always," she whispered as she kissed him under his ear.

Thunder groaned.

"Woman, we need to get inside now before we put on a show for our neighbors." He picked up Isa and carried her to their bedroom. Tonight was the first time they would share his bedroom as husband and wife. After the wedding, they had stayed in a hotel and flown out the next day to the reservation. He laid Isa down on the bed and undressed her.

"I will bring the luggage in tomorrow from the car. Tonight, I am not a patient man. I want you so bad, I can't think straight. When I am inside you, I feel reborn again. You make me feel so alive and loved, Isa. I love you with all my heart and soul."

Isa smiled at him. They were both naked now, and he was lying on top of her.

"Thunder, you are my life, my love, my very soul. Without you, my heart would not beat as it does. Since the day you walked into my life, well after all the misunderstandings," Isa giggled. "You have made my days so happy. Our future will be wonderful, especially now that you have made me not only your wife but the mother of your child."

Thunder quirked an eyebrow. "What are you saying, Isa?"

"That I am pregnant with our child. I am about two months along."

"Are you sure?" Thunder froze and stroked her hair with his hands.

"*Han*, I am. You shouldn't be surprised. We never used protection from the first time we made love. I'm surprised it didn't happen sooner. Are you not happy?" Isa wondered if maybe Thunder did not want a child so soon in their marriage.

"You have made me the happiest man in the entire world." Thunder smiled suddenly. "I could not be happier. Earlier today, I was just thinking about what it would be like to hold our child. Now, you tell me you're pregnant." Thunder had tears in his eyes, "*Mitáwicu caŋté thečhíhila*, I love you, my wife, my heart."

"I didn't know it was possible to love you more every day, but I do. I am so glad you will be the mother of my children. You are so caring and loving. You will be a great mom. I could not have asked *Wakan Tanka* for a better wife." Thunder kissed her gently.

"Pilámaya, Wakíyaŋ Hotóŋpi," Isa responded as tears of joy ran down her cheeks.

Thunder kissed her tears away and gently, tenderly made love to his beautiful wife. It was one of those moments where actions spoke louder than words.

***

Over the years, Thunder's cultural center had the desired effect. People from all over came and wanted to learn more about American Indian culture and history. The tribal council was so happy they opened more around the country, teaching about all tribes, especially whichever one lived in the area before the white man came. They could get money from American Indians and their supporters around the world. And like Thunder's American Indian Cultural Center, once they were open - between the sales of pottery, sculptures, jewelry, paintings, and the restaurant - they became self-sufficient and quite profitable.

Special Thanks

NETZI

I wrote this book almost thirty years ago. Then life caught up with me, so I set it down until now. But back then, I asked for help from several Lakota people. I would like to thank them now for their letters when I asked them questions about the language.

A special thank you to Vivian Spotted Horse and her daughter Patricia Hawk Eagle. In 1997, I wrote to them. They were gracious enough to write me back. Patty answered my questions about the language.

If I have spelled anything wrong, it is my fault and I apologize. I have always been interested in the Lakota nation's culture and history. I even bought cassette tapes back then to learn the language. On August 2nd, 1997, I attended the 12th Annual Oglala Lakota Nation Wacipi & Fair. It was a powwow with rodeo on the Pine Ridge Indian Reservation in South Dakota. It was a wonderful experience which I still remember today. I love to listen to Robby Romero & Red Thunder. Makoce Wakan is one of my favorite albums of all time. I don't understand all that is being said, but I love the music.

I attempted to portray the Lakota culture accurately in my novel. I'm sorry if I made a mistake. As a Cuban, I empathize with the struggle of not being able to live like your ancestors. Despite our different situations, the outcome is similar.

Thank you also, to my reading circle, my husband, daughter, and friends (Michelle and Amy). I would be remiss if I didn't thank my original book editor, McKenzie Gibel. You truly pushed me to write a better book. And to Deb Krickovich, my new editor, who bought this book and edited her signed copy to make me better – Thank you so much! This latest edit led to this 3rd Edition.

About the Author

NERI LOPEZ

Neri Lopez has worn many hats as a stay-at-home mom of triplets, graphic designer, and high school teacher (Spanish, Art, and Graphic Design). She lives in Florida with her husband, grown kids, and their fur babies, Mocha and Chewy. She is a crafter of all trades, including crocheting (several craft shows a year), jewelry making, scrapbooking, knitting, sewing, and painting.

Neri loves to hear from her readers, contact her at:
website: sirenbookandcraft.com
(When you sign up for her newsletter, you will receive a FREE downloadable bookmark of Red Path.)

Please...Don't forget to share your thoughts on Neri's books by writing a review on Amazon and/or Goodreads after reading them. Reviews make it easier for readers to find an author's books on Amazon.

Or follow her on:
facebook: Neri Lopez - Author
instagram: Neri_Lopez_Author
(She is most active on facebook)
The Path Series
Book 1: **Red Path** (available on Amazon)
Book 2: **Unconquered Path** (available on Amazon)
Book 3: **Wagering Path** (available on Amazon)
Book 4: **Unexpected Path** (available on Amazon)
Novella Book 4.5: **Double Trouble Path**
(2025 - This novella will be free for a limited time on Amazon.)
Book 5: **Twisted Path** (2025)
Book 6: **Blue Path** (2025)

www.ingramcontent.com/pod-product-compliance
Lightning Source LLC
Chambersburg PA
CBHW060351310726
48976CB00003B/785